There is nothing and no one in this story that is real. Everything is made up. This is a completely fictional story with no resemblance to anyone anywhere at all, living or dead. This story is ONLY for entertainment purposes.

I would be remiss if I didn't thank my Partner in Crime. From the moment of inspiration to the final product, I've been grateful for the freedom to express myself and be who I was born to be.

I'll just go ahead and apologize to my family here. It may not be the kind of story that makes anyone proud of me, but it's one I had to tell.

Someday, I'll tell the entire story that led me to this point in life where I was able to create this story. But, for now, the only thing that matters is that, at the time of writing, my options in life were incredibly limited. I wrote this on a very, VERY old computer that I bought 2nd hand for about $200 in my "spare time" while working a full time job. I recorded the audiobook myself (because otherwise it would never happen) in a blanket fort made of PVC pipes and old blankets on a $50 microphone.

And I am incredibly thankful that this book has been able to make it from my mind out into the wild. I hope you enjoy it as much as I do, and I hope you are as blown away with it as I have been. After all, it felt more like Ester was telling the story, and I was just taking dictation.

Thank you.

Chapter 1: WTF

Where does one begin to explain the murder of thirty four people in one town on the same day? Especially when there was an undetermined number of killers with a variety of methods? It was a normal town... until it wasn't.

There were no observable common threads. Nothing linked all the victims together other than they lived and worked in the same town. And all the killers were silent.

They all lived and worked in the same town. The dead and the slayers were friends and neighbors and coworkers. There were families that went to church and had dinners together. Some of these people had kids playing sports together. There was no common connection other than they were all part of the tapestry of the town. They were the fabric of the society.

Business men. Loners. Bikers. Mechanics. Bankers. Drinkers. Religious. Honorable. Questionable. Family oriented and hermits. Older and younger. Educated and street smart.

There was no pattern. There was nothing obvious to begin with. There was simply a day where thirty four people turned up dead in one place.

When the state police arrived to investigate, the officer put in charge asked, "Where is your sheriff? Why am I already in charge here?"

The answer was, "He's dead. He was one of the victims."

Captain Bucklem was stunned and speechless as he looked down and shook his head. Where does one begin to investigate almost three dozen homicides with a town full of suspects? He took off his campaign hat and looked to the sky as he rubbed his forehead. He slowly composed himself and muttered, "There's no way the academy prepared me for this."

He looked around. There were people everywhere. They were standing in groups. They were silent. They were staring. They didn't know what would come next. They didn't even know what would come first.

Captain Bucklem huffed out a sigh. He was as stunned and confused as the people of Sherone, Ohio. He nodded a seasoned state trooper nod and gathered his best authoritarian voice to address the mass of people gathered around the courthouse.

"Alright," he said. His voice would grow in volume and command as he began to look for a starting point. "I want all law enforcement in the area to gather around me. If you have a badge, come to me now!" He retrieved the microphone from his cruiser and flipped on the P.A. He used his car as a bull horn to address the crowds. "I can't imagine what all of you are thinking and feeling right now. Hell, I'm more confused than I've ever been in 17 years of law enforcement. Go home. Gather with your family. Pray. Hug your loved ones. Don't leave town. Wait for us to figure out where to begin with this. Once we've had a few moments to assess everything, we will do our best to inform all of you as to what comes next. Thank you."

The nearest deputy, Corporal Wilson asked, "You're just going to let them all go?"

Captain Bucklem looked him square in the eye and asked, "Do you have a plan to herd the entire town into captivity for questioning? If so, I'm listening, son."

Corporal Wilson shook his head.

Captain Bucklem continued, "Hell, I don't even know where to begin with this myself. Nothing like this has ever happened outside of a communist regime. At least there, the government was the mass killer. No one had to gather clues or guess. Let's find out how many are actually dead. Let's... hold on." He began to shout and wave for all law enforcement to gather around him.

Once he could see no more uniforms approaching him, he stepped up on a tool box from the trunk of one of the cars. Since there were only about twenty officers, he wouldn't need amplification. "Alright folks. No need to explain the obvious fact that we don't know anything, and none of us have ever seen anything like this." He stopped when he noticed one man standing at the edge without a uniform. He looked at the man and said, "You got to be kidding me! Get out of here!"

"I'm with the press!" the man barked back.

Captain Bucklem was not amused. "Have you lost your fucking mind? Is there any part of 'active investigation' you need explained to you? Walk away now or I will personally taser you in the face and deal with the fallout later!"

Everyone stared at the man. He looked incredibly uncomfortable as he quickly debated his freedom of press and the promise that was just made directly to him. Captain Bucklem shrugged and reached for his taser. The man's eyes widened as he backed away. The people in uniforms parted like a blue sea as their new leader readied his weapon with steely eyes.

One young man sort of giggled, "This aughtta be good."

As the captain raised the taser towards the face of the man claiming to be with the press, a change came over the person that didn't fit in with those around him. He spun around and ran away.

There were weak laughs and head shaking all around as the taser was holstered.

Captain Bucklem seized the moment. "Any of you that get the bright idea to share anything with that fellow or any other press will take that tase to the face he ran from. Copy?"

There was a disorganized chorus of, "Copy that!"

"Now," Captain continued. "If you have a map of the area, specifically one that covers where all bodies have been found, can someone get that to me? Let's tape off all crime scenes if that's not already done, and if we have enough tape. We need to do a census of sorts to see if there's any more people missing or unaccounted for that we need to be searching for. Is there a town historian of any type? Or has he been killed, too?"

One deputy asked the obvious question that everyone was thinking, "What do you mean by town historian? Like someone that runs a local museum?"

Captain explained. "Historian can be a town clerk or plot map person. It can be the oldest chess player in the park. There's probably a group of old farts that gather for coffee and share one newspaper every morning. I want them. I want someone that's been here long enough and has either been nosy enough to be in everyone's business or has been involved in the town politics for a hundred years. You're local LEOs, do NOT ask for anything from anyone in this town until further notice. Do NOT share ANY information with friends or family. Do NOT trust these people in any way, shape or form. They just killed a bunch of people you know. Do not trust them with anything! Is there any question about that?"

There was silence.

Captain Bucklem looked over the faces. There was fear and uncertainty he had never seen before. It was worse than when he was a brand new marine being sent on his first deployment. He had to address the problem.

"I see you're scared. Don't think I'm not scared, too. They killed your sheriff. Let's get organized on who's going where to round up the dead. We'll need a place big enough, like a school gym. I doubt we can fit them all into a normal location."

Someone spoke up. "We have the old VA clinic that shut down. Can we use that?"

Captain nodded. "You bet. I like that idea. Better than putting them where the kids go. Gather all information. Pictures, statements if anyone is around, and any loose items that might matter. Once we have all the bodies, we'll send you all home to get clothes and whatever you need. We'll try to have a secure place to work from as we begin sorting this out. Maybe the armory. But, we can't have you staying at home unsecured... given the environment and scale of homicide."

There was an unsettled and uneasy mumbling. Sergeant Murtle wanted to let the captain know, "Sir, we've already established a strong hold for command center functions in the city police headquarters."

Bucklem stared at Murtle for a moment, then slightly shook his head. "I don't know why you didn't chose the armory, since it's made to be exactly that, but you all live here, and I'll trust that you did the best thing that could be done." He was questioning several things about the people he had been sent to lead, but he didn't have the luxury of figuring out much. He continued, "Ladies and gentlemen, we don't know anything yet other than people were killed by other people. We don't know how much we don't know. Let's be alert and diligent. Gather up and reconvene. We'll have to figure this out together. Team up if you can. Watch out for each other. Let's get rolling."

Captain Bucklem turned to a female dispatch. "Can you contact someone from another county to put together a team of lunch ladies? We can't trust anyone from here and we're going to need food and other care items. I don't care if we have to borrow people and supplies from 3 counties away. Please, figure out how to take care of these officers when they come in tonight and can't go home."

She looked shaken. "Sir?"

He understood. She needed information and clarification. "We can't take any chances. We need to protect our own until we can figure out what happened here. We need to be safe. If there's a couple dozen killers here and we don't know who they are, we need to trust strangers to help us with food and water and stuff. Please reach out to places outside of here. I'll see about bringing in more troopers from other parts of the state. I'm sure we'll have federal help long before we want it. But, before that happens, we need you to work some magic, please. What is your name?"

"Laura Strong, sir" she answered.

"Laura," Bucklem replied. "I'm trusting you to not be one of the killers."

Laura was taken back. She stuttered, "N-no, sir. I mean, You, you, you...." She took a breath. "You can trust me sir. I'm not one of the killers."

He stared at her. He wasn't sure what to believe in the midst of the most unbelievable thing he'd ever seen. "Alright," was all he could say. "Get on it, Laura."

He turned to a man standing near him and looked at his name tag, "You seem to be the ranking local officer, Sergeant Murtle. Assuming that is YOUR name on the uniform."

"Yes, sir," he replied sharply. "I am Sergeant Murtle and I am the ranking local officer."

"Hmmm," Bucklem was skeptical. "No city chief of police, or is he dead, too?"

"Sir, the chief is on vacation," Murtle responded. "He has a cabin in Wyoming."
"Prior service?" Bucklem surmised.

"Yes, sir," Murtle confirmed. "Six years active duty

army."

Bucklem mulled a moment, then asked, "Here because of a purple heart?"

Sergeant Murtle nodded, "Yes, sir. Only one. No cluster."

Bucklem slapped him on the shoulder, "Glad you made it home."

The veterans stood silent for a moment.

"Alright, soldier," Bucklem said. "Here's your role. Find a public information specialist. I don't care if it's a high school kid from the debate team. The real press is probably already here snooping around, and we both know they will fuck things up just to MAKE a story. We're going to have the entire world breathing down our necks for answers.

I'm going to call the governor and ask for some reinforcements to watch our six while we work and sleep. You understand being in foreign territory and not knowing who's friendly. Get me that historian. You're going to have figure out a way to make your fellow LEOs understand that we are one unit right now till the end of this. Not their wives and parents. Not their kids. Just us with the badges. Got it?"

"Yes, sir," he replied.

Bucklem concluded, "You know the area and the people. You're going to take on a bigger role than you want. I'm going to lean on you for a lot. So, if you're a man of faith, this is your opportunity to pony up and have faith, man. If you're not a man of faith, I need you to be one hell of a man. Ya ready?"
"Absolutely not, sir," Murtle confessed. "But, yes, sir!"

Captain Bucklem looked around. There were police and sheriff people looking at maps and talking and sharing notes. He became a little upset as he felt the marine in him raging to his voice. "THERE ARE BODIES ALL OVER THIS COUNTY!!! PICK ONE AND HEAD THAT DIRECTION!!! WHAT IS TAKING YOU PEOPLE SO LONG?!?! MOVE IT!! MOVE, MOVE, MOVE!! GO! GO! GO!"

He lowered his head. "God, you're gonna have to help me out here, buddy. I'm lost on this one."

He headed towards the police station where he would begin making phone calls and hoping for information to begin coming in that made sense. Because right now, nothing was making sense.

As he reached the steps, he noticed a TV crew setting up their van just a few yards away. He felt a fleeting urge to rid the area of such vultures. But, it was just a fleeting urge. After all, his method would not be legal.

As he choked back his disdain for the media, he slowly became aware of a lack of activity in the police station. His demeanor changed as he went to find Dispatcher Laura Strong. When he found her at her desk, she was eating a tuna sandwich.

She looked up at him, covered her mouth and explained, "I eat when I get nervous or anxious."

He nodded slowly. "I understand. But, I'm wondering... is it always this quiet in here?

She finished chewing. Then, she answered, "Sometimes. But, today, there's a few of our officers that are missing. And all the ones that did show up, you sent out."

"What do you mean 'missing?'" he asked.
Laura replied. "Missing. As in 'no call, no show.' Not answering the phone or radio. They are missing."

"How many officers are missing, Laura?" he almost sounded like he was demanding. Perhaps he was just trying not to panic.

"Two police," she answered. "Sheriff's department is also missing a couple. Plus, as you know, the sheriff."

There was silence. Captain Bucklem was processing. Laura was staring at him. Neither seemed to know what to do or say.

Finally, the captain shook his head and headed to his work station. Laura finished her sandwich.

Chapter 2: The Historian

"Captain Bucklem... This is Ester Wireman. She is the historian you might be looking for."

Sergeant Murtle was introducing the four foot nine inch, 95 year old lady to the six foot four inch, two hundred and forty five pound, physically fit state trooper. They both had their heads angled about forty five degrees. Hers was up. His was down.

He offered a hand shake to the little, old lady as he introduced himself. "Good afternoon, ma'am. I'm Captain Bucklem of the state police. I really do appreciate you coming in and helping me out here."

She placed her tiny hand in his. It looked like a man shaking hands with a toddler. She responded, "So. You need a nosy, old broad that has her nose in everyone's business to tell you who's sleeping with who and what kind of secrets everyone has?" She wore her age like a badge of honor.

Bucklem glared at Murtle. It was a very uneasy moment.

Ester spoke up. "It's not his fault. He didn't explain it that way. I'm just yanking your chain."

Bucklem shook his head in disbelief. "Thank you, Sergeant Murtle. If I need backup while talking with Ms. Wireman, I hope you won't be far away."

Ester smiled at the huge man. "There ya go. Gotta have a sense of humor, even in the worst of times." She walked over to the nearest chair and sat down. She walked quite well and almost seemed... happy. It was like she was in an oddly good mood. Or at least, the bizarre circumstances were not affecting her much.

Captain Bucklem wasn't sure what to make of her on first impression. He simply proceeded as normal. He offered her something to drink and asked if she would like a more comfortable chair.

Ester sat in the chair and accepted nothing. She waited patiently for the captain to ask questions. After all, that was his job and why he was there. She was old enough to know that he sent for her for a reason. So, she was going to let him do his job. And so it began.

Bucklem finished trying to make connection and tried to ease into explaining what he was looking for. He said, "Ms. Wireman. I'm not from here. I'm hoping you can give me some understanding about the area, the town and the people."

Ester didn't change expression. "Anything specific? Ya know you can get a lot of information from the internet. Just put the town name in and a whole page of stuff comes up. Jobs. Elevation. History of who settled the area and how it grew. You can even see how many people live here and what kind of money is considered average income."

"Are you kidding me?" Bucklem shook his head. "I need someone to help me and they bring me you."

Ester smiled. "Now, Officer. I'm guessing you don't need someone to tell you the stuff you can find for yourself. You're probably hoping I can point you in the right direction for figuring out who might have done something like this. You probably want me to list the drunk and dangerous. Maybe you need to know who has marital and money problems and who might hate their neighbor. You may even need to know of the gangs of Hatfields and McCoys."

Bucklem sighed, "Yes, ma'am. You definitely understand the assignment. So, I won't try to patronize you and I sure as hell won't play any games with you. I'll be direct. You already know that I'm like a fart in the wind here with something no one's ever seen before. I'm desperately looking for anything that can help me make sense of this."

Ester continued to smile. She seemed to be enjoying this interaction. She said, "Captain, I've seen it all. I've watched people be born, grow and die. I've watched them fall in love and run from it. I've heard more dirty laundry than can be cleaned and I know the people around here. I don't know every dirty little secret for everyone, but you might say, I know where all the bodies are buried."

Captain Bucklem was visibly in disbelief. Ester didn't really change expression.

She offered to console the rattled officer. "Maybe that was a bad cliché to use today. Maybe I should have said that I have a good idea of all the skeletons in the closets?" They stared at each other for a moment. She then offered, "Maybe I should just stick with the facts and avoid any clever sayings?"

"Can you help me understand the folks and the culture around here a little?" he asked. He really didn't know what else to say to the little old lady.

"Yes, sir," she replied. "You take notes. I'll start talking."

She sat back and looked down. She continued, "Actually, I'll make it easy to understand."

Captain Bucklem moved up to the desk and picked up a pen. He thought he was ready.

Ester looked at him and said, "I know everything. Officer Murtle was right to ask me to come to you. He knew I would know."

Bucklem began to look confused and uncomfortable. "Mrs. Wireman. I don't think I understand. It almost sounds like you're suggesting that you are behind all this."

"Maybe I am," she responded. "But, I'm not making a confession."

Captain Bucklem dropped the pen. He sat back in the chair. He wasn't sure if she was senile or just being a smart ass. He wasn't amused. He looked Mrs. Wireman in the eye while he thought. She didn't look away.

Finally, Captain Bucklem spoke. "Mrs. Wireman, I apologize for dragging you down here today. I believe that Sergeant Murtle made a mistake. You are free to go, ma'am."

He figured that sounded better than telling her she was of no use to him. He tried to not let his disappointment show. But, when the little, old lady didn't leave, he felt almost obligated to explain to her that she needed to leave. She just sat there silently staring at him. He almost felt like she was daring him to question her.

He stood up and said, "Thank you for coming here, Mrs. Wireman, but we will not be needing anything from you."

Before he could continue, she said, "Yes, you will." Her expression hadn't changed.

He began to look puzzled and perhaps a touch frustrated. He wasn't sure she was understanding. He could have easily picked her up with one hand and tossed her out the door. "Ma'am. I'm releasing you to go home. I appreciate your time, but I have an awful lot to work on. So, please, go home."

Ester Wireman didn't move. She didn't change her expression. The state policeman was trying to be patient with her, but was not about to waste any more time. Bucklem frowned and said, "I'll get someone to drive you home."

"No, you won't," she challenged.

Bucklem was now visibly surprised and maybe even looked a little angry at the defiance he was dished. He fought the urge to have her removed from the building. He wanted to believe this tiny, old lady was not about to fight him. He sat down and hung his head while he fiddled his fingers. He finally nodded his head and looked at Ester with earnest in his eyes.

"I'm listening," he conceded.

"Good," she snapped. "I get tired of people treating me like I don't know anything because I'm older than dirt. I didn't get to be this old by being stupid. People should value the things I've learned about life and the world instead of dismissing me for my age. It's ridiculous to watch them make all the same mistakes."

Bucklem realized what was being said to him. He took up a notebook and pen. "You've made your point, Mrs. Wireman. I'm asking for you to educate me because you know much more about this town and it's people than I do. And I'm ready to learn."

Ester finally relaxed. She began to speak. "I'll begin with me."

Bucklem settled into note taking like a college kid on his first day.

She said, "I was born and raised here. A lot of people still used horses and only a few rich folks drove cars. The Great Depression was about to happen. Like anywhere else, times got tough, and we had to get tougher to survive. People did what they had to do to survive. Most of us survived by learning to care for the dirt that grew our food. We learned to take care of nature so she'd take care of us.

I was sixteen when World War II sucked us in. Our little town had crawled out of depression and suddenly, men in big cars came from the government and turned everything we had into stuff to make war machines and food for soldiers and bullets. We were making stuff for war before we actually went to war. Some of our boys enlisted and went to the other side of the world. Most came home. My uncle didn't. And I can still name the others that didn't.

It was during that time that I met one of those government men. He was only nineteen, so he didn't have any authority like the other older ones. He was brought to do whatever they told him to do... set up podiums for their speeches... drive them around... fetch things. He was handsome and smooth with words and charming. And I was just sixteen.

We would sneak around when we thought no one was looking. Before the war ended and as soon as I graduated high school, we were married. I thought he was everything. And then the war ended.

What I didn't know was that once he didn't have a job that made him feel important and we had a baby on the way, that he would change. I'm not sure that he actually changed. I kind of believe that he just started to really become the true version of himself. I think he was the best version of what he could be as long as he had his government job. But, once he married and got left behind to be a good old local boy... we'll he didn't really want that to be him.

He got a job. We bought a house. We raised kids and dogs and a garden. We went to church. We took vacations to the Grand Canyon and Chicago. We were the picture perfect family living the American Dream."

Ester paused while her expression sobered. "And like many others here, and I imagine most towns, he began to drink. And he began to resent his life with me and the kids and the dogs. He became bitter. Then angry. Eventually, he became mean and unbearable. He called us names and said terrible things to us.

I thank God every day that the kids grew up and went to college and found life on their own before he started hitting. It turned out that he was actually a 'good man' because he never really beat his children. Only used the belt across their behinds like a normal father. Never punched them and blackened their eyes or broke their bones.

Noooo.... He saved all that for me. Once the kids were out

of the house, I was in the hospital. I think I spent as much time there as I did in the garden, until I didn't spend time in the garden any more. Most of my life after the children had left was hell and punishment. For what, I do not know.

I prayed. I talked to the pastor. Then, I talked to the priest and another pastor. I talked to counselors from the big city. Eventually, I even talked to the police, the judge and the lawyer. Nothing worked. Nothing saved me. No one stopped him. I didn't find relief until he died 15 years ago. I lived in agony and misery for many years with that man. Now, I sometimes catch myself missing him, and I hate myself for it. I remind myself what he was like and what he did.

After he died, I spent a lot of time learning to live again. I restarted my garden and learned to knit. I started helping at the local shelter and got involved in church again. I've been able to live a somewhat normal life while waiting for death. And I hope he's in hell where I'll never see him in eternity."

Ester smiled. Bucklem looked a little surprised. He wanted to ask what that all had to do with today, but she didn't give him the chance.

"As for most folks around here," Ester continued. "They live normal lives. We have a couple factories. Some of the younger ones make their living off the internet. We have some office jobs. There's one tech company that seems to do well. Their people drive the fancy cars around here. Not many people garden any more. They like to go out to eat, so we have some decent restaurants, plenty of fast food, and a couple chain restaurants. We have the same trailer park trash most towns probably have. We have our share of meth heads and druggies. We definitely have plenty of pot heads. One steals everything. The other barely does anything. Most of us fall somewhere in the middle.

Most of these people live paycheck to paycheck. They're struggling to make ends meet. That's a lot of stress, ya know, trying to just survive. Not everyone takes vacations any more, and if they do, they stay home. They call it a 'stay-cation.' Saves money.

A lot of people have a second job or some home business. But, that's going away because of the government. Kids can't even open lemonade stands because they have to buy a permit and have the health department approve it.

When I was a kid, we shoveled drives and raked leaves and mowed lawns and milked cows and bailed hay for money. Now, everyone is afraid of lawsuits if the kid gets hurt and the kids are all playing video games and watching their tablets or phones.

We've always had a county fair and 4H program, but the carnival is so expensive and the 4H isn't what it was. We had sports for little kids, and everyone played or cheered. Those are still around, but barely. Everyone went to high school sports and cheered and stood by their school. That doesn't happen much any more. We used to ride our bikes all over town and out in the country side. Now, everyone is afraid that their kid will get snatched up in a van and taken away. Kids don't ride bikes except at the bike park with their parents watching.

We used to walk in the park and have picnics. Now meth heads pander for money if they see you there. The social problems we had were out of sight. Drunks and drug users were in the bars with no windows and other dark places. Now they're on the streets in the day time. Homeless hid in the woods. Now they camp next to the stores. Kids were afraid they might get beat up. Now they might get killed.

I can go on and on, Captain Bucklem. But, as far as I can help you is to tell you that nothing is the way it was. We're still a normal town doing all things that any normal town does. But, the fabric of our morals has torn. And our world has lost it's way. The moral compass of America is spinning instead of pointing the way. Normal doesn't mean the same thing it used to mean.

Now, if you really need me to sit here and tell you intimate details of each person I know, I suppose we can do that. Obviously not for all 20,000 people that live around here. But, you asked for a history lesson. I do believe that that is exactly what I have just delivered in Cliff Notes form."

Bucklem had not taken a single note. He found himself listening to someone that could have been sitting on the porch with his mother talking about the world going to hell in a hand basket. He let his head bob a little as he weighed her speech. Finally he said, "Mrs. Wireman, I hate to admit how much I agree with you on what you've said. I thank you very much for coming here and talking with me. I only have one question. Can you tell me who is the one family in this area that everyone keeps their distance from?"

"Come again?" Ester asked.

"You know the type of family I mean," he replied. "They're probably poor. Maybe kinda dirty. Mean. No one messes with them, and when they go to the store, people try not to look at them. They just quietly get out of their way."

Ester smiled. "Oh, yes. You're talking about the Fredricks family. You can find them out on the east end of town just beyond the welcome sign a bit. Just follow Johnson Road.

You'll know the place."

"Oh," he said thoughtfully. "And can you tell me the money family? You know. The family that has a few businesses and maybe a street named for them. They're the ones that come up with ideas that always seem to go their way because no one can stand up to them."

Ester nodded while still smiling. "Yes, yes. That's the Hesson family. They're on the north end of town. They more or less own that end of town. Their family started out with the feed mill and eventually owned the mercantile and then the grocery store. They do have several businesses and last year they got three old oaks cut down in town. No one wanted to lose those trees. They were as old as the town, but they cut them down anyways. Said they were a nuisance and a hazard."

Bucklem asked, "Do a lot of people have problems with these families?"

Ester squinted at him. "I'm sure there are some. People tend to not like extremes, ya know. Some hate the poor. Some want to eat the rich. It's human nature, Captain. I'm sure you already know that."

"Yes, ma'am," he responded rather disarmed. "I do."

Ester frowned. "I'm guessing what you mean to ask me is if those families could be evil enough to do this or have it done"

"Yes, ma'am," he responded respectfully. It occurred to Bucklem that being direct with Ester would be the only way to achieve anything. Common courtesy and pleasantries seemed to be lost on her in an odd way. She was very proper and polite, but she didn't seem to believe in dancing around the matters at hand.

"As for the Hessons," she began. "Not really. I don't think anyone really hates them. A lot of people are probably annoyed with them. And a few are jealous. They have money and they don't hide it. That can get to people who struggle with paying the bills, but I don't believe anyone would go after them for being rich. After all, they really did work hard for it. They were a little lucky. But, they didn't wake up rich. I don't think anyone would wish anything bad on that family. And I know they would never do anything bad to anyone.

Once they wanted to buy out Old Fred Meyer. But, Fred refused to sell. They offered him more and more, but he always said, 'No.' So, eventually, they quit asking and let him be. They just figured out another way to make their plans work without his land. No, I don't think the Hessons pose a danger and I don't think they have anything to worry about. Ansel is good to Madeline and the kids. And everyone knows it."

It seemed odd to Bucklem that she mentioned anything about how Mr. Hesson treated his family. But, before he could process anything or speak, she continued.

"Now that Fredricks family," she shook a finger at him. "They have always been pretty terrible. I always felt bad for them not having money. But, they didn't really make an effort to change their place in this world. Dale was a mean bastard to everyone, family, neighbors, people in line at the store... He wasn't nice to anyone. Darlene was a bitch. Just like her husband, but a woman. There didn't seem to be a decent bone in either of them.

That's why their kids were always holy terrors and not welcome anywhere. The two boys, Theo and Kern were always in trouble with the law and at school. Neighbors would move away from them. The poor girl, Sally, could have been a beauty, but she never had a chance with parents and brothers like that. She was born into hell with no redemption, Captain. Everyone felt sorry for her. But, trying to help her was like trying give a cat a bath with a bunch of junkyard dogs circling her. They've been better, but I don't believe they were killers."

They looked at each other intently for what felt like a long time. Eventually, Bucklem blinked a few times.

"Mrs. Wireman," he quietly said. "I noticed that you spoke of the Hessons in the present tense, but when you talked about the Fredricks, you used the past tense."

Ester never changed and didn't miss a beat. "Of course, Captain. Haven't you been informed yet? They're all dead."

Bucklem was shocked, "All dead? What do you mean they're all dead?"

Ester looked at him with the same fake confusion a parent uses on a child when the kid doesn't understand a clear statement. "Sir, I didn't stutter. The Fredricks are all dead. Everyone knows. Everyone has been talking about it. They were all shot and their property set on fire."

He shook his head in disbelief. She remained undaunted. "It's OK. Your people will come tell you about it soon enough."

24

Bucklem had definitely reach his limit. "OK, Mrs. Wireman! Thank you for all your help and insights. If you don't mind, I believe I'm about to have my hands full."

Ester nodded and smiled. "I wish you the best, Captain. I'm sure you're going to be here for awhile trying to sort this all out. I wish I could tell you who could kill all these people, but I'm afraid I just can't do that. Time will tell."

She stood to her feet, adjusted her outfit and turned for the door. She walked out as a woman that didn't have a worry in the world and all the confidence of a princess. Bucklem wasn't sure what to think, but he wasn't exactly comfortable with the way the first meeting went.

Chapter 3: Ester's Decision

It was two years ago when Ester saw them.

First, she saw Carrie Ann come to the church potluck wearing the uniform of the beaten: the dark glasses and heavy make up with the large hat. Then, at the same social event, each with their respective man, she saw Mary and Susan wear the same uniform. She had just come from the gas station where she had seen Terri still ashamed of what was left of her black eye. And the night before, she saw Theresa in the same condition.

Something changed in Ester that afternoon at the Holy Trinity Potluck. Maybe it was God calling. Maybe it was Satan tempting. Humans have a tough time with whatever it is that makes them do the things they do. Some rationalize. Some blame. Some claim it as their own. But, Ester saw all those women hurting and humiliated and something in her flipped like a light switch.

She had spent a good part of her life beaten as one of them. She relived every horrible moment and suffered an indescribable empathy when she looked upon their faces. She knew every soul crushing feeling. She felt the weight of their despair forcing her to bow her head and lower her eyes. She knew first hand what it felt like to have others look away and a few offer to pray for her.

Somehow, Ester couldn't bear to talk to these women. She couldn't offer prayers, because she knew too much. She had lived long enough to survive the curse of a husband. She knew she couldn't tell them what to do. That would just drive them deeper into the arms of their abusers. She knew she couldn't ask if they were OK. They'd lie just like she did. She knew that if their men saw her talking to the victims, they would snatch their woman away and forbid future contact. Ester knew the hopeless despair and desperate desire for some kind of magical miracle. And that day, in the annex, Ester made a decision that she was going to start a charity work.

She didn't think anything out. She didn't brainstorm or ask for advice. She knew she had to start a charity for these women to help others.

She wasn't going to tell them that it was for them. Nope! She was going to invite them to help others. She knew that if they were asked to help someone less fortunate, they'd sacrifice whatever they could to be there. She knew this, because that's the way she had been. Ester would do anything to help others because she couldn't help herself. And giving someone else hope was the only hope she could feel.

It was an eerie, peaceful feeling that enveloped the little, old lady. A palette of anger, vengeance, sorrow, regret, pain, humiliation, and worthlessness began to paint her in a new image of resolution, strength, hope, faith and love. The irony of Ester's rebirth in the church that day was disturbing. She wasn't washed in the blood. She was seeing red. She knew that she was only saved by grace by accepting the Son of God as savior. And today, she was going to devise a way to save these women. And she would square up with God at the Bema Seat on Judgment Day. Ester was about to become Samson armed with a jawbone of an ass. She had had enough of the abusive assholes.

Ester walked out of the Holy Trinity potluck and cried all the way home. It was the sorrow of a life stolen from her that she was feeling for these women now. She couldn't feel the pain.

The physical pain healed. All she could remember is not liking how it felt. It was the emotional scaring and fears and feeling all the bad feelings that haunted her now. That was the cloak of horrors that she couldn't shake off.

She sat at home all evening alone and into the night thinking and feeling. She didn't eat. She barely moved. She only got up when the need to pee was too much to hold. Inside of her simmered a soup of sensations that steeped into her heart and mind. It flavored her soul with bitter anger and resentment. It swept her humanity under the rug and replaced it with the intense need for justice. The soul of a vigilante was forged in the kiln of oppression and regrets.

As the light faded and night moved in, Ester wrestled with accepting her revealed destiny. She was going to kill them all and let God sort them out.

And once the resolution of the decision fully engulfed her, she slept in peace.

Chapter 4: The Charity

Two years prior to the death event in Sherone, Ohio, the suicide of a young girl broke Ester's heart. She had already made her decision, but that was the final straw.

Ester couldn't shake it from her heart and mind. Someone should have been there for her. And before long, she made up her mind that she would do whatever it took to help the next before it was too late. Ester was going to start a children's outreach.

She just wanted a couple of women to join her. Ester didn't want a huge organization with 501C status and PSA ads everywhere. All she wanted was the ones that needed her the most to come to her. She wanted to help.

Ester had spent several nights thinking and planning. She needed to be absolutely sure about every moving part of this idea before speaking about it to anyone.

Ester presented an opportunity to Pastor Herman Kern of Holy Trinity Church for an outreach program to children previously unreachable by the church. She outlined the idea of being able to bridge the gap between the church and the street so that new kids could hear the good news and be brought into the folds. The program would begin under her advisement with the help of other ladies she would screen and mentor.

It didn't take much to get Pastor Kern to agree with her and pledge his support. The church would host the new program with Ester at the forefront. He would talk to the elders and make all the arrangements for her to begin as soon as she was ready.

Almost immediately, she went to work building a list of ladies she wanted on board with the program. She knew exactly who she wanted on this outreach. She reached out to Lily first.

Lily was key. She was the one that was never broken. She didn't have an easy life, but she always found a way to not allow her circumstances to define her. She wasn't bitter. She was rebellious, yet she was likable. Lily would go toe to toe with anyone and not back down. Ester needed her.

"Why me?" Lily wanted to know.

Ester smiled kindly. "Because, you are one of a kind: pretty as roses in the rain, fierce as a guard dog and stubborn as a mule in the summer sun. And I believe that you will do just about anything to make sure someone else doesn't have to live life the way you suffered and survived like you did."

Lily smiled flatly with anger and compassion. "I'm in."

Ester managed to convince her first choice of partners in this endeavor to join in about sixty seconds by leveraging Lily's life against her. In her mind, Ester knew that she wasn't being fair. Maybe she was actually being rather mean. But, she needed Lily to help. She was sure that nothing else would work without Lily and her life of experience.

With Lily, came Raith. They were best of friends who had survived many, many nights of terror and abuse. Raith more so. While Lily was always learning new ways to fight off her father and uncle, Raith was only able to endure the life her father and his friends had inflicted upon her. There were too many to fight. And when they were drinking, she couldn't fight at all because they'd hit back. The girls would try to sneak away every chance they could and learned to camp out in the woods. They learned about surviving in the wild. They learned everything they could from books and the internet about building shelters, and from foraging to trapping and cooking game. They could catch fish without fishing gear, then clean and cook them without knives or modern fire starters. They were true survivalists.

Lily and Raith were about as smart, cleaver and independent as any woman could get. Ester knew she had the glue she needed to piece this organization together. She took her time talking to them about building a charity outreach through the church that would encourage children to find shelter from life's harshness. They would be able to change the lives of at least a few kids who needed hope in the hopeless homes they were living in. The spirit of these two women would be impossible to put a value on. But, it would be incredible if it could be instilled in others. Lily and Raith could help others as living proof that giving up isn't the only option in a bad life.

Once Ester had Lily and Raith on board, the rest of the recruiting was as easy as asking.

Crystal was the world's greatest actress without a Hollywood contract. From the outside, everything was good... almost perfect. Her husband was handsome with a great job as a contractor. They lived in a big, beautiful house with two dogs, two cats and two kids. She was on the school board and spent many Saturdays providing snacks and drinks along side the soccer fields. Her family never fought in public. She and her husband, Sam, seemed to still be in love after all those years together.

Indeed, the visual cues of the Fausser family painted a

wonderful mural of their coexistence. It might have been the greatest show on earth.

Much like a mirror image, the reality inside their home was a reverse image of all that was seen outside the home. He was anything but loving and caring. He was a monster in sheep's clothing. He kept a separate bank account on "the down low" for his bad habits and woman chasing. The son was the model student, but in the shadows, he was one of the biggest weed dealers in the school. The daughter was the cutest gymnast with eating disorders and cutting issues. Even their handsome dogs had issues. Most of the neighbors wanted to shoot or impound those untrained and unrestrained animals that were constantly digging holes, knocking over trash and causing other mayhem.

But, Crystal herself was resigned to a zombie type existence of survival. She covered up and apologized constantly for every perceived misstep. She no longer yelled. She no longer fought. She looked for a way to make everything appear right or OK. She would let a truck run over her, if she thought it would keep the family facade intact.

Crystal had survived enough abuse of every kind to learn how to survive every kind of abuse. She could be an incredible politician. And Ester knew it. She knew it all. She almost needed Crystal as much as she needed Lily. And getting Crystal to join was as easy as asking. After all, it would look good on the family.

Serena was much like Crystal, but without the polished showcase. Her husband also had a great job as a judge making plenty of money. The only animal they had was their spoiled child. Serena was likely to throw her husband's money and position around to try to get her way without regard for others. Ester didn't believe that Serena would help with the charity other than donating money. But even then, she would need convinced why she should. Serena would likely be a real tough challenge to reel into the cause.

Ester figured that a very different approach would be required for this one. It was very unlikely that Serena would put herself out to help anyone else. No. There would need to be a "Serena reason" for Serena to get involved.

All Ester needed was was one well worded question to bring Serena to the table. "Would your husband mind if you spend a little time away from him to give a few dollars to help some poor, little kids in our area?"

That was the perfect bait. Robert HATED poor people. He was always talking about how many come through his courtroom with poor people problems that should never even be a problem to begin with. He was constantly complaining about how he was locking up as many poor people as possible to teach them the value of freedom that's bought with hard work. Plus, he felt like he owned Serena and all of her time and attention. He believed that her only existence was to serve him. When she said, "I do," at the wedding, that meant that she would do everything he wanted.

This gave Serena the perfect opportunity to spite Robert, the judge, while avoiding him. Not only did she agree to give money, she was all in on giving time. The fact that he cared about his public image would make it easy for her to take up a key role in the charity. It would make him look good. Ester was a bit surprised, but she was well on her way to breathing life into this mission with a solid base to build from.

The first couple weeks were exciting and a little chaotic. Ester didn't seem to be as old as her age indicated. She was always available and always involved. Among the early recruits to the cause, she added Michelle Satori and Onna Kline to the roster.

Onna was very quiet. Not many people knew her. She wasn't involved in things. She didn't go out. She was extremely... ordinary. She was someone that could go unnoticed. But, Ester saw her, and had spoken to her at the grocery store a couple times. Ester had a sort of radar for people who need someone to talk to. Ester didn't know her, but she knew.

Michelle was a lovely person, but low on confidence. She looked like she could be a leader in a Fortune 500 company, but she lacked the drive and personality. She didn't have much charisma. But, she was a wonderful person that would help anyone upon request. And she was actually rather resourceful. Michelle seemed to be a natural at finding and procuring stuff. She was almost like a den mother for arts and crafts. And she was gentle as a dove.

Beverly was a natural fit for the charity. She had been the lead soprano in the church choir for a decade. She almost asked Ester if she could help before Ester could finish explaining the project.

The children's ministry had other women working within it that could have been candidates for the group Ester was assembling and mentoring like Carrie Ann, Mary, Susan, Terri and Theresa. But, despite the bad situations they were each trapped in and enduring, they were clearly not ready to break free from their abusers. They hadn't been abused badly enough nor long enough to come to the reality that they couldn't change the one they saw potential in. They still believed that they could fix him.

Ester had to struggle through the reality that those women would only destroy her vision and turn on the others. Once someone accused their abuser of being an abuser, they would race to defend the abuser at all cost. No. It was crushing to know that she had to let them continue to suffer, but Ester couldn't save them, because they didn't want to be saved. They didn't believe they needed to be saved. They believed that they could save him. So, Ester had to leave them behind to find out.

Ester had her disciples. She had almost effortlessly acquired the heart and core of the program. She had carefully considered several names for the project ranging from generic to very wordy and specific. Ultimately, she settled peacefully on The Krisis Outreach. When Pastor Kern questioned her on why she would name a children's ministry The Justice Outreach, she replied, "Life is unfair. And these little ones deserve at least a little just treatment, don't you think?"

On a Wednesday night, while Pastor Kern held the mid-week service, Ester asked her girls to come together for their first official meeting. She chose a simple white dress that was nice, but not fancy. She wore her favorite blue shoes with it. She didn't care if they matched. She liked them.

She waited patiently for the ladies to straggle into the library of the church away from all the other people that might be there. She had stopped at the store and bought a few bottles of water, tea and other drinks along with a box of small cookies from the bakery. She thought it would be fitting and proper.

Once everyone had arrived, Ester took her place as the spokesperson. The chatter faded out. And Ester began to speak.

"Even though this is a formal meeting, I won't be wasting your time talking just to talk. There won't be any frivolous details or long winded speeches. The obvious things include the fact that we need to raise some money so we can do stuff. We won't be simply giving hand outs. There's plenty of programs for that. This is not a welfare program.

We want to help. And we will. We want to give hope. And we will. At the same time, we don't want this program to take up all your time and become your entire life. I'm too old to waste time and energy. And you ladies have lives to live and things to do.

Krisis needs to be direct and efficient. When we begin reaching out, we need something solid to offer. Not a hand out or candy bar or balloon. We need to be tossing kids a life line. They know their life isn't good. They know that we can see that. So, we should be able to give them something more than a few words of encouragement, a dollar and a prayer."

As if on cue, Lily asked, "Do you already have that planned out?"

Ester smiled. "I like that. No, not really. This group is not about me. WE can come up with something. WE have the ability and the brains and resourcefulness to come up with something."

And to the amazement of all, including herself, Onna

spoke up and asked, "Why did you choose us?"

Serena looked at her with wide eyes like everyone else. And just when everyone thought she would spew some smart remark at Onna, Serena narrowed her eyes and looked at Ester and asked, "Yeah. Why DID you choose US?"

Ester bowed her head with a smile. She nearly chuckled a little as she let her head bob. She now knew that she had definitely picked the right women at the right times in their lives.

With a long, sharp breath, Ester looked around the room with a beaming face and said, "So, you've already figured out that we all share something in common. I knew I was doing the right thing."

Raith was looking around and asked, "What does that mean? Lily, what is she talking about?"

Lily explained with her street smart response, "We're all abused women."

Raith was confused. "How do you know that?"

Lily looked at her. "We develop a type of radar. We just know. We can sense it. It's intuition. You feel it. You just might not know what to call it or you might be trying to ignore it. We do that... ignore it. We know another woman is suffering, but we can't fix our own life, so we ignore it."

It was quiet for a moment. Ester let them process that before taking charge. "You each possess special skills and abilities that will allow this outreach to be a success. But, you're right. I carefully chose each of you for a reason. We've all been beaten and abused by people we love and trust. Or at least we used to love and trust them."

Ester hesitated. "Now, before I say anymore, let me assure you that this outreach is for real. We're going to help kids and we're going to have a very positive impact on this area. We will do good things."

Again, Onna asked the surprise question, "So, that's good that we really are here for the kids. But, why us? What are we going to do here that's for us? You chose us for a reason. We have the same shitty criteria. What do you want us to do for ourselves?"

Ester smiled kindly with pride. "Oh, Onna. No wonder you don't say much. With that x-ray vision, you don't need to. You can see right through the thickest walls to the heart."

It was very quiet. No one could have imagined what the little, old sweetheart had in mind for these completely normal, but troubled beauties. In this moment, it would be completely normal for Ester to be nervous. She should have been having doubts, and she should have been second guessing herself. It was the quintessential moment for soul searching.

But, nope. Not Ester. Ester had heard the call. She was on a one way ticket and not looking back. She had no doubts. She wasn't guessing about anything, and she had spent a lifetime searching for her soul. She was ready.

The ladies were not. They were not ready at all. There was no way they could be ready. They were about to inhale the poison plans of perdition that in the mind of Ester, lead to redemption.

Chapter 5: Ester's Plan

That Wednesday night in the library of the Holy Trinity was a most pivotal moment in the lives of eight women. They were to be the core and heartbeat of a children's outreach ministry. What Ester unveiled would change everything starting with them, ebbing out to other women, and eventually, it would change the lives of everyone in Sherone forever with eternal repercussions.

Ester began with the story of her government issued love of her life, just like she had told Captain Bucklem. However, she was very intimate with details for the ladies. She described the bruises that replaced kisses. She explained how fear displaced trust. She led them through the dark passages of love bombing and gas lighting and all the love horrors that even Mr. Poe never openly ventured to write about.

It became a mess.

One by one, they each openly shared gut punching, face bashing pain and misery. They cried uncontrollably about the way their hearts were teased into believing and loving right before being sacrificed to their lover's ego and selfish wants. It was ugly crying from wall to wall as the dam broke. Regrets about sacrificing themselves and all they believed in surged and raged. All the lies they were choked with, all the promises broken upon them, all the betrayal they were burned with became visceral.

The children were forgotten. The ministry was forgotten. They forgot that they were in a church and that time existed. They talked and cried and howled as they shared a river of tears and spilt blood. Two of them had to run to the bathroom to throw up. One of them had rounded up every box of tissues in every open room they could find. All of them spilled their guts and released all the hidden nightmares they had been hiding.

Ester headed Pastor Kern off before he could come down to the library to check on them and assured him that she would lock up when they left and that he could go home. She kept him away from the most vulnerable people on earth at that moment. She was their shepherd and protector.

It was nearly midnight when the agony and crying subsided enough. They had drained as much emotional anger out of their minds through their tears as they could. The success of the session was a relief. Nothing had really gotten done to help anyone outside that room. But, everything that could be done had begun. They couldn't wait for another meeting so they could move on to the next question.

Raith asked that next question, "What can we do about all this? I mean, crying is awesome! Don't get me wrong! That was the best cry I've ever had, and I didn't even know how much I needed that. But, I don't want to get together and just cry. I want to do something about this. Am I the only one?"

Ester was beaming. Her tears glistened on her wrinkles as she smiled ear to ear. She looked at each one of them. Deliberately. Individually. Sincerely. And she said, "You just did the most amazing thing ever. More perfect than I could have ever asked for. I hope you don't forget how important and powerful this has been. And it will continue to be.

It's late. So, go home and sleep. Sleep well. You've earned

it by crying it out. I need every one of you to think about this very seriously. And no one can make up your mind or convince your heart to do anything except you. There is something we can do. We can help some children. But, we can certainly help ourselves. We can help ourselves and each other and we can help our own kids. We can't change the world. But, we can change our world. And we can make this suffering end. We don't have to die this way. We don't have to live this way.

It's going to take time. And it's going to be hard. It'll be the hardest thing you've ever done. I promise. But when we talk about what has to happen, you'll understand. And you'll have to make the most serious decision of your life. Then, you'll have to make the hardest commitment of your life. I have a plan.

It's late. Go home. Sleep. We'll talk about what's next when we meet again."

As the women filed out to their cars and started for home, Ester felt the most comforting warmth. She couldn't have asked for things to come together better. She may have had no idea what it was going to take to bring such a diverse group of victims together and bond for a horrible task. Yet, there was no doubt that a strange and powerful miracle had happened here.

Maybe it wasn't really a miracle. Maybe it was too sinister to use any holy terms. Maybe it was too dark to be shining in Ester's eyes like that.

But, Ester was sure. She was reassured. She was making the right decision. Her plan was going to work. She didn't need any more signs. She didn't need a golden fleece. She didn't need anything from anyone. She went home with a smile and couldn't wait to sleep and dream about how she was going to be able to encourage these women to do what she had always wished she had the courage to do sooner. She was going to cuddle up in bed with the assurance that she could teach them to be brave and bold. She breathed in the hope that they would all kill their abusers.

Chapter 6: Ester's Plan(s) Laid Out

The next meeting was Sunday evening. Soccer and Little League games, dance and music practice made it challenging to get the girls together again during the week and ten times harder on Saturday.

There were no tears this time. No crying. No sad or brutal stories. It was all business.

Ester outlined the need for Krisis to make money. Without fund raising, there was nothing. There had to be at least a minimum income for there to be a children's outreach. As sad as it might sound, getting money was the first and foremost critical part. No money would mean nothing could happen beyond their personal pocket books. And even with Serena's husband's money, they needed to be objective about money. They needed a business plan that included income and out go.

Record keeping was also important. There needed to be a paper trail for everything. Whether it was paper or electronic didn't matter. They just needed to be accountable for time, money and results. Even the most honest and noble church activity needed to be discoverable in board meetings and monthly updates.

Ester was very efficient at laying out the basic essentials for the outreach. Since she had been on a handful of church committees and community holiday activities, she had a pretty solid base for the basics. A couple of ladies had similar experience and were very helpful in outlining the particulars for the outreach.

No one wanted to waste time with the nuts and bolts part of building a children's ministry. They all knew they were there with anticipation of learning more about what Ester had in mind. Helping kids was great. But, that was not what burdened their hearts. Maybe that was really bad of them? But, they wanted to believe they had good intentions towards the ministry and the children it might help. They wanted to believe that Ester had something good planned for them. They just didn't know exactly how far the little old lady wanted to take them.

They would soon learn.

It took some time get the business particulars in order and lined up, but as the necessary work was completed, the ladies felt more at ease to talk about personal things. They didn't venture down that path of tragedy and nightmare they shared the first night. Rather, they conversed about daily chores, kids being kids and the routines they worked through daily. It was absolutely a typical gathering of women working on a humanitarian project.

Until it wasn't.

When the time was right, Ester encouraged snacks and drinks. With her battered angels around her, Ester began telling the intimate details of how she was able to rid herself of the man who swore to love her and protect her forever when he had become too abusive to tolerate anymore.

It was slow. He still got his licks in on her for awhile. But, he had become a drinker. So, she slowly started "adding stuff" to his drinks. After a few months, he was showing signs of illness and fatigue. His bad reputation had slid even further into the gutter. No one respected him. That's when she gave him a reason to celebrate one night. And she practically forced him to drink more than he had ever drunk before. Each one had more and more chemical in it.

By morning light, he was dead. The love of her life laid wasted on the floor. No breath. No heartbeat. Just gone. She laid in bed a few more hours and made sure that she wreaked of alcohol when she finally called 911. He was pronounced dead on the scene. She was pronounced too intoxicated to be helpful.

When she was declared sober in the drunk tank, she was questioned about what had happened. She explained that they were celebrating. She didn't know how much he had when he stopped drinking. She was consoled and released to grieve. She left the jail with tears in her eyes. She arrived home alone to relief.

Ester had just confided in seven other women that she had murdered her abusive husband.

It was as silent as silent could get. Ester, the sweet, little, old, gentle lady, had just confessed to murder. No one was able to say anything. They wanted to! They couldn't.

Ester allowed the silence to linger. She rather enjoyed it. She gave a smirky grin before speaking. After all, she really just put herself out there in a most vulnerable spot.

She addressed the elephant in the room. "Now ladies, that was a pretty heavy burden for me to unload. I've never said anything about it to anyone. And here I've just bared my darkest, evil secret to all of you." She looked around. Although the faces were a little stunned, there was no condemnation or judgment. In fact, the look could be described as awe... almost adoration.

Of all those present, Serena spoke for the collective. "Ester, that might be the bravest thing I've ever witnessed in my life. I don't believe anyone here will EVER speak a word of this outside of this room." It was pretty clear that that was a threat. They all understood. It was in their eyes that this was binding. The Krisis Outreach ladies were now on a vow of silence concerning Ester's past.

The silence was back. It was almost more silent than before. Eyes were disassociated. Hearts were beating a little faster and harder. The gears of thought were fully engaged. The magnitude of the confession was unfathomable.

Ester smiled knowingly. She could hear their hearts and minds measuring facts and extrapolating a world of information and feelings from there. All heads were angled down a little. All eyes were fixed on the floor or their own feet. Ester knew that each one was examining their own life and situation. As they pictured the terrible trap they were ensnared in, they over laid Ester's final freedom to that image and began to ask, "What if..."

The next few minutes were a blend of imagination and memory seasoned with feelings, aches, pains and regrets. The thoughts whirling through the minds of those girls were a firestorm of reality and possibility. The inevitable, intrusive thoughts of life without fear and pain invaded like The Allies at Normandy. The possibility of living in a world with no one watching and controlling every thought, feeling and movement was titillating. It was the like dancer in the club with the pulsing lights and driving music making them imagine things that couldn't possibly happen. But... maybe they could? Maybe those things could be real?

Sam and Samantha sat a little closer. One by one, eyes began to look up with heads still lowered. They looked around the room. Ester continued to grin as she watched the hearts and minds of battered women awaken to the ancient conscripts that they were not slaves to be treated like property. She could feel their primal nature forming a tribe. Her grin melted to compassion and understanding. She began to worry for these women as she knew the dangerous and destructive journey they would have to commit to taking on the way to freedom. Much like the underground railroad and founding fathers of America, this small band of broken hearted bravehearts would have to struggle with unimaginable battles and challenges.

Ester already knew that this was going to be a long, winding trail of tears that would have massive barriers to cross. The odds were nearly impossible to overcome. There were so many things to go wrong. A million delicate details had to fall in place perfectly. Only one missed step would end it all. But, she wasn't going to talk about that. They didn't need any warnings or bad news. They needed hope and direction. So, she set her heart and mind on that very objective.

Ester had been choosing her words for this moment very carefully for a couple of weeks. It was a cherished moment for her to finally speak to them. "Ladies. Thank you. I had no fears of telling you about how I found peace in this world. And it's not a death bed confession. I have no intentions of laying down in the dirt until I've seen others find an end to the evil in their lives."

Heads began to pop up. Samantha brought the question everyone had on their mind, "Ester? Are you suggesting that you aim to teach other women how to kill their abuser?"

This round of silence wasn't silent. It was charged with gasp and restless rustling and tiny, audible sounds of confusion.

Ester replied, "And get away with it."

Now the room was filled with noise and voices. It was simply not possible to contain the reaction to a tiny, old woman stating that she was going to teach women to kill the ones they loved but hated.

It took a good five minutes of Ester sitting in silence... smiling... while the others lost their minds. There was hand waving and legal discussions and disbelief... however... at some point, there was a weird and comically sinister change.

It began subtly. The frantic, gut level reaction to the ultimate wrong began to simmer down and take on an almost rational tone. And that rational tone slowly began to morph into something that could only be described as indescribable. And yet, Ester knew that would happen. She just needed to pull the pin on that topic and let the smoke clear on its own. And she was rewarded with a conversation taking on the fantastical rift of what life might be like if all the horrible men somehow just all died at once.

At the age of 93, Ester had the brass and tacks to toss a live idea into a crowded room and let it take on it's own life in its own way. Her confession of killing her abusive husband had magically transformed into conversations of how to get rid of abusive husbands, boyfriends and lovers. She had done it. Ester had convinced a group of women to join her in killing their abusers. And she had barely even said anything. It was perfect.

Once the conversations were lighter and on the verge of a teenage slumber party at 2 am., Ester regained command. She looked around the room and deliberately made eye contact with each one of them before talking. Finally, she said, "Now you all understand how it seems awful. It's a horrible thing to wish someone dead. But, it's a much more horrible thing to make someone wish they were dead. Wouldn't you all agree?

As heads nodded, she continued. "Sometimes I really do feel bad about him dying. But, when I remember all the times I wished *I* was dead to get away from him, I realize that it really was either me or him. He was only going to get worse and worse until he destroyed me and erased me from his life. Nothing was going to make him stop. It didn't matter how much I cried. He didn't care how much I begged. No matter how much blood he took from me, he always came for more. One black eye wasn't enough. He had to hit me hard enough that I couldn't see out of either one. He left me no choice."

She looked down for a second with a somewhat somber look. But, there was no sorrow on her face. There wasn't a shred of regret. And there was steel in her voice when she said, "And if that bastard rose from the dead, I'd kill him again."

She looked up and saw the faces smiling at her with an odd, almost proud look. Ester didn't hesitate. "If you want out of here, now is the time. Get up and go. No one will think anything less of you. No one will try to make you stay. If this is too much for you, and you can't deal with it or you can't handle it, please go.

You can go with my blessings and my prayers for you and your safety and the safety of your children. Obviously, I'd rather you not discuss this with anyone outside of these ladies. But, I can't and won't stop you. If someone finds out and wants to lock me up, that's fine. I've lived some wonderful years without the pain and beatings and humiliation. I've been able to enjoy foods and concerts and museums that he'd never let me have. I've been able to take a few small trips that were the most wonderful sights I've ever seen in person that he would have never let me see. And I've made friends with people he'd never let me talk to. I've enjoyed the best years of my life once that bastard was dead, and I have no regrets.

So, if you want to leave, and you want to have a clear conscious before God and man, I understand. You are free to go. No one will argue your decision. No one is forcing you to stay. No one will ask you to do something you are not willing to do. No one will make you do anything. You can stay or you may go. It's up to you."

Ester looked around. No one was moving. She put on the most stoic look she could muster and said, "Last call. If you want out of this group of women that wish their abuser was dead, PLEASE get up and go now. There's no hidden agenda. We want our abusers buried. If you can't talk about it and want to go, please go. Please."

When no one moved for a full two minutes, sitting in tension, waiting to see if anyone ran, Ester finally proclaimed, "Congratulations, ladies! You are now officially the keepers of my secret! And you are welcome to discuss the possibility of your own emancipation."

It was the strangest, sinister happiness to ever fill a room.

50

Chapter 7: From Chaos – Order

There were a few obvious things Ester needed to make clear before anyone left the room that night.

The most obvious: she would rather not spend her final days in prison. So, she had to ask them to understand that talking about anything she revealed would be a death sentence for her. The next: none of them were born killers. They would definitely NOT be going after anyone any time soon. And there was no way they could all pull off the same thing Ester did. Each would have to find their own way. However, it would have happen all at the same time. One by one would raise suspicions immediately and end the plan with a couple women in prison and the rest foiled and arrested with their abuser still free to enjoy their best life. It had to happen at the same time, in a variety of ways.

Thirdly: No accidents. A bunch of men dying in strange accidents at the same time is no coincidence. Besides that, it's cowardly. That's not standing up to the abuser. That would be deceitful. And the odds of success on staged accidents would be too low to rely on. There'd be too many moving pieces and too many chances.

Lastly: when they were out in their individual lives, they needed to only speak about the real work they would be doing for the kids. They would need to do real things for real people. They would have real fund raisers and real outreach. They really would be doing good things for kids that needed it. They could talk about that all day long. But, if they really wanted to be free of the invisible prisons they were trapped in, the things they planned and talked about in secret needed to remain secret. And that could only happen if they didn't talk about it outside of the group.

The next few weeks were utter chaos. For all of them. They found themselves sleepless and restless. They were torn between a lifetime of learning to be submissive in survival mode and finding revelation that they didn't have to live and die that way.

They were trying to juggle a new ministry into their already busy lives. There were meetings and plannings and phone calls and emails. They were learning new things about how to reach out to people that needed help without making them feel embarrassed for needing help. They had no idea that it would only take them six months to get Krisis up and running. But, it would take them a full year to get the courage and resolve to put an end to their abusive misery.

Along the way, some would need time to heal from new wounds and beatings. Each incident only made Ester more steely in her mission. And it helped them accept that it would never end if they didn't put an end to it.

As the ministry gained traction, it grew. The need for more help allowed Ester and the girls to reach out to other women and bring them in. Each was introduced to the Krisis program and folded into the mix. But, the core group remained elusive and secretive about the things they had shared and were planning.

The idea of allowing more women to join the "after party" was insanely risky. They would be coming to something that began organically. They weren't there for the first cry. They didn't feel the fire of Ester's confession. No one else would ever feel what they experienced in that first melt down.

And it wasn't like they were being invited to a bridal shower. More like they would be asked to join some kind of black ops military group that was hidden from the public. But, people are people and people are not very good at keeping secrets.

Ester wanted to be sure whether or not the new women introduced to Krisis were a fit for the smaller group of women meeting in the library. So, she would make a point of working directly with each as much as possible. She needed to know if they would truly want to seek what Ester was offering AND be able to keep the secret. She had to allow most of the new women to go on with their lives without knowing Ester's secret. They were just not ready for those changes.

They were only a couple months into their existence as a group when Michelle invited Megan to Krisis. And it was only a couple weeks after that when Megan approached Ester. There was a collective gasp of panic when that happened.

Megan had been abused when she was young. She grew up to be goth and Michelle thought that she would be able to connect with that demographic of kids whereas the other ladies might not be able to. Megan and Michelle had been friends from long ago and remained in close contact on a less frequent basis as they did when they were younger. This was one of the overlooked weaknesses in the secrecy of the group. Women have that one close friend they share everything with. It's impossible for them to keep something so life changing from their best friend.

Ester only showed mild surprise when Megan timidly asked if there was more she could do and learn. Megan carefully probed for information trying to ask about the group without coming out directly. Being tuned in, Ester understood what was being hinted at and spared the poor girl from having to kick that door open.

She led the young, goth girl to the library where Ester learned about how she learned about the group. So, Ester asked Megan what she wanted to know. This helped Ester understand the group's vulnerability. And it gave her the opportunity to evaluate what might happen in the future as the outreach grew.

Megan told about how she and Michelle had become friends in middle school and gravitated to the goth scene. She needed someone to trust. Michelle wanted to be trusted. They fit. She told Ester how her father had mistreated her as she was growing up; about how he would "help her" try on new clothes including underwear and a training bra. Michelle was the only person ever trusted to tell that to until now. Ester was the second. She broke down in tears with the depth of shame and anger and the whole flood that trauma like that brings. She couldn't hold it all back any longer.

Ester consoled her and explained how she could understand and empathize with her. She was very cautious to lead the younger girl down the path of understanding in the matter of moving from victim to something higher. It was a very delicate conversation with several check points along the way.

By the end of the time bonding one on one, Ester was exhausted, but knew that she had a new ally in this crusade. She also knew that she would need to have a serious talk with the ladies about this exact incident that just happened to work out well. None of them could afford to have someone learn about this where it didn't go well.
One of the first big and successful fund raisers was a Hot

Dog Buffet that they hosted in street vendor style. They raised a good amount of money for the outreach and it was a great experience where the few kids they had involved in the program helped plan and organize the event. The kids even promoted the event.

With a little help here and there and some guidance from those that had experience, Krisis was able to raise almost $1,200 that weekend. Pastor Kern was able to get local radio coverage, but once the first few people found the Hot Dog Buffet, social media did the rest. The only reason they didn't make more money was because they ran out of food even after sending runners to the store three times.

During the next meeting of Krisis after the fund raiser, Ester was gushing about how amazing they were and how they worked both harder and smarter than anyone she had known. She was very generous with praising the women. And she was very proud of them. They went over the impact it had on the kids and how more kids wanted to get involved. They began laying plans for more fund raisers and other outreach tools.

Then, while the "outreach only" girls were leaving, she gathered her disciples together. They had not had very many meetings and when they did, it was more like an odd parallel universe where they were sorority sisters talking about sinister ambitions when they weren't helping needy kids and taking care of their families. Both worlds seemed completely normal and comfortable.

As they locked the last Krisis people out of the building, they settled into the library with one more person. Ester didn't waste time. She began with the introduction. "Ladies, this is Megan. Michelle has known her for a long time and trusts her implicitly. Once I became aware of Megan's knowledge of us, I took her aside and spent a good deal of time with her. At least as much as I could with things going on. She made her story known. We shared a lot. And I'm confident in welcoming her to this group."

There was chattering and welcomes from the ladies formally inducting Megan to the group.

Ester continued, "I believe Megan understands the gravity of our discussions and will protect us as you all protect each other. We are all dependent upon one another to keep our secrets, but also to encourage and strengthen each other.

Now. Ladies, I understand that you may have friends. And you may know someone that needs this more than you even do. As you know, I'm a woman that can truly understand. But, I hope you understand how critical is to not talk about this outside of these walls. The old expression is, 'The only way two people can keep a secret is if one of them is dead.' There are more than two live people here."

Ester explained that they needed to consider the safety and integrity of the group ahead of their friendships and family relationships. If they didn't, they would be exposed. That would mean arrests. And there would not be justice. Nothing would change. Failure to protect the group was failure to protect themselves and those around them.

For Ester, that would mean the end of her life in jail. But for the rest of them, it would be the loss of their kids, jobs, homes... plus it would be the eternal continuation of the abuse. Secrecy was the most critical cloak they had. It was their only way to survive.

The discussion about close friends and family that needed salvation ensued with deep emotion. The ingrained loyalty to those that were not supposed to be abandoned or left behind or have secrets kept from them was impossible to avoid. Ester was in an unavoidable snare. She felt like she was neck deep in quick sand.

Ester explained that it was also impossible for her to have time to properly vet every person one by one. Total silence is completely contrary to human nature and, while sharing important, life altering information with trusted people would be completely understandable, it was not reasonable. They were going to need an incredible method of induction for new people, or they would need to remain silent. And even with an amazing plan, silence was their only real protection.

There was a lot of murmuring. Everyone was struggling with this when Megan finally spoke up. She interrupted the individual conversations by saying, "I think I can help."

All voices yielded and all eyes focused on her. Ester encouraged Megan to explain.

Megan said, "I've worked in HR and have taken a lot of classes. That doesn't make me an expert, but I think I can help.

We're all the same, but all different. That's obvious and everyone knows it. But, it's possible to unite people for a common cause. Look at Krisis. None of you are the same, but you're united in helping kids. You've worked hard to establish a great, unifying cause. And you've been smart about it.
With this group, in this room, there's a common tragedy that's formed a common bond and inspired a common goal. That can be condensed into a script of sorts. It can become it's own outreach.

We can put information together and work out a system of telling our closest friends whom we know are suffering, too.

Not everyone will be approachable. In fact, most won't. Most will show signs of fear and disbelief. They'll think the worst of you and maybe even call the police on you. They're probably in a very fragile state of mind and emotion and will be very unpredictable.

But, IF and only IF they show the signs of being receptive, we can consider more. In other words, if we feed them a cookie, and they choke on it, we don't give them any more. If they devour it and beg for more, we have a slightly bigger cookie ready to offer."

Sam inquired, "So, you're talking like some kind of series of questions that tests them to see if they're OK with this or should be left alone?"

"Yes," Megan responded. "We don't want to reveal ourselves to those that would ruin us. They probably wouldn't mean to and would most likely feel bad later, but they would ruin us. We only want like minded forces with like minded goals. So, we develop a plan... a questionnaire that allows us to test the waters. If they sink, we let them. If they show signs of wanting to swim, we test their desire to actually swim. Remember life guarding classes for a summer job? Never let a drowning person pull you under. You can't help them if you're dead."

There was a propagation of positive murmuring and chatter. Ester was impressed that the new girl might turn out to be extremely valuable. She was also very worried about how many others might already know about the After Party.

Ester interrupted the low key noise again by proclaiming, "I believe that this is a great idea. I would caution that we do not want to give anyone the entire box of cookies at one time. Too much too soon might be poisonous. Rather, it might be wise to give a little at a time. Let them mull it over and see if they want more. Let them decide if they like the flavor. More importantly, see if they can handle it.

If we have a few more ladies that follow that trail of cookie crumbs willingly, on their own, then maybe we can gather them together for their own special bonding party like we all experienced. Almost like their own initiation where they've earned the right to know."

When the overlapping voices returned, they were much louder and even had a joyous ring to the tone. This idea from the new girl, Megan, sounded exactly like the perfect method to find out if there were any more women like them. Surely there had to be. Logically and statistically, there was no way they could be the only ones.

The unanimous agreement to form a list of questions or verbal prompts that would allow any lady to investigate the potential eligibility of other ladies for the After Party gave the women a lifted spirit. It gave them fresh hope. They would all think about what might make them reconsider life choices and begin thinking that there might be a better way. Matching ideas would definitely be top of the list for approval. Other ideas would be tested and voted upon.

As they said their good nights and parted ways for the night, Ester gave a tired sigh. She wasn't sure of anything. She could feel the good in her chest. But in her mind, she saw a need for miracles. She saw a multitude of mess ups. There were so many ways it could all go wrong.

But, the ball had been put in play, and the clock was ticking. At first, she thought that all she could do was have faith. Then, she realized, she could begin to prepare for the next wave of women that would inevitably come to her. And she also realized that she would need to be ready to set a date before the number of women got too out of control. Less than a dozen was already looking a little sketchy. If she ended up with as many as two dozen, she didn't think the secret would be secret any longer.

As she made her way home, Ester let her mind wander all around. She was feeling tired. Age was certainly a factor. Her mind managed to meander down every rabbit trail. She toggled between the past and future. She tried to focus on the matters at hand, but she was romanced by the possible and grappled by the life she had lived.

Everyone that had ever tried to encourage others to break free from oppression had to have struggled with so many conflicting thoughts and feelings. Morals and ethics had to have been an endless debate inside the mind and certainly would have been an exhausting mental tug of war. Emotional flares probably had set fire to feelings that had not been expressed previously.

Ester found herself wondering how the people helping with the Underground Railroad were so resolute in their mission knowing they could be killed for it. She wondered how George Washington & Company were so convicted in fighting for freedom that they were willing to sacrifice everything to wage war with a kingdom. She was able to imagine the depth of the pains this country suffered in the mid 1800s as friends and families chose sides. She couldn't image how Anne Frank lived in fear of neighbors who were willing and maybe eager to see her and her family loaded on a train to death.

She knew she was right. She knew it was wrong. The best sweet and sour dish required extremes that mingled. It was the conflicting that made the most complex and desirable harmony. Ester was allowing all things good and bad to touch on her heart and mind.

As she settled into her chair, Ester allowed all that thinking to funnel back into containment. She closed her eyes and drained her mind. She emptied her thoughts. The zen of nothing became her comfort for a minute.

Then, she realigned her purpose. She remembered all that had led her to this precipice. She wasn't about to throw herself off of it. Rather, she was hell bent on standing boldly on the edge, watching the darkness weaken as the light grew brighter. She knew that she had been called to lead this revolt against pain and suffering. A warrior's spirit had filled her as she accepted the final challenge of her life. What started as messy anger and a chaotic need for justice had slowly welded her soul to bringing this mission to fruition. She was going to rid the world of as many bad men as possible. She was going to make sure that as many abusers as she could eliminate would never hurt another woman or child. Ester was going to kill them all. She figured that God would sort them out.

Chapter 8: The After Party Participants

Sam and Samantha were a package deal.
Sam tried being married. She really did. She loved a lot of the good things about it. Having a wedding was a dream. Falling in love was dreamy. All the courtship and looking for a house and buying a car together was simply wonderful. There was nothing about finding a man, falling in love and getting married that she didn't love. Until it became a nightmare.

How could anyone pretend to be so kind and gentle and loving for so long? He seemed so perfect. He acted so right. There was nothing wrong with him. Until there was. At some point after the honeymoon, when the honeymoon phase wore off, he changed. Or rather, he allowed his true self to come out. The wolf allowed the sheepskin to slip off.

He became bossy. He acted like he owned her. He became demanding. He went from giving to taking. All of his good habits were traded for bad ones. He controlled the money, the TV, the food, the bills, the car and everything else. He didn't allow her to do what she wanted, and he drove away any friends she might have. He isolated her in his domain as his servant. She was expected to wait on him like the old cliché. The only time they had sex was when he wanted to. It had to be the way he wanted. And his way was rough to the point of violence.

It was only after a few years of being held as a marital captive that she finally tried to get away, but he refused to divorce. It took almost 2 years of stalking and beatings and terror before he broke her so badly that he was locked up for attempted murder. Even then, she was left with such debt from lawyer bills trying to get rid of him, that she didn't know if or how she could ever recover.

When she met Samantha, it was an almost instant bond. Samantha had never wanted a man at all due to an abusive father. The only kindness she had ever known was at the hands of women. And Sam needed a kind hand. They became immediately inseparable. Neither had any regrets about abandoning the male species and never looked back.

Onna was the quiet one. That's how one becomes when talking without being asked gets a face slap. She learned early in life to be quiet unless spoken to. And even then, she learned to measure her response quickly. Too much delay was slapped. "Wrong" answers were slapped. Onna developed a survival ability to assess any situation quickly and respond "appropriately" without delay. She almost took pride in being able to manage this special skill, but could never express that pride.

Serena was the bad bitch Barbie hiding Ken's dirty laundry. He had to have the perfect image to hold a high public office. No one could ever know what went on behind closed doors. So, Serena was bound by financial bars to a life of hidden misery. They weren't in love, but they had to appear to be in love for the sake of the image. The image was the brand and the brand brought them financial stability. As long as they could afford to have their individual lives together, they were bound to each other. She learned about his fetish of banging the prostitutes he sentenced when she contracted a cocktail of venereal diseases. His calloused dismissal of her anger was unbelievable. He literally ruined her and acted like it was no big deal.

At least he didn't act like it was her fault. Instead, he told her, "You should have figured it out sooner." He insisted that he had given her plenty of clues. He told her there was no way any woman could ever be enough to satisfy him. He needed the chase and the new body. He liked manipulating the guilty into providing for his fetish.

They slept in separate rooms after the infections. And they only spent time together in public pretending. Serena lived a miserable existence with a pervert that didn't care about her and only used her for his own gain.

Crystal was a good girl hiding the abuse and shame. It made her depressed and humiliated that, at times, she almost secretly liked the total domination her husband ruled over her. He would use her like a play toy. And there were no safe words. There was no consent. Everything sexual was on his terms. No exceptions. Failure to comply or provide as demanded was punished harshly. She was simply so humiliated that she put on the best show on earth to hide it all. She never wanted anyone to know about any of it.

Michelle Satori had been raped. Twice. And both times, everyone blamed her for it. Especially the second one. People accused her of dressing provocatively and drinking too much. They told her she should have been more careful. They told her she was too flirty and invited the wrong type of attention. She was told that she wore too much make up and showed too much cleavage. Even the police told her that she should have never been out late and that certain areas were places that a woman "was just asking for it." Someone even told her, "No wonder, with that hair like that." She didn't even know what that could possibly mean!

Michelle didn't know what to do besides hide it and try to follow all the "advice" she was given. She tried to be plain and conservative as humanly possible. But, she learned quickly that if she talked about it at all with men she was interested in, those men changed the way they treated her. Some avoided her. Some became too touchy and demanding. It was as if being raped gave men permission to treat her like a second class whore. They didn't see her as a victim, but rather an easy target.

Even when she thought she could confide in women, she couldn't. She learned the hard way that women could be just as judgmental, and in some ways, much worse than men. Men only made physical advances. Women were so psychologically destructive. It was more devastating to trust women than to tell a man and fight off his hormones.

So, she hid. She never spoke of it at all and did her best to pretend that none of it ever happened. As far as anyone knew of her life, she had grown up healthy, safe and happy.

Megan was younger and goth. Most would consider it a simple phase a younger girl might go through. But, for Megan, it was a warning to boys that she wasn't afraid to cut them. She grew up abused by men that were supposed to protect her and cherish her. She woke up one day and chose violence. She had done a year in juvie for stabbing her father. Most people didn't understand why. That part was sealed in court records since her father was a police officer.

One day, when Megan decided she had had enough, she stood her ground in a corner with a knife from the kitchen. And instead of checking his hormones, her father thought his police skills would allow him to disarm the young, weaker teen. He required 72 stitches for his under estimation because he was overly confident.

Once released, Megan refused to go back. She stayed with

various friends and other family members until she could land a job that allowed her to save enough money to live in a conversion van that served as her home. She only paid for a lot at a campground where an understanding owner allowed her to keep a generator and stay all year.

She was dating Samual who worked in a factory. But, he was far from a nice guy. He was always trying to prove how tough he was, almost as if he was trying to prove he was worthy of a big titty, goth girlfriend. But, he couldn't seem to control his rage and shut it off. Even with her.

She really loved him. Or she thought maybe she did. But, she hated how violent he could be. And at times she wondered if he would beat her more if he wasn't afraid that she would stab him.

Lily was the one. Lily was beaten but never broken. She was the quintessential country girl that was kerosene and lightning. Her boyfriend had as many black eyes as she did. He would have been more likely to get a blow job from a rattle snake than believe he could beat her ass and get away with it. Because once she got up, he was going to get his.

No one felt sorry for her because she seemed to be able to hold her own. But, no one understood why anyone would live in a relationship that resembled a cage match. People just assumed that they wanted it that way.

What they didn't see were the drugs and alcohol that fueled most of those fights. Neither one was innocent. Lily avoided the drugs, but drinking brought out the fighter in her.

And there was no stopping her mouth. If it was on her mind, it was on her tongue. Lily was never going to be silent for anyone. Those that knew her family, knew that she was the product of her daddy. He was a loud, fighting son of bitch. What they didn't know was that he was abusive in many ways.

Raith was Lily's best friend. Lily was Raith's guardian angel. If there was ever a poster child for the After Party, it was Raith. All she had ever known was abuse. Physical, sexual and psychological. The girls met at a party where Lily pulled two guys off of Raith and beat their asses in front of everyone for trying to rape a passed out girl. Raith was never going to be the "pass around girl" ever again, if Lily had a say.

Once Lily came around, Raith had to learn a new way of living. Friends and family were no longer able to use her. Raith didn't know how stand up for herself. She had never known what it was like not to be used. Lily spent countless hours crying with her, teaching her and propping her up.

Raith was never going to be the woman Lily wanted her to be. But, she was trying. She loved Lily. But, she was conflicted from being conditioned her whole life to be a sex doll or a discarded nobody. She wanted be strong and independent. But, it was like growing up in a dungeon then being set free in a foreign land with strange customs. As much as Raith wanted to be "normal" that was simply not possible. She had been too broken for too long.

The members of the After Party were a mess at best. No one was sure when they adopted the name After Party, but it became their code word. They were just trying to discretely let each other know what they were talking about without telling others what they were talking about. They were all broken and beaten. They had all endured lies and cheating and horrible people close to them. They were a mess.

The only thing perfect about them was that they met. And that they met Ester. And that they met Ester after that little old lady became a monster.

The thing many people don't understand about monsters is the very thing that people who read monster stories are attuned with. The monster is generally not bad or evil. They are treated like a monster, so they become a monster. The ones that are misunderstood become feared because they are not understood. The fear makes people treat them so badly with distrust, isolation and a multitude of pains and rejections that they become monstrous.

Ester was not a monster. She was treated badly. Her husband treated her very badly. She was dragged through mud and fire and forced to survive. All she ever wanted was to be a cookie baking Sunday school teacher who crocheted afghans for her kids. Instead, she was poked and prodded into becoming the sneaky killer that poisoned her husband, and now she was on the verge of going full-on Charles Manson with her new found disciples. So, maybe in some way, she was becoming a little bit of a monster? Maybe her late husband really did create a monster.

Chapter 9: The Trail of Questions

New women. How were they going to bring new women into the group that had been building a ministry outreach since their inception? One that was secretly talking about abuse and the justice never received?

The first months of their existence were almost all group therapy. Albeit informal and very hit and miss, they were self healing and self soothing. It was very unorganized. Talk was never planned and neither were tears. But, both were abundant. The core group of women plus Megan were bonded tight. They had shared everything.

Now they were convinced and convicted to reach out to those who were closest to them. Were. Because once they found the After Party, no one would ever be as close as those in the After Party. But, they didn't want to leave their best friends and closest family behind in finding freedom and liberation.

It was a risky move. It was actually insanely dangerous. But, they agreed that it was necessary and worth the risks. So, they set to work on The Questionnaire.

The Questionnaire was their attempt to ask the ones they wanted to trust some key questions that would allow them to figure out if they could trust them. It took them MONTHS to figure it out. It was not as easy as it sounded. Each question had be designed to elicit a clear yes or no answer. The answer to the question didn't have to be yes or no. But, the feeling had to be definitive.

Questions needed to be tested. They couldn't afford to guess. They needed to be sure that the women they were seeking honest answers from could be trusted to not know that they were being interviewed for the After Party. The goal was for the questions to be so natural that the answers were given without question. They didn't want to conduct a formal interview with anyone. People being interviewed might lie. When they know they're being tested, they may lie.

And they certainly didn't want anyone to feel interrogated. That was the last thing they could afford. Questions that probe too deeply become suspicious. Once suspicion is aroused, guards go up. People shut down. Then, the one asking questions begins to be asked questions. Nope, they didn't want that.

The questions were crafted carefully. They tried them on unsuspecting subjects at stores and gas stations. Funny looks were a clue to try again. Smiles and answers from complete strangers would indicate that they should be good to go. It was a tricky and delicate business. But it was essential.

"How's it going?" That's pretty vague and the answer could be anything, including a lie.

"How is everything?" That's also vague, but allows a follow up question or two that can be more specific.

"Have you been sleeping good?" AH! What a seemingly odd question. But, the answer tells so much. Few people would lie about this one. In fact, it's almost a bragging point when it comes to sleeping badly. It would be tempting to immediately follow up on this question, but they agreed that allowing the person to answer was the most important moment. Not asking "Why?" would be critical. It was critical not to ask them why they were not sleeping well. Remaining silent to wait for an answer would give the person an opportunity to reveal more. And their *decision* to reveal more would be more honest than any answer would be.

"Have you ever known anyone that had to go to a women's shelter?" That's a very direct question and obviously not the first one to lead with. But, if the conversation made it that far, it would give them a chance to reveal so much. Asking if they, themselves, ever had to go would be too personal and an instant shut down for most. But, asking if they *knew* someone would not only allow the person to answer, but it would allow them to ask the same question.

That reflective questioning would be the key moment where certain secrets could be revealed without revealing the After Party. It could be kept between the two of them.

If there became an honest flow of information, the question with the weight of a million broken hearts was waiting. "Have you ever wanted to do something about it to make it stop?" And that could lead to the final question, "If you could do anything to make it stop, would you stop at anything?"

That was the most important question and it had to be asked in that specific way.

"Would you kill your abuser?" Can't ask that. Nope. Just no. It's like tossing a flash-bang in the room.

"What would you do to make it stop?" Not clear enough. Too open ended. It leaves the person looking like a deer in the headlights. It doesn't lead any direction.

"If you could do anything to make it stop, would you stop at anything?" was the perfect question. It was clear. But, it would lead the person to think. It was open to morality. It gave the opportunity to pull the trigger or back down. It allowed them to evaluate whether or not they would stop at nothing to end the abuse. Or if they were just not at that point.

By asking that question, the person was in control of making the decision. It wasn't handed to them. They were not fed the response. It was up to them. The women just needed to be ready to accept whatever answer was given and not ask any more. They couldn't goad the new person or *try* to get a particular answer. They just had to ask and be ready for whatever answer was given.

If they turned away, let them. Do not pursue. Just let them go. It's impossible to make someone do something they are just not willing to do. Sure, some can be tricked or forced or bribed. But, that's not a decision. There's no commitment. And with no commitment, it would make the group vulnerable to exposure. Just. Let. Them. Go.

If they gave something vague, it would be better to also let them go. Half hearted is not committed. Only if they were quick and solid on their answer about doing whatever it would take to end the abuse... only then should any hint about a secret place to find support should be given.

And even then, it was still a question. It was a hypothetical question. "IF there was a group of women who had survived abuse and were looking to settle up with justice, what would you say?"

Then, let them think. Let them answer, but let them think about it for a few days or even a couple weeks. Never lead them into ANYTHING. The ultimate test of self restraint would be to hint that there was a group, but not to offer any information until that person was talking about wishing and wanting a group like that. Then and only then, were the girls to finally ask the final question.

"Let's pretend a group of women were secretly meeting with plans to end the abuse they had endured for so long. And let's pretend that it was super secret, because, ya know, some people would be scared about what a group like that might do to end abuse. What would you think of such a group if it existed?"

The only answer Ester would consider as an agreement to learn about the After Party was, "I'd do anything to be part of it!"

Ester needed them to commit to keeping any secret no matter how shocking. They needed to be willing to hide it all from their friends and families. She wanted them to understand that learning about the group was dangerous and that they would be asked to protect the lives of those already abused. Ester needed anyone wanting to join their ranks to be life and death serious about joining.

There was no room for doubt. There would be no forgiveness for being found out. The girls would need to practice over and over asking the questions and being patient for answers. No one was to begin asking before everyone in the group was satisfied that they were ready. Each person wanting to ask someone to join had to be tested and approved BEFORE asking anything. The failure of one would be the failure, and maybe death, of all of them.

It took them weeks. They wrote and rewrote the questions. They rehearsed and analyzed answers and responses. They learned to listen without talking more. They learned to accept the outcomes they didn't want. Spacing out the questions didn't come natural, so they worked on the self discipline to wait each question out. They demanded patience from each other when asking and waiting for the final answer. It was a slow and difficult trail to blaze.

There were times it looked like they would never be able to invite others. There were arguments. It was rough at times. It was tense and frustrating. But, the goal was always there. They never seriously considered giving up. They'd rather slug it out in the church library than give up. And there were a few times Ester had to step between women that were nose to nose with clenched fists.

It was the most trying and testing time of the their coexistence. Getting from hapless victim to active interviewer was a long, grinding path uphill. Diversity and various backgrounds might ultimately make for a strong group, but not so much in the beginning. Different ideas and approaches can be a stumbling block.

Occasionally, Ester just wished there was a wood shed and a willow tree on the property.

Sometimes she wished they would grow up. But, then she'd remind herself, and them as well, that most of them were robbed of the chance to truly be a carefree child. When tempers flared, she understood that there was a lot of stored, unresolved anger and helped them redirect it towards the abuser and their end goal. When back handed comments sparked petty match ups, Ester would step in with grace and nurturing to sooth the flare ups. She was able to help them identify and deal with many of the expectations and requirements that society had forced them to assimilate and display while growing up as a woman.

She allowed them to be themselves, but not at the cost of others. She explained to them that they didn't have to smile and "be nice" any more. It was up to them to recognize the invisible fence that society expected them to stay behind. She gave them permission to step over it. They could be civil without being fake. They could be decent people without competition and snide remarks. They were allowed to compliment each other and let it be just a compliment. Ester had unintentionally taken on the life coach role of guiding these women to a new mind set.

For a few months, it was touchy and tense and there were times it seemed impossible and on the verge of meltdown. But, somehow, they kept going. They backed up and moved forward. Sometimes it felt hopeless. But, without fail, Ester focused them and led the way. It was tempting to pounce when one fell. It was hard to fight the urge to rub salt in the wounds. None of them realized how far into toxic territory they had wandered until Ester called them out.

There was even a time when Serena stood toe to toe with Ester staring her down. She was shaking and angry at the little, old lady. Ester looked up at her innocently and asked, "Is this what you want, my child?" The tension was pulling at everyone. It was a rather scary scene until Serena began to melt like a child caught being disobedient.

Ester ended up sitting with Serena's head in her lap for the rest of the meeting stroking her hair. It was the most peaceful feeling the group had ever experienced together. It was really the unplanned, unscripted moment that let them all know that no matter what happened, they would eventually be alright.

Chapter 10: The Weakest Link of the Outreach

As the women gained the confidence to begin reaching out to their friends about joining their venture, a terrible and tragic revelation came to light. It was a horrible discovery that threatened to unravel everything. And it was right under their noses.

Pastor Kern may have had an ulterior motive for supporting the children's outreach. An accusation... actually a couple of accusations... were leveled at Pastor Kern about his affinity for kids. Specifically, evidence was mounting that he was a pedophile.

"Let's start with him today!" Lily demanded.

It was the torches and pitchfork moment. They were ready to storm his office and cut off his dick.

Ester had a hard time holding them back. She assured them that she would handle the man and put him in check. The only thing that satisfied the mob was when she promised that if she failed, they could do what they wanted. And she'd help. This gave Ester hope that they really were evolving from helpless victims to those that were angry enough to be moved to action.

Ester became a private investigator. She tracked down the children so she could assess the damage. Fortunately, it had not gone beyond the hopeless point of no return. But, it was an eminent threat. If the parents went public with formal accusations, and if charges were filed against Herman, he would become untouchable. Ester would not be able to do anything to him, because he would be in the public spotlight. And even worse; since he was sponsoring Krisis to allow it to be recognized as an outreach of Holy Trinity, that program would be put under scrutiny. Everyone and everything would be put under a microscope.

She talked to the parents that were making the accusations. Those were difficult conversations. And Ester practically pretended to be an uncover FBI agent setting up a sting for the man of the cloth. She assured the concerned and angry parents that their children would not be sacrificed to the devil in pastors robes. She didn't know if she could keep that promise. But, she needed them to delay intervention until she could give them the go ahead. She promised them that there was a plan in place that would solve this problem, but she couldn't tell them more. Check points and status updates would be all she could give them to make sure their kids remained unmolested. And if they were too worried, she asked if they would quietly withdraw and allow her to complete her work on correcting the pastor.

Once again, the magic of Ester kept the momentum and security of the group. But, that man would need to be put on a short leash. Ester spent some time in prayer before approaching the man of God.

She felt strongly convicted to hold no punches. She went to his office and barged in. The young couple that was there for marriage counseling was surprised, but agreed to leave at her request. It probably sounded more like a demand.

"Pastor," Ester was stern. "I hope you understand the seriousness of my visit. Because, if you don't, it's not going to go well for you."

Pastor Kern played the typical role of ignorance. Ester was not amused. And she was not having it.

"Pastor," she said calmly. "May I borrow a piece of paper and a pen?"

He looked a little confused, but said, "Of course."

Ester wrote the names of the three kids who's parents were making accusations. She paused between each name to look him in his uncomfortable eyes. She could tell that he had gotten good at hiding his sins. But, she was very good at seeing through the bullshit.

She stood upright and folded her hands in front of her. She felt like she was rather pretty in this particular dress that she had found for $1.25 at a yard sale last summer. She was wishing she had bought that cast iron skillet to bring with her today.

She wagged a finger at him and made the shushing lips. She only wanted him to listen. And she outright told him that. Ester explained, "Pastor Kern, we are having a conversation right now where I speak and you listen. If you fail to understand that, I will have no choice but to unleash the parents of these three children and their lawyers.

Now I have no doubt that you have some dirty skeletons somewhere. And I don't want to know. That's between you, God and the Devil. This is my ministry. And I'll personally have a few large, angry dads take you away to a farm I once knew of. And I'll allow the animals and insects and angry parents to have their way with you over and over and over again until you're begging for mercy. Then, I'll make sure it gets really unpleasant.

There won't be any lawyers ruining your name until you're long gone. There'll be no tearful memorial service for you. No one will miss you after a couple months. They'll only wonder what ever happened to you. And I'll take that with me to the grave."

She only paused to make sure he squirmed.

"You see, sir," she continued. "I was a victim of a man like you. He proclaimed Jesus in public and practiced evil in secret. And I just can't allow another man like you to do that to those children that are already in need of good people. I learned long ago that evil preys upon the innocent. It won't cannibalize itself. Evil doesn't feed on evil. This is why bad things don't happen to bad people. Bad things happen to good people because evil feeds on the very thing it's missing. It tries to consume everything it is not. This is why we are to be wise as serpents but gentle as doves."

Kern couldn't help but be amazed and maybe a little terrified. Ester had just answered the question so many people had tried to trap him with. All of his seminary training had never given him a better answer to why bad things happen to good people. Unfortunately, it was coming under circumstances that were promising to ruin his public image and ministry.

Ester concluded, "You certainly have mastered that 'wise as serpents' part."

Pastor Kern put his hands on his desk and looked down with that guilty head tilt. "Now, Ester..." he tried to explain himself.

"Shut up!" She wouldn't let him. "You just shut your whore mouth!" She shook her fist at him. She continued to rail the now startled man. "You're testing my graciousness. One more outburst from you and I pick up the phone! So, you can sit there in silence like you expect your victims to do."

That did it. He was mortified. She felt justified.

Ester leaned on the desk and spoke eye to eye. "If I hear the slightest rumor that you are sniffing around the kids in the Krisis Outreach, that will be the end of you in a very slow, painful payback from hell. Krisis will no longer be symbolic. It will be literal justice."

Kern didn't say anything.

Ester stood up straight. "There's only one answer that will save your hide for now. Nothing will save your soul. But, if you want to live a somewhat normal life doing whatever you do now, you might want to say, 'Yes, Ester.' I'm just saying. It's up to you."

The pastor swallowed hard as he said, "Yes, Ester."

Ester was pleased. She asked, "Will you keep your nose and hands and everything else out of my ministry? You will stay far away from Krisis, it's people and everything about it?"

He knew he was in a bad spot. "Yes, Ester," was all he could say softly.

Ester stood there staring at him for a solid minute. She wanted him to feel as uncomfortable as some men had made her feel as they stood over her with strength and power. She finally said without changing expression, "I suppose if this were a movie, I would caution you to not test me. But, honestly... part of me really wants you to cross that line so I can make that phone call with a clear conscience. Do ya know what I mean, Herman? Can you understand how much I'd like to see someone suffer and pay for the evil they've done? How it might feel good to see someone get what they deserve? And remember, you've already been warned once, you bastard."

That did it. She owned him. He obediently replied, "Yes, Ester."

She stared at him another solid minute. She would have given two more minutes, but he was making her feel sick and dirty.

Ester left his office with disdain and anger. But, she had to be level headed. She couldn't risk losing it all now. She also made a mental note that he would get what was coming to him.

Chapter 11: The Horse Before the Cart

"How do we do this?" Onna wanted to know.

The room fell silent. They had been meeting for months now and Onna laid out one of the most obvious questions.

The outreach had been going well. In fact, it was going great. Their innovative approach of reaching kids with the intentions of only helping them help themselves had garnered attention and headlines around the region and beyond. They were almost in danger of becoming a victim of their own success.

The Krisis Outreach was not focused on giving to the needy. It was built on the cliché of giving a man a fish vs teaching him to fish. The women used their backgrounds and educations to teach kids to garden and can food. They taught them how to find odd jobs for money and how to be professional about it. Krisis was more focused how to help kids develop the tools and skills necessary to help themselves. They wanted these lives they impacted to learn that they didn't need to be victims. They wanted them to take the lead in caring for themselves for a lifetime, not just a meal.

The Outreach had an unplanned success in that as they taught the children skill sets, the kids wanted to teach their new skills other kids they knew were struggling. They ended up bringing more kids to the program than anyone had expected.

Fortunately, fund raising was easy. The kids figured that if they could raise veggies, they could sell them, too. And once they figured out how to get enough money from cleaning cars to buy a lawn mower, they were bringing in money for themselves and the program. It was nearly a self sustaining entity.

The raging success of the Krisis Outreach also gave the women access to more volunteers than they ever expected. Success breeds success and everyone wants to be part of it. They had to turn a lot of women and men away as they simply didn't have enough places for them all to help.

Amid all the hoopla, Onna asked an important question for the After Party: "How do we do this?"

Ester asked for clarification before assuming anything "Excuse me, Onna? How do we do what?"

Onna looked around the room hoping to see how many understood what she was saying without saying it. She timidly elaborated. "How do we do this? How do we get justice for all the shit we've been through? How do we make them pay?"

Lily piped in, "And get away with it? How do we do this and get away with it?"

This put Ester in a bind. She was visibly a little on edge. She was not prepared for anyone to ask that yet. She bowed her head and folded her hands in her lap for a moment. No one bothered her. No one interrupted.

Ester raised her head after a few moments and opened her eyes. She smiled weakly as she looked around the room. This was not supposed to be the speech she was giving now. This was supposed to be happening after the wave of new inductees was in. But, she knew that she couldn't put it off once it was asked. She had to speak.

"I had hoped to do this at another time," Ester said apologetically. "But, I suppose we ought to spend a minute on this now. I don't think we can get away with it."

She allowed the room to buzz and the unsettled fears rise. It needed to bubble a little before she could serve the news.

Samantha asked, "What you mean we can't get away with it? Are you saying we'll go to jail?"

Ester raised a hand to speak. "My sweet ladies, we can definitely do this. I just don't believe we can come out unscathed. We can't get away with it. Not totally. There will be some aftermath."

Michelle said, "Now, Ester! You told us how you got away with it, but you're telling us that we won't?"

"Oh, Michelle," Ester assured. "I won't be getting away with anything anymore. I'll be taking the blame for all of it."

Again, she let the room bubble before explaining, "I've lived my life. I have nothing to lose. I fully intend to take full and complete responsibility for everything. You all will have to protect yourselves and each other by blaming me. When they question you, blame me. It was my idea. I did it. I pulled the trigger. I used the knife. I poisoned him. It was Ester.

No one! And I mean NO ONE is to admit to anything. All fingers point at me. I get all the glory. I take all the blame. None of you know anything and NONE of you accept any responsibility. Do you all hear me?"

There was a concerned grumbling and weak answer. Ester asked again, "Do you ALL understand me?"

There was a more unified but hushed affirmation. Ester did not look satisfied. She frowned and said, "Look. We have new women coming into the folds. They will need time to believe just like you. They will need help, just like you. You will be their help. When this happens, it will be a major, one day event unlike anything anyone has ever seen.

At that moment, this group does not exist. It never existed. And none of you know anything about each other outside of what you might learn while leading a children's ministry. You will all be more silent than monks. And the only cold hearted killer in this town is Ester Wireman.

Now... once we onboard these new women whom you've all been questioning and preparing for weeks, we will set up a retreat. We will spend time welcoming them to the group. And as we are sure the timing is right, we all go on a well earned retreat; a last supper kind of meeting where all the final details are laid out.

We'll talk and sing and cry. We can have movie time and games. And we can eat seafood and pie. Or cake."

Sam interjected, "Uh, Ester. I'm not sure I like the sound of the last supper idea."

Ester smiled a knowing smile. "I know, Sam. I know. But, we have finally come to the point in this journey where there's only one last chance to turn back. Maybe two.

But, once we make the date and set the final plan in motion, this will all have ended already. There will be no more After Party. No more meetings. No more normal.

There will also be no more beatings. No more rapes. And no more abuse for us. And, I'd wager that the men witnessing this will think twice before they lay hands on another woman or child. We can't fix the world. But, we can absolutely rock it. We will make the world take notice and ask the questions that should have been asked long ago. We will make them pay attention, and quit ignoring us and blaming us for what has happened to us."

She could see some slightly dreamy eyes. She addressed that.

Ester said, "Now, before you get lofty dreams of glory or think that it'll all be OK the next day or week, it won't. It's going to take time. It'll take time to sort through the details. It'll take time to get though the investigation and questions and whatever else may happen. It'll take time to get used to life without the abusers.

Ladies, you need to prepare yourselves for a long, hard adjustment from what you've known to what you don't know.

That can be the scariest thing in the world. The unknown. Even when the known is bad, at least we know what we have. Not knowing is terrifying.

This will be the focus of our retreat; preparing for the great unknown. You all know I'm now 94 years old. I'm facing the greatest unknown. But, I'm prepared. After all, I can't bail out of that.

I encourage you to look at where you've come. All of you have grown so much. You've become so much stronger and more vibrant. You have so much more to live for and so much more to accomplish. I wasn't wanting to give this talk now. Not yet. But, maybe we all need a little taste of the good stuff that waits for us down the road. Maybe we need to hear that there's life after all this crap. There's a good life."

The mood was heavy. They had come to the part of the journey where it was no longer just talk. They were no longer meeting to encourage and uplift. All the time they had spent together was becoming real and soon it would become insanely real. It was about to move from hypothetical "some day" stuff to "pick up your weapon and follow me" stuff.

These women were waking up to the realization that they weren't just talking. They were planning. And now, they were getting ready to act.

Yet, Ester's admonishment was helpful. They could still bail out. They had not committed any crimes or harmful acts. They were just women talking. So, they still had time. It wasn't too late. They just needed to keep talking and bring the next line of ladies to the After Party.

Chapter 12: More Women

Beverly was the lead soprano in another church across town for the past 10 years. Before that, she had been with Holy Trinity, but an incident with Pastor Kern caused her to transfer membership. She never talked about it.

When her first husband died in a car accident, she remained widowed for a long time. But, eventually, loneliness got the better of her, and she began dating a handsome man that treated her well. They only dated for about six months before they knew they were in love and right for each other.

Trent was a teacher. He was well respected. He helped with the chess club. Maybe that's why he was so good at hiding his violent outburst. He was always thinking ahead.

As with so many, his hidden demons surfaced within a year of taking the vow to love and cherish and protect Beverly. And like so many, Beverly got really good at making excuses and hiding the evidence. She was Onna's pledge.

Crystal had been working on Faith. Faith said she really loved Scott Harwick. She just wished for that farmer to not be so angry all the time. He couldn't control the weather, or the prices or so many other things. She hated his mean streak. She blamed it on the stress of farming. She just wanted him to change for the better. She just hoped he could be a little more kind and gentle.

Faith was a little bit of a wild card in Ester's eyes. She didn't really want to lose her husband. She wanted to fix him. That wasn't going to happen, and that's not what the group was about. She had been trying to change him for years and was at her wit's end. And she didn't see an end to the anger and abuse.

Not surprisingly, Megan was the bad girl that was good at recruiting. She was pledging Tammy and Candy.

Tammy was with Ricardo in a fiery and tumultuous relationship. They lived together with their toddler. Their union could be called anything but happy. In fact, both of them had a reputation. Either might be found at one of the bars looking for a fight when they weren't using each other as sparring partners.

Candy married Deputy Conner Cain at an early age. She was probably the only married high school senior at the time. With Conner being 21, it was just a little scandalous. When the honeymoon wore off, the stress of a cop's life took over. Candy took to drinking to cope. And all the unpopular problems that accompany an alcoholic life were waiting for her.

Adrianna was unique. Technically, she was mentally handicapped. Most people wouldn't recognize that at first. They would have to spend time with her or be told. Sometimes it took people awhile to fully believe that she was just born different and operated on a different plane than the average person. Raith adored Adrianna thinking that she was the sweetest and most gentle soul alive.

And Raith hated Ken for taking advantage of that. She hated how he would bully her and get her to steal things, then play it off on her "lack of awareness" if she was caught. Raith hated how he talked badly about that beautiful butterfly in public, then he would degrade her in private. But, she REALLY hated how he got off on choking her out and other twisted forms of pleasure derived from hurting her.

Adrianna didn't like how Ken treated her. She couldn't win an argument against him and always felt like she had no choice. He would make her feel like she needed to be grateful to him for taking her. And that was where Raith drew the line.

Bethany loved Dan. At least, she did at first. He was a good old boy that loved to fish and ride four wheelers. But, when she found herself working two jobs to support his fun, that loving feeling began to change. He acted like she could never make enough money to make him happy. And when she wanted more sex than he could deliver, he accused her of being a whore and began to treat her like one.

It took her a couple of years to fully awaken to how bad it was. She looked in the mirror at a stranger one day and asked that worn and ragged girl, "What the hell is wrong with you?"

There were many, many women who were just not right for the After Party. Too loyal. Too controlled. Too scared. Too weak. In denial.

Some helped with Krisis and were wonderful assets to the program. But, they had to be kept in the dark about anything beyond the kids.

Even still, the list of candidates for Ester's Army was rather lengthy.

Randi was a party girl who had been party raped by

friends who then blamed her for it. She was ready to put an end to that.

Meelow's parents had "rented her out to friends." The explanation was as irrelevant as it was irrational. It was sick and wrong.

Brenda was the loyal wife to the high school principal. He had been accused of placing hidden cameras in the girls' locker rooms, but all of the evidence mysteriously disappeared.

Meg was the most controversial pledge because she was only in high school. She had been forced to grow up way too soon and was the protector of her little sister, Julie. Meg's story was too much for the women to hear. They regrettably understood why she looked so disheveled and unkempt. No one could tell this girl "no." She was chronologically too young. But, once she shared her story, she was welcomed with open arms and given sanctuary.

All of this was a problem for Ester. She wanted to help as many as possible. But, there were so many! How in the world would they be able to remain secret with so many women?

The part that was messing with her mind was the sheer number of women whom they were identifying as being abused. It was absurd. She began to wonder if there were any women left that had never been abused. How were they going to make a difference if they were so outnumbered by abusers? It was no wonder so few women fight back. What would be the point if there were ten more just like him backing him up and ready to take his place?

Ester's heart was aching and her mind was racing. She was trying not to question herself or second guess her decisions. She only indulged the pain and doubt a little while, like an annoying house guest who wanted a second cup of tea when you thought the conversation was over.

The stories were all the same, and yet, totally different. The same could be said for the women. The same could be said for the men. Regardless of social status or income or religion they were all the same. She felt like she was watching the same short feature film over and over with different faces and names playing all the same roles.

She shut her thoughts down and went back to that original scene that sparked this entire journey. She returned to the core of the mission. There was no way she could back up or back down. So, she put all attention and energy on the goal. Ester was committed to make sure some evil abusers left this planet before she did.

But, she was still worried.

Then she realized it wasn't worth the worry. It would all work out or it wouldn't. Worry wouldn't work any wonders. Worry could only ruin a lot of things but it could never make anything better.

Ester chose to focus and direct her energy into making sure she did everything she could to help everyone she could and protect them as much as possible. She had to make peace with herself knowing that some might get hurt, some might go to jail, and some might find another abuser to replace the one they had. But, she was not leaving this life without making this vision of hers happen. There were simply too many women in bad shape to stand by and do nothing.

With more women about to officially join the group, some things needed to happen. It was time for some of the women to step up a little more. Ester needed a couple of women to become the next Ester.

Lily and Onna were Ester's first choice. Naturally, Onna immediately refused by sighting lack of courage, capabilities and a few other self abasing traits. Lily tried not to look as scared as she felt, but she was excited. Ester was at peace.

"My dear ladies," Ester spoke as a parent. "There's many reasons I've chosen you. But, the single most important thing that matters is that neither of you really want to be leaders."

There was obvious confusion on the faces of the ones just chosen to be leaders because they didn't want to be leaders. They glanced at each other and back to Ester.

Ester explained, "Long ago, I learned the hard way that those who desire to be in charge probably should not be trusted to be in charge. They tend to want leadership for all the wrong reasons. Ego. Status. Money. Control. They want everything except to lead. Everything is for them, not others.

No. I've learned that leaders who care about those they lead; that comes from within and tends to make amazing things happen. Some fail. For sure, it's not a fool proof thing. Ya learn from those things, too. But, I'm not wrong here.

Lily... Onna... I need you. I can't do all the things that need to be done for those coming to us. You know it. I know it. I need you. And so do they. It's asking a lot, but let's face it, we're all in this way over our heads already."

The nervous ladies giggled. Ester took a hand from each and held them. She smiled knowingly. "You will both do fine.

You'll make mistakes. You'll make a bad decision. You'll have people that challenge and test you. Just as I have. But, you'll do fine.

I will be there with you. You will not be alone. I will help you and coach you. I'll answer questions and guide you. You only need to be willing. Please, help me."

How could they refuse? Really. When a 94 year old killer sweet talks you into helping her train a herd of average housewives and girlfriends into savage vigilantes, how could anyone turn her down?

Once they all agreed that the three of them would work to lead the revolt against abuse, Ester told them, "One more thing. Now that these ladies are about to become aware of what we're planning, we need to be diligent and active in making a date for it. We need to have a retreat as soon as possible and get them up to speed."

Lily asked with concern, "What's the hurry?"

Onna answered, "Once we have more than double the women, we'll have more than triple the chance of someone screwing things up."

Ester nodded. Lily nodded, too. They all understood that once they opened the door to increase the After Party, it started the count down to the Grand Finale. Once they brought more women in, there would be more variables that could go off the rails. And those who were newer were not as invested. It would be too easy for someone who was new and not fully invested with skin in the game to rat on the group. So, once they allowed the group to grow, the group would need to get to the final agenda as soon as possible to reduce the chance of being exposed.

Chapter 13: The Discipleship

And so the training began. Lily and Onna needed to set aside more time to learn and that was a problem. Life with kids and an abusive man was too much for them. So, a diversion was needed. They needed an excuse to be out of the house more. And the outreach wasn't good enough for their men. So, they decided that it was time to get creative and win at all costs.

The reasoning was sound. The reason was heroic. The plan? That was sketchy as hell.

They were going to get girlfriends. Not for themselves. For their men. They were going to get the perfect woman for their man to cheat. That would give the men reason to not only allow the girls to get out of the house, but to encourage them to get out of the house.

It made perfect sense. The guys were abusive assholes. They didn't really love their women. Matter of fact, all love was already gone. They were going to cheat if they hadn't already. And they were going to be dead eventually. Perfect. All that had to happen was open the door to temptation and they would take it from there.

It worked. It worked better than live bait at feeding time in the honey hole of a fisherman's favorite pond. It was easier than a toddler finding all the snacks that were hidden.

Randi and Michelle volunteered to be the Mistresses. They were pretty. They could be tempting. And besides, since they were disappointed in their own men, they figured it would be fun to fool around and get even before killing them.

All they had to do was show up. Lily and Onna gave a couple suggestions on when and where to meet the guys. Randi and Michelle showed up. And it was on. It didn't take much flirting. They showed up and the guys were hooked like fish.

With the men preoccupied, Lily and Onna were able to spend more time with Ester learning her ways. And it didn't take very long. Ester was kind. Plain and simple. Everything she did was filtered through kindness. That was the first and main principal that needed to be handed down.

From there, it was an odd mix of information. For example, the need for secrecy. Keeping the group secret was the kindest thing to do because of all the lives that would be ruined if they were revealed.

Onna questioned that. "OK. But... what about the men? Isn't keeping a secret really lying by definition? Especially if we're keeping a secret from them about the fact that they're going to die?"

Ester giggled. She loved this question. "You are correct. Keeping a secret is by definition deceitful and therefore a lie. I suppose I could make an argument about how much worse the men lie about loving a woman while beating her and cheating on her. But, that's not any way to justify anything. It's a terrible act of a child to try to deflect guilt and justify bad behavior by using someone else's bad behavior as a reason.

In this case, my dear, I'm choosing to keep that secret regardless. After all, a lie about what I'm hiding probably isn't as bad as the fact that I'm going to kill them. Now is it?"

Onna was rather speechless. But, her face said a lot.

Ester went on, "Now, Onna, if you want to, we can talk about how in the Old Testament God used all sorts of good and bad people to kill all kinds of people and entire cities. We can discuss ethics and morals and maybe find the good and right way to think of all this. Perhaps there's even some wisdom and clarity from the philosophers of ancient and modern days. Maybe we can think and reason and come up with some rainbows and unicorn magic to make it all OK.

But, here's the cold, hard truth, girls. I don't care about any of that today. I might rethink that later, but not today. And you can't care about it either.

My husband tormented me daily for years. Many years. He didn't care. He didn't weigh the morality of his actions. He didn't turn to philosophers or God or books about right and wrong. He hit me. Then, he hit me again. And he called me names and he ruined my heart and mind. He didn't care. Not about me. Not about him. Not about right and not about good.

This isn't about right and wrong or being a good person who follows the rules. These men don't care. And neither can you.

Caring is what got us into this. Caring is what made us victims. We were lied to and manipulated and we allowed ourselves to be destroyed by the ones we loved.

We tried to love them into being better. We tried to beg them to be better. We gave them every opportunity to be better. They didn't care. They took every opportunity to take everything from us and leave us with nothing. Because we cared. And we cared about doing what was right. And we cared about feelings. And we cared about everything.

You need to stop that! You need to stop that right now!"

Onna and Lily looked shocked and a little scared. In all the talking and hugging and sharing, they had no idea what lay in the recesses of Ester's heart. They were slowly realizing that they were getting to know a gentle woman who was actually a brutal and vicious victim summoning some kind of Viking code of war. They were awakening to Ester's awakening from helpless victim to resolved warrior. They were getting baptized into the fighting spirit of a little old lady who had taken all she could take and wasn't taking any more. They were witness to Ester stepping away from being used and beaten. They were learning what it took for a loving, caring wife with the most pure intentions to become a killer.

Ester continued to emphasize placing all other feelings and emotions aside for quite awhile. In fact, it was a daily mainstay for her. She wanted Lily and Onna to hone in on justice and lock onto it. She needed them to be more concerned with justice than anything else. If there was no justice, the abuse would just go on and on and on.

In Ester's teaching, she drilled down on the idea that abusers don't care. They take. And they keep taking. And they have no limits to how much they take or how they take it. Abusers will take everything from a person, then accuse them of being worthless because they don't have anything left to take.

Ester showed them how abusers twist everything and use it to make themselves look justified or respectable. They lie and cheat and deceive to make everything look like it wasn't their fault. They lie to make a woman believe they deserve to be abused. They lie and twist everything to make the victim sound crazy or like they're lying about being beaten up.

She brought clarity to the women that they had never seen before. As Ester opened their eyes, they began to realize how much of their life and sanity had been taken from them. They weren't living. They were surviving. And even that wasn't real. They were sacrificing themselves to men who were taking everything from them. And for what? So, those men who were weak in character could feel like kings in their own living room while they were worthless outside of their house?

Ester began to ask them, "What did you want for yourself? What were your hopes and dreams before you fell in love? What could you have been if they hadn't ruined you? What would your life be like if they didn't control you and strip away every ambition?"

Lily could have been a doctor. She wanted a happy home with dogs. She wanted the kind of place where friends came to visit and play cards or enjoy grilling by the pool. It was always her fantasy to be the couple or family where the neighborhood hung out and wanted to be at her place.

Surprisingly, Onna wanted to go to West Point. She had never told anyone. She wanted to be an officer in the United States Army. She wanted to command troops and salute and make strategic plans for battle. She was in love with the idea of rising through the ranks as high as she could go.

Ester raised one eye brow just a little. "Make strategic plans you say? Hmmm... Onna, you might still get to live that part of your dream."

Onna looked very interested, but Ester changed gears.

Ester went further to explain, "When we take these women in, they will be coming from the same type of hell you did. They'll have all the same heartaches, black eyes and insecurities you had. You will have to remember that. They will not be able to walk into our world and join us where we are. Not mentally. Not emotionally. They will have to climb. They will have to work at it.

When they fail, you will have to bite your tongue. You can NOT criticize them. You cannot express displeasure. You can't even sigh heavily and roll your eyes. They WILL fail. I promise. You have to respond with nothing but compassion. You have to catch them and be a soft landing place, like a safety net. If you respond with anything less, you will appear to be just like everyone else. They will see you in the same light as their abuser. And from then on, nothing you say or do will win them over or help them stand on their own.

You will get mad. You'll be hurt and sad. You'll want to give up. You won't understand why they don't understand. They will test you. They will push you. They will do things to sabotage themselves and accuse you of all sorts of stuff.

Ultimately, if they decide to leave, let them. If they chose to quit, just let them go. If you fight to keep them, it will be against their will, and no one can be made to do anything they don't want to do. If you try to keep them and they want to go, you'll be holding onto a lead rope for a horse that's about to run. And if you try to hold tight and force anything, that rope will burn you when they bolt or rip your hand off. Just. Let.

Go.

Do not try to convince them of anything, no matter how true. You will appear as a used car salesman. State the facts. Be prepared to not back down on the facts. But, let the facts stand on their own. The truth will always be true not matter what. And no matter how much they might not want to believe, it will still be true. And be prepared for them to try to prove you wrong. Let them. Just don't fight it. Say what needs said and let them come to believe.

Most importantly, know that I have faith in you. I believe in this mission, and I believe in you. I have literally trusted my life to you. And you must believe in yourselves and each other just as much.

When the time comes for us to dispatch our abusers, you will have to have enough training and encouragement to follow through with it all the way to the end. This is life and death. Once the plan is revealed or in motion, there's no way out but death and nowhere to go except through the flames. And you are going to need to instill that determination in yourselves enough to transfer that and instill it in the rest."

Lily asked, "What happens to you with all this?"

Ester gave a sad smile. "Lily, what has already happened to me? What have I given already? What has been taken from me? My only worry is for you. I'm good. In fact, by age, I'm golden."

The ladies smiled. They couldn't get to a laugh.

Ester finished talking. "You've already heard my story. You'll hear it again at the retreat. You know how I've lived and come to a point of peace. I'm resigned to my final days on earth. I'm fully prepared to enjoy my greatest satisfaction in watching all those evil bastards get what's coming to them. And I will be leading the way with Pastor Kern." That was all the more she was saying at that moment.

Chapter 14: The New Girls

Ester stood behind Lily and Onna like a guardian angel. She was tough and encouraging. She held high expectations with total grace and understanding.

Onna and Lily began encouraging the rest of the ladies in the way Ester had been with them. They explained the needs Ester explained to them. Ester was able to share the hardest and most intimate lessons with all of them by allowing just two women to reflect what was in her heart and mind.

It felt like forever but in just a few weeks, they were ready to open the door and welcome the new girls into the After Party. Perhaps they were opening Pandora's box. Maybe they were opening the opportunity for betrayal.

But, that's what makes a leap of faith: no guarantee for a good outcome and a million chances to fail. They had to trust that they did a thorough job vetting the new girls. They had no choice but to trust that they all were making good decisions, and that the ones they reached out to would come to them without drowning them.

The induction of new energy meant that they would need to schedule and plan the retreat rather quickly. They didn't want to let much time pass between "Welcome to the After Party" and whatever might come after that. Ester needed enough time to get everyone up to speed and fully vested, but not enough for things to unravel and spin out of control.

So, while Lily and Onna were assuming some of the

weight from Ester's shoulders, Ester started looking towards the Retreat. Plus, she knew that Raith would automatically be in with Lily helping faithfully.

Ester chose Bethany, Crystal and Michelle to plan and organize most of the logistics and activities. At first glance, it almost made her laugh. Pairing these three up seemed to have a lack of potential. They didn't seem like the perfect mix for planning a retreat. But, as she thought about them, Ester was somehow sure that they would be able to figure it out just fine. They were survivors, and they had found common bonds. They would get it right.

Ester had to push an intrusive thought out of her head. She laughed out loud when she thought about giving the retreat the title of "How to Kill Your Abuser Retreat." She had to force herself to tuck that one in the back of her mind.

She would be turning 95 soon. She knew time was critical in all endeavors. Baking bread was time dependent. Teaching kids to potty train was largely dependent upon timing. Growing, harvesting, planting were nothing but timing and effort. Photography, camp fires, watching fire flies and showing up to important moments in life all revolved around timing. Almost everything in life needed some degree of it.

Ester was more determined than ever to get things set and rolling in a timely manner. She wanted to make sure she made the most of the days and weeks ahead. As much as she was determined, she was also convinced that a few of her ladies were running out of time. They needed to make the most of the time available so they could save themselves and enjoy the rest of their time on earth.

The only real problem Ester wasn't sure she could conquer was feelings. Feelings were messy. Feelings made people do stupid things. Feelings made otherwise rational people believe lies and give everything they worked for away and even give their entire existence to absolute assholes.

There would be tears and fears and hesitations. She was going to war with the irrational and almost insane imaginary dragons of emotions, uncertainty, and overthinking. Not to mention how often not thinking was the real enemy; or actually, thinking about the facts by squeezing them through a sieve of preconceived ideals that were based on false assumptions and impossible hopes.

After all, she had done all that. She was that girl. She was that wife. She had hoped against hope and wished to God and the stars above. She lay awake endlessly trying to think it all better.

There was a light bulb moment in her mind. Ester sought out a paper and pen, but couldn't locate one. Then, she realized that she could make notes in her phone. So, she slowly typed out the conversation in her head so that she could share it later at the retreat.

That was what she needed. She needed to take them back to where she had been because that would be where they were living in the present. Her past was theirs now. Once she could gather them in that space, she could take them by the hand and gently shepherd them towards the gates of freedom.

Ester immediately set about outlining as much information as she could about what led her to destruction and captivity. She paved the path from an innocent and pure person to the miserable wretch she loathed. Ester typed these things out till she couldn't keep her eyes open. Then, when she woke, she went right back to writing. In just a few days, Ester wrote out her entire journey from sweet young girl, to beguiled lover, to beautiful mother, to betrayed spouse to battered wife.

She finally found an old, partial notebook and transferred everything she had typed in her phone to paper. She didn't trust technology. Her notebook never ran out of electric.

Then, when all the pain had been gathered, she took another path that was less traveled. She explained in writing how she began to understand what had happened to her. And that was a major light bulb moment for her. As soon as she said it, she realized that the magic sauce was in understanding.

The only way she, or anyone could help a woman escape anything bad in her life was to get them to understand that it was bad. They had to come to that conclusion on their own. They had to become aware of the reality that everyone could see except them. Self discovery was the only key that would unlock the hearts and minds of her army. Ester figured that it would be pretty much pointless to try to persuade anyone to pursue any path if they were paralyzed in their old mental and emotional prisons.

So, she set her mind and energies upon that goal. She thought and outlined the way. She made verbal road signs to point the way. She made a list of check points that would take someone by the hand and pull them up the ladder of hope, one rung at a time, from the pit of despair.

It was intensely personal to her that Ester get every word on paper before the inevitable came to take her by the hand and lead her down the final path.

It was exhausting. The writing of every thing that mattered in her crusade against cruelty drained her. It didn't take everything out of her. She gave everything. She laid herself out on paper in words for the good of the goal.

When she finished writing, and she was satisfied that she had done her best, Ester laid down in bed. She hadn't taken care of herself in days. She barely ate. She would only sneak a piece of toast and peanut butter. She hadn't bathed. She was sleeping like a cat. Or more like a front line soldier who only passes out long enough to regain enough energy to move further along.

And finally, she slept. Ester closed her eyes and let everything go away. She melted into the mattress and enjoyed the cocoon of blankets. She let her eyes close as her breathing slowed. Everything was going to be alright. It was going to work out. A gentle smile graced her tired lips and she slipped to slumber.

It was late the next day when Onna, Lilly, Michelle, Crystal and Bethany let themselves into Ester's place. It didn't look like anyone was there. They found the pile of papers she had written on the coffee table in front of the couch. There was an empty jar of peanut butter beside that pile of paper along with a pile of used paper plates and bread crumbs covering the area.

They began searching for their mentor with held back nervousness. It only took a couple seconds to find Ester in bed looking pale and frightening.

Their hushed panic chatter woke Ester up.

"Why are you chattering chipmunks in my room making all that racket?" Ester weakly growled.

The women reacted with a mix of shock and excitement. They had been fearing the worst. They were relieved, but immediately concerned. Ester was obviously not in good shape.

They called for an ambulance. Ester threatened to get up and kick all their asses for that, but she wasn't even able to get up to go to the bathroom. They stayed by her giving her ice chips until the EMTs arrived and took over caring for her.

Before being loaded to go to the hospital, Ester told the girls to take the writings and read them, understand them, and commit them to heart. They needed to be able to deliver that message to the rest. Ester said with a feeble wink, "You know. Just in case."

There were three nervous days of Ester being in the hospital. Even the kids from Krisis were sending her letters and cards and candy. (After all, they were kids.) But, she recovered from her exhaustion and dehydration.

The vivid truth of time running out on the After Party became an intensity no one could have planned. Ester had poured her heart out into these women. And they knew it. Whatever might have been a speed bump, stumbling block or excuse was eliminated. Ester could have told them to wrap themselves in wet blankets and run into a burning building and they would. When Ester returned to the outreach, she was greeted with an emperor's welcome. The captain had taken command of the ship again.

Within a month, the After Party welcomed 18 new women into the sanctum. The energy and conviction of the founding members was infectious. There was a fire lit and the warmth wrapped a force field around all within reach.

As the first few weeks of fresh members found its way, Crystal, Michelle and Bethany became known as CMB. They were the planning committee for the Women's Retreat that would be happening in just a few months.

Once Ester made her commitment known... or rather, once Ester's commitment *became* known... the snowball had been started rolling, and it was gaining momentum quickly. Both Krisis and After Party took on new life full of fresh breath. There was an energy that fueled everything in forward directions.

Krisis wasn't perfect. After all, people are not perfect, and it was being run by people helping people. But, it was reaching kids in numbers that were gaining attention far and wide. The kids were the real champions. As they achieved success and confidence, they were bringing more kids. And as they gained confidence and success, they were creatively reaching for new and better ways of fund raising and life skill improvements.

As kids were overcoming harsh lives, the volunteers that were coming to the program were seeing real improvements in their own lives. Their family lives were improving. Their relationships were improving. Their self confidence was growing. As the women helped the kids, they were helping themselves.

Krisis had started as an outreach to the most under served demographic of vulnerable humans as a cover story for a more sincere, but diabolical purpose. And it had become a success story for the decade. It was becoming so successful that it was on the verge of turning one entire neighborhood all the way around. Fulton St Projects was no longer considered the most poor and dangerous area in town. It was becoming a community.

Krisis really was meant to be a good thing all its own. It was intended to actually help kids. It was never a throw away activity. It wasn't intended to be Ester's legacy, but it was certainly becoming epic. The story of a little old lady reaching out through a church to help kids find better lives instead of a handout was incredible in it's own right.

That was the environment that abused women were coming into. As they were drawn into Krisis to help others help themselves, Ester was able to help those women find hope. And even without the After Party, more and more women (and kids) were realizing that they were living a life that they didn't ask for and didn't deserve. Hard topics that were never spoken about were now on the table and being discussed. Taboos were being broken. The stigma of being a victim was beginning to be seen in new light.

As the poor kids were taught to "turn on the light switch" for themselves, women that were huddled in darkness were given a candle and a match. They were able to strike up a new flame in their lives that was helping them find their own light and illuminate their own path.

The contagious inspiration of those who were finding a way to make the most of the little they had was forcing those with so much more to consider what matters in life. Despite being beaten and controlled and manipulated and lied to, women involved in Krisis Outreach were feeling convicted to do better. As they watched the kids form plans and carry them out, they began to awaken. As the kids did things they were told that they could never accomplish, the women felt a hopefulness they had missed. The kids who were defying the odds and overcoming what this world handed to them was inspiring the women to see themselves as more than victims. The kids and women were learning that a better life existed.

The new girls came with all the same problems and black eyes and bruises that Ester said they would. And much like the first time the initial group of women gathered, there was an outpouring of tears and fears and stories met with support, encouragement, and compassion. It was much like that first experience, but there were twice as many coming in as there was in the original group. The After Party just tripled in size.

Ester was as excited as she was concerned. It was amazing to see such outpouring and bonding. It was heart breaking to see so many living through the same horrors. It didn't seem possible to have so many people together in secret and expect it to remain secret. It was wasn't reasonable.

But all she could do was hope and pray. She would continue to work on the goal, with the highest of hopes and the lowest of expectations. Ester had started something with all her heart and there was no place to turn around. She was on this journey to whatever ending it might take. There was no plan B. No back up plan. No one to call if things went sideways.

For a little while, Ester sat silent in the middle of the room and observed her recruits. She let the air of excitement and emotions fill her. She let herself be lost in the moment. She allowed the women around her to believe that she was old and tired while she felt a peculiar reminiscence of a time in her youth when the world was safe and wild, free and still ahead. Being in this moment took her feelings back to a moment when prom and graduation were her biggest waves of elation and nerves.

Only Ester knew why she was smiling such a radiant smile. She was beaming. And it didn't matter who saw it. Calmness draped her shoulders and confidence filled her chest. The time was coming quickly when all that Ester ever wanted was about to be delivered. She wasn't thinking about repaying evil. She was drenched in the delivery of justice. The idea that the weak and innocent would be tasting freedom and the ones that exploited them were going to get what they deserved, put Ester at peace.

Before the night was over, Ester was able to share emotions with Adrianna. Adrianna was mentally handicapped and was afraid no one would believe her because of that. Ken took full advantage of her, knowing that she was high enough functioning to be considered mostly normal, but handicapped enough to not be fully normal. He knew she couldn't defend herself verbally. So, he could make her do almost anything he wanted.

She met Meelow, who's parents had "sold her services to friends" while she was young, then abandoned her when she was "too old to be wanted." She met Sondra Kendron, the mayor's wife, hiding so much from so many with no safe place. She met women who had been raped and blamed and victimized in every way imaginable and in a few ways no one wanted to believe were possible.

Maybe the hardest story to bear was Kendra's. She had spent six years in a basement prison being starved and abused in a variety of ways for the entertainment of her captor, a friend she had known in high school. Her scars left no questions about her truthfulness. Her eyes left no doubt about her utter destruction at the hands of a sick and twisted man.

Ester wasn't sure if they could reach Brad. He went to prison when Kendra managed to escape and find help. A woman named Tammy said she knew some bikers who would make sure that one way or the other, prison or not, Brad would get what he deserved.

The growth of the group through the careful work of the women willing to risk everything for justice was a wonderfully unsure accomplishment. The risks were insane. The reward wasn't going to feel like a win. There was no way on earth this should be happening.

Yet, as Ester talked and listened, hugs and sobbing assured her that this mission was on point. She welcomed and received each and every woman into the After Party that day. As the evening reached a point where everyone needed to return to their homes, Ester made a passionate plea.

She implored, "Everyone! If I may have a last word before you leave?" She allowed the commotion to settle. "There will be times when this is hard. And you will need someone. You'll want to talk. Call me. Call Onna. Call Lily. I am BEGGING you to NOT talk to ANYONE else about this. Not a word. Not a hint. Not a breath. Those of us with our lives on the line will not be alone in hell if you let word of this group slip.

We are a secret. And it needs to be a real secret. So, go home. Take care of your kids and family. But, you have a new secret family here now that is depending on you to keep yourselves and all of us safe. Please. And thank you."

The room emptied quickly. They had stayed too long. When it was just Ester with Lily and Onna, Onna asked, "Do you think we'll make it to the retreat before someone screws up and reveals us?"

Lily snorted, "Maybe. But, I think once we have the retreat, the fuse is lit and it'll be a short, fast one."

Ester agreed. She was quite certain that once they laid out all the plans and mapped out the final goals with all the important details and information, that would be when they would be most vulnerable. With everything exposed they'd be like a dog lying belly up.

They all understood and agreed that once the retreat took place, they would have a limited window of opportunity to complete the Grand Finale. They would have to ensure that the retreat instilled enough motivation and energy to carry them the rest of the way.

There was one deep question that these three ladies needed to answer. Could they, along with the other original numbers, devise a rally point that formed a covenant of killers that would abandon their victim state of mind and actually pull the trigger to kill their abuser?

Everything they had experienced and shared was wonderful and amazing. That day's induction of new members was a highlight. But, when the ultimatum to "put up or shut up" sounded, how many would do it? Would any of them do it? They could speculate all night. They could analyze name by name weighing strengths and weaknesses. They could think and guess, but in the end, unless or until each was tested, it just felt like being in the rapids with no paddle.

But, ultimately, they could only do all they could do and let the dice roll. They went home. Ester sat alone in the dark in her chair. She knew she had to come up with a way to make sure that no one got in trouble but her. Everyone needed to get away with murder. She reached deep into her past and let her heart and mind battle until she was sure she had the answer. She was now ready to schedule the retreat and the Grand Finale.

Chapter 15: Planning the Retreat

Ester was always calm. She had lived a long time. She was in no hurry and had nothing to prove. Nothing bothered her. Normally.

But, now she had an urgency about her. She was noticeably driven. She wasn't ambling about stopping to smell the roses. She was more like a 40-something woman with ambition and goals.

Planning the retreat became the only objective for Ester. She impressed upon Crystal, Michelle and Bethany that the CMB machine needed to engage in high gear.

The date was easily set for the first week of October. That would allow families to settle back into the new school year. The weather should be more mild than the blazing summer heat, yet warm enough to be pleasant before the fall temperatures took over. It also gave plenty of time to plan, get alibis and prepare the newest members. It was just about the most agreed upon time when the women who would be attending would have the least amount of "real life" to deal with.

Some of the women would have a harder time than others. Some husbands and significant others would simply not allow their woman to leave the house. Kids would get sick, in laws would need help, and a million daily household chores would need done. There would be every kind of reason to not go.

But, for those that were serious about changing their life for the better, there was a reason to go. THAT was THE reason to go... to change their life... and the lives of their kids... and everyone's life that their abuser had affected.

The ladies that had chosen the After Party were very serious about making time to attend Ester's Retreat. They had to call it Ester's Retreat. There really wasn't any other name they could possibly call it. And some wouldn't ever consider any other name. No other name would do.

The time between the decision of when to hold Ester's Retreat and the actual retreat was possibly the most difficult time the After Party had to struggle through. Any retreat is challenging. It takes time. Lots of time. And planning. Extensive planning. Which takes time.

Ester was able to secure the guest speaker. She planned to do the majority of the speaking, but she needed "a ringer" as she put it. The guest speaker was specifically procured for her ability to motivate women to embrace self sufficiency and to reach for goals they never would believe that they were capable of attaining. Bridgette Carandou was a well known motivational speaker and Ester was able to get her to agree to a very small engagement on very short notice. It raised a couple of eyebrows and questions, but Ester deflected everything saying that Bridgette was impressed with the group and wanted to help support them. And that raised a couple of questions with a couple of the women within the After Party, but Ester remained enigmatic.

Ester debated explaining that she wanted Bridgette to have plausible deniability. She wanted her guest speaker to help the women realize their strength and potential. She did not want her guest speaker making national headlines as an accomplice to Ester's plans. She wanted Bridgette to be an amazing guest speaker who knew NOTHING about what would happen once she left the retreat. She figured that she could explain should the need arise.

Crystal sought out a former police officer who trained women in self defense. Carissa Smith loved to help women be brave and fight back. She nearly jumped at the opportunity.

Michelle had convinced an old friend of hers to come and help the women have a good time in a unique way. Hirra Haussen had been a marine. She was fairly well decorated for her time deployed to the Middle East. When Michelle asked if she would be willing to come and teach the women the most basic of basic skills for a combatant, Hirra showed a painful mix of being honored and being a veteran. The scars of combat made her hesitant to teach civilians anything. Knowing how to fight made her want to teach them everything. She really did want every woman to be able to self defend, but she understood the cost all too well. She agreed to setting up a simple obstacle course that would be fun and mildly challenging. It wasn't reasonable to expect to make fighting warriors out of humble housewives and giggling girlfriends in a month, let alone in a week, and absolutely not in a day or two. But, they could certainly have a lot of fun doing things they never dreamed they could do instead of having tea while doing crafts.

Beverly was arranging tea and crafts for the retreat. It wouldn't be exciting and dirty and rugged. It would be a quieter moment where conversations would be able to flow. It was to happen after Hirra's obstacle course so that they would be energized and talkative.

There was a serious debate about having food catered verses keeping that within the group. Some were worried about overheard details and possible exposure to people they didn't know and might not be able to trust. But, no one wanted to miss anything because they were on K.P. Duty.

It became clear to Ester that they would want to cater some meals. An outside vendor would be allowed to bring food and leave it, then come back for their gear. Otherwise, they would figure out a way to make meals where everyone was involved in the making. So, CMB set about to figuring out what foods or meals could be whipped up on the fly by the members. They even decided to make it a group bonding exercise for one meal where smaller teams would be given random ingredients and tasked with figuring out how to make something from them.

A youth summer camp was selected for the location. It had cabins with bunk beds and was very reminiscent of scout camp outings from the 70s. Showers were located in the shower houses down the path from the bunk areas. Almost all the cookware in the industrial kitchen was either cast iron or army kettle style. It was not abandoned, it just wasn't in use much anymore.

The canoes had been updated to kayaks. That was possibly the only modern upgrade. The trails through the woods were still the same. The bonfire pit had probably never been cleaned out. And the grassy areas were not mowed, but more like cut with a farm tractor with a brush cutter. There was an archery range, gun range and other outdoor physical activity areas from long ago. Hirra would not have a hard time adapting those to her program.

The encampment sat a ways off the road down a winding dirt drive. There was a spring fed creek that ran along one side of the property and a pond with a floating dock. The place wasn't secret, but once past the first or second bend in the drive, it felt almost isolated from the world.

Whatever happened back there, wasn't visible from the road. Or anywhere, really.

There were only 27 women scheduled to attend. So, there was way more space available than they needed. And it would be easy to feel like they were just a speck in the sand out there alone. Ester and her CMB needed to make sure that they scheduled events and times in a way that ensured that the women didn't feel tiny in the campgrounds. So, they picked locations for meeting that might have been more suited for smaller groups and avoided the larger halls and auditoriums. They chose to have talks instead of lectures or programs. They elected to do more physical stuff during the day and reserve talks for later when darkness would bring them closer together around a fire or in rooms that would feel more like a sleep over.

There was no music or singers scheduled or planned. They weren't hosting a youth camp. They were not wanting to artificially elicit a "kumbaya moment." They were not looking to lead people to the Lord, but rather inspire women to deliver them to His presence with prejudice.

Ester emphasized to CMB that they had to aim for unification. Ultimately, they needed to have as much time as possible to teach, train, and motivate. After all, they would only have less than a week at the retreat to prepare their friends for the Grand Finale. They were to literally design the week for creating and bonding partners in crime.

They knew it would be a delicate balance between push and pull. It would be a challenge to accomplish the goal. Hell, it was going to be a miracle if they made it to the the end of the retreat without it all falling apart, let alone actually pulling off murder on a grand scale.

They planned a loose program and decided that the best they could do was to not try to control every detail. They would not try to fill every moment and direct every action or thought. They figured that the best they could do was cover the basic needs, plan for the basic events and information, then allow the group to figure it out. It might not have sounded like a good plan, but it was the only plan that made sense to them.

If they tried too hard, there could be push back. If they tried to make anyone do anything, there could be rebellion. If they tried to push anything, they might be turned into authorities.

Ester, Crystal, Michelle and Bethany did the best they could and decided that it would either be enough or it wouldn't. And the best they could hope for was the most unlikely, nearly impossible outcome imaginable. But, they decided to roll the dice and hope. Ester's Retreat for the Grand Finale was set.

Chapter 16: Holding It All Together

The weeks before Ester's Retreat threatened to unwind everything. If there was something that could go wrong, if there was some sort of distraction, if there was any kind of illness or injury or infinite list of things not wanted, it was happening.

It took Ester a couple weeks to realize that with the intensity of the After Party meetings and the opportunity for them to get together for a week, there was an unexpected and unwelcome side effect. The women were getting brave.

As more women were showing signs of abuse and there were more injuries that were more severe, Ester realized that these women were beginning to stand up to their abusers. And they were paying for it. The abusers were lashing out as the women called out and questioned their bad behavior. The women were beginning to see that they deserved a better life and were starting to hint at that. It was not going over well. It was not well received by the ones that were used to being 100% dominate and unquestioned.

Ester was afraid that they were gaining too many of the good traits too soon. They were becoming too confident. This could be a problem. She was afraid that in the moments of duress, one of them might let too much information slip. Even a simple promise of, "You'll get yours soon enough," could derail everything. No one wanted any abuser asking too many questions or getting suspicious.

She wondered what to do. Should she rein them in? Should she try to convince them to suck it up and take it until the Grand Finale so that they could orchestrate in secret? Or should she continue to encourage them? Should she let them grow? They might get more resolve as they see the truth more and more.

They might become more reliable in the mission as they hungered for freedom and the end of the oppression.

Or maybe they'd be broken back into submission. Maybe the increase in abuse would kill someone. It was possible that the abusers might find and employ new tactics that the women hadn't planned for and never experienced. There was so much that could go wrong. There were too many variables to figure out and guess.

So, at the next meeting, Ester asked for a few moments to speak. She cleared her throat and adjusted her hair. When she stood up, the women took note.

She said, "Ladies, I hope by now you all know how much I care for you and adore you. I hope you know how much I want to see you happy and living in peace. It is my most sincere desire that you have confidence in yourself and find a way to live the kind of lives you all deserve.

I know it's getting hard. I can see it in your eyes. I can feel it in your hearts. And I can see the marks and bruises."

There was an uneasy shift in the group. They became instantly self conscious. Ester attempted to put them at ease.

"Now, don't go covering up those battle wounds and scars. We've come too far together. We all know. We've all shared that pain and burden. There's nothing to hide and nothing to be ashamed of here. You're with us. Safe in our love. We are one just like you and you are one with us. This is our safe haven. And we all feel it to our bones.

Some of you are already starting to get excited about the freedom that's waiting for us on the other side of this. Your confidence is growing. And this is a good thing. You're already feeling the strength to stand up to the bullshit.

All of us know what it's like to be hit and beat and hurt. We know how much we can take. And that's the truly sad part of all this. I'm not going to stand up here and tell you to take any more. But, I can't tell you to unleash your anger. Yet.

I will never ask anyone to take one more hit. I never want to see another bruise or cut or burn or anything on any of you beautiful women with hearts of gold. After all, you already know that I'd kick each and every one of those rotten bastards in the balls myself."

There was hushed laughter as the women regained relaxed comfort. They waited for Ester to go on.

With great comfort in her voice, Ester spoke, "My girls. I want the best for all of us. And it's coming soon when we bond together for the Grand Finale. There will be a day, soon, when we will work together to put an end to the misery in our lives that we've had to bear and have been ashamed of for so long. You will all be free.

Because we are all in this as one... because we rely on each other for strength and courage... because we support and protect each other... we need to protect each and every one of us. That means each of you needs to protect yourself. You must train yourself to focus all feelings until that final day. You cannot allow your pain and anger to taunt the bastards. You need to teach yourself to never say anything about this group and this mission to anyone outside of this group. Ever! No matter what.

One way or another, you need to save all those thoughts and feelings for the Grand Finale. You need to redirect all that pain and anger to that day. Never allow a single word to slip. Never give them a clue. Give them no reason. Give them no hand hold. Show them nothing in your hand. Reveal nothing in your heart and mind.

You do not owe them any explanation for anything. You cannot reason with the unreasonable. You cannot get through to them. If you could, you already would have.

Keep everything close to your heart. Keep it locked in your head. Let nothing loose from your lips. Do this for yourself. Do it for me. And do it for your blood sisters here with you.

You will need this skill now and later. We'll talk about that more at the retreat soon. We'll talk about a lot at the retreat. And we'll have fun. And we'll learn a lot.

And when the retreat is over, we'll be ready for whatever the rest of our lives will look like. We'll be ready to be free women with no more shit taken from anyone."

Ester reclaimed her seat. She could feel a strange and wonderful energy in the chatter that grew within the room. There was a mix of emotions, but the movement was towards protecting the After Party at all costs. The women were bonded and united in encouraging each other to take this secret sisterhood to the Grand Finale and even to the grave.

Later that night, when the women had gone home and the lights were turned out, Ester lay in bed and tried to stop thinking. This night was particularly hard on her mind. As the reality of what she had begun began to become clearly visible, she was beginning to feel things she had expected.

There was one thought that was particularly harsh on her. What if she was just creating monsters? What if she was unwittingly behaving like some kind of Jim Jones whipping her cult up into a killing frenzy? What if she wasn't really leading them on some noble crusade? Maybe she was, but just like the original crusades, history would look back with negativity. Maybe she would become one of the worst villains in history that converted Christian housewives into killers.

The idea of being cast in a black light of shame for all the world to read about ate at her like a cat with it's dead master. It was merciless. It had no soul, no mercy, and no off switch.

Finally, around four in the morning, Ester got up. She went to the bathroom and then to the kitchen. She poured a little milk and took a cookie from the jar on the counter. She sat at the table and began to shuffle a deck of cards. Solitaire was the stand by activity of retirees and the bored. It gave the hands something to do and the mind a place to focus.

As she shuffled, a card fell out. That happens sometimes. But, this time it caught her attention. She froze and stared at it. After a minute or two, she set the cards down. She took a slow bite of cookie and a sip of milk. Normally, she'd just pick it up and slip it back into the deck. But, she was tired. And the thoughts had been messing with her mind. She was in that combined state of sleeplessness and thinking.

Fifty one cards stayed in her hand, one flipped out. Jesus had once talked about leaving the 99 for the one. Another time, he asked, "Where are the other nine?" after healing ten people and only one came back to give thanks. It suddenly occurred to her, that there's always one.

There's always one. Judas was the only one to betray. Luke was the only one that could sway Darth Vader. One savior. One Satan. One hero. One evil dictator. There's always one.

Ester had the strangest collision of thoughts that brought her to the realization that with all the women in her group, there would be one. There would be one that would rise above the rest. And there would be one that fell out. There would be one that would betray them or fail them.

She took another bite and sip. Somehow, that thought brought her to the point of control in her mind. She was able to think clearly and not allow the micro pulses to flare wildly in her synaptic gaps.

She needed to identify the one. Ester was going to need to watch the women and identify the weakest link. She would need to know who was going to be the most likely to chicken out or turn them in.

She also decided that she would need to make the very deliberate decision to believe that she was doing what was right. She needed to believe that regardless of whatever anyone would ever say about her, she chose to eliminate evil people for the protection of good people. It was her new mantra that she was defending the rights of those that were unable to stand up for themselves.

Ester reasoned that bad things happen because good people stand by and do nothing. She found a notebook and wrote these thoughts out. She needed to see the words of what she was believing in. So, she wrote for a long time.

She wrote about how the truth is hard to see. And that it needed to be seen in full light. She wrote about how people need to believe that someone cares about them so that they have the courage to fight for themselves because if no one cared for them, they would believe they had no value. She wrote about how often bad things had to happen to bad people so that good people could live good lives. Ester wrote as much as she could about all of this that was swimming in her head.

And once she had written down as much as she could get out of her head, she was sleepy. And there was no more battle in her head. Ester was able to lay down and close her eyes. And sleep quickly cuddled her.

Chapter 17: Ester's Retreat, The Beginning of The End

It really was a miracle.

The entire retreat was paid for using the same things that Krisis was teaching to the kids they were helping. There was no out-of-pocket expense for the women, so they didn't have to fight with their men about money.

Only one was unable to attend the entire retreat. Susan would have to miss the first day and a half due to a funeral. Otherwise, all the ladies were able to make all the arrangements for child care and work and all the 10,000 speed bumps in their way of being there. But, only three women were not able to attend any of the retreat. Well, just one of the newest members, really. Sherry was the only woman that couldn't get away to be there. Meg and Julie were school age, so technically, they were not women.

Monday morning, after putting kids on buses and dropping them off at school and making sure (ironically) that husbands and boyfriends could survive the week without them, ladies began to find their way to the retreat campgrounds. It was very much like the first day of camp like when they were kids. There was excitement and anticipation. There were nervous feelings and worries. And there were the awkward moments as adults looking for their cabins and bunks.

Lunch was the first activity and it was barely structured. A local company brought in sandwiches, chips, and drinks. Since there were only 24 women plus Ester, it wasn't a huge spread in the large dining hall. So, they took their food to the main lodge where there was a large fire place with couches and chairs. They didn't light a fire, but it was a smaller area that felt more appropriate, or at least it didn't feel like they were a dot in a giant place.

It was a fun and casual time to express excitement of being childless and manless for a few days. They complimented themselves on making it all happen. It was impressive to know that they had been able to plan this entire event and follow through with it. It was truly remarkable.

They lughed about the stories they gave their husbands and boyfriends about where they were going. It wasn't hard to avoid a lot of questions when it was free and it was "just a bunch of women getting together for a church thing."

After lunch, they took a walk around the campgrounds to get acquainted with where everything was. It helped give them a feel for the layout and where things would be happening. Being in October, there was a question about swimming in the pond, but not a lot of enthusiasm about swimming in the pond. Even with the nice weather, the spring water would be really cold.

They unloaded cars and settled into the bunk house and checked out the showers. At least there was hot water. It was a bare bones basic shower house. Onna had asked Beverly to make sure there was plenty of "good toilet paper." Crystal went the extra step to ensure that there were plenty of necessities should anyone being needing them for their period.

They were invited to freely explore the archery range, shooting range, and any other areas of the camp they wanted to see. Hirra would be monitoring the shooting sports. Meelow was actually quite good with archery, and volunteered to help others. Carissa Smith found it challenging to find women who wanted to learn to fight as self defense.

A few women went for the kayaks while some went to the creek and some enjoyed the range. Those who had never shot a gun before were very worried about their first experience. But Hirra talked them through the safety part and showed them how to handle the weapon so that they didn't catch their hand in the slide. She taught them to load and cock the gun, aim and gently squeeze the trigger until it fired.

There were six women that afternoon with a new adrenaline rush they never imagined having. The power of a pistol recoiling in their tight grip gave them a sense of awe. The smell of gun powder was sweet. And hitting a target was the greatest prize they never knew they wanted.

Four more women were amazed and confused with the compound bows. They found it challenging and fascinating. Crystal was the only one who really enjoyed it. It was more skill intensive than they imagined it to be. They developed a new respect for those who would dare go bow hunting. It was not as easy as it looked. It was fun and a new skill, but most of them were OK with just the one lesson. Meelow shook her head. It was disappointing to watch people reject what she loved.

There were ten kayaks, so ten women went out on the water. They all got a first hand taste of how cold the water was. Most of them were not great with the floating core exercisers. And the couple that didn't capsize got capsized. They had a wonderful time getting worn out and freezing on the lake like kids at play. They were incredibly happy with the hot showers.

The final four of them went to the creek. It was more of hiking and chatting time. There were some wet feet and cool rocks. Someone found a rusty knife in the water. Megan and Tammy were chasing the others with crawdads they found under rocks. Again, it was like watching kids at play for Ester. It was warming her heart to watch her girls get away from daily life and begin to loosen up.

Eventually, dinner time rolled around. Everyone came in from the activities and cleaned up. Fresh, dry clothes felt good after warm showers. Only mascara was added. The rest of the make up routine was dismissed. The catering company left ham, chicken and a massive salad blend. They even left a tray of roasted cauliflower in case anyone wanted a vegetarian option.

Bridgette, the main speaker, joined them for dinner before she began her program that evening. She went around introducing herself to everyone and taking a few moments to ask about their kids, jobs, and other small talk. She eventually sat with Ester until dinner was over and clean up was taken care of.

The caterer returned for their stuff and it was time for the first official activity. There was a cabin with a room just about the right size for all of them to gather in. Bridgette waited outside while Ester addressed the ladies.

Ester went over the typical basics of being at a rented facility. They had to leave it as they found it. Don't wander off without telling anyone. Forget about your phones. Don't ignore them completely, but leave them alone. THIS was more important. She said she'd take them if it became too much of an addiction for anyone.

Then, she introduced Bridgette and Bridgette took the reins. She marched right up to the front of the group, but did not turn around to face the group. She faced the same wall the women

133

were facing, like she was one of them. She did this until it was confusing and awkward.

Someone finally asked just loud enough, "Aren't you supposed to face us?"

Bridgette had been waiting for that. She asked, "What are you all looking at?" There was predictable confusion. So, she explained, "You were all facing this direction. I was just wondering what you were all looking at. What do you see?"

Randi piped up, "We weren't really looking at anything. We were just waiting for you."

Bridgette turned around and smiled. "Why, thank you! If you were looking for some deep, philosophical metaphor with profound meaning for life in my weird intro, you're going to be extremely disappointed. I was just being a dork wanting to see how long you'd let me look at the wall."

"What?" Megan demanded. "Are you serious?"

Bridgette nodded. "I am. Some groups let me stand there for a long time. Some say something immediately. It gives me a clue as to whether or not the people I'm about to talk to are going to be interactive or just sit there allowing osmosis to occur."

Again Megan demanded, "Did we pass the test?"
Bridgette smiled, "It's not a test. It's just a gauge. And you ladies are going to do quiet well. So, I'm going to ask you the most important question of the week right now. If

there were no men on earth for 24 hours, what would you do?"

Eyes darted around the room. Heads turned. Glances were exchanged. Bodies shifted.

Bridgette elaborated, "Let's say that somehow, some way, every man on earth was magically taken to Mars for a 24 hour fishing trip or rock hunting expedition. You are all left here on earth for a full 24 hours with zero men on earth. What would you do? Would you do anything different? Would you feel different? Where would you go? Who would you see? Would you leave your house, go shopping or what? What would you do if you had 24 hours on earth with no men?"

There was fidgeting. There was quiet confusion as the women processed the idea. That is, until Candy offered the first answer.

Candy was married to Conner Cain. And yes, she hated the jokes. She was an aggressive drinker who spent a lot of time drinking to escape the fact that she was married to a sheriff's deputy, so there would never be anyone coming her rescue. She said, "First thing I'd do is put on the music I love and turn it all the way up. Then, I'd put on the sexist, sluttiest outfit I can find. The one that he hates and would never let me wear to the grocery store."

When the laughter died, Randi spewed out the next answer. "I'd dress up as hot as fire with no bra and go dancing at the best club in town."

And now the answers came rapidly.
"I'd wear the tiniest bikini to the beach all day!"
"I'd go drinking with my girlfriends and not worry about anyone slipping anything in my drink!"
"I'd ride my bike at night."

"I'd walk around the park at night without fear."

"I'd wear whatever I wanted and go wherever I wanted without looking around everywhere."

"I'd get drunk and pass out knowing that I'd be OK when I woke up."

After a few minutes, just before it became a free for all, Bridgette called them back to order. Once she could be heard, she pointed out, "Did you hear what you all were saying? All of your answers revolved around wearing whatever you want, going wherever you want and doing whatever you want. But, most importantly, and some of you actually said it... 'without fear.'

We grow up learning to live in a perpetual state of fear and paranoia. We go to the bathroom in pairs to make sure we all come back and no one disappears while we're gone. We cover our drinks or go without one because we can't trust the crowd around us. We watch out for predators for ourselves and the women around us. It's incredibly sad that we spend our entire lives living with absolutely zero real freedom.

We can't go to the beach without knowing we're being stared at and undressed behind sunglasses. We can't go bowling without comments about our asses. We can't go anywhere without a high enough collar to make sure we're not giving away free looks down our shirts.

Every single action we take, every single move we make, every place we go, everyone we know, affects what decisions we make about what to wear, how much make up we put on and who will be around us. We even call our best friend or mom to tell them our exact itinerary. And we all know that if we've been given that information from our friends, we know what do if they don't check in with us after a certain amount of time."

It was possibly the most stunned group of women anyone has ever seen. Not even 10 minutes into the first meeting of the retreat and they were slapped up side the head with a brutal reality that they felt, but never verbalized. Ester was pleased.

Bridgette didn't give them too long to sit like taser victims. She said, "Now, I know that's a really rough thing to hear. We all know it. We've all been 14 or 15 and had to slap someone's hand away from trying to grab our boobs. We all know what it's like. We've lived it. But, no one has really put it in perspective like that. It's rough to hear.

We don't want to believe it's that bad. We want to put on a great facade saying we'll wear what we want and go where we want. But, we know that we don't really do that. We know that we make every decision based on our safety. And even in our most relaxed and comfortable moments, we're conditioned to slap those damn hands away from our boobs. Ladies, we've lived that life for almost all our lives. And in some cases, all our lives.

That sounds sad and depressing. And it can be. It really is, to be honest. I'm not going to leave that alone. It's just a brutal truth. But, there's an upside. There's something good about all this.

You are all stronger than any man. They have muscles." Bridgette stopped and gave a corny lip bite and eye roll. "Thank God they have muscles!"
That was just enough to cut the tension and elicit a giggle from the group. Bridgette continued.

"Yes, we might love how men are built. But, in a physical contest, there's really no contest. They're bigger and stronger and faster. Physically, we lose almost every time.

So, we learn to be stronger in other ways. Ways that are not always seen as strength. We get mentally tough. We become intellectually tough. We learn to be constantly vigilant and aware. Men may talk about situational awareness, but are they really? I mean, come on! Girls, we run circles around those guys all day long. They don't even know how much we see that they miss.

And don't even get me started on how strong we get to be emotionally. Do any of us believe a man could handle the hormone dump of a period? NO! Are you kidding? They think we're emotional, but if they were to walk a mile in our panties and maxi pads, they'd learn how weak THEY are!"

By now, Bridgette had won the crowd. She was able to get responses and stir emotions. She explained how they were living in constructed walls of expectation and invisible chains of politeness. They were taught to always smile and be a good girl. Never make people mad or to feel uncomfortable. Never say bad things. Always be a good person. Always be the bigger person.

Bridgette explained how they grew up dreaming of Prince Charming while surrounded by village idiots. They were told to never make a man mad because he might do bad things. They had learned the mastery of subtle avoidance and how to kindly deflect unwanted attention. Never were they taught to be confrontational and direct. Not once were they told to spell out expectations and stand strong on them. They were not given the information they deserved to expect better from the people around them.

They were conditioned to be gentle and meek. They were expected to be polite and not stir the pot. The whole world around them imposed an unspoken code of behavior for women that boiled down to being second class citizens: speak when spoken to, perform as expected, do what was expected without being told. Submit. Comfort. Support.

But, why couldn't they be just as free as men? Why couldn't they speak their mind? What was holding them back from enjoying life the way they envisioned it in their heads?

"A back hand across the face," Tammy barked out before she realized she was saying it. She shrank and slapped both hands over her mouth with wide eyes.

Bridgette let the gasping and comments from the group go for a second. Then, she raised her hands and yelled above the noise, "NOW! How many of you are criticizing her?!?!"

All noises faded out. Bridgette asked, "Seriously? Are you all here to support each other? Is anyone going to call her out? Or do you agree? Do you agree that you have to be the way you are because if you don't there will be punishment?"

There was a collective muttering.

The speaker stood silent. The ladies sat silent. Awkwardness had filled the room.

"That's what I mean," Bridgette quietly explained. "That feeling right there. You all feel it. You don't know what to say or do because... consequences. Physical. Social. Emotional. You can't take that chance of speaking right now because you know deep down that you'll pay for it.

THIS is the feeling that holds us down. It keeps us locked up in the prison of our lovers. It drains our dreams as we do nothing but chase the kids, fold the laundry, load the dishwasher, and fill our role as home maker.

Don't get me wrong. Taking care of your house and kids is right and good and blessed. It's the right thing to do and care about. It's the highest calling as a wife and mother. It's good.

However, not being able to pick carpet, isn't suppose to be part of that life. Not being considered smart enough to manage the bills is not acceptable. Not being seen as a good driver that can easily keep the car and kids safe is not right.

We should be fully involved. Having a man that kicks back after work and expects you to keep going so you can take care of him after you've had a full day... that's not supposed to be the way life is. You could both work on stuff so you both could relax later.

Hell, half of you work outside the home and STILL do everything when you get home while he has a beer. At what point in our lives did we sign up to be super-everything? And how did they get a pass on that?"

Bridgette paused. She looked at every face. Then, she changed tones. "I'm not trying to make you feel bad. I'm not trying to make you angry about the life you have. I don't want any of you to get depressed about where you are in life.

Life can be better. It can be more. I'm only making you aware of what life is so you can see where you are. And as we talk more this week, I hope that you can see a bright and wonderful future for yourselves. I'm hoping you can see a way of life that is fun and fulfilling. The whole reason I'm here is to help show you the way from where you are to where you can be more free and full of all the good things. The purpose of this time is to redirect you into a world where you not only know your worth, but you FEEL it! You can BE worthy! You can BE free and still be responsible. AND you can expect to be treated as an equal partner in life.

Now, I know that's asking a lot. I know! I get it! I've been there. You might be shaking your head, thinking that 'he'll never get it' or 'he'll never go for that.' Well, that doesn't mean you can't still have more out of life. That doesn't mean you need to settle.

This might be the craziest thing you've ever heard, but I'm saying it; you already have to fight to survive. Why not make up your mind to fight to live?"

Every face was either stunned or blank. So, Bridgette said it again. "You already fight to survive. Why not fight to live? Really live, not just get by. Not just get along. If you HAVE to fight, if you HAVE to endure the pain, why not fight for something better?

I'm not telling you to pick a fight or get beat up more. Not even close, honey! NO! You KNOW what I'm saying. You know EXACTLY what I'm saying! You may not want to think about it or you might not see what it really means yet. But, you think about this: If your life is an endless string of whatever it is... then, why not take that string and make it a life line and pull yourself up into a better way of life? Why take the hit for no reason? Why not make a plan and fight for that hope? Why not take the risks for better? Why not make every pain pay off in a glorious new life that's free? Why not climb out of the depression into the sun?

There are women that have support. They don't live in fear. They live with hope and joy and enjoyment. Why can't that be you? Why can't that be all of us? You are so much more than you may feel. I want you to feel it and strive for it. Even if it's just a little. There's more good stuff out there for you. Go for it!"

Bridgette went on to answer SOOO many questions about what it would take to break the chains holding these women and what it would look like moving forward. The session went well beyond the scheduled time due to the personal interaction and information. It was a deeply moving, unplanned event.

Everyone wanted to hear about more than just the broad, sweeping generalizations that get people pumped up. They wanted meat and bone. They wanted the nitty gritty. These women hungered for details that would feed them insights.

Bridgette did most of the heavy lifting, but called on Ester to fill in some places where only the wisdom of experience could really put meat on the plate. It was a rare, organic feast of emotions and education for women to gain the elements they needed to grow in ways they never imagined that they could.

Finally, it was past midnight. For a group of soccer moms on their first night away from kids and family and routine obligation, it was incredibly late. And the eyes were showing the tired and the voices were getting a little gravel. Ester finally broke the meeting up and shooed them off to bed.

And as they were leaving into the night to head for the bunk house, Ester called after them, "While you are drifting off to sleep, I want you to all think about what you would do if there were no men on this planet for a day. I want you to take those thoughts, and have the most wonderful of dreams."

Chapter 18: Ester's Retreat, Day 2

Breakfast was light the morning of day two. Doughnuts, cereal, fruit and the usual morning drinks of juice, milk, and coffee were all available. Bridgette would be there later, it was just the After Party.

Ester and Hirra had made sure that all the women were up and present. They needed to talk very seriously about getting very serious. After all, that was the intent and purpose of Ester's Retreat.

So, they kept the ladies in the breakfast area and began to address the elephant in the room. As always, and as expected, Ester went first.

She said, "The time has come, my lovely ladies, for us to talk in a most serious manner. We can certainly enjoy this place and the time together. However, we are here for one very serious reason.

As you know, I was a victim of abuse. I've shared with you my story of my late husband. I did not share with you, nor anyone including him, that I had been raped as a young teen." Tears filled eyes and her voice broke, but she kept on. "I never told my parents. Or the boy's parents. Or my friends. I told no one. That boy was older than me. He knew what he was doing. And I was too scared to say anything. I was too scared to say even a single word out loud.

I lived with that horrible secret that haunted my memory for most of my life. It's been the worst part of me for the largest part of my existence." She stopped to dry her eyes with a handkerchief from her purse.

After a few sniffles, she straightened up and went on, "Now, as you know, I killed my husband. I poisoned him. And while I really have no regrets, there are small moments that I miss him. From time to time I miss when things were good. I miss the touches and gentle kisses. I miss the mischievous looks behind our parents' backs at holidays. I miss his voice when he would sing those stupid jingles on the radio."

Ester smiled with sentimentality for an instant before saying, "I sometime wonder what life could have been like if he would have just tried to be a better man past the beginning."

Her voice and expression changed. "But, I knew that would never happen. He had years to try. He had too many years where all he had to do was decide to be better and try.

And I had never gotten justice for the first violation in my life. That boy never paid for what he did to me; what he took from me. I had that pent up inside, simmering for decades."

Ester stopped talking and looked at the floor for a minute. No one spoke. She was mulling things over in her mind, reliving tiny fragments and bringing the anger and need for vengeance to her taste buds.

With a glance up to the ceiling, she took a stabilizing breath and continued. "I can't tell you to do what I did. I can't even ask you to consider it." She snorted a tiny laugh. "What kind of person would do that? And yet, I'm sitting here in this campground with you, hoping that you make the same decision I made before you waste a decade or two or six... before you waste your life getting slapped around like an unwanted toy.

I used to think that my husband saw me the same way he saw his toys when he was a boy. Fun for awhile. Then, a challenge to see how rough he could get without breaking things. Then, I was sure that just like his plastic toys, he became obsessed with finding out how hard he could abuse me before I broke and was destroyed and became disposable. It was clear that he didn't enjoy having me around. I was only a test of his strength, and I had to be defeated at any cost.

I realized that I didn't want to wait for him to light me on fire or bury me or drown me or run me over like he did all his toys. So, I killed him.

And I see the same thing happening to you. And that is just not acceptable to me. I saw it happening to someone else and I could feel it happening to me all over again. And I just couldn't stand by any longer. I couldn't stay silent again. I couldn't let it happen and not say anything. That's why I've invited you all here."

Ester looked around the room. She locked eyes with every one of them, one by one. "I can't save any of you. If you walk out of here and decide that you like the life you have, I can't change your mind. If you think you can change him and he can be a good man, I cannot convince you otherwise. Hirra can save you from a burning building, a war zone and many other things. But, she cannot save you from YOU! The only thing that NO ONE can save you from is yourself."

And, Ester locked eyes one by one, again.

"I cannot save you from you," she said very solemnly. She

waited just a couple of moments.

"Now," her tone changed. "If you have had enough... enough beatings, enough of being bullied, enough of being belittled and made to feel worthless, then I might be able to help. The only way I know how to save you is to expose the life you have in such a bright light, that it's obvious to see all that it is and you can see what you have ahead of you for the rest of your life.

Once I do that, it's up to you. Totally and completely. You can quietly go back. Maybe you'll be OK. Maybe your kids will be OK. Maybe it'll all get fixed. But it won't. And you know it!

So, you have come this far with me. And this is where you must decide if you want to take the road untraveled. Only you can decide if you want to go any further on my path. Only you can choose to experience a life without pain, or shame or imprisonment. It's up to you.

Quit and go home. Never speak of this. Live the life you're used to. And just let life be whatever it is. Or you can take the greatest risk of your life and join me in freedom. You can decide to wipe the horrors from your life. You can choose to eliminate all that is wrong in your life.

But, I'm warning you! And this is the most serious thing in the world... this will change your life in every way imaginable forever. Killing your abuser really does make you a killer. And once he's gone, there's no 'Oops! I didn't really mean to do that.' This path of mine is a one way road."

Ester decided to stop talking there. She sat down. No one moved. No one spoke.

Ester stood back up and left the room. She took Hirra with her.

147

It was just the women of the After Party. No Ester. No Bridgette. No Hirra. That's when the talking began. And it was loud.

The chatter began in fear and uncertainty and disbelief. But then, it changed. It became a little lighter as they explored some of the "what if" parts of life where there was no abuse. It had began with repercussions and consequences. But, then a new tone took over. The idea of a life free of battery and bad words and bruises and pain began to unfold. A brand new banter began.

There were jokes about walking around without fear or shirts. No more egg shells. They verbally imagined skinny dipping in the pool and shopping braless. It was fun to fantasize about coming home to peace and quiet, propping bare feet up and enjoying a glass of wine. It was fun to replace lawn mowing with having a couple baby goats. It was incredible to imagine going out dancing and coming home without paying dearly for it.

Ester stood outside the door smiling as her girls were seeing a brighter day. They could see that there was another side to the lives they currently knew. She let them go for just a few minutes longer as she indulged in her own personal fantasy. But, eventually she needed to get them moving, or there would be no hope for anything good to ever become real.

The first exercise of the day was gun safety. Once they completed that, Hirra would begin teaching them to use a gun if they didn't already know.

So, Ester reentered the breakfast cantina. The girlish

conversation diminished. Hirra entered and all conversation ceased.

"Good!" Hirra exclaimed. "I'm gonna need ALL of your attention. Please follow me to the classroom across the meadow for the gun safety course."

Some of the women had grown up with guns. They were quiet. Some had never even seen a gun in real life. They were not quiet. They were nervous and chattering. The gaggle of gals made their way across the grassy area to a log cabin that was set up as a learning center. Inside, Hirra had already placed several hand guns and rifles on the desks and tables. She had a presentation on the screen and took her place at the head of the room.

"Ladies! Please come in and find a seat anywhere," Hirra instructed. "We will be learning gun safety whether you already know it or not. So, if you do already know it all... No, you don't! Pretend you forgot, please, including those of you who fired on the range yesterday.

No one touch anything unless told to do so. Once instructed to do something, do it exactly as it is explained. This is not hard. It's just very important."

For the next 25 minutes, Hirra explained and demonstrated what a gun is and isn't. She explained and illustrated what it does and doesn't do. She had fun dismantling Hollywood myths. She showed the parts and workings of hand guns and rifles, along with the advantages and disadvantages of each. She even showed them video of what each was capable of in ballistic gel.

Finally, she came back to the first rule of guns that she had begun the teaching with: a gun is a weapon and should never be pointed at anything that is not intended to be shot. Then, she further explained that it should only be pointed at something if there is a deliberate intention on shooting it. She emphasized why she said the same thing two different ways. She then covered loading and unloading, chambering a round and taking the weapon off of 'safe' using her own weapon to demonstrate.

At this point, the marine stated firmly and clearly, "At this moment, this weapon is live and ready to fire. It is hot. It is now capable of firing a live round, known to you as a bullet. That bullet may be traveling 1,000 feet per second or even much faster. It will be traveling in a straight line from where ever it is fired to where it is aimed, even if you didn't mean it. Even if your aim is off. So, aim carefully. The closer, the better. Close shots are much easier to make. You are more likely to hit what you intended to hit. The further away, the harder it gets to be accurate. No one here is going to be an expert sniper unless they already are."

Hirra emphasized several times that a gun is useless if there is no bullet ready to fire and that every gun needs to be treated as if there is always a bullet ready to fire. She even joked that if there was no bullet ready to fire, it was just a plastic rock for swinging at people's heads. She fielded questions and tried to assure them that it's not hard or dangerous as long as common sense is always engaged.

Once everyone was as ready as classroom possible, it was time to head to the range. She allowed everyone that wanted to carry a gun to carry an empty weapon from the classroom to the range with the promise that if they didn't respect the weapon and the rules of safety, Hirra would make sure they regretted not taking all this seriously. She wanted to make sure that everyone had the desire to be careful and respectful by explaining that she didn't want to be accidentally shot in the back.

Once out on the gun range, Hirra felt a little like she was coaching the Bad News Bears. Or maybe she was in the movie Stripes. Only a couple of women were actually comfortable with a gun. A couple more had at least fired one. But, most were first time shooters.

She gave each a magazine and one bullet. She coached them into correctly loading that bullet into the magazine, then corrected Samantha on the direction the bullet needed to face in order to go into the magazine. It would never fire backwards.

One by one, she had them step up to her, load the magazine into the gun and pull the slide back so that when they let go, the gun would be charged. Now that they loaded the gun and were ready to fire, she had them aim at the target and gently squeeze the trigger until it fired.

Since Samantha made the first mistake, she took the first shot. As soon as she did, it was like they were all nine year olds at recess. Most of them were not aware of the adrenaline rush from the powerful pop of the weapon. The new sensation of burnt gun powder was like a drug.

They eagerly took turns stepping up, loading, charging and firing a gun for the first time. They were giddy. Simply giddy. It was very much like being a four year old and discovering popcorn for the first time.

Once they all fired, Hirra reemphasized safety and divided out five more rounds to each now eager woman. They each loaded their own magazines and they stepped up to the line, five women at a time. Like new recruits, they locked and loaded their weapons, took aim down range, released the safety and fired all five rounds. It could not have possibly felt more like being kids at camp. They may have been full grown adults and parents, but no, they weren't at this moment. They were kids. And they were learning the coolest thing in the world that any kid could learn.

It took them all morning to get through learning gun safety to firing a handgun, a rifle and a shotgun. And of course, the shotgun was easily the scariest and simultaneously funniest venture of all. From the kick of the weapon knocking women off their feet, to the sheer destruction of a watermelon, it was the most hated favorite. It was hard on the shoulder, but it was awesome to wield that much power.

The conversation after the gun range at lunch sounded similar to a junior high lunch room the day before vacation. The merriment of fire arms kindled new feelings in many. And it mostly ingrained juvenile enthusiasm in all of them. Even Ester had squeezed off a few rounds to the cheering of the women she was leading.

After lunch, the chipmunk cheerfulness took a down turn as Hirra led them all through cleaning the weapons they had been firing. Somehow, the maintenance side wasn't as much fun as the shooting side. But, they made it through the smelly gun oil and dirty carbon.

The afternoon session consisted of more fun and light hearted antics. It was pretty recreational. There was kayaking and hiking. A small volleyball game took place near the lake. Someone found a kite in the bunk house, so a couple of women sent it up for a little while. For a small handful of hours, they were like kids with few cares. It was nice.

By dinner time, the conversation was comfortable. The small band of retreat goers were bonding and enjoying the time and the environment and companionship. For a lot of them, it was probably the first time in their lives that they felt comfortable and welcomed and any sort of real peace.

Then came the evening session. Bridgette was back. But, before she could begin, Ester needed to stand before them and ruin the mood. She didn't want to. But, she had to.

Ester had to inform them that Susan would not be able to join them as planned. Her husband had gotten upset that she was leaving for a few days and he began to slap her around. When she slapped back, he escalated his attack. He broke her neck. She was now paralyzed from the neck down with no idea if she would ever walk again or even be able to feed herself.

In just a few seconds, the wonderful atmosphere and lively environment ended. It was like they all suffered Susan's injury with her. It was quiet. It was sad and very quiet. There was nothing that seemed right to say.

As the moments passed and the shock began to subside, the sniffles and tears began. The abuser was in jail, but there was nothing that was going to stop the tidal wave of grief that was washing away their happiness at that moment. The crying and wailing began. Ester allowed it.

Ester allowed them to feel all the pain and emotion. And the predictable evolution took on a life of its own. The tears turned to disbelief. The disbelief shifted to anger. And the anger brewed to rage. That's when Ester knew it was time for Bridgette to earn her pay and take the stage.

But before Bridgette could calm the crowd, a voice rose above the fray "WHAT DID YOU JUST SAY?"

Megan was standing up and demanding of Candy, "SAY THAT AGAIN!! SAY SHE SHOULD HAVE KEPT HER MOUTH SHUT ONE MORE TIME! I DARE YA! *SAY IT!*"

And that's when the fight broke out.

Megan didn't wait for another word. She lunged at Candy. An all out hair pulling, fist flying brawl broke out. Ester just shook her head and frowned. Bridgette stood back in a corner, mortified. Hirra and Carissa inserted themselves trying to separate the fighters.

The actual fighting only lasted a minute or so. But, the emotion and adrenaline ran high for quite some time. Ester sat back and watched with folded arms and disgust. Hirra stood like a referee between the contestants. Tammy held Megan back while Carissa had Candy restrained. Their red faces only had some minor marks and scratches and their messed up hair and clothes were classic school yard scuffle.

Ester slowly unfolded her arms, and with hands on knees style, she pushed herself up. She very slowly parted the crowd as she made her way to the center of attention. It grew more quiet and calm as she did so.

When she reached the epicenter, she scowled at both and

said, "What? No blood? Would you two like to take this outside and go at it till you're both satisfied?" She didn't wait for answers. "SO! Did either of you help Susan today? Did either of you make things better for her? Did you make ANYthing better for ANYone? No. No, you did not.

Now, if you don't mind, it would be awful convenient if you two would decide to make up, and let us get back to some stuff..." At this point, Ester went to full volume, "THAT IS ACTUALLY HELPFUL AND IMPORTANT!"

And very much like a school yard scuffle, there was shameful quiet followed by an exchange of half muttered apologies that led to reconciliation. The meeting was able to get back on track.

Bridgette took the center position as originally planned. She began with an awkward smile and forced tension breaking, "Well, that's gonna be a hard act to follow!"

There was very little chuckling.

So, Bridgette made her next statement. "As you can imagine, and probably no surprise, I had a topic picked out. But, I've decided to make this a simple and direct message."

She paused to look around. "What do you want life to be?"

She stopped and slowly made eye contact with each one. "We... you... can have every excuse in the world for living like you do. And if you like it, that's fine. Own it. More than likely, what happened to Susan won't happen to you. Most likely, you'll live the life you're enjoying now for many years. Exactly. As. It. Is. Embrace it! Go ahead and own that life! Brag about it and enjoy it.

However... Before you do, please... I'm begging you, ask yourself: 'What do I want life to be?'

Nothing else matters until you do. There's no tips or encouragement or motivational speeches. How could anyone encourage or motivate you, if there's no goal to aim for? You have to want something. Either you already have it, or... you need to answer the question. It's totally up to you."

And with that, Bridgette stepped from the stage and exited the building.

Chapter 19: Then Came the Night

They were left standing there. Bridgette just got up and left after a two minute talk, and they were all just standing there post fight. It was like they were all in shock, almost like the moments after JFK was assassinated or when the second tower was hit on 9-11.

Bridgette had asked them a question, but no one was thinking. They were just standing.

Eventually, Ester cleared her throat and said, "Well, I don't believe I have a lot of life left to figure out. I think I can pretty easily decide what I want life to be. So, I think I'm going to have some ice cream." And with that, the little old lady in command walked out.

A couple minutes passed in near silence until Candy stood up and said, "Yeah. Some ice cream really does sound good." And she went the same direction as Ester. It didn't take long after that before the rest slowly followed suit.

Soon, all the women of the retreat were in the chow hall seeking ice cream. The problem was, there wasn't any. This caused some unrest and disgruntled choruses.

The complaining stopped when Sam offered up, "The store has ice cream. And right now, I want my life to have ice cream. They're still open, so, I'm going to the store and bringing ice cream back. I don't want to live a life with no ice cream."

The mood switched instantly to a more lively tone. Sam bumped that up a notch by adding, "Before I go, I'm already thinking I don't want my life to be exactly what it's been. So, I'm changing into my jammies before I go." That got a laugh, but she finished with, "And I ain't wearing no damn bra!"

That's when the mood lit up. Suddenly, there was laughter and more warmth. Sam went to change. Samantha, Sondra, Kendra and Randi decided to go with her, also in pajamas, of course. They were making an ice cream run that would make any college student proud.

While they were heading to town, the rest of the women consorted and came to a consensus that they were done wearing real clothes for the day. Braless pajamas was the new uniform of the retreat. The campground was magically transformed into a man's fantasy of what a sorority might be like. However, they all agreed to a "no pillow fight policy." The only other rule came from Ester: no talking about kids or the abusive partner. She did not want anyone getting depressed and the night to descend into despair.

The carload of ice cream recon women sang to the radio all the way into the supermarket parking lot. They skipped into the store with free boobs flopping as they laughed. The few shoppers watching them raid the ice cream isle were split between trying not to stare in mortified disapproval and watching in total fascination and amusement.

One woman tried to reprimand them. It only made them laugh. Sondra replied, "You can be mad, or you can change how you see life and join us. It's up to you." And they continued on their way with smiles and giggles.

With the money Ester gave them and a few dollars of their own, they bought a variety of ice cream like a bunch of unsupervised junior high kids that found a $100 bill in the parking lot. From plain chocolate and vanilla to fancy amaretto flavors to tubs that had as much "flavor enhancers" as ice cream, such as nuts, chocolate chunks, cherries and such stuff. They had even thought ahead to bring a cooler and even brought it into the store so they could load the cool goodness directly in after check out and keep it in the most delicious state possible.

When the sortie arrived back at camp, they were amused and happy to see everyone lounging in their most comfortable clothes and state of mind. It was a beautiful sight. And of course, they were greeted with cheering. Or maybe the ice cream was greeted with cheering? Either way, it was a joyous moment.

It was a slightly surreal moment of solitude and comfort in the campgrounds that night for Ester's Retreat. Susan was not forgotten. But, nearly everything else about daily life was. No one cared about laundry or dishes and there was no talk of any chores of any kind. No one talked about bills and money. There wasn't a single word about kids and men.

No. The After Party was exactly what the name sounded like. They were chilling. Memory lane was getting heavy traffic. Memories of youth evoked laughs and giggles. Conversations about how far eternity was from earth were usually floating around dorm rooms at 2 am, but on this night, those topics were on the table. Some of the conversation was even getting a bit naughty.

Ester was enjoying the cool comfort of childhood memories on her spoon and the sentimental sensation of child like conversations in her ear. She shifted between the good old days and the happiness of the now. She was choosing to postpone the inevitable.

The shock of alcoholic beverages being smuggled into camp

was just for show. No one was shocked. Probably more than half of them had something they had stowed away. Sam and Samantha were amorously influenced by the alcohol. They took a little teasing about sitting on top of each other and getting a little grabby.

Ester wanted to get a quick but essential item off her chest and into their minds before they got carried away too far. So, she asked Michelle to direct attention her way.

"I'm going to be going to bed," Ester said once she had all attention. "So, before you kids stay up all night like this is a slumber party..." She allowed laughing before continuation. "I want... or maybe I *need* to share an observation with you.

I hope you can actually see it yourselves, so really, I'm not teaching you anything. I just need to make sure you see it. I need to be sure you feel it.

Despair is an evil feeling. You don't feel evil. It's just an evil thing that blinds you. It's that feeling of hopelessness. It keeps you from seeing anything good. It keeps you focused on the bad things in front of you and even makes you see bad things in just about everything. Being in despair doesn't allow you to see anything good because it's a hole. That's why it's called 'the pit of despair.' You only see the dirt walls.

Just above the edge of it, lies hope. And with hope, there's so much wonderful world available to you. You just need to see it. Once you see beyond, you can climb out and live a good life full of good stuff. Despair is more than sad. It's sticky sadness.

So, here's what I believe to be the ladder that gets us out of despair. First, you have to recognize that you're in despair. You might even say you're bummed. Or life sucks. Whatever it is, you have to say out loud that you're stuck or in despair or hopeless. But, why? Why say it?

Because that's the motivation to get out. If you never admit that you need to do better, you never will. Recognize that you are in despair. And when I met each of you, you were. And we talked about that. You told me your story. That was you recognizing that you were in despair.

Then, the hardest part: Want out. It's easy to say life sucks. Then you just shrug and say, 'It is what it is.'

Bullshit. That's not how it has to always be. That's what it may be, but that's not the only way it has to be. You just have to want out. You have to WANT to fix it. And there's no easy way for that. You just have to make up your mind that you want it. You have to want to want it. No one can make you. No speech can inspire you. Nothing on this planet can help you want it. You just have to want it. The fact you joined this group proves to me you want it.

The next hardest thing is making a plan. You have to figure out how to get moving. That first step is a bitch. But, you'll never get anywhere if you don't take it. You may stumble and fall. You might get hurt trying to take that first step. It doesn't matter. You get up and go. You take that step. Even if you have to kick down a door to get moving, figure out how and take that first step. It doesn't even matter what direction. Just get moving! Staying is bad. You already know all about being there. Move! Take that first step.

From there it gets easier. You begin to see things. Your vision clears. Your mind clears. You take more steps and you get a sense of direction. Pretty soon, a path opens up and you can see the way.

Once you get moving and you have a sense of direction, you begin to seek a purpose. That's when you find hope. It's like you're walking along the path and as you crest a hill, you can see the valley and the horizon and the sunset. You take a deep breath of freedom and you can see that you have a purpose in this life. You matter. You're not someone's property. You're not just the house maid or taxi driver. You're a woman with a heart and mind. You have dreams and talents. You have feelings that matter.

That sunset isn't really a sunset. It's a sunrise. It's the dawn of your new tomorrow. It's the rising of your new life. And you can make it amazing. You just have to want it."

Ester sat smiling for a moment. She was very proud of these women. They were her friends and daughters and students. She felt a sense of joy. It was tainted with a shadow of sadness. But, for tonight, she was going to sleep with the knowledge that her ladies were on the path to hope and leaving the pit of despair. She rose from her chair and meandered out of the chow hall. She stopped to look up at the stars and relish the enjoyment of cool air. After a few minutes, the chill convinced her to head on to bed.

The After Party cleaned up the chow hall and moved on to an open concept cabin with a fire place where they had couches and chairs and more of a social environment to sit around and chat. Attached to that building, there was a game room of sorts with ping pong, pool, Foosball and darts. There were also cards and board games, but the mood was more active, so those old timey games sat ignored.

While the women talked and played in their pajamas, there was almost a subtle magic that often creeps into camp and retreat environments. It was that "kumbaya moment" where the camaraderie is so consuming that everyone is almost in a dreamy state of happy unity.

Barbara and Bethany were situated into a love seat like cats curled cozily against the corners. They began talking more about life without men and that led to living a life more forward and unafraid. That led them to what life could look like if they were truly unafraid and able to control their own destiny.

This gathered a few other women from nearby furniture or those who were passing close enough to catch part of the conversation. It had gained traction slowly, and was slowly building momentum. But, eventually, it was the premiere topic of the night.

It was funny and loud. The women were a little more lit from the smuggled booze. They were feeling braver and less inhibited with the retreat and the environment with no men around. Almost like high school kids, the women were "one upping" each other on how carefree and amazing their life would be if the world were a different place... if the world were more like the retreat. It was kind of silly.

Until the conversation changed directions. They began talking about what they would miss if there were no men.

Faith was the one that asked the entire question, "What would you miss the most if there were no more men on earth?"

"Dick!" Serena tossed out instantly.

Sam clarified, "Good dick!" That got a laugh and agreement.

Lily asked, "Of all the people in this room, it had to be you? No offense, but you're over there snuggling a really hot chick, ya know?" More laughter ensued, but some of it was a little cautious.

Sam replied, "I've had my fair share of dick. After all, I tried to be married to a man. Every now and then, one dick would be attached to a guy who actually knew how to use it. Not just random pounding with ugly 'O face'. Not cumming after 3 strokes then crying. Noooo no. There was that 'one guy' that had some kind of magic in that wand. Even though I didn't really want it, yes, I did because I hate to admit how good it felt. Those kinds of guys might have made me straight, if they all weren't a piece of shit for using me like I didn't matter and making me feel worthless."

There was a low murmuring of agreement and understanding.

Samantha spoke up, "Now, don't go thinking that just because we're not with men that every day is unicorn piss and sparkle farts! Loving a woman isn't really any easier. It's just different. Women come with problems, too."

There was a short, but awkward silence before Meelow said, "I would miss the loving moments if there were no men."

Kendra piggy backed on that with, "Yeah. I would miss intimacy. Not really the sex, but the closeness. I would

164

really miss being connected on a deep level."

Beverly added, "Yeah, I really love those special moments with a man. The looks, the jokes and teasing. The touches. That's the part of having a man I love. I just wish there was a way for that to be what the relationship was made of."

Sam said, "Yeah. If the bad didn't come with the good, I'd have never met Samantha. I'd still have a man. But, some of them don't give ya the good without the bad. And they really make you pay for it. After so many black eyes, it's not worth it. There's no good parts. Just the part that's good before it gets bad. Then, it's just OK before it gets bad. And then you're just wondering why it's always bad."

There was an unexpected interjection from Adrianna, "Well, Sam and Samantha, you have each other, so you have good times, right? I mean, you can touch each other and feel good, right? You don't need any men because you have a girl. That's just as good, right?"

This presented an interesting pause in the conversation. Adrianna was so pure in her curiosity. Sometimes it was easy to forget that she was mentally handicapped. Occasionally, her lack of understanding social norms was a gentle reminder.

Megan was the first to speak after that set of questions. "Yeah, Sam and Samantha. That's just as good, right? Why don't you tell us about it? I'm sure there's some curious minds here right now."

It felt a little like some sort of odd challenge. Megan was asking some good questions, but her tone and demeanor felt off. It was like she was trying to publicly embarrass the lesbian couple.

Sam didn't let it bother her. She took it as an opportunity. She said, "Well, since you asked..." She looked around with confidence. "We are people. We have a relationship. So, we have problems. We're not perfect. But, we have a relationship, so we work on things. We disagree, we barter, we bicker and we figure it out. Is it better than having a man? Maybe in some ways. But, not in others.

Let's not kid ourselves. Men are a lot of things women are not. So, in many ways, they complete us. Or at least they compliment us. When a man and woman get together and it works, one compliments the other. It's a good bond.

When two women get together, they can be soul mates. They can be more madly in love and destined for each other than you can imagine. But, in some ways, there will always be something missing. And it's not just the penis.

No matter how big and tough a butch women might get, she'll never be a man. Or at least, she didn't grow up a man. Only a man that has grown up as a man in a man's world understands the world from a man's point of view.

Think of it like this, any man that claims that he feels like he was suppose to be a women will never understand what it's like to have someone grab his boob when he's 14. Anyone who didn't grow up a girl and went through everything we did to become a woman will never understand.

So, a man sees the world through man eyes. He processes the world through a man's mind. Everything is filtered through his being a man. Having a man gives us the other side of things or the other way of understanding stuff. We

166

have someone trusted to help navigate life seeing and understanding the things we don't."

Samantha injected, "Plus, to be perfectly honest, a man tends to be protective of his woman, even when he's the one that hurts her. He won't let anyone else hurt her. He acts as a protector, even when he's the one abusing her and making her afraid of everything. That can be super confusing, but men really do have more strength and aggression. Plus they can understand when other men are looking at us with bad intentions and they're willing to challenge that. Most men will avoid a woman because of the look her man gives him."

Sam regained the narrative, "We're not saying that two women is bad or wrong. It's just a fact that a man and woman together has a lot of strong points. Probably more than two women can have. But, it's also a fact that as long as they're all human, there will be problems."

Candy asked, "So, would you say that having a woman as a partner is safer than having a man?"

Sam frowned for a minute. Then she said, "Yes and no. Obviously, a man can do way more physical harm. And he can do a lot of emotional and psychological harm, but he usually relies on his physical ability to allow him opportunity to inflict those. A man can only damage our hearts and minds because of his physical ability to control us.

I think that women are more dangerous in ways that are not physical. Think about it, we're all women and we know how women can be. We know how WE can be. We can do a lot of damage to another woman, but it's not usually in a fight. It's ugly warfare that involves rumors and reputations and back handed comments and stuff like that."

Michelle Satori spoke up, "Yeah. That's no joke. As bad as I've been treated by men, I've never recovered completely from what my supposed girlfriends did to me. They pretended to be a guy I was really crushing on, contacting me and chatting with me on social media. I was hooked. And I didn't know it was all a joke until they convinced me to go up to him at school where everyone would see. He had no idea what was going on and freaked out on me, calling me psycho and running from me. I was humiliated with the entire school laughing at me and talking about me for weeks."

Sam broke back in before the compassionate comforting got too loud, "Yeah, exactly. I don't think you'd ever want to be with a woman after being done like that by a few."

Michelle shook her head, "No. I barely want to be with anyone. There's no way to know how to trust anyone."

"No one can blame you," Sam said. "And honestly, all of us are kinda in the same boat with trust issues. We've heard some of the horrible ways we've each been treated. Some are worse than others, but we've all been done wrong so bad that trust is broken forever.

I can only tell you that I love Samantha. And because I understand her pain from her point of view, I'll never do anything to make her hurt like that again. And I'm sure she feels the same for me. I'm not sure that's a man or woman thing, but it's the way this works for us."

Crystal interrupted the brief pause that lingered in the air, "I guess that's really how it works for any of us. We just want to find someone who understands what we've been through and wants to never put us through it again."

Tammy tagged in, "Yeah, but it seems like most people take what we've survived as some sort of invitation to treat us like garbage. Like we've been ruined and don't deserve to be treated good. It's like being taken advantage of gives everyone else the OK to use us anyway they want for the rest of our lives."

Lily agreed, "Yep. Like once someone marked me as a target, the whole world took aim at me. But, I refuse to let them."

Meelow said, "Lily, you definitely don't take shit from anyone. You're a real fighter."

Lily responded, "So, are you Meelow. We all are. We might be afraid, but we have that fight in us. It can be hard to let it out. But, I'll be damned if I'll ever let one more person take advantage of me without feeling my resentment and anger. I won't be a helpless victim. If they want to treat me like garbage, they can get treated just as bad.

Roger has pushed every boundary and we've gone 'round and 'round. He knows not to fuck around with me. He's been warned. And yet, he acts like I'm joking. He acts like he'll always be bigger and stronger than me, so he's in charge. He tells his buddies that he can keep me in line and he's the man of the house, and that I do what he tells me to do or else." There were tears in her eyes. "He don't think I know how he talks about me, but I do. I hear it all. And I feel it. I'm not his dog. I'm not his slave to push around and force me to do his laundry and cooking and cleaning. He's acted like he owns me for years." She growled, "Well, now he's gonna get his."

Lily just left everyone a little unnerved. They all knew exactly what she meant, and there was no doubt that she would be taking the lessons from the range home to put to use. Everyone knew what Lily meant and that she really meant it.

Adrianna circled back to her curiosity, "So, is it harder to have a woman than a man?"

Smiles filled the room. She was so cute in her innocence. Everyone was caught off guard and even Lily had a slight chuckle.

Onna spoke up, "Sam, ya wanna fill her in, or would you like me to field this one?"

Sam smiled and settled back into Samantha, "Please, be my guest. Help me out, Sis!"

Onna nodded. "Adrianna, it's not harder or easier. It's just different. Women don't feel the same as men. We're softer. Men don't cry like women. Women don't fight like men. Men don't argue like women. It's just different because men and women are different. Do you need more than that?"

Adrianna smiled. "No. I was just wondering. If it was easier, I'd rather have a woman. But, if it's just different, I don't. I'd have to learn too much."

It felt like an odd statement, but no one could say she was wrong.

Michelle Satori leaned over to Lily and whispered, "Are we sure she can keep our secret? She's mentally handicapped. She doesn't always know what she's saying."

Lily whispered back, "No one can really know. Hell, I don't know if any of these women have kept quiet! Adrianna has given the names of her abusers and they'll be dealt with. That's all that matters."

From somewhere in the middle of the group, a voice drew attention by saying rather loudly in alcohol speed, "So, is anyone gonna kiss me so I know whether or not girls are better?"

Tammy was issuing a slightly drunken challenge and further explained, "I just wanna know if I'm missing out on something. Ya know?"

Sam shook her head and laughed, "It's way past bedtime. Someone help me get her to her bunk." She was expressing the general consensus.

But, before anyone else could move, Candy popped up and wobbled a little. She walked over to Tammy and leaned over. They bumped foreheads and giggled. Sam and Samantha moved to break up the party before it got out of hand, but before they dragged Candy away, she gave Tammy a peck on the lips.

To the mixed reactions, Candy called out as Samantha walked her away, "I'm a pretty good kisser! I think she'd like me!"

It was clearly time to head to bed. So, Sam helped Tammy up and off to her bunk while everyone else tidied up loose ends and the After Party shuffled off to slumber. They had made it through a long day with a huge emotional moment. And they had no idea what the rest of the retreat held in store for them.

Chapter 20: Ester's Retreat, Day 3

Breakfast was very low key. No one had gotten totally wasted, but there was definitely a "morning after" feel in the air, if not from the booze, then from the bad news.

Even the time at the gun range and cleaning weapons was low key. There wasn't a lot of chat. It wasn't very lively. It was almost somber. By lunch, Ester had grown frustrated. She was afraid that her girls were becoming disenfranchised and might be slipping into a resolution to go back to their lives and settle for whatever that might be.

She took Hirra and Bridgette to another building to talk about what was happening and what might need to be done. They only had this day and one more before they either went back to their old ways or were going to eliminate as many abusers as possible and begin new lives. Ester had a weird moment when she realized that she no longer afforded Bridgette the luxury of plausible deniability. But, she'd just have to make sure that she apologized and explained herself to Bridgette before it was all over.

Ester expressed her concerns to the other two and asked about options. It was a stale mate. Ideas did not come easily or quickly. According to Bridgette, the women were acting like normal humans. What Ester was asking them to do was not normal. And the only way to get someone to do something extraordinary that is contradictory to their nature is to put them into extraordinary circumstances or training. That wasn't very likely to happen in four days at a Bible campground in Ohio.

Hirra concurred. She explained that people may joke about waking up and choosing violence, but when it comes to actually pulling the trigger, stabbing or otherwise seriously harming another human being, very few people are able to make that decision and follow through. Even with trained military personnel, there's a certain percentage that freeze up when face to face with the reality of actually killing another person, even when that other person is trying to kill them.

Ester was a little dismayed. She frumpled her eye brows and lips. She had invested everything of herself in getting other women to understand that they don't need to put up with abuse. She did everything to make it clear that abusers do not change. They only go away. She didn't know how to make it any more clear and imperative to the After Party that they would never escape the abuse unless they made it stop. She was trying to figure out how to get them to understand that living in an abusive environment was never the right way to live.

Bridgette took Ester's hand and explained to her that she had made all of that clear. She said, "Ester, you have done more than any other human could have done to explain it to them. You have led by example. You have laid it all out there for everyone to see. You have talked and talked and talked. You even have Susan laying in a hospital room. It can't be made any more clear! There couldn't be any more visceral example than their friend lying there with a broken neck.

Ester, they're just not killers. You can't make them do it. They know. They know how bad it is and they know they should do better and they know that what they are enduring just isn't right. But, they just aren't going to bring themselves to do it. I'm afraid we can finish out the retreat, but ultimately, they're going to go home and nothing will change."

Ester was very angry and sad. She did not want to admit that she was on the cusp of defeat. She didn't want to admit that there was no real hope of saving an abused woman from an abuser unless she decided to get out of the relationship. She also knew, that most go back or go on to another abuser.

This was the struggle in her heart and mind. All of her life, she had watched women take what was dished out to them and never fight back. She had witnessed one good woman after another become a broken slave to a degenerate and ungrateful man. Broken bones and broken noses were as common to her as broken hearts and broken promises. She wanted justice.

Hirra and Bridgette were watching Ester process the inevitable collapse of her plans. The little old lady that had survived abuse and ended her torment by ending her abuser was struggling. She was struggling to understand why the facts didn't seem to matter. It was hurting her to image what was going through the minds of the women that were enduring such terrible treatment. She could see and feel the terror of being cornered and beaten as she pictured each of them. She was weakened by the helplessness they each felt every time their abuser snapped. She could feel the burning sting of every blow they suffered. And she teared up as she was swept under the waves of shame and guilt and the aftermath of each attack.

She couldn't let them go on like that. She needed to find a way to make them understand that killing these horrible men was the only way. The problem was that they saw their man as horrible only when he wasn't the love of their lives. He was only a bad man when he was abusing them.

She began to realize that they had not suffered enough to realize that the "good" wasn't worth the bad. They didn't see that they were only treated good enough to stay so they could be used for punching bags again at a later date. Ester finally saw the 10,000 foot view of what was happening.

From above, or from the outside, she was finally able to comprehend that the only way these women would believe it was bad enough would be when it had been bad enough for long enough. Until they had been completely destroyed, they would never fight for themselves. They would always love him because he was "so good to me" at other times. It finally made sense to her that even she was guilty of believing that she could help him change to become the man she saw him as and wanted him to be.

Then, it occurred to her that once the women left this campground, they would be able to be seduced back under the spell of their abuser. Once they were away from the support and encouragement of the group, they would be isolated and vulnerable and weak. They would be victims again and forever.

No, no, no. Ester couldn't let that happen. She couldn't let them leave camp without being ready to end the abuse once and for all. In her mind, Ester was determined to do whatever it took to follow through with the plan to kill the abusers.

Ester realized that the only way these mild mannered housewives and girlfriends would ever fight back would be if they were more afraid of her than what they had at home. They would rather sacrifice themselves than see their abuser harmed. The only way Ester was going to create a killing army over night would be to create such a hostile environment, that they would have no choice but to go along with her plan.

Her problem was that the military took months to break a person down and build them up as a warrior type killing machine. She had 36 hours. She was stumped. This was the most troubling challenge of her life on several levels. The ethics and moral dilemma was solved in her mind. The abusers were already judged to be guilty and worthy of death. She had led the horse to water. She had taken these women right up to the river. She showed them the problem and sold them the solution. But, now she was wondering how to get them to drink. How was she going to convince them to take that final step and plunge into the waters that would wash away their pain?

Ester didn't take long to see through the fog. She could see clearly. Her eyes were open to the one option that would allow her to take control of everything. She knew what she had to do. She called Pastor Kern to join them at the retreat for the next night's closing ceremony of the retreat.

Hirra got a cold shiver. She knew that asking what Ester had in mind was a terrible idea and a burden that she did not want to know. She knew she'd find out soon enough, just like everyone else. So, for that day, she quietly decided to proceed as if everything was normal. But, she knew that inviting a man, especially one with Herman's reputation and history with Ester, was not on the agenda. She knew it couldn't be good. She and Bridgette were worried about whatever it was that was brewing in Ester's mind.

The afternoon proceeded as originally planned. There were some fun activities and games and casual recreation. The women of the After Party were obviously enjoying the cool but decent weather. The freedom from the daily grind and normal day to day life was something to be soaked in like the Caribbean sun on an island beach. They were enjoying life that afternoon as if they were carefree teens with bright eyes and lofty dreams. But, in the deepest part of them, they all knew that this relaxed fantasy world would very soon implode. They were ignoring the monsters at the end of the rainbow.

Dinner time that evening was completely normal, except for the conversation. The topic: could you kill him for real?

Onna had been staring off into the distance when Lily asked her if she was alright. Onna responded, "I dunno. I just don't know if I could really kill him. Or anyone. I don't think I could do it."

Lily asked back, "Like, for any reason? What if he was coming at you, drunk out of his mind with a knife, promising to kill you?"

Onna just shrugged.

Lily asked, "What if someone was trying to kidnap your child? Could you kill them?"

Onna looked conflicted, "I don't know. I just hope that nothing like that ever happens."

Lily began to look a little concerned. "Wishing and hoping won't work very long. We all hope for the best, but we don't always get it. The fact that we're all here is proof of that."

That made Onna think. The wheels in her head were obviously turning.

Lily came back with, "A man takes your child. You KNOW

he's going to do the worst before killing her. You have a gun. There's that moment where he's so close you can't miss. You shoot him or your child dies. Do you pull the trigger? Or do you let him take her and hope for the best?"

Several others had tuned in for Onna's answer, "That's an impossible thing for me to answer. I'd fight like hell to stop him, but I don't think I could shoot him."

"But!" Lily pressed. "He's too big and strong. He's faster. Do you kill him? It's the only way you can save your daughter. At that moment, no one but you can save her?"

Onna was sad. She was conflicted more than she had ever been. The scenario was too much for her. She couldn't allow the abduction of her child, but she couldn't bring herself to do whatever was necessary to stop it. The ethical dilemma of taking one life to save another was too much for her. She cried.

While some of the women tried comfort her, others began to speak up.

Barbara offered, "You wouldn't have to do anything, baby. I'd take care of him for you."

When Michelle Satori said, "I'd shoot him in a heartbeat. No questions asked," three other women agreed and said they would do the same.

Faith answered, "I don't know. I would hope for a good Samaritan or police or something. I don't think I could do it either." Two other women concurred that they would be in the same boat.

Meeelow said, "Anyone that comes at my baby is going to meet Mama Bear. No way on earth I would allow anyone to do my child like was done to me. Hell, naw! They would hear my roar and the roar of my gun!"

Kendra interrupted the conversation with a low and disturbingly quiet statement, "I'd shoot him, gut him and hang him in the town square as a warning to anyone thinking they wanna try."

Faith responded, "That's a little dark, Kendra."

With no additional emotion, Kendra responded, "I know what it's like to be helpless, wishing for a hero, a cop, a dog... ANYONE to come help. I remember what it felt like to need to be saved and no one came. There's nothing on earth that could stop me from doing everything and anything necessary to make sure someone I love never has to know what I know... what I live with every day."

Faith quietly said, "Not all of us have been through what you went through, but..."

Before she could finish another syllable, Kendra came unglued. She snapped up, screaming, "You're right! You weren't held hostage in a basement for two years and used like a toy day and night! You didn't get humiliated to the point of not being human anymore! You never begged for death because you knew that every day forever was going to be worse than the day before, and your soul was murdered while your body kept being beaten and raped!

I hope you never know what's like to be talked about and looked down on for being a victim! I hope you never know what it feels like to hear people whisper about you being used and broken because you were a victim! People think of me as less than human because someone did all that to me! It was NOTHING I ever did or chose to do! I didn't go drinking and kill someone in a car! I didn't get stoned and make a bad decision! I was a targeted, innocent woman! Wrong time, wrong place and now I'm labeled and worthless and nothing but a leftover that society makes fun of!

So, since you never went through that, you're too afraid or holy or whatever to kill the fuckers that want to do that to your kid?! You would allow your child to become ME?! You would let them suffer the rest of their lives like me just because it wasn't you that suffered?! FUCK YOU!! FUCK ALL OF YOU!!" And she raged out of the building.

The women were silenced.

Ester was hiding her smile. She couldn't have planned a better guilt trip. She went to consult Bridgette.

The evening session got a late start. It took a bit to get everyone calmed down and back on an even keel. Bridgette was a little nervous. She hadn't planned for anything other than delivering a normal seminar, so far there was zero normal. She hadn't planned for such a charged environment. How could she have planned for this? How could anyone have possibly planned for it?

And now, Ester was asking her to alter her message and tailor it to the occasion. When Ester made the request, Bridgette nearly quit and left. But, Ester was so sincere and passionate about helping her girls, that she consented.

Now, she was about to take the stage to deliver an improvised set of information that was supposed to inspire. She was nervous. It was show time.

Ester called the After Party to order and introduced Bridgette, emphasizing that this would be her last night with them and that the final night would be a very special guest. Bridgette took a deep breath, walked up and began speaking.

She said, "Thank you all for listening to me these past few days. It's always an honor to speak for people, but this opportunity has truly been a privilege. When I took this gig, it was initially for the money. After all, this is what I do for a living. As Ester explained to me that you all have something in common, I was more passionate about being here, because I fit in.

Yes. I was molested, too. And I'm not going to share the whole traumatizing history, because, let's face it, we've all got a story and we've all heard the stories. We've lived it. We get it. We don't need more of it.

I can tell you, that it's one of the main reasons I became a public speaker. Kind of a weird twist of fate, I guess, but in a round about way, it made me want to help people. And this seemed like the most obvious way to help as many people as I could.

This has been an incredibly weird week for me in terms of speaking. Normally, it's very uneventful. People gather. I speak. They get glassy eyed waiting for lunch or dinner time. I don't really try to get their attention. I just talk. They either take notes or they dream of sandwiches and beer.

You ladies have challenged me. You're not here to listen to me.

There's no glossy brochure about this retreat making promises of happiness and finding purpose in life. You've found purpose. You already are way ahead of anywhere I can lead you. You have each other.

Whether you know it or not, finding each other and bonding like you have done is possibly the most incredible treasure you could ever have worth more than gold. In the world, this never happens. Yeah, there are support groups. Do you know what they do? Nothing.

They talk. They do nothing but talk. They commiserate. They share stories and cookies. Maybe they share a few tears. But, in the end, they do nothing. It's just a place to talk.

Even if you never find a way out of whatever situation you're surviving, you at least did this retreat! I've never seen another group do anything like this. This is amazing! You really do need to be proud of yourselves.

But. And they say there's always a 'but.' And yeah, there's a 'but.'" She paused. "But, you may have come as far as you can." She watched them shift in their seats.

"Yeah," she continued. "I know the end game." Now, she was watching the faces. The reactions were very telling.

"And, no," she made clear. "I will not be joining you on your purge." She waited for that to register in everyone. "What I'm going to talk about tonight is not something I planned to say. Everything I had on paper went right out the window.

Normally, my job is to inspire people and motivate them to do better with their lives. But, I don't know if that's possible here. Hell! You all are inspiring ME to do better with MY life!! How am I supposed to top THAT?" She waited for the subdued giggles and bashful smiles.

She resumed, "What I want to do right now is tell you a story. And we'll see what you all get from the story. I think it'll help you all understand yourselves. It'll help you understand the situation you're in. And I hope it helps you embrace what you need...." She couldn't say another word.

There was a man in the back of the room.

That man wasn't supposed to be there. No man was supposed to be there. Men weren't even supposed to *know* about this retreat. Yet, there he was. Six foot four inches of muscle, looming at the edge of the lighted area.

The women were gasping and frozen in fear. They experienced the "deer in the headlights" sensation collectively. The man in the back stepped forward a couple steps. But he wasn't exactly a man.

Larry was only 17. He was the All American linebacker from one of the local schools. Despite having the build of a Greek god, he had the face of a school boy that barely shaves. He was handsome for his age without being a "pretty boy." He looked just as scared and nervous as the women.

Everyone was frozen. He wasn't supposed to be there. He wasn't supposed to know they were there. He shouldn't have even known that the After Party existed, let alone was at a retreat. Yet, there he was. There was a sharp, icy feeling in the room as everyone tried to figure out how this happened.

But, they all knew how it happened. Someone told him. Someone had been talking about the After Party. Everyone felt the instant wave of betrayal and vulnerability. Except the one that told Larry what was happening. She just felt awkward.

Ester pulled on the back of Hirra's shirt and waved her off before the marine could approach and confront the young man. This was Ester's Retreat. Ester would deal with him. She didn't want the marine testing the young lad.

Ester wobbled up to Larry and titled her head almost all the way back to look up at him. "Well, young man. It seems that you have been privy to some information that wasn't intended to be made public. I have to surmise that one of my girls has been talking with you." She turned over her shoulder to the After Party and said, "Despite the endless admonishments not to talk about our group outside of the group."

She looked back up at Larry and said, "Before I throw you out of here, I need to ask you some questions. So, how about you and I step outside?"

Larry looked a little surprised and a whole lot confused when he replied, "Did you just challenge me to a fight?"

The laughter was slow coming, but it grew in volume once a couple of snickers could no longer be contained. The image of tiny Ester standing half the size of this man-child was already amusing. The idea of her wanting to tear into him gave the mental image of a purse dog going after a rottweiler.

Megan finally confessed to having confided in Larry. They had known each other a long time and were well acquainted with each other's horrible histories. Ester was not pleased. Not at first. But, she tried to put aside normal thinking to find out what would make this young lady risk so much for so many by telling Larry about the group, right down to when and where they would be.

Sadly, Larry was holding back on his emotions so hard he couldn't talk. He was fighting to control his breathing and refused to let his teary eyes leak. His face was flushed red and his forehead was sweaty. If he were in a movie, the sound track would cue up a full orchestra for an emotional crescendo.

Megan spoke for him, so Larry wouldn't have to take a chance of breaking down. She said, "He's here because his dad has been as bad to him, his brother, and his mom as any man has been to us. He's here to help."

Ester's face went through a myriad of expressions. The faces in the room remained mostly frozen in shock. They were all trying to process how anyone could have possibly done bad things to this handsome, boy faced man. Mostly, they were wondering how big someone would have to be to get away with mistreating this lad.

Ester turned towards Megan with a very perplexed face. "Help how?" she asked.

Larry took in an immeasurably deep breath and growled through his clenched teeth, "Once I've taken care of that bastard I've called 'Dad,' I want to help anyone else that can't go through with it or needs more strength than they have. I'll stand there with you to make sure you're safe. Or, I'll take care of them for you. I've had enough. And it's time to end this shit for good."

He was shaking. He was young and hadn't learned the art of self control in stressful and emotional times. Football had taught him to build up rage and adrenaline, then direct it at the opposition and unleash it all at once. No one had ever taught him to cry. Only to redirect feelings into workouts and performance.

Ester began to settle into acceptance with this young man crashing her retreat. She was very slow to move and very deliberate in her words. She didn't want Larry to respond in a physical way. But, she needed to let him know that, "Young man, you are way too young to even know about the Guardian Angels of New York, let alone remember them. But, you just offered to fill that role for us without us asking. Which would make those fellows very proud of you. Come with me and we can talk about how you might be our guardian angel."

"No, ma'am," Larry refused to follow. The shock in the room went up another notch, even though it seemed impossible for there to be another notch. "Respectfully, I only want to tell this story once. So, if y'all can let me do it right now, I'd feel a whole lot better. Please."

Ester looked at him with warm, motherly eyes. She wondered how such a marvel of a young man could be in such a messed up state. She decided to give him the floor. After all, they were all a bit messed up. Why should he be treated any differently than a victim like them?

Ester took him by the hand and led him to the front of the room. He didn't need to be on stage. He could be seen clearly.

Larry began his story, "People tell me that my dad was a hell raiser in school. Then, he was even wilder in the marines. But, supposedly, he became a whole new man when he met Mom.

She straightened him out. Made him go to church and stop drinking and fighting. They tell me she turned him into a good man.

I don't know when that changed. I don't remember a good man. He was always a mean drunk that fought and yelled and hit everyone for any little reason. When my brother was about 11, Dad hit him so hard that he went reeling across the room and fell down the stairs to the basement. I remember his head was bleeding so bad that I couldn't see his face.

Jason had brain damage and has never been OK since. Dad turned him into a mentally handicapped mess. He's beaten Mom into a drunken slob of a woman. She can barely function."

He had been fighting emotional breakdown with every word. Now he was gritting his teeth and forcing the final sentence out as he fought off tears with every ounce of strength he had in him as he growled, "And every time he hit me, I swore that I'd take it, and save it, and give it all back to him one day! And now, I'm not afraid! And he's going to pay! And once he's dead, I want to make sure that every man that's treated someone like my old man did to us... I want that bastard to get what he deserves!"

The tension was more than intense. It was at the breaking point. Ester very quietly stood beside Larry and with all the compassion of a mother watching her child hurt said, "It's OK to cry here."

Larry looked down at her. His entire body was hardened and prepared for war. He was huffing hard. He began to tremble as a guttural sound welled up from within his chest. Every one clapped their hands over their ears as he unleashed a primal scream like a viking sending his fallen to Valhalla.

Everyone had flinched and was boarder line cowering. Except for Ester and Hirra. They stood on either side of Larry and helped him sit on the stage as he broke down into tears, wailing and gasping. They stood like protective angels over the broken man while he was helpless. Someone brought tissues. Some women broke into sympathy crying.

Ester shook her head. She thought it was rough to watch the women break and cry and get emotional. She wasn't ready for Larry. Watching this majestic mountain of a man reduced to a sobbing child was worse. It was so much worse. She wanted to comfort him, but she couldn't control her own situation. She was feeling everything he was crying out. It was possibly the worse feeling of painful helplessness she had ever experienced.

It felt like he cried all night. The room was burning in an emotional train wreck. Ester couldn't even clear her head. Her heart was breaking. But, finally, she was able to get Larry to sit up and catch his breath so she could say to him, "I promise that you will be able to fulfill your promise to yourself very soon."

Ester turned to the ladies. She lowered her head and forced her mind to focus and put together coherent thoughts. "I promise that this will all come to an end. It'll be over soon." She raised her head and looked around at the blood shot eyes and weepy faces. She said, "You women are not helpless. This young man isn't any stronger than you. He's just as hurt and abused. He's survived just like you. You have endured as much as he has. You are stronger than you know. You are more than you believe. All of that has been stolen from you, but not anymore.

You're not helpless. You are going to take back your lives. You are going to quit being victims and you are going to kick some ass.

I can't watch this one more time. I will NOT watch another person be treated like this! NO MORE, LADIES! You are NOT going to go home and be beaten any more! NO MORE!"

Ester was approaching rage. The little old lady was not acting like a Sunday school teacher. She was becoming a commander of warriors. She was taking her throne as the Queen of the Killers. It was time to turn these broken cherubs into avenging angels.

Ester couldn't project her voice like Larry. She was too weak for that. But, she delivered fire and brimstone nonetheless. She was barking mad. "I'll start kicking ass myself. If you go home and let those bastards treat you like a rag doll, you'll have to answer to me. NO MORE! You are not trash! You are NOT weak! You are not a victim! You are women, and you are damn good women at that! You deserve to be treated good! You deserve to be treated with decency and respect! You do NOT deserve to be treated like you're nothing, because you're NOT! You're amazing! You're beautiful! You have loving hearts and kind spirits! You are mothers and protectors!

It's time you get off your knees and act like the hero you need! The time for being afraid and being a coward is gone! NO

MORE! You are NOT going to take it anymore! No more pain! No more tears! No more fear! No more bruises, no more being controlled, no more being talked to like an idiot, because you're NOT! NO MORE!

I will not tolerate one more day of this shit! And if you're too afraid to kill that bastard that is killing you, I'll do it myself! And I'll kick your ass for not doing it yourself. It's your life! Act like it matters!"

Tears were gone. Eyes were still red. Breathing was heavy. Fear was real. The women were in all new territory. They were getting yelled at by the kindest, little old woman they knew. And it had them paralyzed.

Ester glared at them one by one. "I'm heading to my room. You all need to search your soul. Tomorrow is the last day here, and I promise not to waste it. I'll make damn sure that you all understand in no uncertain terms what this has been all about. By tomorrow evening, you will know for sure if you are all in, or..." she paused and glared around again. "You will know that you will keep your damn mouth shut about all this forever. Whether you sit back and watch, or do what needs done, NONE of you will EVER say a word to ANYONE about this retreat, the After Party, or anything we talked about. In fact, you will deny knowing each other. Tomorrow, this ends. I will not put up with one more day of this and neither will any of you."

Ester hugged Larry and asked if he was OK. She let him get up and she offered to find a place for him to sleep. She left Hirra and Bridgette to clean up the crew and get them settled enough to head to bed.

Whatever Bridgette had hoped to talk about didn't matter one little bit at that point. No one could possibly follow that. No one could change the mood. It was going to be a tough night of sleeplessness and tough conversations. Few would sleep. All would think. And all would wonder what was coming next.

In reality, the bunkhouse almost held the atmosphere of an army barracks the night before deployment. Ester had promised that "tomorrow, this ends." There was no hiding the unrest and fear. The women were worried. They were guessing and conjecturing and trying to figure out what she meant.

It had been a long day and a lot had happened. It had been the most emotionally charged day any of them could remember that didn't end in a hospital visit. They were exhausted. But, they were chasing sleep like a child chasing a rabbit. Tomorrow was coming, ready or not. Ester's promise was looming and tomorrow would be there soon. The women appreciated the few smatterings of sleep they slipped in and out of. The final day was about to dawn.

Chapter 21: Ester's Retreat, Pastor Kern

Before the retreat had begun, Ester had planned for the catering to bring a grand buffet type breakast for the final morning. The women of the After Party woke, or rolled out of near sleep, to find the chow hall being decorated and stocked like royalty was coming. But, it was all for them.

The tables had everything. There were even stations set up to make fresh pancakes and omelets. It seemed like there was EVERYthing! There were several types of donuts, every type of breakfast meat, cereals and bagels with cream cheese and lox. They had nearly every breakfast option. Everything was there. Except Ester.

Ester was in her room. Alone. With her thoughts. She was in prayer. She was in pain. She was talking out loud and silently. She was singing the saddest dirges she knew, and she was crying. She was pacing. She was sitting, lying down, and kneeling. Ester was possibly the most tormented soul on the planet at that time. And she didn't want the others to see.

Breakast was a strange mix of delight and uncertainty for the women. The almost festive feasting was shadowed by the unknown events coming from an unseen horizon. The ample spread of various good foods was festive and welcomed. But, the unclear future was looming.

The morning went quickly. There was little activity. Very few went walking. Very few went to the gun range. No one was in a "camp mood." They were a long way from the first day of the retreat. Just a few days seemed like a lifetime of experiences. And a lot of those experiences were intense. No matter what else happened before they left the grounds, some of them would never really be the same. At least they wouldn't be 100% like they had been.

The morning morphed into some sort of "Girls' Day Away." After such a marvelous breakfast buffet, there was a lot of lounging around. Showers were slower, more luxurious of sorts. Hair and make up were joint ventures. There was a soft tone to the activities of prepping and preening, perhaps faintly reminiscent of teen sleep overs in a way.

An unspoken phenomenon was blanketing the campgrounds. It was unspoken, because they didn't realize it was happening, or rather, that it had already happened, and they had become part of it. They were no longer who they were. They were no longer what they had been. Meeting Ester had changed them.

This camp solidarity would have NEVER been possible with these women before Ester. They would have been catty and gossiping. They would have been broken into cliques or just each doing their own thing. It wasn't that they were "of one accord," but they were not just broken and lonely individuals forced to gather. Maybe it was Ester's ominous promise that brought them together this morning. Maybe it was the course of events. Maybe they were secretly bonded through mystic means unspoken.

Whatever it was, anyone coming to the campground would have been hard pressed to believe that these were abused women plucked from their harsh lives and dropped in together. Even Larry was fitting in. He was surrounded by five or six women at any time exchanging questions. He was a bit of a novelty for the ladies, but not the center of attention.

In fact, no one was the center of attention. And no one was

alone. It was very tranquil and... comfortable. Actually, it was more than that. It was comforting.

Eventually, lunch time rolled around and nothing had been accomplished. Nothing had been done. No speeches. No organized activities. No organized anything. Just a lazy, enjoyable day. And even if it they didn't put words to it, they were relaxed and, to some degree, happy.

Then, Ester returned to camp with Pastor Kern in tow.

The mood changed instantly with the introduction of yet another man. The lazy day was done. They were on alert. The mood became more like when unexpected company comes over and they're not only unexpected, but really, unwelcome.

Lunch was rather light. The breakfast feast was enough to stave off any large lunch options. It was more of a peckish event where nibbling and light snacking was more the vibe.

Ester kept Pastor Kern in conversation. A few women stopped by to greet him, but for the most part, he was far from popular. He was a strange guest in a strange land.

Eventually, Ester stood up and called for attention. She announced that everyone should prepare for their final session together. She was going to take the pastor to the meeting hall to prepare. She wanted them all ready to come as one when she let them know that it was time.

It was odd. It felt weird. It was uncomfortable. It was almost cold. No one could put their finger on it, but something was off. Bridgette had been sent home. Her time with the After Party was over. But, even Hirra didn't know what Ester was doing. She had gone off script. This was not on the agenda. After all, she was taking Pastor Kern to the main meeting hall that they had not used.

The ladies went to the bunkhouses and prepared themselves for whatever was coming. That meant that they cleaned up, packed bags and stripped beds. They were dressed and presentable. That was all they could do.

It was all down to Ester and whatever she had planned with Pastor Kern.

Pastor Herman Kern had almost always had a question mark hanging over his head. Everyone knows that no one is perfect, but Herman didn't really seem to be making any effort to be the best version of himself. He hid most of his bad habits pretty well. His breath was the biggest tell he had. Cigarettes or alcohol seemed to commonly generate a terrible fog from his throat. Obviously, he wasn't into fitness. And in spite of not being obese, he had probably never missed a meal.

He was very likable. He wasn't mean or cruel when he drank. Rather, he was quite funny and charming. He was very helpful and full of information that he shared freely. And since he seemed to always be drinking, he was almost always funny, charming and likable.

The only real problem with the pastor was that occasionally, he seemed to favor a particular child. He would befriend an odd kid and spend time mentoring them one on one. It would take on a weird friendship/relationship vibe that didn't seem malicious or malevolent. But, it just didn't feel right. It didn't have the most innocent vibe.
No one could say he was doing anything wrong. But, his

attachment to kids seemed off. It wasn't completely normal. And those kids would never say anything bad about him. It was almost as if they adored him. No one knew of any wrong doing by Pastor Kern. Except Ester.

Ester was naturally involved in the church. So much so, that she had been given a key. Often, she would come in and clean or set up for groups and events. And as fate would have it, there was one early evening where Ester let herself into Holy Trinity unannounced for an unplanned cleaning session on a Friday. Pastor Kern's car was there. She went to his office to ask what he was doing, and to see if he needed any help.

Nope. He didn't need any help. And she was mortified at what he was doing.

The sound of sex coming from his office stopped her in her tracks. She was sickened in a way that she had never been before and could have never imagined. She froze. She wanted to run. She wanted to know who it was in there. She wanted to throw up, scream, cry, and everything else a body might do at such a discovery.

She had to know. Was it one of the choir ladies? Was it someone's wife from the congregation? Maybe it was someone from another church? Nope. Peeking in through the tiny, narrow window of his door was the worst mistake she had ever felt like she had made.

She could not be silent when she saw the grown man naked with that boy. Both scared faces looked up into the tiny, narrow window in that door that separated Ester from the heinous sin she was witnessing. It was hard to tell who was more horrified.

The pastor was too drunk to chase Ester down. The kid was too scared. Ester hurried away in tears and terror. Everyone knew, but was too scared to say anything. It went unspoken. That was years ago. And Ester was too weak to do the right thing. She lived with his horrible secret all this time. But, when he started sniffing around her kids in the outreach, she had no problem putting her foot down and ending that.

Ester had killed her abusive husband sometime after that fateful day that changed her. Something *changed* in her. Seeing the "man of God" fall so far and hard from grace altered her view of the world. It changed how she saw life. It changed how she saw *her* life. The way she saw life and everything and everyone changed.

She made up her mind that she would protect these young ones that she considered her responsibility. And now, she made up her mind that he should never be allowed to groom and molest another child. And she decided that she would not be gentle and kind like she had been with her husband.

No. Ester was going to make sure he got a taste of what he deserved. She bought the most powerful taser she could find. Then, she found an old extension cord and stripped several inches of insulation from the end furthest from where it plugs into the wall. She stopped at home and put those things in the car along with some rope before she went to get Pastor Kern.

Ester had decided that today was to be the Judgment Day. Today was the Day of Elimination. If there was ever going to be a right time for those abusers to die, today was the day. And it was going to begin with Herman.

While the ladies were getting ready for the afternoon session after lunch, Ester was leading Herman to the place where the afternoon session would take place. Pastor Kern was under the impression that he was the guest speaker, and he was honored. He never thought to ask her what was in the bag.

Ester had plans. She was going to make him the sacrificial offering that would ignite the After Party to action. She was going to use him to make the women more afraid of her than they were of their abusers.

Upon entering the building, Ester asked Herman to sit in the chair up front on the stage. Figuring that she was going to perform some kind of light and sound check, he placidly complied. Once he was comfortably seated, Ester opened the bag. She pulled out a large bottle of water and the taser. Pastor was confused. Ester was not.

She took the lid off the bottle and squeezed a large stream of water onto the seated man. As he was gasping in shock and disbelief, he tried to stand up. Ester was ready with the taser and zapped him back into the chair. His eyes spoke of horror and pain. His voice was just an indistinct sound through clenched teeth as he stiffened. When she relented with the taser, he went limp and passed out.

Ester shut off the taser and cocked her head at him. She muttered, "Hmmm. I hope I haven't killed him already."

She got out the rope and began tying him into the chair. It was slow going. Her hands weren't young and strong like they once were, and she worried that he might be able to escape. But, she did her best. Once he was tied up as best she could muster, she called Hirra to bring the ladies to the

Great Hall. Before she hung up, she asked if Hirra would send Larry down ahead of the rest. Hirra thought it odd, but having Larry at the retreat was odd. So, the young man trotted off to Ester's call.

Just as Larry was walking into the room, Pastor Kern began to moan and awaken. So, Ester zapped him again, right in the neck. This made his eyes roll back and his head to droop again.

Larry stopped. He was unsure that what he was seeing was real. He called out cautiously, "Ester? What's going on in here?"

"Oh, good!" Ester replied. "You made it! I may need your help making sure Herman stays in the chair. My hands are old and weak, and I'm not sure I have him tied down good enough."

Larry's eyes were wide as his heart beat increased with every step forward. "Ester, I'm asking again. What's going on in here?"

Ester's eyes shot from the taser to the pastor and up to Larry and she asked, "Is this a trick question?"

"No, Ester," Larry replied. "I'm serious. What's going on? What are you doing?"

Ester smiled. She got a warm glow about her as she explained, "Oh! I'm zapping the good pastor into submission, so I can tie him up and make him an example for everyone this afternoon."

Larry looked confused now on top of being shocked. "ESTER! WHAT ARE YOU DOING?" He was afraid that he was going to have to disarm the little, old lady.

"Larry," Ester spoke with an almost motherly comfort in her

voice. She was calm. Creepy calm. And she explained, "Pastor Kern has been molesting children for years. I was too weak to stop him. But, not today. The time has come for him to stop. And he's going to pay for that. And it's just convenient that he can die as a testimony to what happens to those that hide behind innocence and abuse those that are trusting them. He will be the example to the women in my care. And we will end the abuse tonight. For all of us."

Larry was frozen in place processing the words. Visually, he was watching a crime. But, Ester's explanation was causing him to think through a lifetime of events and information and feelings. Larry had come prepared to kill his father. He had offered to kill for them. Now, suddenly, it was real.

Ester went on, "You see, it's a proven fact that those who are abused when they are young tend to grow up to become abusers. They learn it. They hate it. But, yet, they become it. It doesn't happen to everyone. But, it's what happens for most. Because they don't know any other way. Larry, I can't let this monster create new monsters." Tears welled up in her eyes and her voice got shaky. "I was too weak and scared and I allowed more children to be ruined. He destroyed more lives because I couldn't stand up to him and put an end to it. Now, the only way to end it is to destroy him. He'll never change. He was caught, and never changed. He will never change. He will always be a child molester. He will always be a monster."

Larry closed his eyes as he processed that. As a kid that had been molested, he knew what she was saying was true. It began to cause a change in him. His blood began to boil and redden his face. He began to feel the rage his father had beaten into him. The young man was face to face with the exact thing that had brought him here. And he was seething. The revelation that someone in a position of responsibility where he was supposed to help, he was supposed to stop the abuse, but he was actually inflicting abuse was causing Larry to burn inside.

Pastor Kern began to wake up again. Ester turned on the taser again. Larry stopped her.

Larry walked towards the man in the chair. As the pastor awakened and saw the massive youth approaching him, he regained consciousness only to wish he hadn't. Larry was clearly angry, like Hulk angry. But, Ester was in control of the beast.

She introduced the two. "Herman. I'm glad you're awake. This is Larry. His dad used him like you use little boys. Larry, this is Pastor Kern, the child molester."

Larry instantly unleashed an open handed slap across the man's face that laid him sideways on the floor still tied to the chair. Ester was impressed with her rope work. It held up! Pastor was in extreme pain as his entire face turned bright red with a hand print. Larry was unapologetic. But, he righted the man in the chair back to a seated position.

While Herman pleaded and Larry struggled not to hit him again, the After Party began to arrive. The women were not prepared for what they were walking in on.

Ester raised her hands and shouted for them to come in. But, her voice was getting drowned out. Larry stood behind the bound pastor and bellowed, "PLEASE BE QUIET!!!"
Ester thanked him, and asked him to instruct the ladies to come in and be seated. He complied. Ester was almost giddy

201

with how helpful the young man had been already.

Herman was frantic. The ladies were scared and confused. Larry stood like a sentry. Ester was happy as could be.

Ester stood beside Herman and began to address the After Party, "Ladies, I know you have questions and there's a lot of confusion in your minds."

She was trying to talk over Herman as he grew louder and more agitated. Finally, she frowned at him and tased him again. The women jumped and gasped with shrieks as the old man convulsed in his bindings. But, he did quiet down to a whimper.

"Now," Ester went on undeterred. "The final lesson of the retreat is that you need to break out of the cycle of abuse. I know first hand that even though we hate the abuse, it's the only thing we know that makes sense. We know the patterns. We anticipate and adapt. We try to manage it. But, in the end, we get our asses beat. Not any more. That ends today.

Pastor Kern is here to help get the ball rolling. I'm sure you're all wondering about why he's tied up and I'm shocking him. Well, I'm glad you ask. I'm going to tell you.

You see, Pastor Kern has a thing for children. Oh, sure, in the public eye, he's a good man that helps kids. But, behind closed doors, he's not that way. Oh no.

Long ago, I went to the church on a Friday evening. And there in this office, he had a young boy, naked on the floor, and they were having sex."

She let them mull that over a bit. It was a hard pill to swallow.

She went on, "I was scared. I couldn't say anything. I just ran. But, I couldn't un-see it. I couldn't stop thinking about it. He had groomed a child so he could molest him. I knew it. But, I was too weak and scared to say anything, let alone do anything. I did nothing. And I allowed him to do what he did, because I did nothing. And I had to live with that.

Actually, I didn't have to. I chose to. I was too afraid to do anything to protect the child. Someone's child. I was too much of a coward. I was too weak and ashamed and scared to protect someone's baby boy from a man that was willing to take away that kid's innocence. I allowed this man to rape a child."

The room was staring in scared silence. Ester turned from looking at the meek faces to the face of the man that was guilty of horrible things. She exhaled. She let out all of the guilt and shame she had been harboring for years. Everything she had been hiding that caused her to suffer was blown from her being. The next deep breath in was the beginning of her next incarnation.

She let her head drop, but only for a moment. She felt the new spark of life light her eyes. She took another deep breath of determination. Ester was feeling a strength and fire in her chest that she had never felt before. That moment, the frightened women of the After Party at Ester's Retreat were watching the transformation from a little old lady to a warrior. The helpless victim and silent witness to molestation was being transfigured into a fearless and determined crusader. Ester was taking on the spirit of every one that ever cried for salvation from their tormentors. Every cry for a hero who never arrived echoed in her ears and rattled in her heart. In that moment, Ester decided that she would be the hero she needed and never got.

With a living fire in her eyes, Ester turned her face to the women she loved and empathized with. She said, "I've cried with you. I've listened to your pain. I've lived your nightmares and I want nothing more than to watch you live better dreams. What if that was your child in his office on the floor?"

When Ester stopped talking at that moment, faces began to change. Eyes began to change. Expressions and posture changed. She asked again, "What if that was YOUR child on the floor with that man on top of him or her? What would you do? Would you want me to stop it? Would you hate me for running away and allowing it? Because I hated myself for that. I hated me. I really hated me for that."

She was beginning to draw them in. She could sense the connection. Having a live offender was so much more personal than conjecture.

She made eye contact with each one. "What would you do if he was raping your child? Would you let him? Would you turn away? Would you be too afraid to stop it? Would you break down the door? Would you pull him off? Would you? Or would you just stand there and cry? Would you just watch and weep? What would you do?"

She could see the shame and guilt. She felt their helpless distress. She had pressed them as far as she could. It was time to take them to the goal line.

Ester straightened herself and summoned the angriest look she could put on her face. She only hoped she could finish what she started nearly two years ago when she spoke. "No more. I woke up one day and knew that I couldn't let it go on anymore. I couldn't allow any more abuse. I wouldn't let my husband touch me with hatred and violence anymore. I would never allow anyone to abuse another woman. I would never allow another child to be molested.

I decided that I had to be the hero that never came to my rescue. I had to save myself. No one would come for me. No one was going to help me except me. I was the only one standing between living and being killed. I was the only one who could stop me from being abused and beaten.

No more abuse. No more pain. No more living in fear. No more walking on eggshells. No more would I allow someone's child to be used and molested. I will no longer allow *your* child to be treated like trash.

That means that I must save myself from myself. I have to be done being afraid. I have to kill the coward in me."

Ester stopped to take a temperature check of the room. It wasn't clear, but it looked to be warming.

She couldn't stop or slow down now. She went for a slow crescendo. "I was hurting. When my husband was beating me, it hurt. But, I was allowing him to hurt me because I was hurting. I was in pain and misery. And when he hit me, it allowed me to feel pain that covered up the real pain inside that was eating me alive. That black eye didn't hurt as much as the feeling of failure and shame I felt. The bloody nose allowed me to blame him and talk about him and everything was about him and what he was doing. I didn't have to talk about me and what I was really feeling.

I don't remember when or why. But, I remember waking up

one day and realizing that I was allowing myself to be beaten because I was broken. I don't know why. But, it seemed easier to be beaten than to admit that I was a mess and needed to fix things. I needed to fix ME. And I was really afraid of that.

It was honestly more terrifying to realize that I didn't need a hero. I just needed to be better. I needed to work at being a better version of me. I needed to be stronger and braver. I needed to speak up. I needed to stop being a scared little girl and grow up. I needed to own my life and my mistakes and make every effort to become the woman I was meant to be. It would be easy to be saved. It felt impossible to save myself.

Once I realized what was wrong, I could see what needed to be done. I saw that I could be so much more. But, I was still being abused."

Ester turned to face Herman while still addressing the women. "I needed to get away from the abuse. I couldn't become the woman I was born to be as long as that man was beating me into nothing. So, I decided to end it all. It was him or me. I knew that as long as he was reining over me, I could never take control of my own life. As long as I allowed him to control my life, I would have none.

So, I couldn't die knowing that he ruled my life. I couldn't die knowing that I allowed one man to ruin me and make me nothing for no reason other than to make himself feel bigger. I decided that I would not trade my life for him to live some kind of fantasy where he was some sort of king of his domain. I wasn't going to be his source of a big ego by allowing him to break me to pieces and use them to prop his ego up. I wasn't his dog! He was treating me worse than the damn dog! And I decided NO MORE!

That's when I made the decision. I started reading old books. I learned about the old ways of poison that left no trace. I learned what would kill my husband and set me free. And that's what I did. I poisoned him. I killed that son of a bitch!"

Ester fired up the taser and aimed it to Herman's groin. He only had a split second to panic before the blue arc made contact with his zipper. His body folded so hard the chair cracked and the ropes cut hard into his body. The room full of women jumped and yelped and said things.

As Herman slumped into his bindings, Ester got loud. "I won't take it any more! I will never allow one more child to suffer! No more!"

She zapped him on the shoulder. He stiffened and screamed through clenched teeth. Ester rallied, "NO MORE! I will never again allow this monster to touch another child! I saw the destruction my husband created. And he wasn't destroying as many people as this molester!"

Ester zapped him in the ribs. Herman bent sideways as much as the ropes allowed with another gritty cry of pain. The women were teetering between terror at watching the little old lady tase a man, and the revelation of what Ester was proclaiming as the justification for this torment. They were struggling with their humanity and the sense of justice for those that violated humanity. Ester needed them to fall on the side that demands that men pay for their crimes.

Ester handed the taser to Larry. She began walking through the ladies seated in the room watching her administer justice to a pedophile. Herman was a bit slumped, breathing hard. His eyes were showing the fear and pain as he was crying and begging.

She walked the middle isle and asked loudly, "A man... any man, whether you know him or not... is taking the clothes off of your child and laying on top of him or her. His penis is hard. He's about to stick it in them. What would you do?" One by one, Ester locked eyes with each woman and asked them, "What would you do?"

One by one, she asked them to their face. She made them feel the intensity of how personal it is to be violated. She looked them in the soul, asking them if they would come to the rescue of their own child. She wasn't asking if they would save their kid. She was interrogating their value system. She was forcing them to self examine their own beliefs.

She knew they knew. Obviously, they knew what it was like. Obviously, they had all been victims. They had all been violated.

Ester returned to Herman's side. She looked over the ladies and asked, "What would you do if you knew then what you know now? If you knew then, would you do the same things? Would you run? Imagine being that young and innocent and unable to defend yourself. Imagine knowing it was wrong, but remember what it was like being so young that you were afraid to say so."

Suddenly, Ester had made it even more personal. She was putting them back in that scared little kid. She demanded, "Imagine being too young and scared to fight him off, afraid to fight because you would get in trouble. You want to run. You want to fight. You want to scream. But, you couldn't. Because if you did, you somehow KNEW that you would get in trouble. And it would be worse.

You are NOT that kid! You are a woman. And you know better. You know it's sick and wrong. You know! Are you going to let that little kid become you? Knowing all you know now, are you going to deliberately allow that man to turn your child into what you have carried and hidden and suffered all these years?"

Ester paused with tears in her eyes and her voice was beginning to crackle. Then, she went savage. "What kind of monster would you be to allow that?"

She let them absorb that dagger.

She had them hooked. Ester could see their eyes. She made their hearts bleed. And she wasn't about to let up.

"HOW COULD YOU?!?!" She screamed. "How could you do that to your child? How could you allow that, knowing what you know? Because you did."

Ester just bitch slapped the whole lot of them. That was the most painful truth anyone had ever laid on them. Everyone of them felt that stab to the heart.

"You allowed it to happen to you," she stated. "You knew it was wrong, and you allowed it. You did nothing except go along with it. You were nice. You did what you were expected to do. You did what you were told. And you allowed that child to be abused. Because you were that child.

Now, you need to decide. Are you going to let it happen again? Are you going to allow that child to become you? You have the power and the tools to prevent that! You KNOW! You have the ability to act like you know!

THERE HE IS! The man that wants to put his hands and penis on your child! He's right here in front of you wanting to screw you into oblivion! That man right there wants to destroy you and your child and your world and your future and everything about you that could ever be worth living for! WHAT ARE YOU GOING TO DO?!" She paused and whispered. "Will you let him?"

Ester stopped talking. It sounded like everyone in the room stopped breathing. Hearts weren't even beating. Time wasn't moving and the universe was on pause. This was the moment where heroic action would arise to battle for salvation or humanity would fall and spiral into despair and nothingness.

Without a word, Lily levitated from her seat. She marched with full determination past everyone seated. Herman was shocked and scared. Larry was simply shocked when Lily snatched the taser out of his hand. And Herman received the shock of a lifetime when Lily jammed it up under his jaw and pulled the trigger.

The jolt to the pastor was so much, that he kicked the chair backwards and landed face up to the sky. He was out.

The jolt to the room was so visceral that no one could breathe, let alone move or speak.

The jolt to Lily was so strong that she dropped the device and stood frozen in fight or flight mode.

Ester was smiling with approval.

Heaven and earth were not colliding. They were blending in that room. The souls of women tormented and tortured were ripped wide open. The bleeding hearts were creating a river of blood that was contaminated with all they had suffered and endured. The brains that had been infiltrated and twisted by beatings and mind games were whirling in directions never imagined.

Lily just shocked a man into another realm. She was absorbing all the adrenaline. She was fighting the fear. She was grappling with the morality. She was ditching the ethics. She was wondering if this was what super villains felt when they decided to go bad.

She slowly turned towards the women of the After Party who had been talking about being abused and what it would mean to be free from every part of that. She faced her peers of survivors and felt life pulsing in her veins for the first time. Her face washed through a host of intense emotions. Her lips started out tight, but slowly curled into a smile and opened to an excitement she had never experienced before. And she burst out, "You have GOT to try this shit!!!"

Ester was grinning. She wasn't feeling bad. She believed that a man reaps what he sows. So, in Ester's heart and mind, there was no reason to feel bad for the man who was a bad man doing bad things.

For 45 minutes, Herman's life was hell. It was truly not worth living. Most of the women took turns slapping his face, punching him in the chest and tasering him. They called him names like "slut", "whore" and "baby raper." Sondra even called him by her husband's name before punching him full in the face. There was more talk about never being abused again.

Some didn't follow the mob. Sam and Samantha sat with a couple of others who couldn't bring themselves to torture the man tied in the chair. But the mob ruled. A feeding frenzy of revenge was initiated and Herman was the only offering.

Ester was complete. The After Party was ready for the Grand Finale. Before they set out to finish the mission, it was time for Ester to finish Herman.

She had everyone back up from him. The once revered pastor was fully disgraced. But, there was no way Ester could allow him to live after all that. He was not a man of character. He was a weak coward. Herman was a pathetic man hiding behind his degree and pulpit. He would promise anything to make the pain stop. He had never suffered a day in his life. As soon as he could, he'd be running to the police.

No, Herman couldn't live another day past this one. Ester had already planned on that. She took the prepared extension cord and with an audience that was horrified and mesmerized, she wrapped the bare wires of one stripped side around one of his wrist and then mirrored that on his other side.

Disbelief filled the room. The anger and aggression was still there, but now, the ladies were having a hard time understanding what they were seeing. Ester was explaining why Pastor Kern couldn't be allowed to leave, but they were so off guard at the actuality of it all that they were frozen in disbelief. They couldn't believe that Ester was actually going to kill him.

Women screamed and hugged each other when Ester plugged that cord into an outlet. They were terrified! Herman went stiff as a board, grinding out sounds of pain. His teeth were involuntarily clenched. His rigid body tried to slide out of the chair. He wet his pants. Ester could hear his skin sizzle. But, she reminded herself not to care. She informed Herman that she didn't care how bad it hurt. She unplugged him from the electrocution after about 30 seconds and left him panting awkwardly.

The witnesses were still frozen in panic. They could see everything: the burns on his wrists, the wet center of his pants, the fear in his eyes, Ester's strange calmness... they all had a front row to the most horrifying show they could never imagine.

Ester began explaining to Pastor Herman Kern, "I have an obligation to rid the earth of you, and anyone like you. It's my duty to ensure that no more kids will ever be manipulated and corrupted by you. And it's my pleasure to usher your soul on to its next destination. Perhaps God will have mercy on you. But, I've lived with the guilt and shame that you should have never put on me. And I have no mercy for you as I send all that with you. With God as my witness, I will make sure that EVERYONE knows all about what kind of man you have been."

She wasn't sure how much he was hearing. She might have fried his ear drums. He was crying. He was realizing that he was about to die a horrible, electric death. Most of the ladies were sure Ester would stop. She had more than made her point with him, as far as they were concerned. Ester didn't care. She was done with the scumbag.

Ester plugged the cord back in. As Herman arched involuntarily, she squirted water on him from a large bottle. There was a massive fireball of a spark across Herman's body and his wrists began to smoke as the lights went out. The emergency lights came on after a moment of darkness.

"Oh, dear," Ester said. "I may have used too much water." She unplugged the man.

Herman wasn't moving. He didn't appear to be moving. Ester was not about to take any chances though. She walked over to a table where she had set a large kitchen knife. She took the pointy knife to the limp man. She positioned it on the side of his neck and leaned on it. As the blade glided through his skin and into his muscles and through his veins and arteries, the women were nearly hysterical. Blood oozed out in a small river while Herman gave no response. Ester withdrew the bloody blade and repeated the positioning on the other side of his neck, then leaned on it.

While she was close to his ear, leaning on the knife in his neck, Ester said loud and clear, "You earned this, you son of a bitch!" She pulled the kitchen tool being used as a weapon from his neck and watched his blood run out. She stepped back and gave him one last look of disgust and said, "Goodbye, Herman."

Pastor Herman Kern was dead.

Ester just killed Pastor Kern. Right in front of 23 women and Larry, the sweet, little, old lady became a stone cold killer. She called him out as a pedophile and murdered him for it. She was his judge, jury and executioner.

The ladies of the After Party were poised like mannequins around the room with heavy breathing, subdued crying and fear. Ester wasn't about to let the fear go anywhere.

Ester laid the knife under the chair that was holding Pastor Kern's body. Ironically, as she stood up, his dead weight pulled the chair over. He crashed face first into the floor and rolled over to his side, chair in tow. Some women jumped and yelped. Ester just shook her head in disapproval.

She said, "Even in death, you're a disappointment. I was hoping you'd be sitting here when the police or whoever finds you. Not fallen on your face. Oh, well."

Ester looked up at the women huddled in front of her. She looked almost surprised at first, as if she had nearly forgotten that they were there and suddenly realized that she wasn't alone. The simple act of the dead pastor falling over caught all of her attention for a moment. Then, as she saw all faces were painted with a mix of concern, fear, shock, confusion and more fear, she became concerned.

The woman who had just killed a man and criticized him for failing to remain upright in his chair reverted back to the caring, motherly, little old lady who only wanted the best for her girls. She spoke with a soothing sentiment, "Oh, ladies. I'm so sorry. I know that was a lot. And I know you've never seen anything like that in real life, only on TV. But, I don't want you to be afraid. Herman might have seemed like a good man on the outside. After all, he was a pastor. He was supposed to be a man of God. He was supposed to be the kind of man any of us would be able to trust and turn to when we needed someone trustworthy. If we needed a protector, he was supposed to be that kind of man.

But, he wasn't. He was hiding what kind of man he really was. He was abusing young boys and girls. He was using that trust to lure them into his care so he could take what he wanted from them. He was a monster hiding in clerical robes. That man wasn't a man. He was a rapist. He was worse than a rapist! He was taking the innocence of children, and trusting them to never tell anyone about how he was grooming them for sex with him. He was tricking them and lying to them and covering up his sin. Then, he was hiding it from us and lying to us about it.

Ladies, the worst thing he's been doing is the same thing our own abusers do to us. He was making sure that no one would even ask about what he was doing to those kids. That way no one would help them. And he would be able to do whatever he wanted to them forever and no one would try to stop him."

Ester became clearly emotional. But, she went on, "When I needed someone to save me from my husband using me and beating me like a worthless piece of meat, and degrading me, making me less human, no one ever questioned him. They blamed ME for what he was doing. They blamed me for what he was doing to me, as if I caused it or somehow deserved it.

Those kids didn't deserve that. They didn't make him take his pants off and put his hands on them. They did nothing to deserve any of that. The only thing they deserved was to be a kid, to go to school and play at recess, to laugh and make friends. They only wanted to be kids. They wanted to do kid stuff. Not adult sex stuff. That's not what they

216

wanted. They didn't ask for that.

And they never asked for what comes with being abused. They didn't want people to look at them like they were dirty or broken or worthless. Like I was looked at." She looked around at the ladies. "Like you've been looked at, too, I'm sure. We know what it's like to be treated without respect because of what was done to us.

A lot of those kids will end up doing to others what was done to them. And the only reason they do is because it was done to them! What would you do if YOUR child began abusing others? Would you look at them different?

Ladies, what would you do to protect your child? What would you do to make sure that your child never becomes the same abuser as the one that abused them? Would you even bother to help your kid live a life better than ours?

Please don't tell me you'd rather see your baby grow up to become just like your abuser! You can't possibly think it would be better to let them take the punishment than to prevent it! What? You think hoping and wishing that they'll overcome it and be better than you will work? You think they'll have some magical super power to do better than you?"

Ester was frustrated and desperate for the women to understand the importance of eliminating the evil. She needed them to make up their minds that they had to get rid of the abusers in their lives and that killing them was the only way.

"COWARDS!!!" She screamed as loud as she could muster. "We've all been cowards our whole lives! We've been afraid of everything and everyone. We just hope and pray no one yells at us. We just hope and pray no one approaches us. We hope and pray that no one raises a hand to us. We cower. We live with fear and walk on egg shells with our tails tucked between our legs like cowards!

NO MORE!!

Ladies, I'm tired. I've had enough. And I refuse to live like a coward anymore. I decided I wouldn't take any more. No more. I killed that man who beat me. I ended his life to save my own.

He took everything from me. My heart. My dreams. My love. My self worth. My confidence and passion and love of life. He destroyed my hopes and dreams and everything my future could have been. Until I said, 'No more.'

No more abuse. No more beatings. No more name calling and putting me down. No more taking from me. No more making me feel worthless. No more making me a coward, afraid of my own shadow. No more. I refused to be a coward one minute more.

So, I killed him. And the abuse stopped. The beatings stopped. My confidence began to return. My hopes and dreams came back to life. I wasn't worthless any more. Making me afraid of everyone and everything was one of his most evil accomplishments. I ended all that. And every single one of you can go from being a coward to having a life again.

You can live free of abuse and beatings and worthlessness. You can be alive and free with hopes and dreams that you can work on to make real! You can save yourselves and your children. You can end the shit you've put up with and live a real life where you can love and grow and be amazing. You can become anything you want to be, for real! Not just talk. Not just a fantasy. For real! You can live. Love. Dream. Become.

Ladies!" She pointed at the body on the floor. "That man was a pedophile. He was pure evil. He was destroying children. I ended that tonight. From now on, no one will suffer because of him ever again. He can't hurt any more kids. He will never rape another little boy or girl. No more victims because of him. He will never have the opportunity to create another coward that abuses more children. Your children are safe from him. The kids of the ministry are finally safe from him.

Oh, yes! He was eyeballing them! You didn't know? How could you not know? He was drooling over those kids we were helping. He wanted to rip the clothes off of every one of them and put them under him on the floor. You didn't know because he didn't want you to know. He wanted to hide his sins. And you weren't going to ask because you would have been afraid to. You were cowards afraid to ask. And even if you found out, what would you do?

I'll tell you exactly what you would do if you found out he was raping a young boy! You'd have run away and remained silent about it for years because you were afraid, just like I was."

Ester began to cry, but she wasn't stopping. "I was a coward. I let them suffer. All of them. I let him rape all those children because I was a coward. I was too afraid to say anything because I didn't want my life to get any harder. I was afraid to save anyone because I was worried about me. What would happen to me? What would they do to me? What would become of me? I was a selfish coward because all I could worry about was me. And I allowed all those kids to suffer. I didn't save them when they needed help."

Ester began to bawl. The women were torn between wanting to

hug her and scared to touch her. They wanted to tell her that everything would be okay, but they were convicted of being cowardly as she accused. The little old lady sobbed over the corpse of a child rapist that she had murdered in front of abused women who were being given the training and motivation to go murder those that they knew were doing evil things, too.

Maybe Ester would have relented had someone hugged her. It was entirely possible that she might have had an epiphany about all that she was thinking and doing. She might have melted. She could have realized that she wasn't thinking clearly about life and death and what would happen to the younger women in front of her should they also kill someone they swore to love for all time. Had someone just thrown their arms around the little old murderer in compassion, she might have had a similar experience to that of the Grinch's heart growing three sizes larger.

But that didn't happen. They really were cowards too afraid to act.

They let Ester cry. And when that woman had released the bitter things that had brought her to tears, the void allowed a back flow of resolve and resentment to fill in. Her heart and mind tempered into a singular focus of mission completion. She had set out to rid the world of as many abusers as she could, and now, she was going to see that out to the end. In that moment, Ester became Ester 2.0.

In that moment, something shifted in the universe and an unseen delivery of the strength and power of a giant filled her tiny frame. Whatever it was that fuels super heroes and super villains charged Ester's heart, soul and mind.

Kids learn that not all monsters are bad. Godzilla wasn't evil. He was a monster, but he was the monster that could save people from the bad monsters. Sometimes it takes a monster to destroy monsters. Good people can't do it. Even superheroes have to kill in order to save. Ester killed a monster. She became a monster. Ester was the monster they needed to save them from monsters.

In the time it would have taken to hug Ester and calm her down, a new version of Ester booted up inside the frail frame of an aged survivor. And in this moment, Ester was in full control. The time had come for talking to cease and words to turn into actions. Ester cried herself into battle gear. And now she was about to lead the charge.

"Those of you that were too afraid to do anything to Herman, go over to that side of the room. Now!" Ester demanded. She was assuming the role of the commander of troops on the front line who had been awaiting marching orders. She needed to separate the weak who would chose to remain cowards. They would be of no use to her and her army in the heat of the moment. They would buckle and run. She didn't need them.

The few ladies that never laid a finger on Herman while Ester and the rest were shocking and beating him shamefully shuffled to the west side of the building. They huddled, heads down, eyes down. The rest of the pack watched, heads up, eyes curious and focused.

Ester moved towards the separated members. It looked like a small animal cornering larger ones. It resembled a honey badger about to take on a pride of lions.

Ester glared at them and said, "If you want to return to the life you've always had, go over to that corner. If you don't want anything to happen to the one that beats you and molest you, go to the corner right over there."

No one moved. Everyone was frozen. Ester repeated, "If you want to go back to all you had, go to that corner RIGHT NOW!! If you don't want me to kill your abuser, go to THAT CORNER right now! I will not give you another chance. I will not ask again. If you stay right where you are, you are telling me to kill your abuser because you're too weak and cowardly to do it yourself. So, if you want to save their life, move now."

Ester looked from face to face. Or more like she looked from top of head to top of head. One moved. Faith went to the corner. She started to explain that she just wanted him to change, but Ester shut her down immediately. Faith didn't want her abuser to die. Scott Harwick would live. His life would be spared that night.

Ester moved Adrianna to the group not going hunting. She still had enough humanity to spare that poor girl. But, not Ken. Ken would pay for what all he had done to the mentally handicapped girl.

Crystal was the only other one from the original group standing with three of the newest members. She just didn't have it in her. But, she couldn't move to the corner. She couldn't kill him. But, she couldn't go back. She was easily the most conflicted. She was a statue of confusion. She was locked up in her own emotional container.

Ester looked at Crystal and took her hands. Her tiny, age spotted hands barely covered half of Crystal's. She reverted back to the motherly tone, but it was sincerely more sinister. Ester asked, "You understand that I'm going to go to your house and kill that monster you've been living with, don't you?"

Crystal began crying. She nodded her head. Ester dismantled the hand holding and pulled Crystals arms around her to hug her as she embraced the sorrowful and terrified woman. She squeezed Crystal despite her face being practically buried in the taller woman's bosom. Ester held her. Crystal slowly hugged her back.

Ester softly assured, "It's OK, child. I know you're scared, and it's a terrible world for you right now. And I know it'll take some time to recover. But, after tonight, you will be free. No more beatings. No more painful recoveries. No more shame. None of that will be your life or legacy. Tonight, you will be free. It'll only hurt a little while longer, and from then on, your life will be yours to make into a beautiful journey full of wonderful things as you choose."

Crystal sobbed as she nodded. She was understanding and agreeing, but couldn't speak. If she spoke, she'd break down into pudding. She just nodded and squeezed Ester one more time. Then, she turned to the others in her small circle and held all of them at once as they all sniffled and cried.

The time had come. The Grand Finale. Ester rode tonight.

Chapter 22: The Grand Finale

When Ester turned from Crystal to let her cry with the others who would be losing their husbands or boyfriends that night, she had the look of a fearless captain about to take on a hurricane. She ordered the rest of the After Party to assemble in the chow hall. They were ordered to dress for the hunt and prepare all weapons from guns to arrows to knives. She put them all on high alert.

She instructed the remaining women to pull themselves together enough to clean up camp, except for the Great Hall with the body. They were to pack everyone's bags and have the camp ready for all of them to leave for home once they were done.

Once the After Party was finished with the Grand Finale, they would be back and head for home as if everything was fine. They would all return home, shocked to find their beloved abuser dead, even if they were the one that killed him. They all knew that sticking to the same story was crucial. It had been discussed for months before the retreat and hammered home during the retreat. They were not to "act" like anything. They were to return home genuinely believing that everything there was completely normal and they were going to react in the most honest shock and horror as anyone would when they returned home to a crime scene they were not expecting. They knew that once they left the retreat and the campgrounds, nothing that happened during the Grand Finale had happened. They KNEW it. They knew NOTHING.

The stay behinds began cleaning and purging the campgrounds, except the Great Hall. Ester addressed the armed women of the After Party. They needed to be prepared and organized to act without hesitation. If they stopped to think, bad things would probably happen. They didn't need that. They certainly didn't want that. They needed to go, kill the abusive monsters and regroup back at camp.

The rules of engagement were simple and clear:
1. No long shots. Everything was to be close with no chance of stray bullets or innocent bystanders getting hurt.
2. No hesitation. No conversations or witty lines. No explanations. This is not a movie. Show up, do the job and leave. Period.
3. Once it started, it wasn't over till it was over. No chickening out.
4. No backing down. No running away. Finish the job and meet back at the campground.
5. If you couldn't kill your own, say so. Don't let anyone get hurt. Don't let anyone fail. Everyone is all the way in.

It was going to be a wild ride. And they all knew it. It was as exciting as it was terrifying.

The only rule that was disputed was number six. Rule number six was: Ester did it.

And Ester wasn't having any argument. She insisted that from that moment forward, whatever happened, any questions, anything at all, Ester did it. NO ONE was to take any blame themselves. Everything was to point to Ester. And she wasn't about to allow anything else.

They had already made a list of men and a couple of women that were to have their ability to abuse others terminated. Ester divided them into teams according to how she believed they would work together to compliment and complete each other. She then gave each team part of the list.

The strongest team in every way was Larry, Megan, Lily, Michelle Satori and Candy. They would be going after the most dangerous abusers. One of them was Candy's husband, Conner Cain, the deputy. They were to begin with him first.

The idea of killing anyone in law enforcement first was clearly an important strategy. Once the first event was called in, they would be wanted criminals. They didn't want to be chased by cops. They needed to take care of them first, and give the rest of them something to think about and deal with. Candy would kill Conner.

Barbara and her team of Sam, Samantha and Sondra would take care of Barbara's husband, Sheriff Ronny Justin, and Sondra's husband the mayor. They were willing to pick up the men that those staying behind would not be killing. After all, this team had two lesbians, so they had fewer husbands or boyfriends to go after.

A third team would start with Bethany's husband, Tom Burns, since he was a sheriff's deputy. Beverly had her husband, Trent who was a teacher. Meelow wanted her parents. Kendra and Raith each had targets in mind, too.

The fourth team was Tammy, Serena, Randi and Onna. Serena's husband was a judge, so they planned for him first. Then, Henry, who was a mechanic and Perry who was a high school teacher. They would finish with Tammy's husband, Ricardo.

The newest ladies to join the After Party and not separated into the "will not kill" category were huddled together insisting that they would be a team. They really were more afraid of Ester than their abusers. Yet, Ester had her doubts about whether or not they would follow through with the mission, or turn traitor and run to the police. Maybe they would just defect and run back to their abusers. But, Ester sanctioned them as a kill team, and decided to give them the opportunity to prove themselves or fail. After all, she already had too much to worry about and whatever choice they made would matter infinitely more to them than anyone else. All the others were already aboard the train of fate with one way tickets.

That only left Ester, Hirra and Carissa. Carissa had not started out as part of the After Party. Nor did Hirra. But, when Ester explained her mission, Hirra couldn't turn down the offer. She was a marine. But, she was a woman. She had seen more than her fair share of sexual abuse while she was on active duty. She was absolutely all in. Carissa was the same way, but with law enforcement.

Ester, Hirra, and Carissa would take out Cory and Zach from the police force. But, then they had a very special list. They were going to kill a priest, a youth pastor, and the high school principal. And before they returned to camp, Ester would make sure that Crystal's husband, Sam would be dead.

The teams split up and set out on their individual missions around 4pm. Darkness would be coming a little earlier since it was getting to be Fall.

Each team had at least one law enforcement person to take out. That would be the beginning and the true test for each. It wasn't actually that hard to get each officer into the trap and shoot them at point blank range. On duty or off, the ones that were abusing their wife or girlfriend were all dead by 4:30.

No one besides Hirra had ever killed anyone. So, the first kill for the members of the After Party was the ultimate test and challenge of all they had been talking about and learning. The first kill was the hardest. Pulling the trigger felt like pulling against a truck. But, once they had made their first kills, they were killers. And there was no option other than to kill them all.

By 4:30, all the monsters with badges were dead. And the women who had never killed before were reeling from the reality. They were shocked at themselves. They were appalled at what they saw. They were sickened at it all. And yet, they were energized once they got through the initial wave of emotion.

Killing someone was such a gut retching act for them. It was truly gut retching, as in, they could feel their innards churning. A few of them actually threw up. But, by 4:45, they had survived their own emotional tsunamis. It was very much a bend or break moment. And they all bent as far as they ever had. Some of them nearly broke. But, the unity of the group kept them from snapping. Against all odds, against all sensibility, against all natural instincts and against all social norms and consequences, the women of the After Party really were killing abusers in their long talked about Grand Finale.

They were no longer victims. They were no longer fantasizing about being saved. They were done talking about it all. They had crossed the line. They weren't witnesses to the murders. They weren't accomplices. They were killers. They were all in. They literally had blood on their hands and there was no turning back. There was no denying anything. They were on the hunt to kill as many abusers as they could that evening. They all had become

Ester.

From there, it all became a frenzy of racing to the next house or business to kill the next victim. Each team had a list. Each team had a plan. And each team followed through.

The 911 dispatch lines were overloaded with calls. The police and sheriff departments were immobilized. They only knew that some of their own were missing, not answering their calls or dead. They thought they were under attack as law enforcement, so they had called all remaining team members to their headquarters to basically circle the wagons and protect themselves. They were not responding to any calls anywhere.

Ester and her army were on the warpath and they were making the most of it. By 8:00 pm, teams one and two were back at camp. They were in the showers, cleaning the blood and gun smoke from their bodies, showering away the shaking nerves and crying away the emotional overload.

Ester, Hirra and Carissa arrived just after them. They were much cleaner than the amateur killers. And much calmer. The women needed that.

Bloody guns and knives that were not left at the scenes were gathered in a box for Hirra to figure out what to do with them. There were even two bloody ball bats. Sam had found one at Julie and Meg's house and used it to beat their father. She kinda wanted to keep it.

Around 8:15 team three came back. Meelow was almost completely covered in blood from head to toe. She was sitting on trash bags in the car. From what her teammates could describe, Meelow was hell bent to inflict enough pain on her parents as she felt that they had inflicted on her. No one asked anything more.

The team of newbies arrived without incident claiming that they had killed their abusers. They admitted that they had sat in the parking lot of a liquor store with a quart of moonshine trying to decide what to do. They admitted that they had thought about backing out and going home. But, between the moonshine and talking about what would happen "down the road," they realized what had to happen. So, they did it. Ester was impressed and proud, so she congratulated and comforted the terrified and traumatized girls.

About 8:30, Serena, Randi and Onna arrived without Tammy. The three women were blood covered and crying uncontrollably. They were shaking terribly. When they had gotten to Tammy's house, Ricardo had come out of the house drunk with a gun.

Tammy had tried to shoot him. But, Ricardo shot her. While he was standing there in disbelief, Randi shot him in the head. Then, she shot him in the chest five times. Then, she emptied the rest of the magazine into his face.

They took Tammy to the hospital, but they knew she was dead. They just couldn't leave her there with that animal. They couldn't leave their friend behind. But, she was gone.

The campground was very much like a military unit comprised of new recruits returning from their first fire fight. Any gratitude of returning safely or feelings of success at having completed the mission were muted severely by the death of a close comrade. Killing is hardy an event to celebrate. But, losing one their own was sobering. It was more sobering than anything they could have imagined.

Bloody clothes were loaded into garbage bags in Hirra's truck while women cried and moved like terrified zombies. They didn't have the luxury of shutting down or freezing up. Much like a combat unit, they had no choice but to keep moving.

The Grand Finale was complete. The participants were shaking, pale, feeling sick and weak. All but one was alive. The targets were all dead but one.

Ester was quiet. She felt as if she failed. One of her girls didn't come back. Tammy was dead. And Ester knew that it was her responsibility. Like the others, she cleaned up and placed bloody clothes in a garbage bag in Hirra's truck. She didn't know how Hirra would dispose of the evidence. She didn't want to know. So, she didn't ask.

No one talked about anything. They were in shock. They had just killed people. It didn't matter if they were evil people. They were people. And they had killed them. Just straight up murdered them without warning. It was such a strange feeling that none of them had any idea what they were actually feeling. The tangled mess inside of them was too complicated. It was too much. It was too much to explain. It was too much to process. It was too much in every sense.

They cleaned up their clothes and bodies and weapons. They cleaned up the mess hall and bunk house. They didn't try to wipe down every finger print like some kind of Hollywood crime show. They had been at the retreat. Everyone knew that. They were definitely going to be leaving evidence that they were there. Cleaning up too well would be weird.

Before they all gathered in their cars and vans to head home to whatever might be waiting for them there, they gathered around Ester one last time. It was the most unusual moment of their lives, both collectively and individually, as they were about to re-enter their lives with no possible predictable outcome or direction. They knew. But, they had to make sure that before they got home, they didn't know. And not knowing was going to be all they knew.

Ester stood with her head down. They all did. It was cold. It was dark. They were tired and exhausted and messed up. They just wanted to go home. But, no, they didn't want to go home.

Ester was really at a loss for words. For once, the little, old lady who had assembled and forged a small army to combat abuse wasn't sure what to say. So, she said, "I really don't know what to say. I'm incredibly proud of you all. And I'm just as sorry for what has happened. I can't fix anything. Tammy... Well, I'm responsible for Tammy. And I don't know what I'm going to do.

You have all been the best thing to ever come into my life. But, right now, you all have to go your own way. And I'll be turning myself into the police and confessing that I did all of this. Every single bit of everything.

I can only beg you to do better in the future. Please, never let yourselves get trapped by another abuser. Don't let this be for nothing.

It'll take some time for the smoke to clear and the dust to settle. But, never confess anything to anyone ever. The only thing you dare say is, 'Ester did it.' Do not test me on that! This was not your fault. It wasn't any fault of yours. This was me. This was all me. Ester did it. That's the only thing you need to say. Do you understand me?"

There was a grumbled answer. Ester demanded a clear answer, which she got. She asked them to all look at her one last time.

She said, "You are all beautiful women. You are amazing. And you are much stronger than you know. And you will have to be strong for awhile. Everyone will want to know what happened. All you have to do is tell them that I killed all those people. And that's all you know.

Go home. Be amazing. Be ready to live like free women with goals and dreams and ambition once we get past this ugly business. I have faith in you. I've seen how awesome you can be. And for the past couple of years, I've watched you grow and mature. This will be ugly for awhile. But, you will be free. No more beatings. No more names. No more of any of that shit you've suffered through. Be free! I love you all. And I want you to live the lives you deserve. I did this and I'm turning myself in so you may all be free to live. I did this. None of you did anything. I did everything. Confess nothing. Ester did it! Be free!"

Ester lowered her head again and turned towards her car. She hobbled to it and slowly worked herself into it. It was a silent exodus. Ester drove off down the dirt lane and disappeared. The After Party was over. It had served its purpose and was no longer needed. At that moment, it became defunct. The women quietly shuffled off to their cars and one by one, they headed home.

As the women returned to their homes, they were stumbling upon the scenes they knew not to know about. In some cases, an ambulance was on the scene. In others, a neighbor had taken the body to the hospital. And at most homes, the abuser lay where he had been dropped.

There were no police cars, no sheriff deputies nor any law enforcement anywhere to be seen. Those with a badge that were still alive were hiding, hunkered down to protect themselves. The moment the sheriff was found dead, word spread quickly. Self preservation became the standing order as soon as the next officer was found. They remained gathered at the courthouse and barricaded themselves in. They were not answering calls. But, they did order pizza.

Other first responders were nervous, but continued to show up and do their jobs. Fire and rescue teams became the overseers for the community. EMT and medical personnel were cautious, but slowly working through the list of victims. They had become the crime scene detectives. They were not good at preserving evidence. In fact, they were not concerned with evidence. They simply accepted the fact that they were essentially on their own with no one there to protect them. So, they did what they had to do to get to the bodies.

However, once the body of a medical rescue responder was discovered, all rescue activity slowed or stopped. Even the medical people were scared to go to the scenes being called in. Perry was the head EMT for the southwest township. Now, he was a dead body with one gun shot wound to the chest.

The Grand Finale was complete. Ester had done it. They all had done it. They eliminated as many abusers as they could in just a few hours. They created a climate that allowed them to return home without police questioning them. And the only thing left to do was to return home and figure out what the rest of their lives would become.

Chapter 23: Going Home

Leaving the campground was surreal, even for the women that did not go out on a kill team. Life had just changed – dramatically – forever – because lives had just ended. Nothing would ever be the same. They were crying. They were numb. They were scared and panicky. They were relieved. They were sad that they no longer had the one that they loved, hated and feared. They were confused.

Heading home was the longest ride of their lives that took no time at all. The feelings and emotions were overwhelming in ways none of them could have imagined, let alone prepared for. There was a strange sense of relief and pride mixed with loathing and worry.

How were they going to live now? Not only was the abuser gone, but so was his income. How could they keep this to themselves forever? How would they tell their children that Daddy was gone, and that it was the worst good thing to ever happen?

They worried about what the neighbors would think. They worried about what their families would think. They worried about what the abuser's families might do. And they somehow were impressed that they finally did something insanely brave for themselves. It might have just been insane. But, for once in their lives, they had stood up to a lifetime of terrible pain, humiliation, and bullying. For once, they were not a helpless victim. This one time they were raging animals that refused to be eaten.

They had fleeting thoughts of how much more peaceful life would be. They would be able to dress, eat, go to the store and talk to people without fearing the consequences. They wondered what that looked like. They wondered how it would feel.

They feared the nights alone when thoughts and feelings come knocking. They were afraid that it might feel good. They were scared that it might make them sad beyond repair. They were concerned that they might never find redemption. It was the strangest mix of thoughts and emotions and unsure, undefined possibilities imaginable.

It didn't take long to get home despite the eternal feeling of driving home. Each was greeted in different ways. Some were greeted by neighbors who were scared. Some were welcomed home like heroes from neighbors. Some had parents or relatives with their children because neighbors called. Some parents were mortified. Some couldn't be prouder.

Some women arrived home to a quiet house with a dead lawn decoration. Some had to avoid the mess in the house. Some women needed a drink. Some just sat in a chair and hugged the cat or dog or kids who had been home alone crying.

The one thing all the women had in common was the "talk with the neighbors." Whether it was calm, excited or angry, they all had to confront the witnesses to the murders.

One of the seminars or workshops at the retreat was "The Talk With the Neighbors." Ester knew that there would be witnesses. It would be impossible with all the gunfire to hide the killings. So, they all had to do their part to make sure that the neighbors at least understood why there were dead people.

A couple of women were greeted by the neighbors with shotguns. Several were greeted with hugs and asked why they had waited so long. The interactions were as varied as could be imagined, but one thing ran true through all. The women were able to plead their case.

The ladies were able to explain what had been happening to them and how it was killing them. And they were able to finally tell people without fear of being beaten or killed. The women of the After Party were able to reveal the horrors of their secret lives, and ask or beg for understanding.

Once those near them understood the situation, the women had been instructed to only ask those that might have seen the murder to not make things worse for the victims. If they had any decency, if they had any compassion in their hearts, if they had any respect for those who were being abused they would "mind their own business."

The women were practically reading Ester's words from a piece of paper. They all said the same thing in their own way. "Let us be responsible. Let the law deal with all this and with us. Do not make our lives worse. If you have any decency in your soul, you know that God will pass judgment on us and that we have to live with what we've done. And we will pay for it. We've survived hell. Please don't make us live in another level of it. Just mind your business. And when they ask you about it, it was a little old lady who did it. That's all you know. That's all you say. Please! Don't destroy what's left of us!"

They didn't have to recall a memorized script. They really were begging for their lives. They really were fighting for the lives of their children. Ester was giving them a way out, an alibi. It would be up to their neighbors to give them a chance to live without setting fire to their chances at a life without abuse before they could even get a day of relief. Or the witnesses could turn them in like they were wearing scarlet letters.

This was just one more wild card in the mix. It was one more variable beyond Ester's control. All she could do was all anyone could do. She planned. She set the plan in motion. And she hoped and prayed for the best. Only once the smoke cleared and the police made the rounds would anyone know if it worked.

Chapter 24: The Sheriff

Sheriff Ronny Justin was a pretty good elected official. He was well know and well liked. He seemed to be pretty reasonable, as he was very articulate. He spoke about reducing crime and protecting the people of the county as any political law enforcement officer should. And as far as the average citizen knew, he was doing that kind of stuff.

What very few knew about Sheriff Ronny Justin was how he treated his wife, Barbara, when no one was around. And the friends and family who knew didn't say much. They knew better. They knew that if he didn't confront them directly, he would make sure their lives were inconvenienced by traffic stops and civil complaints, but not enough to prove harassment. And even if they complained, no one was going to listen. Those in his charge would never dare go against the man. His subtle retaliation was too much to deal with. And even if it made it into the hands of someone above him, Ronny was good friends with the mayor and the judges. Plus, it was rumored that he had a certain amount of "material" on those men that would ensure that he would "never go down alone."

The only thing Ronny was harder on than crime was Barbara. There would never be a dirty dish left in the sink. Laundry was always done and put away neatly. Dinner was always perfect. The flower beds were always weedless. And his desires were always fulfilled. Barbara was always the perfect wife. Or else.

Barbara learned very soon and very quickly after saying, "I do" that she would be held to a very high standard with high expectations. Failure to keep the house in order or to comply with expectations would result in what Ronny referred to as "swift and severe corrective action."

The day after their honeymoon was the first lesson when she

"ignored the dishes" to spend time with him. Ronny slapped her harder than she had ever been hit before by anyone and screamed at her about how the house was to be kept neat and orderly. From her perspective, he was screaming at her like a drill instructor, but hitting her like a prison guard.

And from that day forward, he was consistent. Black eyes and bruises were expected if she took a nap instead of cleaning. She could count on a bloody nose if she said anything at a social event that Ronny found embarrassing. Questioning him was out of the question unless she wanted a trip to the ER. And she never had a headache when he was in the mood. Refusing to service him would be "regrettable."

Barbara lived in an invisible cage. She was on an unseen leash. She was a silent servant. She was his everything: maid, whore, caretaker, and trophy wife. Ronny defined her daily life and managed her like a chain gang of one. Barbara was in a living nightmare of perfection.

Had Ester not formed the After Party and inspired the Grand Finale, Barbara might have. Ronny had broken her long ago, but she always kindled a tiny spark deep inside where she swore that one day she would be free. One day she would end this nightmare and awaken to a better life. It seemed nearly impossible to escape a man who was well connected and intimidated everyone around him. She had no idea how she could ever escape his clutches and live to tell the tale.

So, when Ester came into her life, Barbara was ignited. That tiny spark was fueled and given breath. Two years ago, when she was invited to be part of a youth outreach program, she had no idea what that would open to. She only knew that it was an opportunity to get out of the prison home for a little bit without arousing suspicion. And without paying a price. She realized that she had spent most of her adult life in servitude to an abusive man that ruled her life. She was living as a slave, but she wasn't living. She was existing, hoping to avoid punishment each day. Life was passing her by. She had considered suicide an option to escape it all.

Barbara was awakened by Krisis and slowly revived by the After Party. She realized that her life was only over if she continued on the path she was trapped on. She realized that she was dying every day. She realized that she wanted to live, but didn't see any way for that to happen as long as Ronny Justin was alive and in control. There were only two options. Take back control from Ronny. Or get rid of him. Neither of which he would allow.

Talking about what she had been through with the other women was the most alive thing Barbara had experienced in years. The idea of killing the bastard that was making her suffer daily began as a quiet suggestion. But, it grew into a raging desire. Over the course of two years, Barbara was all in. She wanted to kill Ronny. Badly.

So, when the talk began to look like it could eventually become action, Barbara was always right there with the watering can making sure that flower of hope grew. She felt like it was her job... no... her privilege to foster the idea of the Grand Finale and to ensure it's roots took hold. She knew that it was a long shot. She knew it was wrong. Murder is wrong. There are laws that say so.

But, those laws don't account for years of abuse. Laws don't consider emotional torture as justification. The law clearly

says, "Thou shall not murder." But...
What if it's not murder? What if it's self preservation? What if a person is holding another hostage? What if a person is holding another as a slave? Murder is defined as the unlawful, premeditated killing of a human being by another.

Well, the Grand Finale would definitely be premeditated. It's not reasonable to talk about killing the bastard and learn to fire a gun for the purpose of killing the bastard, then try to claim it wasn't premeditated. However, that part about "unlawful killing" was another story. That would suggest that there's lawful killing. It was just a matter of making sure that any killing was justified or necessary. Barbara was pretty sure that was her defense and justification for killing her husband. It was necessary.

He was abusive daily. He would never let her live her own life. And she was certain to her core that he would kill her if he even thought that she might leave him. Yep. It was necessary for him to die so she could live.

When the time came, Barbara was first in line to kill her abuser. And since he was friends with Sondra's husband the mayor, she was all in to help get rid of Rich Kendron, too. They just had to begin with Ronny.

Barbara and the girls headed to the Justin residence just outside of the east edge of town. There were neighbors, but they weren't as close as in town. Barbara knew the neighbors. She knew they would come to their windows to see what was going on. But, she also knew that they had had enough of Ronny's bullish behavior that she was absolutely sure that they would just mind their own business.

When Barbara pulled up to her house, Ronny came storming out, madder than ever that she had left him home alone when she could have been fixing his dinners and taking care of him. She stepped out of the car and waited with the gun tucked behind her hands. About the time he demanded that she get down on her knees and suck his dick, she shot him in the knee.

Barbara point blank shot her husband, the sheriff, in the knee as he was reaching to pull her hair. She looked down at him as he rolled around on the ground screaming and cursing. He was still wearing his brown sheriff pants and a black t-shirt with some law enforcement slogan on it. And he had his slippers on despite the colder weather. He didn't bother to put on shoes. He was just running out to abuse his slave wife. So, she shot him in the foot of the opposite leg.

Sam, Samantha, and Sondra finally exited the car and joined in the condemnation of the sheriff. They stayed back. They did nothing to the man but stare at him. Barbara did the talking with a ball bat in her hands.

One of the neighbors came out with a shotgun. He hollered, "Barbara? Is everything alright?" When Ronny hollered back, Barbara struck him in the good knee with the bat.

She replied loudly, "Yes! It will all be just fine in a little bit. You just go back in your house and forget you came out here. I'm going to be here explaining to Ronny about all those years he beat my ass over all those little things. And he's never going to hit me again when I'm done explaining. OK?"

The man waved with the shotgun lowered and slipped back inside his house where he closed the blinds. The sheriff knew he was in trouble.

She stood over Ronny and took a deep breath that reached all the way to the heavens before saying, "Your days of beating me are over." Before he could say anything, she brought the bat around like a golf club and hit him in the left arm. She was pretty sure she broke his wrist. From there, nothing he said mattered. It wasn't even heard. He was crying and screaming and begging. No one heard. Or maybe no one was listening. Maybe no one cared. No one was coming to his rescue.

She beat him over and over, breaking bones. And with each swing, she shared a memory with him. "You remember when you blackened my eye for not having dinner ready? You remember when I didn't weed the flowers because I had the flu? You remember when you slapped me into next week for telling you not to fuck me in the ass?"

Finally, she straddled his weakened body. He was barely conscious. He was broken and bleeding. The others just stared blankly at him. Neighbors tried to hide their peeking through the blinds. Barbara leaned down and slapped his face till he opened his eyes wide at her and she screamed, "WELL, I DO!! I REMEMBER EVERYTHING!!" She raised the bat as high over her head as she could and she began raining blows down upon his face and head. She beat his face in.

As she slowed and weakened, Sondra approached her and calmed her. The mayor's wife took the bat from a breathless woman who had just viciously killed her abuser and said, "It's my turn. Let's go get my husband."

As they turned away to get back into the car, Barbara

screamed at the body of Ronny one more time. Then, she shot one final bullet into his chest. And then, she used the rest of her energy to get back into the car. She closed her eyes and fell asleep covered in the blood of her now former abuser. And when they arrived at Sondra's house, Barbara awaken: revived as a young woman with her entire life ahead of her.

Chapter 25: The Mayor

Sondra was up to bat. Her story was just about a mirror image of Barbara's. She knew that she was signing up for a certain amount of showmanship in her relationship when she fell in love with a man who had political aspirations. But, Rich went way overboard on his expectations and demands.

Unlike Ronny, Rich didn't feel like he could afford to be overt in disciplining his woman. Black eyes and visible marks were not good optics for reelection. Rich needed other means to control. He would poke her in the throat with a finger if she said something he didn't like. He would whip her across the butt with a wire coat hanger like he was beating a smart ass teenager who would laugh about the wooden spoon breaking. And if he was really pissed at her, he would extinguish his cigar on her inner thigh.

Sondra particularly hated sex with him. Although his penis was on the smaller side, she had to pretend that it was huge. If he didn't feel like she was inflating his ego enough, or that she was insincere, or faking anything, he would pull out the sex toys and use them to abuse her. He would make her lay on her back on the floor with her legs spread. If she refused, he would straddle her and use his feet to pry her ankles apart. Sometimes he would use ropes to tie her ankles to things to hold her legs wide open. He would then explain to her why he felt like she had left him no choice but to correct her and punish her in this manner. Then, he would wrap both hands around one end of a long, double headed, silicone dildo as if it was an ax, and he would swing it as if it was an ax to slap her between the legs. He would beat her pussy with that dildo as if he was splitting firewood until she wasn't able to cry or scream any more.

Other times, he would shove a non-lubricated dildo into her while she was still dry. Sometimes, he would sodomize her with sex toys or bottles or whatever he felt like she deserved to be punished with.

Rich Kendron was a very sick and depraved man. And his loving wife, Sondra, kept his secrets and always stood by his side as he smiled and waved to the people whom he wanted to like him and to vote for him. While he provided a decent financial life, he failed at being a decent human being, let alone a good or loving husband to her. No. Sondra was not happy. She was tortured.

That night, once Barbara unleashed years of pent up fury on her abuser, Sondra couldn't wait to get to Rich. Their home was the cliché large house on the golf course. She would not have the privacy and neighborly respect that Barbara had. So, she had to think about what she had to do before she pulled into that driveway.

The house was a modern rendition of Victorian styling. She thought about how she had loved this house when they had it built. Now, she only saw it as a prison. It was a place where she was receiving an ongoing and permanent death sentence. Finally, the time had come where the death sentence in that house was for him.

She just needed to get him in front of the door to the basement and wine cellar. She didn't figure that would be too difficult. Rich was tough when he was clearly the strongest in the room. Or when he had his buddy, the sheriff with a gun, standing by. But, he would always turn to diplomacy when confronted by a stronger man. He had never been a fighter, just a control freak.

So, when he went to assert his manly superiority over his wife, Sondra allowed the women to help put him in his place. Rich stormed out of his recliner with all intentions of reclaiming his wife after her absence from her place in the kitchen or on her knees before him. He could not have imagined that he would be staring down the barrels of four guns. Well, staring down three barrels. One gun was pointed at his zipper.

The vigilantes directed him to the doorway for the basement. They allowed Sondra to explain to her husband how much she hated him for all the horrible things he had done to her and that her only regret was that she didn't have time to return every moment of pain to him.

She kicked him in the crotch and when he bent over in pain, she brought a knee up to his chin that sent him tumbling down the stairs. She hoped he was still alive.

While he was unconscious, they took his clothes off of him and positioned his body face down, bent over a table. They tied his wrists and ankles to the table legs and threw water on him to wake him up. As soon as he was coherent enough to start yelling and threatening, the lesbians grabbed his butt cheeks, one on either side, and pried them apart. As he began to realize what was happening and what was about to happen, Sondra slapped his face with that same long, double headed, silicone dildo that he had slapped her with so many times. Then, without a single word, she began to shove that fake penis up his ass.

It didn't matter how much he squirmed or fought against it. She didn't care that he shit himself and started crying. And when he screamed, she walked to the dirty laundry and brought back one of his dirty socks to shove in his mouth.

Sondra worked that penile penance into that man's asshole until she was sure that it was "deep enough." There was enough sticking out that she could grip it with both hands. And she began to ram it in and out of him like a plunger in a clogged toilet. She sodomized him with prejudice as he had raped her. When she finally stopped and backed away, he was covered in his own blood and feces. He was crying uncontrollably. She took the bloody, shit covered dildo around in front of him.

She growled, "Shut up and take it like a man!" And she slapped him across the face with the disgusting rubber penis like she was swinging for the fence.

Barbara tapped her wrist indicating that they needed to move on. Sondra acknowledged her. She leaned over and pulled Rich's head up by the hair. She said, "I wish we could do this for a few more days. Or maybe a month or two." The women all moved away from Rich. Rich trembled in pain and panic. Sondra finished saying, "But, we have a few other men who require our attention."

She let go of his hair. She put the gun in his face and let him realize that he was about to die. She forced the barrel into his mouth and hesitated. When she pulled the trigger, the bullet went down his throat and came out of his torso somewhere. They heard it ping off of the furnace. The women had turned away. They didn't want to see that much carnage. Sondra fired one last bullet into his head for good measure. And with that, the women left the basement and Rich's body with the bloody, disgusting dildo on his back.

Chapter 26: Conner, Cody, and Zach

The city cop, Zach, had been sitting in his squad car smoking pot most of the afternoon. He appeared to be keeping an eye on the city, but he could barely keep his eyes open.

Ester, Carissa and Hirra were passing by his hiding spot on the way to their intended targets when they noticed the car with the sleepy officer. Ester asked Hirra to circle back and pull up beside the police car. In her mind, Ester thought about how much a person can learn by listening, including things like what someone's abuser might do for a living and where to find them.

Without any questions, Hirra complied. With Ester's window positioned next to the officer's window, the women could see the confusion on Zach's face. He rolled down his window as Ester did the same.

Zach asked, "Are you OK?"

Ester smiled and nodded and replied, "Yes. Everything is just fine for us. But, are you, by any chance, Officer DeGassi?

The man confirmed that he was Sergeant DeGassi of the Sharone police department. When Ester asked if he was Zach DeGassi, he looked a tiny bit suspicious, but again confirmed his identity. Ester told him that she would need him to step out of the car.

"Excuse me?" he replied. He sounded both offended and puzzled. Hirra moved the car forward so that both Ester and Zach could open their doors to exit the vehicles. No one had ever spoken to him, an officer of the law, like that. It was like she was mocking him, using his own lines against him. He slowly rose out of his car.

As Ester climbed out of the car to speak to the waiting officer, she asked, "Are you the same Zach DeGassi that used to be friends with Raith Sizemon?"

Zach recognized Ester from her work with Krisis. He became relaxed, but confused. "Oh, hey! You're that lady doing that awesome work with those kids! Well, ma'am, I have no idea why you'd be asking. I haven't see Raith in years. And we were never really friends. I mean, I liked her, but she would never go out with me."

Ester stood before him with one hand over the other, low in front of her looking up at him with a most serious glare. "Is that why you raped her?" she demanded of him. She stared at him while he processed the question. As expressions changed rapidly on his face, defensive panic overtook the man.

Ester said, "I'll take that as a 'Yes.'" She slowly raised the gun concealed in her hands and shot the frantic man in the stomach, he fell back into his car. As he reeled and buckled, she continued to shoot him (and miss him a few times) and move around to face him more, until she finally placed one round in his chest and one in his head. Hirra informed her that he probably was wearing a Kevlar vest which would mean that the head shot was most likely the only one that mattered. So, Ester reloaded and shot him twice more in the head. Then, she waved at the car that had stopped on the other side of the street, got back in the passenger seat, and the three women casually drove away.

The team of Ester, Carissa, and Hirra didn't waste any time.

They went to Candy's house and knocked on the door. Conner answered wearing gym shorts and a baggy, raggedy t-shirt. He had obviously been drinking.

"Whatever it is, I'm not buying or donating anything," he managed to slur. "Unless it's more whiskey. I could use another bottle."

Hirra looked at Ester. Ester shrugged. Hirra proceeded to activate full marine mode and subdued the drunken sheriff's deputy. Once she choked him out, they hog tied his wrists and ankles and left him on his stomach on the floor.

When Hirra kicked his feet to wake him, he didn't awaken. Rather, he vomited. The vile puddle covered his face and he began choking on it. Hirra and Ester just looked at each other and shook their heads. Conner managed to roll his head to the side enough to save his own life. Before he passed out again, Hirra kicked his feet again. He was dazed. He was too drunk to talk to. So, she shot him in the arm.

Ester flinched. Hirra said, "That got his attention."

Carissa rubbed her ears and said loudly, "That was really loud!"

The adrenaline brought Conner to a nearly sober state. He began to scream and curse. So, Hirra shot him in the other arm.

Ester slapped her arm and yelled, "That's really loud in here, you know!?!"

Hirra nodded her head and agreed. She said, "You're absolutely right." She knew that with that much alcohol in him, Conner would be bleeding out quickly. He would be passing out quite soon. So, she hurried to the kitchen and brought several knives back. She knelt over Conner and spoke to him, "Look. We know what you've been doing to Candy for all these years. We know about the black eyes and broken arms. We know you hurt her so many times. So, we're here to end that."

Conner shook his head. His eyes were already drooping. He scowled, "That lying cunt! She deserved all of it."

Hirra shook her head and looked at Carissa who shrugged, and without another word, she pushed a steak knife into the right side of his rib cage. As he screamed, she plunged another one into the left side of his ribs. And as his cries began to get faded, she stabbed both sides of his neck with force. One side got the bread knife. The other the large chef knife.

Ester removed the knives from Conner's body and made sure that her prints were all over the handles. Now they had one more bad cop to find.

Cory had been at the precinct most of the day. He was easy to find, but they couldn't just walk into the hive of police and start shooting.

His girlfriend, Trina was one of the newest members, and was one of those who was unable to kill her own abuser. Ester noticed that those who had the least about of time with her and the After Party were mostly the ones who were not able to follow through on their own. But, she understood that the newest girls had not had as much time to fully understand and own the abuse. They didn't have enough talk and support to come to terms with it all being wrong. They hadn't had enough time to see and feel how that life was not real. Those that had not been part of the initial experience and worked through all the tears and fears and emotions had not had enough time with the After Party to reprogram their thinking and feeling. They had not been able to unlearn everything yet.

Ester put that out of her mind as they approached the headquarters. Ester went in and asked if officer Cory Martin was still available. She was asked to wait after explaining that she had some follow up information for him. After a few minutes, she was told that Officer Martin had left for the day. She thanked the officer who helped her and said she would try again in the morning, citing that it was sensitive information, and she wasn't comfortable sharing it with anyone else.

Hirra drove them to Cory and Trina's apartment, but Cory wasn't there. This worried Hirra. She was afraid that they may have aroused suspicion. Ester smiled and assured her that everything would be fine.

Just a few minutes later, Cory pulled into his parking space for the apartment. Ester was smiling. Hirra was a little scared that Ester was so calm and collected about killing these men. It was almost as though she was enjoying it.

Cory was on the list to die because of how often he hit Trina. Trina painted a picture of a wild bad boy hiding behind a badge. She described him in such a way, that Hirra wasn't sure this was the guy. He seemed too... nice. He didn't walk with arrogance. He didn't come off as aggressive. He didn't look like a bad boy. He looked rather... nerdy. He was kind of slouchy. He didn't even have a decent haircut. He put off a "bare minimum" vibe.

Hirra and Ester watched him get out of his car and enter the apartment. Hirra asked, "Are we sure Trina was talking about THIS guy? Is there any chance she's not being one hundred percent honest with us?"

Ester thought about it for a minute. Then responded, "Is anyone ever totally honest?" She looked at Hirra and shrugged and said, "I don't know. I'm not sure. I'm sure that as I look back at my life, there's probably times where I didn't describe the events exactly as they happened. I probably put too much emotion into it. I may have missed something. It's entirely possible that my emotions told part of the story.

I know that people who have been traumatized can forget. I know they can embellish. I know they can only tell the story they experienced and their emotions will play into that. I also know that they can lie.

But, that's Cory. And we only have what we have to go on. What would you like to do? Would you like to let him go? Let her come back to him and hope he's learned something from the others?"

Carissa offered her experience from being a police officer. She was pretty sure that Cory was one of those that was cheating on his woman and not very honest. When asked how she was sure, she blushed brightly.

"Oh! You know first hand." Hirra sat quietly for a minute. Finally, she said, "I think I can figure this out. This one's on me. I'll be right back."

She got out of the car and walked up to the apartment door and knocked. Cory answered with a beer in his hand.

"Hi. I'm Hirra. I need to talk to you about Trina," she

introduced herself and an opportunity to talk. She could smell perfume on him.

"She's not supposed to be back till tomorrow. Is she OK?" Cory asked. "Did something happen?"

"Well, I'm not sure if she's OK," Hirra said, watching his eyes. "She said something happened."

Cory looked confused. "What do you mean 'she said something happened?' What is that supposed to mean?"

And then, he started to figure it out. He became animated and agitated. "Now hold on there just a minute! I don't know you and I don't know what she told you, but whatever it is, she's a damn liar!"

Hirra stared hard at him. "Oh, really? How come you smell like perfume? Do you cross dress?"

"Now hold on! That bitch was on drugs when I met her!" He yelled. "I saved her ass!"

Hirra continued to stare. "You haven't been here long enough to be drunk yet. Are you OK? Do you need help?"

"What?" Cory began to look panicked. "Who are you? Are you a fed?"

"Hmmm, I don't know, Cory," Hirra smirked. "Is there any reason the feds might be looking at you?"

There was a moment of silent calculations as the law enforcement officer debated his options and the marine prepared for what she was trained to do.

Ester chuckled in the car and said to herself, "Well now, that didn't take long. Good bye, Cory."

Maybe Cory made a move towards Hirra. Maybe he tried to run back inside. Maybe he blinked at her funny. Whatever sign he gave, she got. The two tangoed through the door and few seconds later, Hirra came out. No blood. No signs of struggle. Just a very angry look as the adrenaline ran through her.

Hirra slammed down into the driver seat and gripped the wheel tight. Ester had been looking straight ahead. She turned very slowly towards the marine, eyes first, then head. Ester softly asked, "Do you need a hug?"

Hirra growled out, "I need the next asshole to kill!"

Ester remained soft spoken. "OK, dear. Let's go get the next bastard."

Hirra looked over at Ester and said, "That douche bag was dealing drugs."

Ester asked, "How can you be so sure?"

Hirra said in a tone of disbelief, "The bags of coke and heroin on the coffee table!!"

Ester replied, "Oh! Yeah. I don't think I'd question Trina. Let's just believe she was totally up front with us. Let's go kill the priest now."

"YES!" Hirra was loud. "Let's definitely kill the child molesting priest!"

"Oh, no!" Ester protested. "He's not a pedophile."

"What?!" Hirra became wide eyed. "I thought the catholic priest was on the list?"

"Oh, he is," Ester assured. "But, not for children. He doesn't like kids. He's sleeping with so many women from the choir and the congregation."

Hirra pulled over, stopped and put the car in park. Turning towards Ester, she asked, "Are you telling me that he's on the list because he's fucking women from the church?"

Ester looked as innocent as she could. "Why, yes, of course. He's not a good man. He's sinning."

Hirra lowered her head and eyes. "Ester. Come on now. Is he abusing them?"

"Well, yes. Indirectly." Ester offered.

Now, Hirra was tilting her head. "Ester. Really? Is he locking them in his office against their will? Is he raping them?"

"No, I don't think so," Ester said. "I mean, he has to be doing something evil to get them to have sex with him. I just don't know what it is."

Hirra shook her head in disbelief. "Ester. If he's not molesting kids, and he's not raping or beating women, he can't be on the list. Maybe God has a beef with him, but we certainly do not."

"But," Ester tried to protest. Hirra cut her off.

"Ester!" Hirra got firm. "Up till now, I've had no reason not to trust your judgment. This is NOT the time to put a doubt in my head. You might believe that he's sinning. And I can agree. But, you know damn well that we are not the judge and jury for every man for everything they do. He's making bad choices. But, those women are making bad choices, too. Maybe there's something he says that plants ideas in their heads. But, they are grown adults. And they have to decide how to act. If they decide to do dumb stuff, that's on them. We are NOT going after them for that. Let God deal with them. We have more than enough serious shit to deal with."

Ester was displeased. But, she was rational. She acquiesced. "Alright. You're right. We can't kill him for whatever voodoo he might have over women. But, if I ever find out that he's locking anyone in his office and taking advantage of them against their will..."

Hirra interjected, "I will drive you there myself and hand you another extension cord."

"Thank you," Ester responded. "I guess we might as well go get that high school principal."

Hirra shook head with disbelief, "Excuse me?"

"He was caught hiding a camera in the girls' locker room," Ester said.

Hirra squinted at Ester. "Try again, Ester. He was caught. They fired him. He never touched anyone. Bad man. Not bad enough. Besides, he's in jail for that."

Hirra was a little unsettled when Ester grumbled about

thinking this would be more fun. But, Ester still had a youth pastor on the list that was confirmed to be sleeping with high school girls. And Crystal's husband, Sam was their final stop. Plus, they still had one very important visit, to a family they would be meeting.

Chapter 27: Deputy Burns

The team of Beverly, Raith, Bethany, Kendra and Meelow were heading to find Bethany's husband, Deputy Tom Burns.

Tom had graduated high in his class. He had natural leadership skills that he displayed as a high school quarterback. He had high hopes and aspirations of joining the state police and moving as far up the food chain as his abilities and charms would take him. But fate had other plans for Tom.

A football injury not only hurt him, but it took him out of college. He lost his scholarship when he couldn't play any more. And a car accident on a rainy road left part of his face scared and took away his pretty looks. It also crushed his arm. It was reconstructed, or whatever doctors do to make it functional again, but he would never be able to throw another spiral. In fact, it wasn't horrible, but it never really looked right after that. It was kinda odd angled at a spot, and didn't move smoothly,

Although they had met in school, Bethany didn't really care to date Tom until after his football injury. He had been too arrogant for her. That mellowed him out enough. And she stuck with him through thick and thin, including the car accident. She didn't mind when he took a job with the sheriff's office. In fact, she was proud of him.

Tom, however, was embarrassed. That was not what he felt he was born to do. He never had any ambition to be what he considered a "local yocal." He was meant for the big time. He should have been state level or even federal.

At first, he was grateful that she felt attracted to him. He always liked her, but never understood why she turned him down. But, as time when on and he lost so much of himself in his own eyes, he changed. Or really, the alcohol changed him. He became depressed. So, he turned to the bottle. And the bottle lied to him. So, he became bitter. And eventually, he became violently angry and bitter about how his life was turning out. He felt it was all passing him by.

Bethany tried to help him see the positive things and to appreciate what he had. But, all he could feel was resentment. And he felt like she was only with him out of pity. He never understood that she loved him once the arrogance was gone. At first it was just anger, depression and quiet resentment. But, it grew in intensity and volume until it was directed anger.

For a long time, Bethany tried. She tried everything. And always believed he could beat it. He could get better. He could be happy. She knew the boy he was and she knew he could become a good version of that as a man. She could see what he could be and just wanted him to see it, too.

But, he couldn't see it. Shot glasses and whiskey bottles don't correct vision. They blur it. They distort it. And Tom went way off course. He became loud. Then, he became belligerent. Then, he became rough. And then, then he became violent.

It began with a drunken backhand. It was followed with profuse apologies and love bombs. But, eventually, there was another backhand. Slowly, but surely, the cycle had begun. Over time, the apologies grew less and less, while the backhands became open hands which became closed fists. Tom became a ticking time bomb for Bethany.

She could usually predict when he was going to blow up. But, he kept becoming more and more out of control. He became less and less predictable. By the time the After Party adopted Bethany, she was at her wits end and was thinking about ending herself. Ester saved her life without knowing or trying. But, having someone to talk to about it all was the light in her darkness.

Now, she was storming up the driveway, screaming at her own house for Tom to come outside because she didn't want to clean up the mess inside. The neighbors had long ago learned to tune them out.

Tom made it to the door to ask what her problem was, but he stumbled and/or fell back in. Bethany hung her head and shook it. She was not happy that she was going to need to clean up the house after killing him.

She stormed into the house and screamed at him to stand upright. She kicked his legs while he tried to pull himself up on a kitchen chair. He muttered something about kicking her ass when he got up. But, just as he got all the way up on his feet, Bethany walked over to the butcher's block and pulled out the chef's knife.

Tom reacted with silent surprise as she stomped towards him with the knife. She lunged, trying to stab him in the neck, but missed and plunged the point into and through his cheek. He was so drunk, he couldn't scream. He just made pain sounds through his now bleeding mouth.

Bethany was now bouncing between rage and horror as she reeled back from her failed attack. Tom pulled the knife from his face. The blood dripped, spurted a little and poured down his face, neck, and onto the floor. He tried to get undrunk as he advanced towards Bethany, ready to attack her with the knife she just provided him.

Raith was waiting in the doorway. She fired one shot that hit Tom in the shoulder. He dropped the knife as he stumbled sideways. The wall held him up. Bethany shook off any fear she had and snatched up the bloody knife. She quickly ran at him and stabbed him repeatedly. She stabbed him in the gut, the neck and chest. She stabbed him like a wild, possessed woman over and over and over.

No speech. No warning. No dramatic moment of any kind. Bethany killed him. She stabbed him to death with the help of one gunshot from a friend. She was full of rage from all the rage he had beaten her with. He beat the anger into her. Now, she had returned it all back to him. And she was leaving it there on the kitchen floor with him.

The After Party had swept into town with each kill team ending at least one uniformed abuser. No other lawmen would die that night. Tom was the last.

Neighbors or a passerby would be calling the police about something terrible happening. The police would be finding dead police. And the police would become worried about the police. They would be worried for themselves. After all, one of their own was trafficking narcotics. And all that evidence was left on the table for all to see.

The local police and sheriff offices would not know if they were under attack from some cartel somewhere. They had no way to understand what was happening. It would appear to them that drugs were involved. And where that volume of drugs can be found, there would be drug cartel.

They could only assume that they were the target, and take precautions.

All remaining local law enforcement was called in or dragged from their homes to the police headquarters downtown. They locked and barricaded the doors. They armed themselves heavily. And they waited.

They did order pizza. And since they knew Doug, the delivery guy from the nearest place very well, they let him in and back out. But, they prepared themselves for the war they believed was coming for them. They were prepared for battle.

Little did they know, that there was no war. The battle was being led by a tiny 95 year old woman who was sick and tired of abusive people getting away with being abusive. The entire town's trained officers were hiding from a four foot, nine inch woman who ran a children's outreach. And they didn't know it.

She might have been small in physical stature. But, she was huge on brilliance. Whether she planned it or not, she had successfully cleared the streets of everyone with a badge and a gun. Once the first bodies were found, all bubble gum lights were heading back to downtown. Ester and her army were free to do whatever they wanted to do and no one was going to chase them. No one was there to stop them. They were free to finish what they had begun.

Chapter 28: The Judge

While the other teams were focused on the sheriff and officers, Tammy, Randi and Onna were set on Serena's husband, The "Honerable" Judge Robert Coccnine.

Serena had had enough of Robert long ago. Like many young women, she was smitten by his charm, intelligence and charisma. He was tall and handsome and when he walked into a room, all attention turned his way. He could command an audience. He was usually the life of the party.

It didn't take long to fall in love with him. And Serena was a tall, well built beauty. He was instantly attracted. Their dating was intensely romantic. He had the money and connections to make her feel special. They always got the best reservations, the best tickets, the best seats... It was dreamy.

But, dreams can change quickly. A nightmare is a dream that slipped on a banana peel. Often, the very thing that attracts someone becomes the wedge that drives them apart. That which draws a person in and melts their heart, becomes the most repulsive resentment that turns the heart cold.

He had a wondering eye, but she couldn't blame him. Women can be incredibly beautiful. And he was the man that women would notice. Robert and Serena were beautiful people that went to places where there were many beautiful people. Of course he was going to notice the beautiful women. But, she was sure that once they were married, he would settle down. After all, he would be making a sacred vow that she would be his one and only love. And he was known for being a man of integrity. Naturally, once he made the commitment, he would be a man of his word and honor that. He would only honor her.

Yeah. That was all an illusion. It was shortly after the honeymoon when she discovered that he had never been faithful to her for a single day. He was a sly and sneaky player. He always had a side chick somewhere.

Serena was bound to find out. But, when he gave her chlamydia, she learned quickly. When confronted, he was unapologetic and unrepentant. In fact, he accused her of being the unfaithful one bringing disease into their relationship. So, why didn't she leave him?

Well, being included in certain social circles is a privilege. And reputation is everything when that's the currency of upper society. Reputation was her golden ticket. If she ruined his reputation, hers would also burn down, too.

In many high society relationships there's a mutual coexistence where he does his thing and she does her thing. They silently agree on a "don't ask, don't tell" policy. They put on a happily married show for the sake of the money and notoriety, but live separate lives together. Most people would say "for the sake of the marriage," but the reality is not as it appears. The marriage is a facade for all that brews behind.

That wasn't exactly the case here. Robert was living his best life. But, he wasn't about to let Serena just "run wild." She was not allowed to live as he was living. Robert made it clear that she was HIS wife, and his alone. She was his trophy. He would essentially keep her on display or on the shelf and only take her out when he wanted to show off.

She was forbidden from dating or even flirting. The one time she attempted to have an affair, she took a sudden "unplanned vacation" when he found out. Robert told everyone that she was being spontaneous and visiting distant relatives in Europe while exploring the roots of her family tree. She was actually recovering in a low cost hospital in India from the beating he had given her while in a jealous fit of rage.

After he had beaten her till she was unrecognizable, he risked her dying to take her to a hospital out of state where she could be stabilized. Then, he had a private jet take her to India for six months of surgery and rehabilitation. She was able to walk again. And eventually regained almost all of her motor skills and cognitive capabilities. But, she would end up taking medication for nightmares and anxiety for the rest of her life. The man she had dated and fell in love with had been a figment of her imagination. She fell in love with a monster. And the man of her attempted affair had disappeared mysteriously, and was never heard from again. Presumably, the monster got him.

Even though that was the only time he had ever laid hands on her, he had done a lifetime of damage. And he controlled her emotionally and mentally. She knew another affair would be the end of her life.

The After Party was Serena's answer to her prayers. It was ironic to her that she had to stumble into a Christian outreach for children in order to find a way to kill her husband. What seemed wholesome and healthy was actually rather twisted. But, then again, that fit Robert. He seemed like a good man, but he was definitely twisted. Serena needed the After Party. Now she couldn't wait for the Grand Finale.

Predictably, Robert was watching sports in his chair. When he heard Serena enter, he requested that she bring him a drink. He had no clue that she had been studying Wiccan and Pagan ways for quite some time. She had been learning about natural plants and extracts. She studied how they affect the body. She had secretly been planning on how to poison him for quite some time, but could never see an opportunity that would get rid of him without being suspicious. Tonight, she had no fear. Tonight was the night she employed all that learning.

Serena spiked his bourbon with the distillate she had made from natural plants nearby. She only gave him a small shot glass, knowing his behavior. He would get mad, down the shot, throw the glass at her, then demand a proper pour. He delivered a predictably flawless performance.

He became outraged when she dodged the glass and simply stood still staring at him. He stood up to make her do as he instructed. She didn't move. She was nervous about how long it would take. He started towards her. She started back pedaling. But, his face began to change. He stopped. His face was nothing but confusion. He began to look disoriented.

"What did you give me?" he asked.

She shrugged. "Well, I was remembering how amazing you've been to me. All the whores. The STDs. And especially how you nearly killed me."

"Did you just poison me?" His body was beginning to falter. The poison was doing its job quickly. Serena was relieved.

She said, "It's kind of sad, really. It's far too kind. I wish I could repay you for all you did to me. I really wish I could tie you up and cheat in front of you every day with a different man for a couple years, and beat you to death slowly every day. But, after tonight, you'll be dead. And I'll be able to tell everyone exactly the type of man you have really been. Good bye, Robert."

There was so much more she wished she could tell him. She wanted to tell him about suffering and pain and justice. But, Robert slumped to the floor. Serena turned and walked out of the house with her head held high. She seemed almost happy. She got back in the car with Onna, Randi, and Tammy and asked, "OK, who's next?"

Chapter 29: Meelow

When she was seven years old and could run fast enough, Meelow's parents smuggled her across the 48th parallel to defect and escape from North Korea. A couple of U.S. Soldiers had helped them get to America to complete their emancipation. They were free.

But, life in America was not. They were able to get by on hand outs. But being from North Korea, hand outs were very limited. They had been sent to a community of South Koreans, but since they were from the north, they were not warmly welcomed.

It didn't take long before a business man explained a way for Meelow to make enough money to support the family. He explained that it would need to be a bit of a group effort. Meelow would not be able to arrange business transactions on her own. She was too young. She was only seven. However, she had everything some men would gladly pay top dollar for. All her parents had to do was set her up as an escort.

Meelow didn't understand why her parents cried and fought and were sick for weeks. She couldn't have known that the business devil had petitioned the community to not help them. He made the community stop reaching out so that the family would be forced to prostitute their young daughter. They held out as long as they could. They offered to work everywhere around them. They tried to get jobs and offered to clean homes. They tried everything to make money. But, they were living on dandelion greens and crickets they found.

Then, winter came. They had no food, no heat and no hope. It was the saddest, ugliest, and most gut retching day of their lives when the only hope of saving them all was for Meelow to become an escort. She would have to "service" grown men.

Nothing the business man said mattered to them. He promised to provide condoms and healthcare and more. But, nothing could pay for or justify the innocence of their child. Since he would be the first to have her, he promised $50,000 to them. It only made the feelings worse, because any dollar promised made the inescapable reality sink in and burn.

The first night he took her was the worst. Until the second night he took her. And every night after that. There was no way to describe the horror of trying to welcome their violated daughter home after what was done to her.

The only "consolation" was that the business man kept his word. Suddenly, they had a very nice, little house with all new appliances. They even had a dishwasher. They never imagined such a contraption existed. They could buy food. They could even go places where food was cooked and served to them. It was the strangest experience.

But, they didn't want to eat. They had no appetite. They had very comfortable beds, but they could barely sleep. They got a car, but they didn't want to leave home.

For months, they all cried all the time. But, eventually, Meelow didn't want to be held. And she didn't cry with her parents. She began to form a new personality. She became someone else. Very slowly, she learned more and more about men and how to navigate their wants, demands and expectations. She learned how to give the least she had to give in order to take their money.

Some men were good to her. Some were terrible. But, they all paid. By the time she was nine, she began managing more of her own business. She had enough experience to pick more men she preferred. She picked those who were good to her. She learned to avoid the bad men who hurt her.

But, the terrible and mean men paid more. And her parents had grown comfortable with having money. All the tears, guilt and sick feelings were eventually replaced with enjoying a better life. They distanced themselves from those early days of selling their daughter. She was now the family business.

They were enjoying a better life. At least, her parents who were not selling their bodies and being violated by vulgar men were enjoying a better life. And from all outward appearances, Meelow was doing well. She had nice clothes. She looked healthy. And she always put on a great display of being happy.

Inside, she was dead. And she wanted to be dead. As she got older, she understood more about what she had become and how people thought of her. It was insanity to be so young and have been forced into a life of prostitution. She didn't get to be a kid. She was a working girl before she even had boobs. There was nothing about her or her life or her family life that actually made her happy. Every smile was fake. Every happy emotion was just acting. Her entire existence was pretend.

When she turned twelve, her father used some of the money she made to start a business. It was a legitimate business. He created a real job to make money for himself. Her mother had become ingrained in the Korean society. She helped with many humanitarian aid projects and neighborhood improvement committees. Her parents had become U.S. Citizens and developed respectable lives for themselves. All because they had made her a whore.

When Meelow survived to the ripe old age of fourteen, she had had enough. She devised a scheme with the help of a few acquaintances from school who allowed her to run away. She took as much money as she could hide from her parents and ran as far away as she could. No note. No goodbye. No looking back.

Sadly, fourteen is a terrible age to be on the run. And she couldn't escape her only means of making plenty of money. So, she set about on a new plan. She did what she had to do to make a lot of money, and she used that to set up a life for herself. She hid it as much as she could.

She finished high school early. She got a college degree in business management in just three years. She then went about finding a good job that was just out of reach of her parents and far enough away from where she had run so she could start over.

It was a complete and total "do over" in her life. She created the chance to have a life, an actual LIFE, for herself. It was a life with no men paying her for sex. There was no one taking anything from her. She had a job, a house and a car. She got a cat and a dog. She mowed the lawn and raked leaves. She paid her bills from a paycheck issued from a corporation. She didn't make the illegal, tax free money prostitution provided. But, she loved having a real life! Finally... she was free.

She struggled with the nightmares. The scars of all she had been through and all that was done to her kept her up at night. She missed her parents. Not the people that slutted her out. She missed the parents she had when she was six. And she often wondered and dreamed about what it might have been like if only....

Meelow was struggling. She loved the new life she worked for. But, she was desperate to escape the life she had physically escaped. There were many days and nights that she very seriously contemplated ending her life to end the seemingly eternal effects that engulfed her. It seemed that she was only holding out hope in the hope that somehow, some day, she might find hope to keep living.

When she heard about Krisis, she asked about more information. She didn't have a good reason to ask. She didn't really have any reason to want to know more. She had been thinking about ending everything. So, why would she want to know more about anything?

But, she asked. That led to her being invited. And some strange, unexplained something happened. It wasn't a lightning bolt. It was mostly a revelation. There was no sudden epiphany. She simply found herself going through the motions of joining the outreach and reaching out to kids. There was no sweeping change, no alter call, no deep convergence of the cosmos. It just felt right. It just made her feel good. And that was something she wasn't sure she had ever felt.

No one helped her. Now she was helping others. When she needed someone desperately, no one came. She was showing up for someone. And it felt good. It made her happy. And it gave her a feeling that she couldn't name. She described it to someone and they called it "satisfied." Yes. She felt satisfied by helping kids learn about having a better life.

When she overheard a couple of ladies whispering about their abusive relationships, her face gave away that she was tuned in. They asked her about her own experience. She lied. They left her alone. But, then... Ester. They had sent Ester to Meelow.

Ester knew. As soon as Ester took Meelow's hand and wrapped her aged, tiny mitts around it, Meelow melted. She couldn't stop herself. Ester had magically disarmed the expert. Meelow was truly professional at hiding her painful past, but not from Ester.

Before she could understand what was happening, Ester had her in the After Party. For the first time in her life, Meelow had support. She had accidentally found a group of women who understood her. Maybe it was providential? At least they understood her as much as they could, more than anyone had ever understood her. When Meelow finally broke and poured out her heart about her past, it was possibly the most ugly cry any of them had ever endured.

As talk about the Grand Finale crept up, Meelow was clearly conflicted. She loved her parents. She hated her parents. She hated what they had done to her for money. She loved them for risking their lives to save them from the horrible life in the communist regime. There were many push and pulls, but in the end, she couldn't get past the facts of what they ultimately exposed her to and the wheels of merciless fate they had started rolling down a mountain side.

After all, no matter what they saved her from, did they really save her? It didn't feel like it. What if they had stayed? Would they have been dying every day in a mine or sweat shop? The questions and doubts ying yanged in her mind over and over.

Finally, she consulted Ester about her duality of feelings over her parents. Ester listened. And then she sat quietly for a few minutes. Meelow became concerned that Ester hadn't understood. Or maybe she had lost focus and drifted away in a day dream. But, when she tried to speak, Ester spoke first.

Ester said, "Meelow. You've suffered a life no one should even *hear* about, let alone should have survived. I cannot put myself in your shoes. No one can. No one could. The only thing I can offer is this: whatever could have been will never be. Whatever might have been possible, never happened and never will. All you have is what has been.

There's only one question that I can imagine that might matter. If there was some cosmic event where God himself took us all back to when we were so much younger, when we were young again, when you were seven... would anything be different? Would the same decisions be made? Would you have to relive the life you've known, or would there be any way for a different path?

In other words, knowing what we know now, would your parents do the same thing?"

Meelow became quiet. She thought about that for a long time. She thought about it for days and days. She thought about it every night. And the more she thought about it, the more she realized that there was only one conclusion based on the things her parents had said over the years about her ability to make money with men; they would do it again.

Once Meelow stopped thinking, she started simmering with an evil disdain that began to overtake her mind. She was sure that they would sell her into prostitution. It always came back to the most bitter backhanded compliment they continuously doled upon her, "You are the gift that saved us."

Gift? Saved? What about her? Was she born to save them?

Why was no one there to save her? How was she supposed to be happy about that? How was that supposed to make her feel good?

She *knew* that her parents only meant it in a good way. But... how long were they going to use her as their gift? How could they not see what their choices were doing to her? How could they be OK with that? It became an endless string of "How could they...?"

Over the course of a year, Meelow began to feel like the "gift that saved her parents" had the right to revoke everything. They seemed to believe that they were giving her everything. They never seemed to realize that they had taken everything from her. They failed to understand that they destroyed everything in her. And they eventually began to act as if she owed something to them. That was her breaking point. If anyone owed anyone, *they* owed *her*!

The woman who probably had the most reason to kill someone for the abuse they intentionally inflicted upon her took the longest to reach the conclusion that her abusers deserved to die. But, like just about everything else she ever did in her life, once Meelow made up her mind, she set her intentions at a level of ten. She was all in.

Bethany, Beverly, Raith, and Kendra could only stand back and watch in fearful amazement when they pulled up to the house Meelow's prostitution money had bought her parents. They never moved. They were still enjoying what they had put her through for them. Meelow approached like an international assassin.

The other four in the car were locked in place with eyes wide. They couldn't help their colleague if she needed it, because she needed no help in any way from anyone. Meelow tossed a rock through a window as she kicked open the front door. There was screaming while the muzzle flash from the gun filled the doorway. Then, there was crashing like breaking furniture and glass. The kill team felt like they were watching a live action movie. In less than a minute, the only screaming was Meelow's voice in Korean. Then, it went quiet. It was another nearly two minutes before Meelow came out covered in blood.

The kill team shreaked and shrank away from her. She directed them to get back into the car. They immediately complied without asking any questions. They drove in very quiet tension to the next abuser.

When the law would finally get to the house where Meelow terminated the luxury her parents enjoyed off of her being on her back, they would be horrified to enter the crime scene. The couple who had fled North Korea and established a successful life in the U.S.A. were found with multiple gunshots, stabs and slices across their bodies. Their arms and heads were more or less still loosely attached to their maimed bodies. And their blood was used to spell out a message on the walls: "My body was not your gift."

Chapter 30: The Fredricks

They were terrible. Maybe they were that way because of the way the world treated them. Maybe that was just the way they were bred. But, they were truly awful people. They were the stereotype of trailer park trash, just without the trailer park.

They lived in the woods in an old, old house that most likely should have been condemned two owners previously. The yard was cluttered with automobile carcasses and junk of all sorts. They never seemed clean and deodorant may have been a foreign word to them. They were so rude that manners were wasted on them.

Dale and Darlene Fredrick produced Theo, Kern and Sally just far enough apart in age to keep each level of public schooling terrorized for years. One would leave elementary to junior high and the next would show up. The one in junior high would go to high school and the middle one showed up in junior high. Principals and teachers called it the Fredrick Plague.

The list of women harassed by the Fredrick family was long. There were probably fewer women in the county that had NOT been harassed (or at a minimum, freaked out by) them. There were stories about a few women that they had kidnapped for their personal pleasure of torture and ritualistic killing.

It sounded crazy, like urban legend. It was serial killer bizarre to think that a whole family could possibly be collective killers. But, there were enough rumors of Sally trying to lure schoolmates home with her, telling them that her parents would "love to play with kids like them."

The rumors were so bad, most people considered them urban legend. They were so wildly disgusting, that they sounded made up. Almost no one knew that Samantha could confirm that many of the rumors about the Fredrick family were true.

Samantha never wanted anyone to know that she had been stupid enough to let Kern and Sally talk her into going to their house. It was spring break. Her parents were going on a cruise without her. And she was a lonely loner. She had separated herself from people so much so, that she didn't have friends to hang out with. If she had friends, she probably wouldn't have been targeted by the Fredricks and her life would have been so very, very different.

The worst part of being locked up, chained down and abused for a week by an entire family was that the Fredricks knew that they could get away with it. They knew she'd never tell anyone because it would be too humiliating and no one would believe her. After all, no one would be dumb enough to go near that family, let alone walk to their house. The Fredricks even joked that she would have a better chance of convincing people that she had been abducted by aliens than try to explain that she had willingly gone to visit them.

When they finally released her, Samantha didn't go back to school. She checked herself into a hospital under the guise of having been kidnapped by a biker gang. She told the staff that they had taken her away and brought her back blindfolded, so she couldn't tell where she had been or who had done what to her. She had an abortion and healed physically, but Sam was the only person she ever trusted to tell the abysmal story of that deplorable family doing horrible things to her because she was so stupid that she put herself in their hands.

281

Samantha formed a bond with Sam when they met at work. For whatever reason, they were placed side by side in an area that allowed them to talk without anyone listening. But, even without words, their energies meshed immediately.

It didn't take long for the two women to form a bond that was indescribably intimate. And while they were labeled as lesbians and were often seen kissing and holding hands, they had never had sex together. They embraced all the characteristics and displays of a romantic relationship without it ever becoming sexual. And they never once tried to explain it to anyone. They never confirmed nor denied anything. They just wanted to live their lives together. Sex was unwanted due to their traumas. They only needed each other.

Barbara and Sondra were shocked when Sam and Samantha asked to go to the Fredrick's house. That wasn't planned for. But, the couple insisted adamantly. As they were heading that way, Sam and Samantha asked if the other girls would sit this one out. It was personal.

But, Barbara and Sondra agreed that if this needed to happen, they weren't going to sit back and watch or take a chance for things to go sideways. They would not allow anyone to get hurt due to their inaction when they would be outnumbered.

The four women made sure their guns were loaded and ready as they approached. Predictably, all five of the Fredricks were either sitting on the porch or milling around the junk piles. That's just kind of the way tweakers are.

It could have been a modern day reenactment of the OK Corral. The women got out of the car in unison. They each selected and targeted a family member as they approached the uncivilized people.

Barbara headed to the porch where Darlene was braiding Sally's hair.

Sam locked eyes with Dale and walked towards him with apprehensive determination.

Sondra picked the oldest son, Theo, so Samantha could have Kern.

The moment Kern recognized Samantha, he hollard out, "Hey, look! She came back! She was the one that said we was the meanest people she'd ever met. Haha! I remember her! She was delicious."

Dale went for his shotgun that was leaning against a pickup truck near him. But, Sam made sure he never made it there. She began running up on him firing as she let out a screaming war cry.

Sondra followed the lead as Theo tried to run. She fired on him till she was putting the last bullet from her magazine into his corpse.

As the gun fire started, Barbara walked up to the panicked women on the porch and cold blooded executed them Dirty Harry style. She shot Sally first. Then, she looked at Darlene and said, "This is for Samantha," before firing into her chest three times.

Samantha was having a hard time with Kern. He was much faster and more athletic than the others. He had rushed her as soon as he realized what was happening. He was drawing a nine millimeter handgun from his holster as he was charging. He was trying to fire, but she managed to get one shot off quicker than him that hit him somewhere in the torso. That caused him to shoot the dirt and drop his gun while his momentum carried him to her. She couldn't tell where he was hit, but he was definitely bleeding as he tackled her. He was trying to wrestle her gun away from her.

He was bigger, stronger and faster, even with a bullet in him. He managed to get Samantha's gun away from her when he elbowed her in the face. She was dazed and weak trying to keep from getting shot with her own gun, but she was fighting back.

Kern knocked her around till Samantha was on her back. He had her pinned to the ground by straddling her hips. Sondra and Barbara were frantically trying to reload as they raced to try to save their friend. But, they were scared to even take a shot. What if they missed?

But, before they could get close enough to try anything, Sam had gotten Dale's shotgun. And she wasn't afraid. Kern turned to face the barrel of his father's gun just in time to lose his head. Sam had pulled both triggers on that double barrel.

At Samantha's direction and insistence, all five bodies were hoisted into the large oak tree out back behind the house, upside down like the deer they used to poach. Samantha cut each one's stomach open just like they would have done to the deer they killed. And before they left, she made sure there were three holes dug at twenty five paces southeast from the old oak tree. That way, when the police came to investigate, maybe they would dig up the three bodies Samantha knew that family had buried out there.

As the bloody crew reloaded weapons and got back into the car, they were engulfed with a strange mix of adrenaline and being mortified. They had essentially just survived their first combat style mission, complete with fire fight. They now qualified for PTSD as defined by the military, as if they had never had any form of it before. They were jittery, excited, nervous and quiet. Their heavy breathing was its own conversation.

They drove to Adrianna's to kill Ken. They were a quivering mess of extreme emotions. They agreed to get it over with as quickly as possible.

Poor Ken didn't stand a chance. He opened the door in his underwear acting surly. All four women opened fire on him before he even realized there were four of them. He fell dead back inside the open door. The women scurried away like trick or treaters who had come across one of those jump-scare ambush pranks.

Once they had completed all of their assignments and were heading back to camp, they were happy to be alive and successful. They were, however, fearful of the killers they had become.

Chapter 31: The Lesbians

The whole reason Samantha was vulnerable to fall into the clutches of the Fredrick family was because her parents weren't really parents. They definitely created her and gave birth to her. But, as far as being loving, nurturing parents that sheltered and cared for their kid? Not so much.

They kept her alive until she could survive on her own. They made sure to never have any more children. They really didn't want this one. And it was as though they went out of their way to show her that. She never had a chance to grow up like any of the other kids. They didn't have to get their own cereal when they were three. They didn't have to make their own meal by the time they were five.

It wasn't that her parents were abusive to her. Well, they were not physically abusive. They just never cared for her. They never cared about her. They never hung her school art work on the refrigerator. They never played games with her or sang lullabies to her. They never had birthday parties for her, or took her skating. They never beat her. They just never paid attention to her.

Being raised so differently, she didn't know how to fit in. So, she was never invited to parties. She was always called weird. And the other kids ignored her almost as much as her parents did. They didn't hate her or pick on her. She just didn't matter to them.

She was invisible. No one knew she was there. She just never existed anywhere. Her entire life was so locked inside her head that she often wondered if she was just imagining that she existed. She was a figment of her own imagination.

She was so isolated, that it was easy for Sally and Kern to choose her. No one would stop them. No one would stop her. She was the perfect target. And it made it OK to release her back into the wild once they were done with her. They knew she didn't have anyone to tell.

Sam's life was very different. She was also an only child. But, she was not left alone. She was very much the center of attention. She had been born a "crack baby" and adopted by two very loving gay guys. They cared for her night and day until she was through the addiction her birth mother had gifted to her. And once she was "out of the woods," she became their pride and joy.

When she was little, it was fun to braid hair with her two dads. They would do make up together and try on clothes. It was fun. But, as she got older, other kids treated her differently.

They lived in an area where there were not very many gays. Very few ever bothered or harassed them. But, they were definitely a novelty. So, no one really harassed them. But, everyone would talk about them.

Kids do not possess the social filters or checks that adults might have. So, when Sam went to school, the jokes and questions and insults grew in volume and intensity year to year. Her dads might not have had much negativity. But, as a kid, Sam sure did.

The last party she ever went to was the worse experience of her young life. It was fifth grade. She ended up in the middle of a large circle where they took turns shoving her back and forth to each other. They called it "Question the Queer."

Whoever she was pushed to had to question her about her sexuality, or her dads's manhood, or something insulting.

She had fought her way out of the circle when a boy had grabbed her butt and said, "See! She doesn't even know what to do when a boy touches her because she doesn't have any men around to teach her anything!" She ran away from the party in tears. She was devastated. She couldn't hate her dads for adopting her and loving her. But, she couldn't face the harsh reality that went with being so very different in public school.

Private school was not without it's problems, too. In fact, it was more intense. The small, close knit environment made it even more personal. So, she ended up going to military school.

There, she excelled. At first, it looked like the same old same gay bashing she was running from. But, at the academy, they taught fighting arts. Sam was a natural. She learned quickly. And she was good. So, by the end of her first semester, no one made bad jokes to her about her fathers. They didn't want to have to spar with her when she was mad.

Sam didn't have a lot of enemies. But, she didn't have any real solid friends, either. She was a bit of a loner, but she got along at military school.

One night during Christmas break of her senior year, a group of kids that had picked on her years ago, recognized her out on the street walking. They pulled up along side her and began the same crap they had never outgrown. She tried to walk away from them, but they made it obvious that they were not going to leave her alone. They were going to pick up where they left off.

Sam gave them three chances to leave her alone. And they reject all three. So...

By the time it was over, Sam was beat up badly. She had a black eye, broken nose, fat lips, and a broken arm. But, when they all got to the same hospital together, she had obviously come out on top. She looked around the ER at the five guys and three girls that were put ahead of her by triage and she nodded with pride in herself. She even made sure to stop by each of their rooms the next morning including the two in ICU.

She had told the staff that they were all friends that had gotten jumped by thugs while just out having a good time. But, she was the only one treated as an out patient. All the others had severe compound fractures and internal bleeding. So, when she came back and was let in to see her "friends," she made sure to record their faces as she approached them, then posted the videos to each of their social media accounts. She thought it was funny since their phones were all missing. Seems someone took them all while they were knocked out. She smiled as she wondered out loud to them about who could have done such a thing. Seems that whoever had their phones could post anything they wanted, and there was nothing that could be done to stop it.

Sam was a tomboy who could rival any boy. Yet, she was clearly feminine. She could wear a ballgown with the best of them. But, she was tough as nails. Samantha was a girly girl. She was the epitome of sugar and spice and everything nice. Together, they were balanced. There was no surprise that everyone assumed that they were lesbians. Their relationship was clearly intimate enough.

However, their bond wasn't sexual. It was much deeper than that. They completed each other in ways that they could never achieve alone. They didn't know if they really were lesbians or not. They just never saw any point to arguing about it with strangers, or even friends. Maybe they really did like girls. Or maybe they just loved each other. They didn't know and didn't care. They didn't try to figure it out.

Sam had her share of sexual harassment, but probably never had anything happen to her as bad as many of the others in the After Party. A few boys had tried to grab her boobs. A couple of girls had tried to seduce her at a Senior Year party to the point where she had to fight them off of her. A couple of boys had tried the same thing and she had fought them off, too. But, Sam was never sexually assaulted in gross or violent ways. In fact, as far as she knew, she was still a virgin.

Sam came to the After Party because of Samantha. Samantha wouldn't go without Sam. Samantha needed someone. Sam was granted as her guardian angel. Though some might say their relationship was not right or sinful, in some ways, they shared the purest form of love. People only assumed that they were sexually involved.

But, sex was never part of their relationship. And they could not care less what people thought or said. They had each other. And that was enough. It took someone like Ester to be invited into their world.

Ester, as always with everyone, provided a warm, safe landing spot for them. She was more than accepting. She was welcoming. She made them feel like daughters. She was the "made for TV" mom who they never had. In the time they had met and gotten to know each other, the little old lady and the lesbians became like family. For Christmas, Ester had made them sugar cookies that looked like boomerang shaped cats. When the girls asked why the cats were bent like that, Ester smiled and told them to push two of the cats together so they fit like a puzzle. There were dorm room giggles and laughing when they saw the cats made a perfect 69 together.

Sam and Samantha grew to trust and love Ester. And eventually, they agreed that they would do anything for her. Ester adored the girls, and admired their love for one another. She wished there was a way she could protect them from the world and preserve their innocence. She saw them as young girls that loved like kindergartners. And she wanted them to always have that, and keep them away from the big kids picking on them and trying to ruin them.

Of all the women in the After Party, Sam and Samantha had the least amount of reason to be there. They could just as easily be part of any support group anywhere for almost anything. They were not without reason. Aside from Samantha's run in with the Fredricks, they were simply not the most abused women in the group. They did not need to risk anything for the Grand Finale.

But, Ester knew. No one else could see it or figure it out. But, Ester knew these girls would fight like Vikings for their fellow women. Those girls shared the same loyalty as kindergartners who have never been betrayed. Once they considered someone a friend, that person was a friend. It was sincere, and it came with all the rights and privileges that friendship could afford.

Sam and Samantha considered the women of the After Party more than friends. They were sisters by proxy of Ester. Most of the women would underestimate these women. Few would understand how loyal they would be. And only Ester would understand why. If Ester asked them to donate a kidney, they'd be on the operating table that day.

For the happy couple, killing abusers for their fellow women was just part of being there for each other. If some horrible person had to be killed in order to save the life of a friend, that person was 100% going to die.

So, when it came to killing Richard, Sam and Samantha were more than willing to rescue Meg and Julie. They were almost happy to help.

Chapter 32: Richard

Meg and Julie were just kids. They couldn't protect themselves from a grown man. And if there was anyone that should fight for them and protect them, that should be their father.

But, no. Richard wasn't that kind of father. He was big and mean. He was cruel. And he had no conscious. Maybe at one time he did, but alcohol had eroded that long ago. He could slap either girl for any reason and continue his beer or conversation as casually as scratching his elbow.

Larry had every intention of explaining to Richard a father's role in raising daughters. Having suffered enough himself, he imagined and internalized how horrible it had to be for a couple of little girls that couldn't fight back. The feelings it conjured in him were unbearable. He had to set that man straight. He was going to to MAKE him understand.

But, Sam heard him talking about it. And she assured him that she and Samantha would take care of Richard. They would be able to explain things to him in a way that was impossible to not understand. It took a little convincing for the giant boy-man to relent, but he agreed to allow Sam and Samantha to go after the Goliath of the targets.

Larry made sure that they understood that he didn't like the idea of two girls going after such a large, muscular man. He was worried about them. They made sure Larry heard their confidence when they assured him, "Larry. We will not fail. Before he dies, he will understand to his very core. And we will be fine." Larry still had a tiny doubt. But, he couldn't doubt their confidence. And he had total confidence in them.

Meg had managed to survive to high school. By the time the After Party held Ester's Retreat, Julie was in junior high. It wasn't easy. At times, she didn't know how they made it that long, nor how much longer they might make it. But, Meg had assumed the role of mother and protector of Julie after their mom died of cancer. Meg was never really convinced. Richard always told the girls that their mother died of cancer. Meg always had a terrible suspicion that her father had a role in her mother's death.

Richard had been a star athlete in high school. He basked in the glory of the school colors every time he helped bring home another victory. He had a lot going for him; good looks, good parents, decent grades and great friends. He had no problem getting the best looking girls to go out with him. One might say he was living the dream as a high school super star. He was even voted "most likely to succeed" by his graduating class.

He was in college on an athletic scholarship where he met Rhonda. She was beautiful and smart. They were such a natural fit right from the day they met. It was all so perfect. Until it wasn't.

Richard's knees were not indestructible. He wasn't Superman. He took a crushing hit on the final drive in an important game that blew out his knees. Two surgeons assured him that there would be no more sports for him. They told him that maybe with surgery and physical therapy he might be able to enjoy golf for a decent amount of years. That news from the doctor hit him hard, but not as hard as the news from the doctor that informed him that Rhonda was pregnant.

They both dropped out of college and took factory jobs. They started a family instead of getting degrees or professional sports endorsements. They worked a lot. They worked a lot of overtime. They fought. They drank. They fought a lot when they drank. Richard and Rhonda became the burned out remnants of all the dreams they never attained.

The drinking was combined with smoking to help age their bodies and faces much faster. They gained weight. They became unhealthy in every way.

More than one person had mentioned or hinted to them that they should probably not have a second child. It was rather remarkable to them how some people felt almost obligated to tell them how they had aged, gained weight and would have been better off not having kids. People didn't realize how hard they were grinding salt in the wound every time they speculated about "what could have been" had it not all gone wrong.

Richard became a very angry and bitter man. Year after year, it grew deeper and more bitter. He became more angry. It grew beyond his ability to check it and control it. He lost friends. He lost jobs. He spiraled down the wrong hole of life. Rhonda understood. She was there for it.

No one else understood. Everyone else saw a drunken asshole. Richard wasn't liked any more. He wasn't welcomed. He once stood head and shoulders above the crowd, but now he was more or less shunned. No one wanted to hear about his glory days from almost two decades ago while he guzzled beer. No one wanted him at their barbecue or around their wife and children. Richard was a reject.

He knew it. He felt it. He had failed at life. He wasn't the man he thought he was. He failed to become the hero he believed he could be. There were opportunities to change direction and make something of himself. But, it would have been hard and foreign to him. He was used to everything coming to him easily. He knew how to work hard in the gym and on the playing field, but he never learned to scrape and scrounge for his existence. He never learned to drag himself through bad times and rise above the fray despite the odds. Once his golden ticket ripped, he fell from grace.

Meg couldn't remember ever being truly loved and wanted. She felt like a mistake from early on. Probably because she could hear her parents fighting. And she could hear her dad blame her mom for getting pregnant. And when she was older, she heard people talk about her and her parents.

In his isolated dungeon of self loathing, Richard eventually began to take out his ruined frustrations on the only ones available to him. It began with a single slap across Rhonda's face followed by love bombing and tears and sorrow. But, over time, it became more slapping and less of everything else. It spilled over to Meg and eventually Julie. Richard was a wretch of a man.

The only good thing he ever did was get a vasectomy after Julie was born. Which was a horrible thing, because it made him feel like there were no consequences to having sex. Since he could no longer create children, he didn't have to be careful.

For awhile, he was able to land a local bar fly or two without much effort. But, as he became known in the bar community, his reputation spread. It became harder for him to go home with someone. Plus, he didn't have the money to drink at the bar every weekend. So, he turned to the only ones that couldn't shut him down or walk out on him.

Rhonda and the girls were terrorized by Richard. They never knew when he would blow up or get horny. Either way, they didn't want him around. Even when he wasn't at his worst, he wasn't good. Between beatings and rape sessions, it was the worst life imaginable for Meg and Julie to be born into.

When Rhonda died, it didn't get better. Richard didn't find Jesus or the light. He was the same rotted shell of a pathetic man he had been. Only now, he didn't have a wife. And he didn't have any hope of finding a new wife. The girls were trapped in a living hell.

Meg had plans to run away with Julie as soon as she could find a way to have money and a place to go. Ester had no intentions of allowing young girls to attend the After Party. But, when she met Meg in Krisis, she quickly realized that Meg as not a girl. She was forced to become a woman way too early in life. She was not a kid. She was a grown up victim in kids clothes.

Even with all that Meg was suffering, Ester could not allow her to get involved in the Grand Finale. She would have to sit out on the killing spree. She was under strict orders to run, hide and save herself as soon as she knew that the After Party was coming for her father, and get Julie into a protected place.

A protected place? Meg had been asking about shelters and restraining orders and emancipation. She thought there were places to go and people to help for anyone in her position. She was too young to know that society makes it sound like there's help. But, there's really red tape. And there's nothing to prevent the damage. The laws and courts and advocates are only there to clean up afterwards. Being under age, she had no real options.

No. Ester wasn't going to let her learn about killing. She was going to encourage the children to endure, because she could promise that the end would be coming. Ester gave them her personal promise that she would make sure Richard would never hurt them again once the day of judgment came. She would not allow those girls to be shuffled around the system and split up or end up in the hands of someone just as bad. She would not allow the court to sentence them back to that encampment of torment. Nope. Ester promised the girls freedom. They just had to do whatever they had to do to survive till the Grand Finale. On that day, Richard would never hurt them again. Ester promised.

Sam was the fulfillment of that promise.

She was still riding high on the adrenaline from killing the Fredricks when they pulled into Richard's drive way. Sam was already keyed up like an assassin in the midst of the mission. But...

Richard was drunk that evening. He was beating and raping his daughters. And Sam showed up. Samantha began crying instantly. Barbara and Sondra couldn't keep up with Sam. The moment she heard the screaming and crying, Richard only had moments to live.

Sam was on his back like a spider monkey beating on him. He was still strong enough to pull her off and smack her across the room. That's when Barbara made it into the house and shot him in the hip.

Sondra said, "OOOOOHHH! That's gotta hurt!"

Barbara replied, "I was actually aiming for his dick."

Sam had regained her footing and fury. Meg and Julie were too injured and too scared to move. They watched in horror as Sam smashed their dad's face into the floor over and over. She kicked him in the head and neck and stomped on his back and chest.

Just when everyone watching thought it was over and Sam had worked out all of her rage, she slipped out to the car. She came back with the rope. She tied it around his neck and demanded that her three cohorts in crime help drag him out the door. Meg and Julie felt a strange, terrified relief as his their father was removed from their prison home.

Sam laid under the car and tied the rope around the axle. Sondra started to question Sam, but Sam's face made it clear that asking anything was a bad idea at that moment. They all knew exactly what was about to happen.

Sam dragged Richard around the block by the neck behind the car going as fast as she could. When she pulled back into the house, he was just a bloody, lifeless mess. But, after cutting the rope loose from the car, she still shot his remains in the head.

The other three women of the After Party silently got back in the car and waited. Sam went into Meg and Julie. She hugged them and cried with them. And reminded them of the strict orders from Ester to make sure that when someone came to investigate Richard's death, they were to ONLY tell them that Ester did it. Nothing else. No other names. No explanations. Just that Ester did it.

She told them to clean up and dress nice. She gave them what money she had and said they should walk somewhere to get something decent to eat. And then, she gave them one more hug with the promise fulfilled that that man would never hurt them again. And that they should NOT go look at him.

The women drove back to camp in mortified silence. Except for Sam. She seemed to be glowing. It wasn't a happy glow. She just seemed... proud.

Chapter 33: The Hessons

The Hessons were the all American classic rich family. Ansel was a big wig at a good, solid company making lots of money with incredible benefits. Madeline had taken up real estate once the kids were older and spending more time in school. She discovered that she was really good at it. She was doing really well. Her income allowed them to take some incredible vacations to Caribbean islands and foreign countries.

Arlin was the stereotype spoiled rich boy growing up on the lake. The genetics of a basketball scholarship father and prom queen mother were incredibly unfair in his favor. He was tall, muscular and handsome as any movie star had ever been. He drove ski boats and rode jet skis all summer. He went on ski trips and snowmobiling expeditions in the winter. Anything he wanted was always at his disposal. He literally had just about everything going for him. He had an easy, dreamy life.

His sister, Deborah, was much the same. She was gorgeous, popular, and athletic. They always had plenty of friends. They were always invited to everything when they weren't hosting the best parties. They were always welcome everywhere. And they were mean.

The Hesson children grew up in a rich home with everything they could ever want. People wanted to be accepted by them and wanted to be their friends. Being born, bred and educated in the world of the wealthy, they learned fairly young that people would go along with just about anything they suggested. They discovered that people would do just about anything for them. People wanted to be liked by the Hessons so they could enjoy the riches and good life that surround that family.

Raith and Arlin were in the same grade. She was shocked

when he invited her to a pool party at his house the summer after their senior year. She was fairly sure that she wasn't ugly. But, she was invisible to him. She had a hard time believing that she was pretty enough for Arlin Hesson to invite her to his house. He had barely acknowledged her most of their school days since seventh grade. She wondered why he suddenly invited her.

But, he was so sweet and sincere in inviting her. He explained that he always kind of liked her, but was low key about it because of his parents. Now, he was older and more confident and able to make his own decisions. He no longer cared what his parents thought. He liked her, and he wanted her at his party.

It was a typical first opportunity to make a great impression for Raith. She spent way too much time picking out a swimsuit and doing her hair. She was equal parts nervous and excited. She thought it was a little odd that Mr. and Mrs. Hesson were extremely warm and kind when meeting her at the door. But, she wrote it off as rich people just being polite regardless of their feelings.

As more and more people arrived, Raith got pushed further and further from Arlin. It was frustrating, but she understood that he was popular and already had a lot of friends. She was an outsider. She was getting uncomfortable to the point of nearly ready to leave. Some of the boys had been staring at her, and with no one to stand beside her, she was ready to get out of there. She was feeling too vulnerable.

While she was looking for the opportunity to excuse herself and run, Deborah popped up beside her. She introduced herself as Arlin's older sister and that she was happy to see a "real person" at the party. She explained that a lot of rich kids can be predictable and boring, just talking about their parent's money. It was always a bragging competition of dollars.

Deborah seemed genuine. She sounded like she really wanted to talk to Raith and get to know her. Looking back, she should have realized that it was too good to be true.

Deborah led Raith away from the pool so they could talk more. They went to the entertainment room on the lower level of the house and sat on the couch with drinks and a bowl of chips. As they talked, Raith noticed that her hostess was getting more comfortable and moving slightly closer. She was facing Raith more and smiling and tilting her head. It was as if she was flirting with Raith.

Raith finally asked, "Deborah, I have to ask a really weird and awkward question, and I hope you can forgive me, but.... if I didn't know better, I'd think you were flirting with me. Are you flirting with me?"

Deborah smiled with bright eyes. "Yes. I thought you'd never catch on!"

Raith silently slipped into shock. She turned to face straight ahead at the giant TV. She couldn't believe what was happening. She couldn't stand up. Her head was getting spinny. Deborah was beginning to look a little cartoonish. She had never been roofied before. But, as they say, there's a first time for everything. She just never believed it would be by a girl.

From there, she only remembered bits and pieces and strange faces. She vaguely remembered handcuffs at one point. She had the bruises to confirm that she wasn't hallucinating about those. It was surreal. She knew that people from the party were doing all sorts of sexual things to rape her, but she couldn't stop anyone. She faded in and out of consciousness. She knew. But it was all a blurry, horrible dream.

When she woke up, she was naked between Arlin's naked, drunken parents. She was still loopy. She stumbled and fumbled to find a towel in the bathroom. She had to pee really bad. The feeling of semen oozing out of her when she sat was horrifyingly disgusting. She couldn't cry. Her feelings felt broken and confused. She just needed to get out.

She found her way out wearing only a towel and managed to make it home. She soaked in the longest, hottest shower she could. She finally began to cry as she dried and dressed. She went to the police station where she couldn't tell them who or how many raped her at the party that she willingly attended. She had showered, so they told her she destroyed whatever evidence she might have had. They told her they could only file her report, but there would likely be no investigation.

She eventually figured out that she had been set up by one of the wealthiest and best connected families in the area. They had baited her and led her in so they could rape her for fun. She wasn't sure if the parents had raped her. She remembered Arlin and some of his friends. But, she would never forget Deborah spiked her drink to give them all the chance with her body. She was pretty sure she remembered Deborah touching and kissing her at some point. But, it was all sketchy, messy memories.

She went to be treated at the hospital. She needed a few stitches down there. And she was told that there could be some long term damage because she had been raped so violently by several offenders. Only time would tell.

And time did tell. She would always have trouble with physical intimacy and sex. She would most likely need a hysterectomy before she was thirty. And the psychological damage was beyond description. The term "trust issues" wasn't big enough to cover it.

When Raith became a part of the After Party, she nearly quit. She was revolted at dredging up all those partial memories that were attached to such completely despicable feelings. But, Ester had a way of making her feel like something good would happen if she stayed. Ester gave her a tiny fingerhold in the hope of pulling herself back up, like there could be real hope and comfort. Raith was given the possibility of escaping this life sentence of guilt and shame.

The After Party gave her hope and real acceptance. The Grand Finale gave her a promise. Raith was hooked on the promise of justice. She might not have been able to get to everyone that deserved it. But, that family would feel her wrath. They should suffer and die so she could feel that justice was delivered. She wanted to repay them for what they did. And she had learned that she was not the only one they did it to.

As badly as Raith wanted to kill them herself, she was pretty sure that they would have cameras and might recognize her. So, she elected to let the team of Larry, Megan, Lily, Michelle and Candy go to the Hesson house. Besides, since she didn't know who all attacked her, it seemed to be a somewhat fitting and poetic justice that they would also not know who was attacking them without provocation or why.

After they had killed Conner Cain, the team dispatched Lily's

Roger and Megan's Sam on the way to the Hessons. That gave Ester time to get there first.

They needed Ester to get in the door. They needed that sweet, little, old lady to disarm and distract the family for them. The kids had gotten married. So, Ester could get the alarms turned off by being there and get the spouses to leave before Larry and the women pulled up.

It almost worked. Deborah's husband refused to leave the side of his pregnant wife. Arlin's wife left the family dinner immediately when Ester waved the gun. Ansel thought he might disarm the tiny, old woman because he had trained in Jiu-Jitsu. What he didn't train for was Ester. Ester wasn't about to let anyone get close enough to disarm her. So, as soon as he started inching towards her, talking the whole time, trying to get close enough to lunge, she shot him.

Ester wasn't a professional hit-man, so it wasn't a kill shot. She wounded him. But, it was a lucky hit for her. Larry's team came running in immediately after the gun shot along with Hirra and Carissa

Ester looked at Deborah's husband and shook her head. She told him, "You poor, dumb bastard. I gave you a chance to live. How did she ever land such a fine and noble man as yourself? You really did deserve better."

The man looked confused. "What?"

Ester probed, "You didn't know she drugged young girls for her brother and parents to rape? Or were you one of those that was here on one of those days taking advantage of a poor girl? Maybe there were too many girls to remember any one in particular? Maybe you would never remember because there were too many."

The kill team was already emotional and outraged enough. Lily gently touched Ester's arm to lower her gun. The show down was tense. There was a moral dilemma. Deborah was pregnant. She appeared to be much more than half way along.

Megan asked, "Ester. What do we do about the pregnant one?"

Ester looked at Megan with discernment and concern. She replied, "That child would be born into a swarm of monsters and learn to become a monster." Deborah began to cry. Ester continued unfazed. "No baby deserves that. And no monster deserves a baby. Monsters should not be allowed to reproduce."

Ester told Deborah to stop crying and asked her, "Do you believe that abortion is a woman's right?"

"What?" the crying woman asked with confusion.

Ester repeated the question. Madeline tried to intercede. Ester raised the gun at her. Deborah responded with confusion saying she didn't understand why that mattered here and now.

"This will be the last time I ask," Ester stated. "Does a woman have the unequivocal right to abortion?" Tearfully, Deborah nodded.

Ester asked the same question to the mother, who snapped back, "Of course she does! But, you have no right..."

Ester turned while the mom was yelling and shot Deborah in the baby.

As the screaming subsided, Ester said, "That ends that debate. Problem solved."

Arlin tried to run, but Larry snatched him right up.

Hirra attacked Madeline. It was a very short battle ending when Madeline's neck broke.

Candy jumped at Ansel and cut his arms as many times as she could before finally going for his neck. She thought about how it was a little unfair for him that Ester shot him. But, he deserved it and it worked in her favor. She cut his neck again, as deep as she could. Then, she used all of her weight to drive the knife into his temple all the way to the hilt.

Ester had allowed Deborah to bleed out.

Arlin always acted like he was a big stud, but when Larry was holding him, he was screaming like a scared, little girl. Megan and Lily undid and removed his pants. He was completely helpless against Larry. And he knew it. Everyone knew it. And Arlin really was scared about what was about to happen to him.

Larry re-positioned himself to Arlin's side and Carissa tapped Arlin in the nut sack to bend him over as Michelle brought a toilet plunger out of the bathroom. Arlin's screaming changed in pitch and intensity as she centered the end of the wooden handle on his anus. The noises he made as she forced the dry wood into his rectum were almost indescribable. It could best be described as the sound of a thousand regrets mangled into one voice.

They let him fall on his face and flop like a fish for minute while he tried to remove it. Michelle remarked, "Kind of ironic that a tool for unclogging shit has been stuck where the sun don't shine and packed his shit."

Even Ester gave her a dirty look as they all judged her for that corny line.

Larry finally knelt down, placed his big hands around Arlin's throat and squeezed the life out of him. They left him face down with his pants around his ankles and a plunger up his ass.

Deborah's husband was standing solid as a statue. He wasn't moving. He was barely breathing. He didn't appear to be blinking.

Ester suddenly looked up at him and said, "Oh! I'm sorry, young man. I really am. I came in first, alone, hoping you would be spared. But, you were too good of a man to leave her. And that's probably because you didn't know who and what she really was."

The man who had just witnessed the vigilante murder of the town's most horrible, rich family raised his hands in surrender. He said with fear and tears, "She only told me that if I ever saw the DVDs, she'd have to divorce me. I thought it was a joke. I had no idea what she and her family ever did."

Ester replied, "Oh, there's DVDs? We'll find them. But, I'm sorry you stayed. Because we can't leave a witness like you here."

Ester and everyone with a gun put two shots into the man. He collapsed in a bloody pile to complete the massacre of the

Hesson family of rapists.

Larry quickly smashed through walls until he found the hidden control room. Once they exposed the recording network and the dozens of discs that the Hessons had made of victims, the After Party's work was done. They left the bodies on the floor and furniture.

They walked out and got back into the cars. They went their separate ways. But, Larry's kill team went to Larry's house.

Larry stepped out of the car and began yelling for his father to come out and face him like a man. As he walked towards the house, the women got out of the car.

The older man came to the door and slapped it open. He was just a big as Larry. There was a resemblance with graying hair. He was loud and rude and crude. He was obviously angry and appeared to be full of violent intentions. He was screaming and pointing at Larry as he leaned on the rail at the end of the porch.

Larry walked towards the loud, angry man without a word. The women slowly began to move in behind Larry. They stopped, frozen in their tracks when Larry got to the the porch and began shooting his father in the chest.

No words. No speech. No fight. No warning. Larry just opened fire. He put every bullet he had in the chest of the man that had tormented him. Then, he reloaded and shot every round of the second magazine into the dead man's face and head.

Larry's younger brother was standing in the open doorway with open mouth and wide eyes. Larry told him, "You didn't see anything. You were never out here. You know nothing. You hear me? Go back in. Forget that this man ever lived. He's never going to hurt us again. And you have no idea who did this. Got me?"

His brother nodded and slowly retreated into the house. Larry stomped back to the car and stopped in front of the women and said, "He wasn't worth the fight. We fought all the time, he just needed to die. And he never gave us a chance. He never fought fair"

The girls all nodded. They all piled back into the car in quiet and headed for the campground.

Chapter 34: Tammy

The kill team of Tammy, Serena, Randi and Onna were doing well until they weren't. They had killed the judge without incident. Then, they killed Onna's boyfriend, Henry. Since he was a mechanic, he was pretty easy to find.

Onna shot Henry in the leg while he was under a car, then explained why she was lowering the jack to crush him. It was just a symbol of how he had been crushing the life out of her for years. She told him it was nothing personal, just something that had to be done. They left his body pinned under a 2007 Cadillac. No one asked what exactly she meant when talking to him before releasing the jack. They knew.

Perry was an EMT. He was the only first responder on the list who wasn't a cop. But, he had beaten and abused the other Michelle in the After Party long enough and bad enough to earn a spot in the Grand Finale.

Michelle Randell was the quiet, nervous type. As a late comer, she was definitely not the killing type, but, she was solid about her resolve that he deserved to die. She just couldn't do it herself. The After Party had some doubts. They were not sure of her. A few felt that if there was going to be someone who blew everything out of the water and turned them into the police, it would be her. However, when she told about Perry's drunken confession that he often would sneak a peek down a victim's blouse or feel them up "accidentally on purpose," that was the tipping point. Perry was unanimously invited to the Grand Finale, and Michelle Randell promised her silence.

They wanted to do something grandiose and fitting for Perry, like administer every drug available in the back of his ambulance to him. However, they had to settle for just shooting and stabbing him to death at his home in his recliner. They pulled up, walked in, and did him in without any problems.

The glitch came at Tammy's house. Ricardo Ibarra was a mean man. He was very manly. He was fast and strong. And he ruled his house like he was king of his castle.

Ricardo acted like he owned Tammy. She was his servant. He usually only referred to her as "woman." He would command her by yelling, "Woman! Get me my dinner. Woman, come here and suck my dick. Woman, clean this place up before I beat your ass!"

When Tammy met him, she loved how strong and independent he was. He didn't listen to anyone. No one could tell him what to do. He was a true bad boy on a motorcycle. But, he was good to her. He protected her and treated her well.

It was once they got married that he began to change. In reality, once they were married, according to his friends and family, he wasn't changing. He was finally relaxing to be himself.

How did she miss all that? How could she have been so blind? He wasn't a bad boy with a good heart for her. He was just a bad man who had pretended to be everything she wanted him to be so he could own her. He played along with her dreams long enough to get her to give herself to him. And once she was his, he wasn't letting go.

Neighbors had commented that even a dog got better treatment than Tammy did. But, no one would dare talk to Ricardo about his attitude or treatment of his woman. One neighbor tried. He never tried again after getting punched in the face. Especially, when the police did nothing about the "misunderstanding."

Tammy endured a live of slavery. She had fallen for the make believe life he promised her. And once she was in his castle, there was no prince coming to save her. She was the cook, maid and sex toy. He used her any way he wanted to whenever he wanted to.

He was such a horrible husband, that when one of his buddies was feeling lonely and sad because of a divorce, Ricardo invited him over for drinks. Once they were drunk, Ricardo forced Tammy to have sex with his buddy. He didn't want the guy to feel bad. So, he made her have sex with the man. He didn't care that she protested. He didn't care what she felt. He didn't even care what she said. In fact, he told her that if she didn't do what he told her to do, he would give her a beating worse than any he had given before.

Ricardo was a terrible husband. He wasn't a good man. He was pretty awful. And the After Party had him in their sights.

When the kill team pulled up, Ricardo came out of his house, drunk, with a gun in his hand. He was yelling that she had run away to go that retreat even though he told her she wasn't allowed to go. And now he was going to teach her not to disobey him.

Everyone in the After Party knew he was dangerous. They had all heard all the stories. Tammy made them stay in the car as she approached him with a gun hidden in her jacket pocket with her hand on the trigger. She and her husband stood in the lights of the car like they were on an old western street ready for a gun fight.

The girls in the car watched hand and arm movements spell out an argument of epic proportions. They watched heads nod and shake while fingers were pointing. Shoulders shrugged and their postures got more rigid. Neither was going to back down this time. They could hear the arguing voices, but most of the words were indistinguishable. It didn't matter what was being said. They all had been in arguments of their own. They had a pretty good idea what was being said.

When Tammy's gun came out, tension in the car hit an all time high. The couple was now in a stand off with guns pointed at each other. They were screaming and nervous. The women in the car had hands on the handles, but were hesitant to open the doors.

It was minutes. It felt like hours. It went quickly. It was in slow motion. It was the most surreal engagement any of them had ever experienced.

Ricardo began to stand upright and relaxed. He was telling her that she wouldn't hurt him. She would never shoot. Doors opened from inside the car.

Tammy fired at Ricardo. He flinched as she missed him. She fired a second shot, but now he had dropped to one knee and taken aim. As the girls flew out of the car screaming, the bullet from Ricardo's gun hit Tammy square in the chest.

He didn't seem to notice the women coming at him as the reality of shooting and killing his wife instantly began to register and sink in. Ricardo stood up and lowered his gun. It rocked loosely in his hand at the end of his swinging arm. Slowly, he looked towards the screaming women rushing him from the car that had brought his wife to him. He looked confused as they raised their guns and opened fire on him. The first few shots whizzed past him. He began to snap out of the trance and tried to return fire, but a bullet hit his arm that held the gun. He lost his weapon as the women continued to shoot and bear down on him.

He started dancing around in pain. But, as the women got closer, more bullets hit him. They shot him in the back, the side, the leg, the other arm, and the belly. They had all ran out of bullets as he dropped to the ground. The enraged women began kicking him and pistol whipping him until he stopped moving.

They moved away from him. He started to grown and move. Onna had already claimed his gun. With tears running down her screaming face, she fired every bullet left in his magazine into his evil face.

They were a mess. They were hot and bloody from beating him. They were crying in disbelief. They had allowed their friend to die. They failed. They sat and held the hands of their fallen team mate. They needed a few minutes with her before they could do anything.

Neighbors were watching. One started coming towards them. Serena reloaded her gun and ran to meet him. The man held his hands in the air. He was trying to tell her that he knew Ricardo was a horrible man and wanted to know if there was anything he could do to help.

Serena addressed him. "You saw nothing. You saw no one.

You make sure NO ONE on this street saw anything. Leave his sorry ass in the mud. No one touch him. Let the vultures eat him. If you're serious and you want to help, then keep your mouth shut about what happened here and don't tell the police anything." she turned away then back. "Can you remember Ester?"

He nodded and gave her two thumbs up with his hands still over his head. She backed away and ran to help get Tammy's body into the car. The man went back to his house.

The team drove Tammy's body to the hospital through their tears. They pulled up to the door of the emergency room and laid her body on the cement. Then, they piled in quickly and sped off as someone in scrubs came to the door. Tammy was taken into the E.R. The car of women was drowning in tears of disbelief all the way back to the campground.

The After Party had lost one woman earlier to a broken neck from her abuser. And now they lost another to her abuser who shot her. It was hard to call the Grand Finale a success. But, they had, in fact, successfully eliminated many abusers that night. Vengeance and justice were dispensed to the fullest measure.

The final hour at the campground was somber. They showered, changed and cleaned up the buildings in near silence. The reality hadn't fully set in yet, let alone the aftermath and consequences of their killing spree. This was the lull in between storm surges. These women were in transition from normal, abused housewives and lovers who were desperate to escape the horrors of abuse to women who had killed. They were barely on the edge of realizing that they were all murderers.

Did they really just kill a bunch of people? Like for real? They were focused on how they were going to go home to murder scenes. How were they supposed to act going home to murder scenes *that they created*? How could they keep from saying anything that incriminated them? How were they supposed to act innocent? What would that even look like?

Questions flooded their minds. Their skulls were too packed with worry and questions to feel anything yet, or to even talk. It was kind of a numb feeling, but really more like a vibrating feeling. It was like they were jittery, but too overwhelmed to speak about it.

There was some fear that someone in the group might talk. Someone might betray them and turn them in. They all knew that no one was supposed to tattle, but they also knew that there's always someone weak. There's always someone who can't stop themselves. Someone would get drunk or stoned and run their mouth. They were scared. They just couldn't talk about it.

As they finished cleaning up, and gathered at the vehicles, Ester delivered her final speech of Ester's Retreat. She gave the final instructions from the Grand Finale. And she admonished the After Party for the last time to only point all fingers at her and she left them. Each left for their own home and crime scene as the After Party was officially disbanded.

Ester stood alone under a slightly cloudy sky at her home. She worried about what would happen to her girls. But, she took comfort in knowing that she had done everything in her power to make sure that they would never have to face their abusers again. There were times she was sure that it would fall apart. She could see all the weakness that threatened to have them all running back into the arms of their abusers. She had been sure they would cave. There were times she didn't know what to say or do to get through to them. The plan was always on the cusp of failure. Ester was always standing on the edge of despair, expecting to watch the women crawl back into their individual POW camps.

Tammy's death was a terrible tragedy. Every commander has to know that casualties are part of war. And Ester was in a war against their weakness and the abusers who exploited that. Nothing can truly prepare anyone for losing a friend and companion. Ester was no exception. She cried for Tammy. She cried hard. She cried for Susan, too. And she cried for all of them.

Ester ended up on her living room floor crying alone in the night for almost an hour for the dead, the wounded and the ones that now had to live without their "loving abuser." She cried in hopes that they could all rebuild lives that were better. She begged God to let them all be stronger and never fall back into abuse. She cried knowing that there would be a long time of consequences and repercussions for this night.

Ester finally ran out of tears. Her sorrow drained away. Her head hurt. Her body was weak. She was tired in a way that she had never felt before. So, she sat for awhile on her porch under a blanket in the cold night air until snow began to lightly flurry around her.

She finally forced herself to her feet and went back inside. She sat wiping her face and blowing her nose while she warmed up. She had actually managed to do something miraculous. She began to own the fact that she had met a group of women on their own turf of subservient humiliation and pain, and led them to a battlefield of victory over the ones that oppressed them, used them, and had beaten them down. As she thought about that, she realized that she needn't be sad. Somehow, over the course of two years, the entire saga had formed and played out without being derailed or exposed. Somehow, Ester was able to form and complete this vision.

As she thought and breathed deeply, Ester began to believe that somehow, this would all be alright. Somehow, something would happen that would allow these women to escape the legal system and it's twisted sense of justice. She became quite certain that real justice would win this once.

That's when she got the idea.

Chapter 35: Ester Takes the Long Way Home

Ester Wireman.

Ninety five year old lady.

Tiny in stature. Barely able to see over the dashboard.

Lovable grandmotherly woman who started a children's outreach ministry.

Ester Wireman was the mastermind of a one of a kind mass murder. And she felt completely justified.

Most of the time, Ester felt like she was just lucky. Every time things looked about to go off the rails, something kept things on track. But, now that she was able to see her mission through to the end, she felt like there was one more thing to do to top it all off. There was one way that Ester could make sure that everyone gave her the credit or blame for the entire Grand Finale.

She got back in her car and Ester headed to the nearest crime scene that she and her girls made. She had already mapped out each of the houses and trailers where someone would be found dead. She was fairly sure that there would be no law enforcement running around, so she wasn't worried about speed limits or getting stopped.

One by one, Ester visited the dead. The closest one was Ricardo. When she pulled up, she could see a few of the neighbors staring. So, she called for them to come closer so she could introduce herself.

The man who had been sent home with two thumbs up saw Ester and didn't know what to think. He and a couple of the other men had been sitting in lawn chairs drinking beer and waiting for the law enforcement that wasn't coming. They approached the little old lady with curious caution.

"Hello. I'm Ester Wireman," she said. "I was wondering if any of you knew what had happened here?"

One of the men began to ramble about the shoot out, but another guy smacked his ribs and said "that must be Ester."

"Uh, huh," Ester said. "Get this through your heads right now, boys. I'm Ester, and I killed this bastard. No one else was here. Understand me?"

The men looked at each other with confusion as Ester walked closer to the body. She pulled out her gun and shot the corpse. The men jumped and stood ready to run in panic, but were frozen in fear and confusion.

Ester said loudly, "I killed this man! Did anyone see anything else?"

The men answered, "NO, Ma'am!" in unison.

Ester turned to face the men with the gun in her crossed hands in front of her. "If I hear that anyone tells the police anything else, I'll be back. Now, make sure the rest of the neighbors know."

The men nodded furiously and scurried. Ester smiled. She thought that she could get used to having this much authority. But, she had a long way to go.

Despite being sleepy and ragged, Ester visited each of the places where her girls had left dead bodies and reenacted that scene with Ricardo's body and neighbors. In some cases, she had to shoot the body on the gurney of the

EMTs. The medics were confused as to whether or not they could move the bodies since there was no law enforcement to investigate the scenes. So, Ester had no problem tracking them all down. By morning, Ester had been to every single site and put a bullet in every single body. Almost all of them.

Ester had made it clear to everyone she could reach, that she and she alone was responsible for the deaths around the area of Sharone, Ohio. She gave no reason. She explained nothing. She only demanded cooperation.

When Ester finally got home, she went to the bathroom. Then, she crawled into her bed, fully clothed and fell asleep on top of the covers. She was exhausted, but, she could sleep. She was done. She was at peace. She had done what she had set out to do. Ester had nothing left to prove in life.

She was able to sleep like a rock from the wee hours till about mid-morning when Sergeant Murtle came knocking on her door informing her that the state police wanted her help. It was the best wake up call she had experienced in decades.

Ester asked Sergeant Murtle to wait for her to get cleaned up and dressed properly. This also gave her time to make sure she was fully prepared to meet the man in charge of her investigation. She wanted to be sure he got the facts straight.

Chapter 36: The Police Response

When the first call came in, police knew what to do. They were trained. They had been training on a regular schedule. They were well trained, well equipped and well prepared. They were ready for the first call. What they were NOT prepared for was the second, third, fourth, fifth calls and those beyond.

The night of the Grand Finale was the most bizarre night in Sharone, Ohio's history for the police. The small city wasn't without crime. They even had a couple of murders in their past long ago. But, when the call came in about something going on at the Sheriff's house, no one was prepared for what unfolded.

The first call of something wrong was when a couple of stoned teens looked into Zach's squad car and he didn't wake up. They began messing with the radio and trying to turn on the lights and siren. The closest officer in the area discovered the body and called it over the radio immediately. This brought in every officer from any place even remotely close to the scene of Zach's car. One was Tim Ollunden, who was off duty, but lived close.

The neighbor who had nearly interrupted Barbara while she was killing her husband, didn't call 911 right away. In fact, he called his brother and had him call after the women had left. This caused the 911 calls to arrive close together at the dispatch switch board.

While there were more and more officers from sheriff and police gathering around Zach's car, the 911 call about Sheriff Justin broke over the radio. People were racing to the their cars when the call about Deputy Tom Burns came right on the heels of it. The 911 calls were beginning almost at the same time.

As the calls quickly mounted, those on the scene at Zach's patrol car began to freeze up. Any officers who were en route to investigate, stopped. They just pulled over and stopped. The mounting 911 calls were quickly becoming a mountain of calls. The officers began to wonder if they were being led into an ambush. Radio chatter became a wild conjecture about a plot to kill all law enforcement. And then came the call about the one with drugs on the table.

Whatever was happening was not something they were prepared for. And since they had zero information with no way to begin to see the big picture, they were blinded by the forest for all the trees in the way. They couldn't even begin to understand what was happening. They began to panic.

Those first 911 calls were all dead law enforcement. Then, the call about the mayor being attacked and killed came in. Everyone in uniform jumped to the "obvious" immediate conclusion that they were all a target. Each of them could be next to die. They believed that they were under attack. They ALL believed that they were *under attack*. Even most of the other first responders were nervous and worried, even though, eventually, Perry would be the only EMT dead. Fire and rescue crews and ambulance drivers began to refuse to respond.

That was exactly what Ester was hoping for. She wasn't sure she could count on it, but she was hoping for it. By killing all the police and deputies who created victims that found their way into Ester's care, she was hoping that the rest of those in positions of protection and power violating trust would know what it felt like to be scared and have no trust. And by making sure that the sheriff was first, she was hoping there would be confusion throughout the ranks. For once, she was thankful for all the war movies her late husband had made her watch. And she was thankful for all the crime dramas and documentaries she was able to watch after his passing that had given her valuable strategy and insight.

She would later become thankful for how much better the police response panned out compared to what she was hoping for. She simply wanted enough time and confusion to allow her girls to complete their missions and get home. They granted her so much more.

Sergeant Murtle decided that he needed to start making leadership decisions. The chief of police was on vacation in Wyoming and the sheriff was reported as dead. He was the next highest ranking officer in the county with the most seniority. He was relying on his experience while in the army. He was concerned that in some foreign territories, a small attack would be launched in order to draw troops and first responders to the scene where a larger wave of explosions and attacks would be initiated.

The first knee jerk reaction to the 911 calls was for all officers on duty to respond and for all those off duty to stand by. Things changed quickly as the calls flooded in. Those already on duty were ordered to report to the police headquarters downtown and dress in riot gear. The town was too small to have a S.W.A.T team, so they immediately called for their marksmen to report as soon as possible with their favorite weapon. The sheriff's team was to transport the inventory of their armory to the city building and close ranks with the police.

By the time all law enforcement was gathered at the city's

core, the Grand Finale was finished. But, the panicked calls were still coming in frantically. By the time the 911 calls were starting to slow down, the After Party was home, blending into the river of callers.

Ester was a 95 year old mastermind. Simply by using a logical order to the elimination of abusers based on job description, she was able to clear the roads of all police for her kill teams to travel freely. In fact, every team had been passed by at least one patrol car while moving from house to house. And it was clear that all of those cops were way more interested in going somewhere in a hurry than they were with the women in the cars driving around killing people.

The city police building was full of law enforcement in body armor. And there was lots of pizza. Because, naturally, if there's any chance of imminent danger that could force a full lock down, there needs to be enough food in the building for a couple of days. To the army veteran, pizza seemed to be the most logical choice to make on the spot.

It was estimated that there were almost two large pizzas per person in the building. There was a variety of pies delivered from a variety of parlors. In fact, there were pizzas from every joint in town. Why? Because one giant order to one place would take longer and risk the store not being able to fulfill the requests. And once all food and drink was delivered, Murtle intended to "shut the place up like the Lord did to Noah's ark."

Once the final pizza was delivered, the city police building went into full tactical lock down. All windows and doors were blacked out and barricaded. All officers were assigned lanes of fire and surveillance. Watch and rotation lists were drawn up as teams were defined. Rest periods were designated. And so the night had begun for the law enforcement community of Sharone.

There were no sirens chasing the gun shots. There weren't even any traffic stops anywhere. There were no speed traps, no random patrols and no police presence. Other than the city building, there was no sign of law enforcement anywhere. Once the killing stopped, it was a very slow crime night.

All night long, the police HQ resembled a sort of combat bunker. Some officers kept watch while others ate or slept. All of them tried to appear confident despite being nervous. Conversation was minimal. Every ear was tuned to the radios waiting to hear some shred of usable information.

By 4am, it appeared that the police were hiding in fear from a threat that did not exist. 911 calls had died down long before. Nothing more seemed to be happening, and the city seemed uncomfortably quiet.

Jacobs and Murr were assigned to one truck. Washington and Prewskowski were given the other truck. The decision to send only the trucks to perform recon seemed reasonable. Two teams would follow a mapped route around the city and surrounding area to survey the situation. One team would follow fifteen minutes behind the other. The idea was that once police presence was seen by the public, any "bad guys" might be flushed out where the second team could spot them. All four men felt like there were going to be rolling targets.

The patrols went out. They followed their prescribed map. And they returned without incident. So, around 6am, Murtle called the state police post to request help after sorting through the call log and counting up the number of possible crime scenes. The State Highway Patrol hung up on Murtle four times before they finally confirmed that he was not calling in a hoax. It took great effort to communicate that he was a real police officer with a dead sheriff and 33 other crime scenes. Then, he was filtered through several layers of red tape. He was finally put through to Major Tatum who actually listened to Murtle explain what little he knew. Major Tatum assigned Captain Bucklem.

Captain Bucklem arrived in Sharone (after his hour plus drive) to find that he was placed in charge of the town's only mass murder since it's incorporation. It was the largest mass murder of his career. The only other one he had been part of was six bodies, and there was only one killer. And outside of a train derailment, no one he knew had even heard of anything that could compare to what he was walking into.

Upon arrival, he met the surviving law enforcement members. Shortly after, he was introduced to Ester per his request for a historian. During that hour and a half, Bucklem was trying to imagine if there was any real and logical way to handle this investigation. All he could do was resolve himself to the fact that he would have to work it piece by piece as the pieces were presented and hope they all fit.

Once he was sure that there was no clear and present danger, or at least it seemed that no one was actively hunting down everyone with a badge, Bucklem ordered teams of two to visit each of the crime scenes. The dispatchers had been setting up a hand scribbled spreadsheet of sorts to help make sense of the nearly two hundred 911 calls. They were able to coordinate with EMT and paramedic units to arrive at the same scenes.

State troopers were rolling in from all over. When asked about support from the National Guard, Bucklem said that he would only consider it if the unit was from at least two counties away.

He didn't feel like anyone near Sharone could be trusted.

Trust is a funny thing. People survive on it. They trust the other drivers, ALL of them, to stay on their own side of the road and obey traffic laws in the same, consistent manner. They trust their neighbors to be decent humans, or at least not a menace. No one wants to live next to someone that makes everyone worry that they'll burn the whole neighborhood down. Trust is shared and compounded. The more trust is shared and confirmed, the more trust is validated and given. It's also expected. Shoppers are trusted to pay for things they pick up.

But, because a few people steal, loss prevention is paid for to ensure that people can be trusted more. After all, if there are consequences for betrayal of trust, people are less likely to violate the trust, because the end result is very negative and very undesirable. Stealing is considered a violation of honesty and integrity. Doing so may result in fines or jail time.

Lying betrays trust and the result is that the liar is never trusted again. Every statement from their mouth will always be questioned. Children are trusted to clean their room. If they fail to keep that trust, punishment may be rendered in various ways from time out to denial of treats to spanking.

People are trusted not to kill other people. And the consequences for murder are quite severe. It could even result in forfeiture of the life of the perpetrator. Whether it be through electric chair or imprisonment, choosing to kill a person also ends the life of the killer. It's the trade off of a life for a life. It would seem to be a substantial enough penalty to deter murder.

But, what is a life worth if it's stolen? What is the value in living if it's at the cost of merely existing? Life can be meaningless and devoid of worthiness if it's reduced to forced servitude. Is not a person imprisoned if they have no choice of their own, only those choices made by the one controlling them?

Should there not be consequences for enslaving someone? Slavery is certainly stealing someone's life from them, from what they wanted to be, or from what they could have been. Once a person's freedoms are removed, their only freedom is that they are free to reevaluate all natural laws and consequences from behind the bars of their captivity.

Trust is attained by the conscious decision to do what is collectively considered morally right. When people have free will, it becomes a pleasure to choose to do good things. They don't get satisfaction from not doing the bad things. Rather, pride and satisfaction is the individual reward of doing good. Those that do not feel forced into any decision or choice will most often claim the societal rewards that doing good works and charity lavish upon them. People speak highly of them. They are respected. They are welcomed because they are trusted.

Inversely, when free will is diminished or quelled, when a person feels that they have no choice, there is no reward. There is only the avoidance of punishment. Any human that is forced to obey, comply, or do what is commanded of them is not free. A person that does not experience freedom and the rewards of making good choices that improve the world around them does not have a reason to make any choice.

In fact, if their situation is limited enough, and they are

punished for even the smallest infraction for violating the commands of their captor, the only decisions they are inclined to make are based upon self preservation. An abusive spouse can rob their victim of life. The helpless one may be alive, but they're not living. They have no life of their own. Their only existence is trying not to be abused or killed. They have nothing of their own. Because all of their time and energy is spent satisfying their abuser. It's stolen by the wants and desires of the abuse. The victim is already dead. They are just a living shell filled with dead. They have nothing to lose. It's all been taken from them already.

And the most dangerous person on the face of the planet is the one with nothing to lose. Unfortunately for Captain Bucklem, he had no way to know that he was beginning an investigation into a bunch of abused women who felt enslaved and had nothing to lose.

Officer Zach DeGassi had been found dead in his patrol car. His body had been extracted and taken to the morgue. Which meant for Bucklem, that any chance of recovering evidence that was viable was most likely ruined by the dozen or so fellow officers that were traipsing around the scene.

Once all officers had been assigned to crime scenes, Captain Bucklem made it a priority to tend to the sheriff himself. He would trust everyone else to take care of the rest. But, as a professional virtue, he felt it was only right and respectful to check on Captain Justin himself.
On the way to the Justin residence, Bucklem began to question whether or not any of the officers from Sharone were involved as killers. It was a pretty awful thought that

drained the color from his face and left him feeling a bit queezy. He had not allowed the thought to enter his mind and affect his judgment earlier. Now, he was trying to get it out of his head. He told himself that it would simply not be logical. If any agent of the law were involved in the killings as an active participant, they would have been sniffed out their fellow officers.

But, Bucklem had not been with them locked up in HQ all night. He didn't know these people. And the next thought was the worst. What if it was the entire force doing the killing? What if they were the collective killers?

Captain Bucklem had just let his imagination run away. There was no logical way that an entire police force could become killers. Plus, they would all have to have become amazing actors. The idea that the cops were somehow the killers was just insane.

Then again, there didn't seem to be any sanity in the county at the moment. The idea of 34 dead with an unknown number of killers and no discernible motive seemed just plain insane. He couldn't imagine how insane it was going to get.

Captain Bucklem thought that he might learn valuable information by visiting the home of Sheriff Justin. Nope. He only became more confused and astounded. He was amazed that that was even possible.

First he met the 911 caller, Ben, who was the brother of Wilson Linden. He was no help. He just kept saying, "My brother said..." and kept filling in the blank. He said nothing that was not already on the 911 call.

Wilson, on the other hand, told the story of how a car pulled up and the sheriff came outside. He told how he heard very little before the gun shots, because 'they were too far away and not yelling.' He told how he remained hidden in his house because it was none of his business. But, the last thing he saw was a little, old lady getting back in her car and driving away.

The officers who had taken Wilson's statement could only shrug when Bucklem looked at them with incredulous eyes. He asked Wilson three times if he was sure. Each time it was the same answer.

Bucklem pulled his team that was investigating the scene out of ear shot from everyone. He asked, "Do you buy any of this BS?"

Deputy Warren replied, "Not really, sir. But, we don't have any other choice."

Bucklem looked at the man like a marine drill instructor about to go off an a recruit. "What do you mean, 'don't have any choice?' The man looks like he was beaten with a bat like he owed money to the mafia!"

Warren leaned over Bucklem's shoulder and hollared at Wilson, "Hey! Did you see the old lady hit him with a ball bat or anything?"

Wilson looked down and nodded before replying, "Yeeeaaahh. She sure did. Never seen an old lady so mad in all my life."

Warren and officer DiNeogun looked at Bucklem and shrugged again. The captain was obviously agitated and irate.

Bucklem growled, "Have you checked with the other neighbors. Have you done any police work?"

Officer DiNeogun said, "Yes, sir. We knocked on every door. And almost every account has been at least similar. Everyone says they saw a little, old lady shoot the man and leave. The description of the woman is consistent."

"Almost?" Bucklem as not amused.

"Yes, sir," DiNeogun said. "That's where it got weird."

Bucklem shook his head and glared with wide eyes of amazing disbelief.

Warren took it from there before Bucklem could say anything. "Ya see, sir, there was one neighbor over there, name of Christy Smith, that started to tell us about a car full of women showing up. But, that's all she said before getting a weird look on her face and changing her story. She looked at the ground and all she would say was that it was one little old lady that pulled up," He looked at his notes and continued, "'Whacked him with a bat, then shot him and drove off.' That's what we got, sir. From everyone."

Bucklem was rubbing his forehead like he had a headache and asked, "So, what made her change her tune so drastically and suddenly?"

DiNeogun answered, "We're pretty sure it was the other neighbors. When we looked around, they were all out staring at us. I think they were staring at her."

Bucklem asked, "Do you mean to tell me that a gang of women coerced all these people into telling us a fabrication about a lone, old woman murderer? And they were so effective, that the neighbors are coercing each other into telling the same lie? You gotta be kidding me!"

A third time, the officers shrugged.

Bucklem shook his head. "I don't even know what to say right now."

Warren responded with, "Neither do we, sir."

The three men stood looking at each other with blank disbelief. They were baffled. They had all been lied to by suspects in their pasts. But, they had never seen anything on this scale. Nothing like this even crossed their minds. But, now they were in the middle of it.

And Bucklem wasn't sure what "it" was that he was in the middle of. Were the cops in on it? Was there mass hysteria? Was there a vicious gang of killer women on the loose? He was beginning to understand what it might feel like to be the only sane man in an insane world. As calmly as he could, he finally asked, "Evidence? Did anyone find a bat?"

Warren pointed to the trunk of his car. "There isn't much. We gathered whatever shell casings there were and they all look the same. It looks like most of the neighbors were over here wandering around like tourists."

Bucklem stared at him for a second before dropping his head and shaking it like a wet dog.

Warren started, "We can check the casings..."

Bucklem held up a hand and sounded very angry. "Do you mean to tell me, that the neighbors are not only lying about a little old lady killing the SHERIFF, a trained professional still in good athletic shape supposedly beaten and shot to death by an old woman half his size, but that they also intentionally contaminated and corrupted the crime scene?!?!" He stared at the sheet covered corpse of his contemporary. He whispered to Justin, "Just how hated were you in this county? What did you do?"

DiNeogun hesitantly answered in defense of Justin, "Actually, he was pretty well liked."

Bucklem was glaring at DiNeogun with anger in his eyes.

DiNeogun didn't flinch. He said, "He had his problems. He was human just like anyone. But, he was a good guy. He had given me some good advice when I was new, and I ain't even one of his guys."

Bucklem simmered down and asked, "What sort of human problems might the well liked sheriff, who is now dead, have had?"

Both cops looked sheepish. DiNeogun said to Warren, "He's your boss. You do it."

Warren frowned and said, "Thanks, buddy." He cleared his throat. "Well, sometimes, he might have had a little too much to drink and would get a little rough on the wife."

"'A little too much,'" Bucklem echoed. "And 'a little rough on the wife.' Can you possibly be a little more elaborate? Like maybe you could give some details here to help us all out? How rough is 'rough on the wife?'"

Warren was now embarrassed and hated being put on the spot. He may have even felt like he was betraying his deceased boss. "I don't mean to speak ill of the dead, sir. But, he got pretty rough with her. He smacked her around pretty hard sometimes."

"'Sometimes,'" Bucklem was echoing again. "Like two times? Or two times a week? Two times a day? What is 'sometimes'? And I don't believe that he was married to this mysterious, little old lady that allegedly beat and shot him. There has to be something in the water here."

Warren begged with confusion, "Sir? What do mean by that?"

Bucklem put one hand on his hip as he rubbed his eyes and said, "Warren, this feels like some weird, mass hysteria, Twilight Zone shit. My grandpa used to watch 1950s SciFi, and that was a common theme in those old shows, large groups of people losing their minds or being subjugated to mind control. I feel like I'm standing inside one of those old shows right now."

DiNeogun asked, "Do you think we were all poisoned through the water supply?"

Bucklem shook his head. "I don't know what to think at this moment." He closed his eyes and took a deep breath. On the exhale, he requested, "Where is your description of that little old lady? Is there any chance she's really, *really* little? Like about four foot nine inches little?"

Both local officers asked in unison, "How'd you know?"

Bucklem put both hands on his hips and looked around like a man trying to retain composure, but he was losing the battle. He stormed off to his car and slammed the door. He began rambling to himself, which got louder and more angry as it went, "You have GOT to be kidding me! There is no WAY! I asked for a historian, and that Murtle son of a bitch brought me the prime suspect. I must be living in a movie. I'm just the main character and no one told me. There ain't no way this is real. I have GOT to be dreaming! It just can't be real!

How in the actual hell could Ester kill the sheriff? There's no way. The bat would be as big as her! This whole town has got to be kidding me! This is some sort of psy-op game by the CIA. Yeah. That's it! That's gotta be what's happening here. I'm being tested for recruitment into the CIA. That makes more sense than to believe a four foot nine granny just beat down a six foot three man, capped him and drove off. I need to wake up from this nightmare.! This ain't funny! I want off this bad trip!

That's it! Someone slipped me some magic mushrooms! I'm hallucinating. That makes sense. I got 'shroomed, 'cause this can't be real. There's no way this shit is real!"

Captain Bucklem talked to himself, searching for some thread of clarity that he could pull on to make sense of all that was happening around him. But, he wasn't finding anything that made sense.

And it got worse. Once he was back to HQ, he began getting preliminary reports that sounded remarkably similar to the situation he saw for himself. One by one, every crew reported that a little old lady matching Ester's description had shown up, killed the person or people, and got back in the car and drove off calmly.

Captain Joshua Bucklem was probably the most confused man on planet earth. As the bodies were transported to the old V.A. clinic, everyone investigating was already growing tired. Most of the police and deputies had been awake for most of the night. Most of the rescue folks and responders were, too. Anyone that was plugged into the 911 system had been awake and on pins and needles all night. Bucklem was awakened from a wonderful dream of fishing on a river in Alaska to come take charge of a town full of sleepless and traumatized people who may or may not be criminally involved in the case they were working. Evidence at almost every scene was compromised or destroyed. Eye witnesses didn't seem to actually witness anything. And there was stale pizza in random places. He wondered why there was stale pizza everywhere.

As the day wore on, the investigating teams grew more confident that they had found every crime scene. There were too many to take the time to properly question all the witnesses, so all accounts and reports were pretty thin compared to a normal murder investigation.

Captain Bucklem and those he tasked were able to secure proper meals from volunteers outside of the county. He was granted a small platoon of National Guardsmen from three counties south to come and stand guard around the headquarters so that there was at least a minimal feeling of safety for those working the case. The soldiers and the State Highway Troopers gave Bucklem a little confidence that there would at least be no more murder of law enforcement. But something was off. He just didn't know what was missing.

It was late afternoon before a legitimate news crew came

knocking on his door. That's when Bucklem realized what was off. Where was the press? This was the murder scene of the century and there was no press. He could barely issue a citation to a jaywalker without a reporter showing up. How did they go all night and day without reporters? There should have been an entire media camp set up across from the headquarters. But, there had only been one. And it was there all day.

He didn't want to be in charge anymore. Bucklem could handle the shoot outs and stabbings and drug runners. He could deal with the gruesome car crashes and murder scenes. He was trained to deal with people hating him for being a cop. But, when the press didn't show up to this murder scene, it scared him. That unnerved him more than anything ever had.

There was a natural flow to everything on earth from air and water to traffic patterns in the street and planes in the air. There was a natural pattern to behavior and events. Life has a tendency to be predictable. If there's a shooting, the police know the press will be there in a certain amount of time. Where were they? How could they miss this? Why would they not be there like vultures on a rotting water buffalo? That scared him. It didn't make him nervous. It scared him.

When the presence of a news crew from the nearest bigger city was announced to Captain Bucklem, he needed a minute to sort through his feelings and put on his professional public relations hat. He straightened his uniform and adjusted his campaign hat.

"I'm Captain Bucklem of the Ohio State Highway Troopers" he greeted the news crew.

The one with the microphone responded, "Sarah Weathers with Action3 News." There was one cameraman sporting what appeared to be an antique piece of gear on his shoulder. One person was directing rather obnoxious lights his way. And the reporter looked like she could still be in high school.

He was wondering if this was a joke. Bucklem wore confusion on his face that was unmistakable.

Sarah Weathers began her job. "Captain, we understand that this is just a training exercise, but there definitely seems to an awful lot of realism from what we're seeing here. Can you tell us a little about how you've been able to make it feel so real?"

Bucklem was stunned. He didn't say anything. He just looked at Sarah Weathers and the crew. He was trying to maintain the best poker face he could while processing the information that the media outlets were informed that it was a training exercise. He needed to quickly decide to reveal the truth or play along. The truth would result in a circus of media and a whirlwind of crazy that goes with it. He knew this from experience. They were always annoying and in the way.

He made the hasty decision to play along. Maybe he could catch a break by at least being able to get a solid day or two into things before the media came storming.

"Well, Miss Weathers, seeing how you've been patiently waiting all day, let me be honest," Bucklem tried to sound as if he wasn't just making things up. "I'm pretty sure that your station and others were told about this being a training exercise so that we could train without interference. After all, training is hard enough. I don't believe I would be out of line to suggest that having you and other crews like yours here might complicate things, would I?"

"Sir," she was insistent as young reports can be. "We are only wanting to get your take on how things are going and what it took to make an exercise this big work. Can you at least give us a little nugget of insight? You clearly have the experience to run a great program."

"Thanks for the butter up," Bucklem smirked. "But, I'm going to have to disappoint you. Just like a regular investigation, this is ongoing and there is nothing we can disclose at this time. Thank you."

He turned to walk away with a smirk. He was pleased at how well he handled that. He appointed a small team of officers to ensure that the reporters didn't get into anything that would lead them to the truth too soon. He wanted to take advantage of the quiet. He needed to be able to investigate before the media came and created havoc. But who could have had the power to stay the press? That was yet one more investigation for him to be perplexed with.

When he was just about to reenter the building, Bucklem was asked about how to proceed with the two families that had been killed. He couldn't believe his ears.

Bucklem asked Corporal Wilson, "Did you just tell me that there were *two* entire families killed last night?"

"Yes, sir," Wilson answered. "Mom, Dad, kids. One family had a pregnant daughter. She was shot right through the stomach. And the son has a plunger sticking out of his... his rear end."

Bucklem hung his head. Thirty four dead people. No common

threads. No motive. Bad information. Bullied witnesses. Individuals and families. The only thing to go on was that the victims were mostly men. Some were rich. Some were working class. Some were not so well off. They held a variety of jobs. There was nothing obvious to put any pieces together.

It was just a matter of time before the junior high news crew figured out that this was not an exercise. Everyone was tired. Everyone was shaken. Everyone was worried. There was way more to do here than could possibly be done even if they had twice the personnel. Bucklem was trying not to think about how overwhelming it was. He was trying to remain calm and figure out the next step with each new piece of information coming every minute all day. And nothing made any sense.

If Bucklem didn't think it could get any worse, he would have been wrong. Ester came knocking.

Chapter 37: Ester and the Captain

There she was, all 81 pounds of kindly, old lady. Ester Wireman was asking to speak with the captain who christened her as the Historian.

The captain was frozen in his tracks. He looked more like a man that had come face to face with a grizzly bear than the commander of a small army investigating the murder event of a lifetime. Everyone that noticed the bizarre, silent interaction between Ester and the captain got quiet and quizzical.

It was a tense showdown. No one could name it. But, they could feel it. Bucklem stood like a redwood while Ester shuffled up to him. They stood there looking up and down at each other.

Ester finally spoke first. "Captain. I wouldn't want to be in your shoes. But, I've had a lovely nap, and I'm here to help."

This couldn't be more awkward. Captain Bucklem was standing face to face with the mass murderer that every eyewitness placed at every crime scene. If it was true, he was looking at the most violent criminal of his career, but he could hardly ask for assistance, let alone protection.

"Ester," he began. "I don't even know where to begin with you. I don't know if you've lost your mind or I have. I've got almost a hundred people here to lead, but I don't think I can afford to leave you alone for three seconds. Do I need to search you for weapons?"

Ester smiled, "If I were you, I would certainly think it would be wise."

Bucklem called for a couple of officers to come search Ester.

She held up her hands and surrendered her purse. Ester insisted that the female officer search her purse while the male officer frisked her.

The deputy, Jerry Coalwine, looked a bit disgusted at being ordered to paw the old lady down looking for weapons, but performed his duty vigorously. When Deputy Coalwine and Deputy Sasha Engle announced that there were no weapons found, Ester announced that she had been hoping that the captain would search her himself.

Ester said with a large grin, "Thank you, so much, young man. It's been a long time since a man has handled my body like that. It was lovely."

None of the uniformed officers could contain their shock. Coalwine announced that he needed to go wash. Engle dismissed herself with a giggle. That left the Captain and Ester.

Bucklem let out a long sigh. He shook his head and said, "Ester, I have a feeling that I'm in for a really rough interrogation here, and I'm out matched already. You probably don't want to come back tomorrow for this, do you?"

Ester was smiling. She replied, "I can come back as often as you'd like if you have more men to pat me down like that."

He didn't try to hide his feelings anymore. Trying to keep a stone face with this woman just wasn't happening. He said, "Alright. Let's go find a comfortable office. I'm going to bring a couple people to take notes for me. So, don't be getting any funny ideas. I'm not going to frisk you, no matter what you say or do, OK?"

Ester shrugged. "You might be missing out."

Bucklem replied, "I will have them throw you down and cuff you if necessary. Even if we have to find child sized cuffs. Got it?"

She shrugged again, "Yes, sir."

Bucklem pulled Laura Strong away from the phones and a couple of male officers to escort and accompany Ester and the captain to an upstairs office with large, soft leather chairs. They lowered the plush office chair all the way down for Ester and tried to find something for a foot stool so her feet weren't dangling.

Ester joked, "When I was a girl, I'd have loved this chair. I'd have crossed my legs up in here and been so comfy! Now, I'd be in pain and become part of the chair."

Bucklem was not finding her sense of humor funny. Ester didn't care.

Ester was in front of the desk which was in front of the large window. Bucklem was seated behind the desk. Laura Strong was at the end of the desk ready to take notes. The male officers found chairs and sat in front of the door. Just before he began to say anything, Bucklem got a weird feeling. He looked over his shoulder at the window then back at Ester. She was still smiling. He moved to the opposite end of the desk from Laura.

Ester said, "If you're worried about me having placed a sniper out there somewhere, that's a very wise and insightful move on your part, Captain. However, since there's no way I could predict where we would be talking, I don't believe you would need to be fearful."

Despite the shared alarm, no one said a word. Ester managed to instill a very uncertain and uncomfortable atmosphere in the improvised interrogation room.

Bucklem was still struggling with what would be the right way to begin this interrogation. What would be the best lead question? How was he going to get her to open up and trust him so he could sway her into giving him useful information? He didn't have to wonder long. In fact, Ester made it easy for him.

"I did it," she said. She still smiling.

There was stunned silence. No one knew what to say. No one knew if she knew what she was talking about. There was no way in the minds of the police that this ninety five year old lady who could barely make it up the stairs had just murdered almost three dozen people in a variety of ways all over the county. They just couldn't image why she was saying it.

Ester was almost enjoying herself. "You're all thinking I've gone mad. You're thinking that this old lady has lost her mind. There's no way on the earth that someone like me could have possibly gone around the whole county in one night killing all those terrible people. You're saying to yourself, 'This sweet, little grandma couldn't hurt a fly, let alone kill ONE person. There's no way she did this. No way possible.' Yet, here I am. Red handed, so to speak."

Ester asked for her purse. When they didn't want to give it to her, she snapped, "Oh, for the love of God, you already went through it! Just hand it here! Don't be a cowardly dick!"

Captain Bucklem's eyes popped open as he couldn't contain his surprise. Ester responded with, "Get use to being surprised, Captain. It's going to get very interesting."

Now Bucklem was trying to hide the worry that was creeping up on him. He allowed Ester to have her purse. The officers behind her had their hands on their guns. But, Ester only pulled out a zippered plastic bag with some paper inside. She opened the bag and carefully removed the papers. The officers relaxed at the door. Bucklem looked very interested.

"Captain," Ester said as she opened the papers and spread them out on the desk. Each paper contained several red marks. The marks appeared to be finger prints. The red appeared to be blood. Everyone looked shocked and shaken. Except Ester. She simply explained, "You see, before I left each of those dead bastards to rot, I took a finger print of each of them using their own blood. I knew you might have a hard time believing that I did it, so I needed to be able to prove to you that I murdered all those evil people."

Bucklem shook his head in disbelief. "Ester, where did you get this? I simply can't believe that you drove all over and got these prints, let alone that you did all this."

Ester reached into her purse again. Hands went to guns again. She pulled out another zippered plastic bag that looked just like the first with more papers inside, just like the first. She explained, "I knew you wouldn't believe me. And you wouldn't want to believe me. So, I made this list of those people with my finger print. Each of those finger prints is mine. The blood will match each of the victims. You will find one finger print of mine with the blood of each and every victim. I had to use baby wipes between each one, so I hope that doesn't ruin the testing."

Everyone that was not Ester looked back and forth at each other with befuddled expressions. They were just beginning to wake up the fact that Ester was playing 3D chess with them, but they weren't quite there yet. She had just presented them with irrefutable proof that she was at least present at each location and had touched each body.

Ester nearly blew their minds when she said, "I'm sorry. I didn't get every single body. Obviously, I couldn't get you a print of the unborn baby I shot."

The guards came up out of their chairs. Laura dropped her pen, and pushed away from the desk. Captain Bucklem sat back in his chair as if he just lost his queen early in a chess match. This little old lady really was dropping an iron clad confession in his lap. And he was so far behind her, that he was beginning to wonder if she was just bringing him along for the ride.

He waved for the guards to sit back down. He looked at Laura, shrugged and motioned for her to continue taking notes. He looked at Ester with an almost defeated expression. They were only three minutes into an interrogation, and Ester already had the upper hand. Hell, she had them on the ropes! Bucklem never wanted to be anywhere less than where he was at that moment. He knew he was in trouble. But, then again, just about anyone would have been.

Ester smirked around at all of them. "OK. So, now that

you all know I did it, let me give you a few clues that will help in your investigation."

There was a sinking feeling in the room. They were actually a little afraid of what was coming because they couldn't know what was coming.

Ester said, "Eventually, you'd figure out that I was hosting a retreat this week. It was mostly women I had met through my outreach ministry, Krisis. I'm sure most of you are familiar with it on some level."

"Yes," Bucklem replied. "It's remarkably impressive. You didn't just give things to kids that need stuff. You actually found a way to help them help themselves. You were teaching them to find a better way or something like that, weren't you? That was kind of your slogan."

Ester was pleased with the captain. "Yes, sir. We didn't tell them that we were doing that, but yes, that's what we were doing. We were helping them become better people with information and training that would allow them to find ways to get out of the hole they were in. Their parents failed them. Their schools failed them. Some might blame society. But, what is society? Aren't WE society? I wasn't going to fail them. My ladies and I were not going to fail them. We would never treat them the way everyone else did. We treated them like little people with big hopes and dreams. We treated them like people with bright minds and full capabilities. We taught them that they were not victims of society. We taught them that no one had failed them. We showed them that everyone is born into a different set of circumstances. Some are good. Some are not. Some are bad. It's not their fault. They didn't choose what world to be born into. But, they could chose what to do in that world. And they could choose to change that world. They could take control of all that was around them and make something wonderful. We taught them that stuff doesn't happen TO them. It just happens. They have to decide what to do about it. They can lay in the gutter and cry. Or they can take up a book and learn about tools and how to use them and build whatever they want. They can grow food instead of begging and going hungry. They can learn to fight instead of being beaten up all the time. And they can learn to defend themselves from anyone trying to take advantage of them, whether it be mentally, emotionally, or physically. They don't have to be a slave to the world they found themselves in. They can be free. They just have to want it, then make it happen."

Bucklem took a moment to stare at Ester. He still couldn't see where she was going with this. But, he finally said, "Damn, Ester! That was inspirational! That is some amazing stuff right there! Two more minutes of that, and you could have me signing up to be in your outreach." That's when it clicked in his head.

He got more serious. "Is that how you did it? You got a few women inspired to change things? You mentioned 'terrible people.' Are you trying to tell me that you inspired some women to help you kill some 'terrible people?' Is that where this is going?"

"Well, Captain," Ester smiled. "You might catch on quicker than I had given you credit for. But, no. I killed those horrible people.

Where I was going with that, is to tell you that eventually, you'd figure out that I was hosting a retreat. You might even begin to think that I led those women around killing people. But, when you get around to doing police work and checking cell phones, you'll find that everyone one of those women were at the retreat while I was out killing. You'll see that my phone was the only one that left the retreat campgrounds. And you'll find that it went to each of the murder sites."

What Bucklem didn't know, was that Ester anticipated this problem. So, she had everyone leave their phones at the campgrounds with those that were not going out on a kill team. Those women were to walk around camp with various phones to various buildings and move them around once or twice while everyone else was gone. Ester's phone was the only one that left the campground and visited every location.

"Uh, huh," Bucklem said. "What about the woman that showed up dead at the hospital?"

Ester finally looked very serious. In fact, she was very saddened. "Yes. Ricardo had demanded that Tammy come home immediately or he would hunt her down and kill her and whoever she was with. She was too afraid he would hurt some of us, so no matter what we said or how much we begged, she went back to him. That rotten bastard killed her as soon as she got there. I was following her, but didn't get there in time. I had to just leave her at the hospital, because I had more people to kill." Ester sniffled a little with tears in her eyes. Tammy's death really did hurt her. But, she was resolute to make sure it didn't derail her intentions.

In fact, when she visited Ricardo, she took his phone and sent a threatening message to Tammy's phone back at camp. Despite her sadness and anger, she didn't over look that detail. She knew she would need to be able to explain it.

"I need a tissue, please," Ester sniffled.

Laura pushed the box near her over to Ester, who thanked her. Laura definitely felt that pain from Ester talking about Tammy.

Ester blew her nose, apologized and wiped her eyes. She composed herself and sat up straighter. She looked at the captain for a moment. He said nothing. So, she took charge.

"Captain," she said. "You're going to figure out all the facts. You'll count how many bullets were fired. You'll figure out how many times they were hit with a bat or how far they were dragged behind a truck."

Captain Bucklem was a little disturbed at how many details Ester knew, but he was still having a hard time believing that she could have killed everyone. But, she was making a pretty solid case for herself.

Ester went on. "You'll have labs matching blood types and finding finger prints and all that stuff everyone sees on those crime shows on TV. One day, they might even make a show about you. They might even make a show about today with you as the lead detective." She smiled gently at him. She rolled her eyes just a little as if she was day dreaming. "I think your character should be played by someone just as handsome as you. But, maybe with a touch more charisma. Don't you agree?"

Bucklem frowned at Ester. She didn't mind. She enjoyed the moment.

"Oh, don't be upset, Captain," she said. "I don't think badly of you at all. Our meeting is definitely not under the

best circumstances. You might even say, it's a little stressed."
Bucklem raised his eye brows at Ester. No one else knew what
to think. They were all waiting for whatever she was about to
say next.

Ester continued undeterred and unbothered, "Why? Everyone
wants to know the why, don't they, Captain? That's really what
all those TV shows are all about. The killing and gruesome
details are just there to get people wondering why. The entire
show or movie is focused on the why. Why did they do it? And
whether in real life or in Hollywood, if there's no why, people
get upset. There's no closure. People can't stand not having a
reason.

Think about it. If those people were as horrible as I could
make them sound, maybe some folks would forgive me for
killing them. They would be able to understand because there
was a reason. And if it was a good reason, they would
definitely understand. In fact, they might even agree with the
killing.

Did you know that in Texas, there was a law that allows
justified killing? It called the 'He Needed Killing Law.' It's
when   a   person   is   so   horrible..."

Bucklem raised his hand to cut her off. He said, "Yes. But, no.
There's no such law and never has been. It's just something
lawyers do to make a jury feel like they should ignore
evidence in a murder trial because the victim was such a
terrible person, no one feels sorry for them getting killed."

Ester looked impressed and responded, "I didn't realize that.
That's good information to have, Captain."

Suddenly, Bucklem felt like he had been led into a corner and
victimized. He tried not to show it. But, he was sure she knew

because he felt that she set him up for that exchange.

"Well, mister lawman," Ester became more serious. She was no longer smiling. "I could tell you all about my late husband. We could spend hours talking about how he was once a good man, but over time, he became a drunken, rotten wreck of a man that would beat me and do horrible things to me. I could give you every detail of what my life was like with that horrible man, because I REMEMBER EVERY SINGLE MOMENT OF IT ALL!!"

No one in the room was prepared for Ester's raging scream. She set them all back in the chairs as she raged on.

"I remember every hit! I remember what it was like feeling scared and waiting for him to hit me again! Do you know what that feels like, Captain? Do you, Miss? How about you dummies back there? Huh? No? WELL, I DO!

I know exactly how many nights I spent crying myself to sleep. I remember lying in the dark wanting to die rather than live another day wondering if today would be the day he beat me to death. I can tell you how many black eyes I had. I lived with shame and guilt all day every day. I was angry, but I was helpless. I wanted to fight, but I couldn't win. I needed help, but NO ONE WAS THERE!!

And do you know what I got when the police asked me what happened? DO YOU?"

Bucklem was very, very uncomfortable as were the others.

Ester was merciless. "You already know that they made it sound like I deserved it. Don't you! 'What did you say to him that made him so angry? What were you wearing? What did you do to make him feel like it was alright to hit you?' They treated me like I was the CAUSE!

I DIDN'T DESERVE ANY OF THAT!! NOT ONE BIT!!"

Ester was shaking. Tears were flowing down her face. Her voice was getting raspy. The officers were feeling the weight. Ester's pain was visceral. They could taste it.

Ester shook for a moment then, went on. "I was a good woman. And maybe he did kill me. Maybe I was already dead when I killed him. He beat the life out of me. He stole life from me. He took my joy and my love and hopes and dreams and he set them all on fire in a hole and pissed on them! He stomped on everything that mattered to me and broke it till he broke ME.

By the time I poisoned him, there was nothing left of me. He had taken it all. He destroyed it all. I had no hope. I had no dreams left. Every single day, the only thing I could think about was how to survive. How do I keep from getting beaten? How could I make it from waking up to going to sleep without another bruise or broken bone? That was all I was. A punching bag.

Captain, if I had come to you with a black eye, what would you have told me? Would you have come to my rescue? Would you have taken him away from me? Would you have been the hero I needed?"

Now, Bucklem and the crew were beyond uncomfortable. None of them wanted to be in that room with that woman. She was savage. And she was tearing them apart.

Ester glared at him through teary eyes. "I know you want to

tell me something noble. But, you can't. Because we both know it'd be a lie. You wouldn't have done anything to help. Maybe you would have locked him up for a night. Then, he'd just beat me even worse when he got home. Maybe you'd tell me to leave. And go where? No money. No one to help. And for what? So, he could track me down and kill me? Some help that would be, right?"

Ester wanted to keep railing him. She wanted to unleash a lifetime of hurt and rage. But, she needed to stay the course and finish the mission.

She had already made all the women of the After Party swear to tell the police that they were at the retreat, and that they didn't know Ester was out killing their abusers. She made them swear to tell the courts that she promised them that all they had to do was pray and believe, and that God would take care of everything for them. She even had them practice that at her retreat. She had prepared them. Now she needed to deliver. She was way ahead of the captain on their shared invisible chess board.

Ester blew her nose and wiped her eyes. She fought back the primal urges and refocused herself on the finish line. She had those in the room with her in her palm. Now, she just needed to clear her head and make the final move.

"Captain," Ester was quieter. "I see a ring on your finger. Do you love your wife?"

Bucklem was silent. He wasn't sure what she going for.

Ester kept on, "Have you ever argued with her? It is a 'her,' isn't it?"

Bucklem was displeased, but answered, "Yes to both questions."

She asked, "Have you ever hit her?"

"No," he answered.

Ester leaned towards him and peered into his eyes. "Have you EVER hit your wife?"

Bucklem was very confident in responding, "No, ma'am. I have not. I may have been mad enough once or twice, but I have never laid hands on my wife."

Ester relaxed. She was satisfied that he was being honest with her. "She is very lucky. She's far more lucky than any of us." Ester stopped talking. She was waiting for them to connect the dots in their heads. Then, she continued, "Let me ask what you might recommend for Hope. It was a sad and tragic irony for that poor angel to be named Hope by those demons that were her parents. Her mother, Andrea, was probably as much a victim, but she never stopped anything. Bill was a horrible bastard. He beat and raped that girl from before she could talk. What would you recommend, Captain?"

Bucklem was clearly uncomfortable while he was thinking.

Ester didn't give him much time. She said, "Never mind. I'll help you out. After all, you wanted to meet the historian. You wanted someone who knows everyone and knows what goes on around these parts. You wanted someone that knows everyone's business. Let me make this easy for you, because I know everything.

When Hope was in school and showed up looking used and

bruised, what should she have done to make it stop? Should she have told someone?"

Before he could stop himself Bucklem said, "Schools have people that are trained to help."

"Really?" Ester pounced on that. "Are you sure about that? Because she tried to tell them."

Bucklem asked cautiously, "What do mean 'tried?'"

Ester explained, "Well, her father played cards with the counselor and went hunting with the principal. They were all friends. And Bill liked to share with his friends."

Bucklem became a little emotional as he realized what Ester was saying. Ester let him.

Ester said, "Maybe she should have run away. Do you think that would get her out of the situation, Captain? Or do you think maybe Bill was buddies with the cops that found her and brought her back? Do you think maybe Bill went fishing or played cards with those cops? Maybe he even went hunting with a couple of state police? Is that possible, Captain?"

Bucklem was nearing a breaking point. He was supposed to be the one asking the questions in an interrogation. But, he was the one getting grilled and Ester was in control. The worst part for him was that he couldn't think of anything to ask her that would put him back in control.

"Captain," Ester asked. "Are you OK? Maybe you'd like to stop and get some fresh air. Maybe you'd like to talk to some of the women that were at my retreat?

You see, you asked for a historian. You wanted someone like me that knows everything. Well, I do. I know how those dead bastards beat the women I took to that retreat. They told me everything. And everything they told me made me relive it all. I felt every beating they ever took. Just like I remember every beating from my husband.

Don't worry. You can talk to them all you want. You can hear every one of them tell you how they were prisoners and walking dead for yourself.

You see, you can fight. I'm small and weak. You can call for back up. We had none. No one was coming for us. No one came for me. No one helped. I couldn't fight back. I could never express rage like men do. I had no one to take it out on when I had a bad day. I couldn't beat someone up till I felt better. I had to find another way. I had to find a constructive way to express my rage. We'll talk about that.

But, Hope didn't have hope. You see, all those men that were abusing her had each other. She had no one. They were sharing stories of how they raped her over and over and over. Just like the men that have been abusing my girls drink beer and brag about how they beat us and what they did to us.

And if any of us tried to fight back, those men just encouraged each other to teach us a lesson and put us in our place. Hope couldn't fight back. It only made things worse."

The room went silent. No one wanted to breath, let alone speak. Ester was in command here. She let them suffer before changing gears.

She asked Bucklem, "Have you ever been knocked out cold?"

He was caught off guard. "Excuse me?
She repeated the question and he answered that he had.

She asked, "You didn't really feel it till later, did you?"

"That is correct, ma'am" he replied. He wondered how brutal the point of this line of questioning would be.

Ester said, "Usually, you wake up and didn't even know that you had been knocked out. You just... stopped. You didn't exist for a moment. You were talking. Then, you were shut off."

Everyone was visibly confused.

Ester read their faces. "Most of those people that I killed last night were shut off. They didn't suffer. They were talking. Then, BANG! They were gone. No pain. No suffering."

Ester began to break down. Her emotions had already been dammed up too long. And it was coming to a fury.

"We suffered every day of our lives. In fear. In tears. In shame. Without hope. Every single day. We had no one. We had no heroes and no saviors. There was no fairy tale. Only a never ending nightmare that would only end in death.

Well, sir, I decided that I would show them the way. I would show them the light at the end of the tunnel. I decided that it would not end with MY death. So, I killed my husband. And I was set free.

And I showed my girls that they didn't have to die for it to end. All they had to do was tell me everything. They only needed to pray to God and believe that everything would be OK. And I promised them that it would end. And they would live. They would be able to have a life. A good life. A life without abuse. No more beatings. No more tears. No more shame and no more fear.

I told them that we would not wait for those abusive bastards to put us in the ground. They would go free.

Because Hope chose to die. It was her only way out. She was fourteen."

Ester was fighting the tears and screaming in her head and heart. She took a few deep breaths. Everyone was afraid to speak.

Finally, Ester said, "That young, beautiful girl ended her suffering the only way she knew how. And I decided to poison my husband. I had suffered under that monster for 62 years, long before the beatings started. He beat me down in other ways before he used his fists. My only regret was that I didn't do it 50 years ago. The first decade wasn't so bad."

The silence was painful.

Ester sighed. She was spent. But, she spoke once more. "So there you go, Captain. I did it. I'm the killer. I murdered my 'loving husband.' That's what they say, right? 'Loving husband?' He loved me so much that he showed it with his fists and belt and dick. And I killed every single one of those bastards I could last night here in this town.

I promised those women that if they prayed and believed, they would have a life worth living. And that's exactly what I gave them last night. I ended their nightmares. I was the only one that came to their rescue. I was the one that showed them that life could be worth living. I showed them that they didn't have to be slaves and take whatever was dished out to them. I promised them that one day the beatings and shame and pain would stop. That was last night. I showed them no greater love. I showed them that they didn't have to be like Hope.

So, you can strap me up in the electric chair and give me the lethal injection while I fry, because I killed those rapist and abusers. I killed those terrible, horrible people. And if God sends me to hell for killing those miserable sacks of shit, I'll kill them again every day for eternity while Satan laughs."

Everyone in that room wanted to crawl under a rock. They had never wanted to be anywhere besides where they were more than they did at that moment. Ester had broken them. From Ester's seat, the interrogation had been successful.

Ester sniffled. She wiped her eyes and blew her nose again. She had accumulated a pile of tissues on the desk. She stared at it for a moment then said, "I would say I want my lawyer..." She looked around the room and almost smiled. "But, that won't work since I killed him."

It was the most impossible, awkward silence ever recorded. It was then, that Ester revealed that her phone had been recording and uploading a live feed to her social media.

She stopped recording. She sniffled once more. She looked around the room, and smiled awkwardly. Then, she stood up and stretched. She adjusted her outfit. She said in a matter of fact tone, "By the way, I called the news before I got out of my car when I got here."

Ester stated, "I'm going home now. You can stop me if you want. But, you have my confession. There's no where for me to run to. And I have no reason to run. I knew what I was doing. I knew the price. And I have been willing to lay down my life to save all of them from the beginning.

If you want to tackle me and throw me in a jail cell right now, by all means, be my guests. But, know that while I was recording a live feed, one of the recipients of that was the news team outside. So, while you would be right in your actions, I'm willing to bet that you would be condemned in the court of public opinion. You would be judged by your friends and family.

So, if you have an questions, write them down for me, please. I'll be available all day tomorrow. After all, I've been retired for a long time and I've had plenty of freedom since my husband has been gone. I've been able to live a good life without him. It's been wonderful to be able to think things through in all that free time.

So, I think I'm going to have a nice bowl of soup at the drug store lunch counter and go home to watch some Gilligan's Island. I've had enough serious stuff here lately. I need a laugh. Gentlemen, Laura, good evening."

With that, Ester stood in front of the guards until Bucklem waved them off. He couldn't say the words out loud. He was too worked up to speak.

Ester refused any help down the stairs and out of the building. She only stopped long enough to wink at the reporter. But,

Ester answered no questions. She only said into the microphone, "I did it. I killed them all." And she left.

That was another gamble she was hoping for, but couldn't guarantee. In her free time, with all that time to think, Ester decided that she didn't want the press there too soon. She was afraid that they might add unnecessary pressure to arrest someone. Plus, she also realized that if she could convince the local news outlets that there was going to be some sort of joint forces disaster training exercise that they should not interfere with, the police would most likely be concerned that someone with power was pulling strings. It would help give her an edge in telling her side of the story if they were worried about who was really in charge.

It was just a gamble. It was a total wild card. She didn't think it would work. But, being Ester has it's perks. With the creation of Krisis, she was able to make new connections and rekindle some old ones. She was such a wonderful breath of fresh air for the news outlets with the success of Krisis, she might have made a good and trusted ally somewhere in the media world.

And with getting news coverage, she might have reconnected with an old friend who had retired from the military and then from the State Troopers. He might have been helpful in her ruse. It was entirely possible that Ester had friends in the right places to convince the media that they would be wasting their time trying to cover a training exercise the night of her Grand Finale.

As Ester hobbled into her car, Captain Bucklem watched from the office window he had moved away from. Laura

Strong asked him why he didn't arrest her, and what he thought was going happen to Ester and the women she was protecting.

Bucklem said, "All those women need to do is stick to their story that Ester did it. She thought of everything. She was playing chess while we were still trying to figure out what game board to use.

No jury is going to convict any of them. There's too much doubt and too much emotion. Plus, there's so little evidence and a lot of that is messed up. She became a vigilante that targeted sexual predators and wife beaters. She's going to be a hero to a lot of people and every woman that's ever been abused.

Even with all the so called evidence she gave me, I honestly don't believe her. I don't know who or what to believe. I have no idea what's real. Locking up a little, old lady before having REAL evidence would be a PR nightmare. Should I? Probably. But, there's no way I'm going to put Ester behind bars today.

Maybe she'll get sentenced for killing her husband, but they'd have to exhume the body and start from scratch. Ester is going to take all the blame to the grave with her one way or the other. She might not even live to see the beginning of the trial, let alone the end of it. Those women are going to go free because of Ester. The ones who abused them are dead, and those women who were their victims will all be free. That's what's gonna happen. Just like Ester planned."

This story is 100% fictional and is based on no people, no events and no facts. Any resemblance to real people or events is purely coincidental.